OLD SOLDIERS
SOMETIMES LIE

RICHARD HOYT

A TOM DOHERTY ASSOCIATES BOOK

NEW YORK

THIS BOOK IS DEDICATED

TO MY DAUGHTER,

TERESA NELLIE HOYT.

OLD SOLDIERS SOMETIMES LIE

This book is printed on acid-free paper.

A Forge Book
Published by Tom Doherty Associates, LLC
175 Fifth Avenue
New York, NY 10010

www.tor.com

Forge® is a registered trademark of Tom Doherty Associates, LLC.

ISBN 0-765-30331-0

First Edition: October 2002

Printed in the United States of America

0 9 8 7 6 5 4 3 2 1

OLD SOLDIERS
SOMETIMES LIE

"OLD SOLDIERS NEVER DIE.
THEY JUST FADE AWAY."

—GEN. DOUGLAS MACARTHUR

To the Reader

In the early 1980s, American intelligence operatives secretly sold weapons to Iran, a so-called rogue state, using the profits to illegally fund the Contra opposition to Marxist Sandinistas in Nicaragua. In the nationally televised Iran-Contra hearings that ensued, members of Congress ignored allusions to an older, far more believable secret operation to obtain money for anti-Communist causes.

When Gen. Douglas MacArthur, the Supreme Commander of Allied Powers in occupied Japan, explained why he would not be prosecuting Emperor Hirohito as a war criminal, the American public believed him. MacArthur was, most Americans thought, a man of honor. But what if that storied old soldier didn't tell the whole truth?

Here, a trio of fictional characters, a scholar, a former CIA operative, and a Filipino intelligence officer, seek to unravel the historical mystery of what really happened to the booty collected by the Japanese Imperial Army in a territory it occupied in East and Southeast Asia from 1931 until its defeat in 1945. The mixing of fiction and history is advanced with apologies to purists of form. Should the CIA respond to the subpoena of public opinion and declassify this historical black hole, mainstream scholars can write a conventional, definitive history that should satisfy the most demanding skeptics.

Contents

OLD SOLDIERS
SOMETIMES LIE

Tomi's Find

Dr. Tomiko Kobayashi began her adventure into the continuing, lethal loop of unexamined and misrepresented history by placing a one-sentence query on an academic website. *The granddaughter of Gen. Yamashita Tomayuki, the storied Tiger of Malaya, seeks personal records or recollections bearing on the 1946 conviction and execution of her grandfather for alleged war crimes committed against the Filipino people.*

Tomi, an assistant professor of Modern Asian history at Washington State University, received a reply from seventy-four-year-old Edie Compton, a Denver woman whose uncle, an Associated Press reporter, covered Asia and the Pacific from 1930 to 1948. Wim van der Elst had died of a heart attack in Tokyo, after which his private journal was shipped back to his family in the United States, where it had lain for more than fifty years in an attic.

Mrs. Compton, a widow crippled by a stroke and confined to a wheelchair, had tried unsuccessfully to get the journal published. Through e-mail exchanges, she told Tomi that van der Elst's handwriting was borderline impossible to read, especially with her bad eyes, and literary agents had all said the same thing: A foreign correspondent's wartime journal might serve as a primary source for a scholar, but was hardly an exciting prospect for an overcrowded, shrinking book market.

In agreeing to send Tomi a photocopy of the journal, Mrs. Compton gave her two leads. She should begin by talking to Avi Feuer, the Asian Affairs editor for the *New York Times*. She should also contact Roderick "Roddy" Baker, a retired foreign service officer with long experience in Asia, who could put her in touch with a former CIA operative who had pursued the story for years.

Edie Compton wasn't kidding about the handwriting. Van der Elst had developed a private form of slanted, nearly illegible shorthand that eliminated most vowels and conjunctions. Wondering if there might not be a treasure of revelation buried in the scrawl, Tomi inched though the manuscript line by line, sometimes spending five or ten minutes deciphering each word, which she keyed into her computer.

Now a flag went up on the corner of her monitor. Tomi had mail. She opened her Hotmail account. It was from Edie Compton. The e-mail contained a short note and an attached file. She read the e-mail:

> *Is Imelda Marcos lying to Ms. Herrera, do you think? Easy to pooh-pooh Imelda but what if she's telling the truth? Also if you haven't read Herbert Bix's meticulously researched biography* Hirohito and the Making of Modern Japan*, you should. I've given you three pieces of a puzzle. Think about them. What do they suggest?*

She downloaded the attachment and opened the file. Mrs. Compton had sent her copies of a series of articles published in December 1998 by the *Philippine Daily Inquirer*. In her interviews with reporter Christine Herrera, Imelda Marcos claimed that Ferdinand Marcos had sold four thousand tons of gold that the Japanese had buried in the Philippines. He gave most of that money to friends who secretly bought up shares of major Filipino corporations. They were his shares, not theirs. After his fall in 1986, the friends declined to acknowledge what they had done and refused to return the property to the Marcos family, to which it rightfully belonged. Mrs. Marcos wanted it back.

Yes, Tomi had read Bix's Pulitzer-Prize–winning biography. Until its publication, most historians had accepted the official line that Hirohito was a reclusive innocent, duped by the military. Bix demonstrated that, to the contrary, the emperor had encouraged Japan's incursions into Korea and China in the 1930s and supported the post-1937 expansions that led to war with the United States. He actively participated in all major wartime decisions from the bombing of Pearl Harbor to Japan's prolonged refusal to surrender when it was clear the war was lost. By the standards applied to other German and Japanese wartime leaders and military officers, Emperor Hirohito was a war criminal. No question.

As the occupation wore on, MacArthur and his "psychological warfare" advisors implemented Operation Blacklist, effectively absolving Hirohito of responsibility for war crimes so that he could be retained as a constitutional figurehead, a move thought necessary for the Japanese people to accept their new American-imposed system.

Now, wondering who Edie Compton really was, Tomi reread Bix's book. As she closed it, she sat up straight, momentarily stunned. Her eyes wide, she muttered, "A necessary move? Was it really, Mac?" Her heart thumping, chewing on her lower lip, she again called up the van der Elst journal entries on her computer.

My God, she thought. *Did Wim van der Elst have it figured? Could it be?*

Prime Minister Nakamura Yoshi rode pensively on the rear seat of the Meiji Limited stretch limousine custom manufactured by the Mitsubishi Corporation for use by the prime minister and members of the royal family. As the Meiji eased silently down the Ginza, Nakamura was aware that the well-dressed, prosperous passersby on the crowded, wide sidewalks were watching the vehicle with curiosity. Although they couldn't see through the tinted windows, they knew the car. They certainly had no idea of the vexing dilemma that had Nakamura's stomach twisting with anxiety.

The efforts to find the phantom "Edie Compton" had been in vain. Not good. "She" claimed to have Wim van der Elst's journal in her possession. How did she come by it? What did it say about the activities of Kodama Yoshio? Did it mention Prince Chichibu? General Prince Higashikuni? Emperor Hirohito and General MacArthur? Did it contain direct links to the Golden Lily and the M Fund?

For Prime Minister Nakamura Yoshi the question of whether or not to approve of the Chiba mission was not merely an issue of saving face or the future of the Liberal Democratic Party. There were deeper problems that would not go away—living in the shadows of unexamined history and a lingering, corrosive lie that was in part maintained by the United States of America. That was not to mention the fading reputation of Emperor Hirohito. The Japanese people cared passionately about the image of the royal family.

The question for Nakamura was what, if anything, was to be done at this late date and at what cost to Japan's national pride. There were passionate factions on either side of the question. Nakamura had given Chiba Wataru his instructions, in the process placing an unprecedented responsibility on a single Japanese. Was Chiba up to the responsibility?

Nakamura wished he had never heard of the Golden Lily. The secret was as a cancer growing in the maw of Nippon. Despite all the energy and intelligence and good will of the Japanese people, they remained locked in the grip of the mythical past. Would the conniving never end? Or would the damnable M Fund continue its power unchallenged?

Nakamura wondered if the *Hagakure* might not offer a solution.

Was the truth, or at least part of it, hidden among the leaves of Yamamoto Tsunetomo's imagination? Yamamoto's code of Bushido required a *samurai* not to think, but to act. A fanatic's death was not dishonorable. It was the Way of the *Samurai.*

Nakamura knew that those currently in control of the fund did not trust him. It had been foolhardy in the extreme, under the influence of his boon companion, Jack Daniels, to express his misgivings to the American ambassador at a diplomatic reception. Sweet Jack was powerless to stop Nakamura's opinion from spreading to the wrong people.

The Meiji glided to a stop in front of the Imperial Hotel, where once more Prime Minister Nakamura would have to go through the humiliation of being lectured by pedigreed foreign economists who knew nothing at all about Japanese culture, much less what was really the best way to manage a national economy.

A doorman in a blue uniform and wearing white gloves sprung open the door for the prime minister. Nakamura stepped out of the car, digging briefly at his testicles. He straightened the jacket of his blue pin-striped suit.

From somewhere across the street, the past pulled a trigger. A bullet slammed into Nakamura's neck, pitching him sideways. He landed on his shoulder with blood pulsing in red loops from his carotid artery. Nakamura-san remained conscious for several heartbeats, during which he was aware of red and warmth and people shouting. In this fleeting, floating zone between light and dark, the long dreaded passage where ambition and fate are at last resolved, a single thought for Nakamura-san:

The color of gold is crimson cubed.

Still staring at the screen of her Dell, Tomi Kobayashi picked up her cell phone and dialed the number of her older sister in San Francisco. Munching on her Whopper, she said, "Miho, I've got it all deciphered and keyed into my computer. Finally."

"You figured out van der Elst's handwriting. At last. You nut-ball!"

Tomi laughed. "There's no figuring his handwriting at a glance. Hard to believe even he could read it. But I finally deciphered it, word by word. Three weeks, it took me! This all has to do with a gap in the history of post–World War II foreign policy that's been shrouded by self-interest and embarrassment. A huge chunk of the story dropped in my lap—including the motive for blaming Grandfather for what Admiral Iwabuchi did. I can hardly believe it."

"Give me a minute will you, Tomi? Laura's lower orifice just leaked and I've got to get a diaper."

"Take your time, Miho."

Scrolling through the document on her computer monitor in Pullman, Tomi took another sip of coffee. The Japanese generals and their officers could have the good food and beautiful women. The noncommissioned offers could take such peasant girls as they pleased. And the enlisted men could have their prostitutes. But all the counts, princes, earls, barons, and dukes of whatever royal family, in whatever far flung empire of whatever era, had to have trusted lieutenants in the field doing what really mattered, collecting the booty.

"Okay, kid's butt cleaned," Miho said. "Tell me more."

Tomi tapped the scroll bar, chewing and reading. "Van der Elst took special interest in the spectacular, favored rise of an ultra-nationalist thug named Kodama Yoshio. The Kodama entries that van der Elst later sorted out begin in 1931 in Tokyo, which he spelled T-O-K-I-O, the style of the day, not Y-O. His final entry is an interview with Kodama in Sugamo Prison on November 12, 1948."

"Kodama who?"

"Kodama Yoshio. Van der Elst believed he was the man in

charge of Kampei-tai units charged with transporting the war booty collected by the Japanese Imperial Army in Manchuria, China, and Southeast Asia. The Japanese code for the treasure was the Golden Lily. Van der Elst called Kodama 'The Great Patriotic Bagman.' "

"Wow! That all sounds exotic. Kampei-tai units being?"

"A kind of secret military police. Kodama wasn't in charge of the operation. Emperor Hirohito's younger brother was. That would be Prince Chichibu. And the emperor's uncle, General Prince Higashikuni Toshihiko. In short, the Japanese royal family, ultimately Emperor Hirohito. The story of the SS thefts of art and treasure in Europe is well known, Miho, but the fate of the Golden Lily has never been detailed." Tomi snagged an onion ring.

"The Golden Lily? Ooh!"

"Van der Elst even figured out the location of a stash of part of the treasure, golden dragons the Japanese buried in the Philippines."

"Golden dragons? Ooh, ooh, Tomi! Tell me more."

Tomi tapped the scroll bar. "I say dragons; the Chinese call them the alchemist archers. How they got that name is fun. A grateful Chinese warlord had golden dragons struck to honor martyred archers, hence the name alchemist archers. It's all explained here."

"Archers in the form of dragons. Say what?"

"Five-hundred-pound solid gold dragons! Eleven of them. The alchemist archers of Xhingsui Gap. Fun, huh? Maybe not the lost Ark of the Covenant or the Holy Grail, but still pretty exotic. I bet Indiana Jones would do a double take."

Miho laughed. "Tomi! You're making this up."

"Hirohito was a war criminal. We now know that . . ."

"We do?"

"Believe me, yes, thanks to the efforts of a scholar named Bix. Hirohito began a series of wildly popular public tours in 1946 to rally the Japanese people to thwart Republican sentiment. On October 10, 1947, the chief war crimes prosecutor Joseph B. Keenan let it be known that 'high political circles' had decided not to prosecute Hirohito for war crimes. What 'high political circles,' Miho? On November 14, 1947, MacArthur held his fifth and last face-to-face meeting with Hirohito, in private, for ninety minutes. Nobody knows what was discussed. It was one of those maddening historical meetings the content of which we can only guess. Following that, and contrary to official prohibitions by MacArthur's headquarters, Hirohito redoubled his efforts to rally the Japanese public to support the Chrysanthemum throne. Beyond mild objections, MacArthur did nothing to stop him."

"Tell me about the alchemist archers. I want to know about the golden archers."

"Dragons, actually. I'm getting to that, Miho. Patience, patience." Tomi scrolled through the document in her computer. "MacArthur's people hanged Tojo and six other war criminals on December 23, 1948. The next day they quietly released Kodama and eighteen of his Class A war criminal friends from Sugamo Prison."

"Nineteen war criminals?"

"Including the Japanese civilian in charge of Nanking during the rape, and the governor of occupied Manchuria when Unit 731 conducted chemical and biological warfare experiments on human subjects. It was a crass, even grotesque release of moral monsters. Why did MacArthur do that?"

"Ooh! Very mysterious. Good for you, Tomi!"

"I say again, Miho, what do you think MacArthur and the emperor talked about in their cozy little chat on November 14, 1947? The Japanese had already surrendered unconditionally. No bargaining chip there for Hirohito. What was left for MacArthur and him to talk about that was so secret?"

"Don't have the foggiest."

"After The Great Patriotic Bagman was released from Sugamo Prison, he went to work for the U.S. Army's Counterintelligence Corps, then later for the CIA. This is a matter of record. Nobody denies it. Isn't that something? Now what or who on earth do you think would compel or convince a racist, xenophobic, nationalist, militarist, American-despising *yakuza* hood like Kodama Yoshio to work for American intelligence services? Remember, this man had spent the war collecting and transporting the Golden Lily for the emperor." Tomi took a bite of her Whopper and munched contentedly.

"I don't have any idea."

"He would certainly cooperate with the Americans if Hirohito told him to, wouldn't he?"

"I suppose he would. How does our grandfather fit in?"

"In a minute, in a minute. Did Emperor Hirohito use the Golden Lily to buy himself a walk? MacArthur's G-2, Charles Willoughby, would have had a year to negotiate the details before Kodama and the others were actually released. What do you think?"

"Beats me. *Now* are you going to tell me about our grandfather?"

"All right. Okay. If I read this all correctly, MacArthur allowed Yamashita to be railroaded in order to pacify Filipino fury over what the Japanese had done to them. The Americans tried him by kangaroo court and executed him. CIA operatives later used him as part of the 'Yamashita's Gold' myth, a canard of disinformation they maintained over the years to pooh-pooh reports of Japanese treasure being discovered in the Philippines. Fascinating theory, huh?"

"All right, Tomi! Do it! Go for it!"

"I carry our grandfather's genes, Miho; I never quit."

"Not to change the subject, but have you, uh, you know, scored?"

Tomi wadded up the wrapper of the Whopper and threw it in the wastepaper basket.

After a moment, Miho said. "You want to stay single forever?"

"This is Pullman, Washington, not the Bay Area. What do you expect me to do?"

Miho said, "Men are men, whether they're in the Bay Area or Pullman. You're smart as hell. You've got a Ph.D. from Yale, for Pete's sake. You're petite. There's something to be said for that. Those American women have big boobs and rumps but everybody knows what will happen in a few years. They'll turn bovine. You've seen them walk down the sidewalk. Lucky they don't crack the concrete."

"Miho, please."

"The closer to the bone, the sweeter the meat. Everybody knows that."

"You want me to walk around in a low-cut blouse with a sign on my back saying, 'Single Nisei. No kids. I speak good Enrish.' Spare me."

"How about, 'General Yamashita's granddaughter.' That'd be a conversation starter.'

"Please!"

"They must have a faculty club at that place, right? A place where tweedy guys with pipes sit around drinking coffee and arguing about obscure journal articles. Pick a good time in the late afternoon and go there. Become a regular. Maybe you can find someone skilled in the marital arts, if you know what I mean."

"Miho!"

"Okay, okay. So what are you going to do about this war criminal business and our grandfather's reputation?"

Tomi took a sip of coffee. "What kind of granddaughter would I be if I didn't find out what this is all about. This is exciting, Miho. An historical mystery waiting to be solved. Why not me? I'm pumped."

"Aren't these guys all dead or senile old geezers? Besides us, who's to care?"

"Defenders and detractors of Douglas MacArthur. Anybody who professes to care about truth. History buffs. Lovers of mysteries and detection. All thoughtful people should care, Miho," Tomi paused. "I can hear a kid squalling."

"Tim. He's got red spots and a fever. Measles, we think."

"Then call me later." Tomi hung up.

After she hung up, Tomi Kobayashi spent a full hour staring out of her window, thinking of the unsettling possibility of what she had discovered by simply matching Herbert Bix's biography of Hirohito with Wim van der Elst's story of Kodama Yoshio's extraordinary wartime career. And then there were the suggestive claims made by Imelda Marcos. Yes, Mrs. Marcos's assertions were likely self-serving, but what if, as the mysterious Mrs. Compton had suggested, they were true.

Outside snow began billowing out of the slate gray sky in great, tumbling whorls.

Tomi knew that revisionist Japanese writers and the historian Chalmers Johnson and others were convinced of another secret of the American occupation of Japan that was as unexamined as the details of Hirohito's wartime activities: the alleged existence, with American complicity, of the phantom M Fund that had financed the oligarchy of politicians, bureaucrats, businessmen, and gangsters that had run Japan from the early 1950s to the present day.

When the State Department announced its intention to write a history of American foreign policy in East Asia from the late 1940s through the 1960s, the CIA refused to declassify documents detailing its postwar activities. The acting director of Central Intelligence, Adm. William O. Studeman, justified the secrecy in a letter to the *New York Times*, saying that the CIA had an obligation to keep faith with foreigners who had "received legally authorized covert support from the United States."

A group of academic historians advising the State Department then recommended that the State Department leave blank official accounts dealing with postwar Japan rather than publish documents so scrubbed of the embarrassing truth as to amount to government-sanctioned fiction.

Tomi called up the first page of van der Elst's journal entries on her computer monitor. Was Hirohito's Gold a resource of the M Fund? The CIA wanted to "keep the faith" with foreign nationals given legally authorized covert support in postwar Japan. Keep the faith with whom? War criminals? Was legally authorized covert support of Japanese war criminals the secret that continued to frustrate historians of the period?

Tomi was no fool. To learn the truth and restore her grandfather's honor, she would be obliged to enter the confusing, duplicitous zone of *kuroi kiri*, the "black mist" of corruption that permeated the political cultures of East and Southeast Asia. If she could but peer back, back, back through the obscuring mist to November 14, 1947, she suspected, she would see the shadowy figures of a living god and a patriotic old soldier conniving to fix the verdict of history.

Tomi took another sip of coffee. With the encouraging ghost of the Tiger of Malaya at her side, Tomi Kobayashi began her inquiry into the mystery of the past by rereading Wim van der Elst's journal entry dated September 19, 1931, the first mention of Kodama Yoshio.

BOOK ONE

Kodama Yoshio

September 19, 1931, Tokio - Well, yesterday was some day, I have to say. At the very same time that Colonel Lindbergh and his wife flew off for China from Fukuoa after a week of passionate nonsense and spectacle, the Japanese army finally went and did it in Manchuria. As the Foreign Office version has it, Chinese soldiers commanded by Marshall Chang Hsueh Liang blew up a section of the Japanese rail line between Darien and Mukden—this in revenge for the Japanese having blown up a train carrying his father, Marshall Chang Tso Lin. Having written off their killing of Chang as a "mistake," the Japanese used the blowing up of Japanese rails as an excuse to capture Mukden. The Kwangtung Army's commander, Lt. Gen. Hayashi Senjuro, enraged by the dastardly Chinese, allegedly ordered the reprisal. A manly Japanese can only take so much from the cowardly Chinese. Lower than worms, they are.

It's obvious to those of us covering the story that the killing of Marshall Chang had been no mistake at all. There was much self-righteous emotion in the Japanese Foreign Office, where we were told that Japan has a railroad in Manchuria and the United States has a canal in Panama. When someone blows up part of their railroad, the Japanese are obliged to respond just as the United

States would if its canal was attacked. So there. The capture of Mukden was entirely logical.

Good old Shiratori Toshio was agitated to the point of getting shrill when he gave us the Foreign Office version of what had happened. He was apparently loaded with the evil Western martini that he has come to love, and so held nothing back. Old we-will-study-the-matter-further Shiratori actually said something. There was no further studying to be done in reply to Colonel Stimson's charge that the Kwangtung army was running amok in Manchuria. Shiratori said it was Stimson who was running amok, not the Japanese army. And we all noticed that he didn't address Stimson as Colonel, his usual practice.

While it may have been indelicate of the secretary of state to point out the truth, it was embarrassing to the limit to the Foreign Office in Tokio.

After four years here, my understanding of the *kanji* is now getting good enough to sort out all this craziness in Japanese newspapers. This or that leader, or passionate followers of this or that ominous-sounding, high-minded organization are combined in a parade of patriotic confusion. The Japanese appear culturally incapable of doing anything if it is not in a group, and this heated rhetoric is the result. The true believers keep popping up, waving banners, and repeating claims of the glorious Japanese destiny. I wonder if a true-blue patriot joins as many of these organizations as he can.

For example, there is one particularly noisy young Japanese, Kodama Yoshio, who is relentless in his protest. First he was arrested for scattering handbills into the Imperial Diet calling for the masses to rise and overthrow Parliament. But since he was such an ardent, patriotic lover of country, he was released. Then he threw a bucket of excrement on the participants in a May Day Parade. The throwing of manure on chanting lefties is demented inspiration.

Now there, I thought, is a young man to watch.

September 17, 1932, Tokio - I was right about that enthusiastic lover of country, Kodama Yoshio. He's someone who will not yield. He has been arrested for attempting to give Emperor Hirohito papers pleading for increased patriotism.

Kodama is associated with Kenkoku-kai, which translates roughly as the Association of the Founding of the Nation. I know this because I looked his name up in the files after I read an approving article quoting him as saying General Hayashi is a hero and a patriot taking the first bold steps to a new Japanese destiny. What I found was a lover in extreme of patriotic organizations. Kodama has himself founded something called Dorkuritsu Seinen Sha (Independence Youth Society). He is said to be a member of the Kokuryu-kai, which means the Amur River Society, whose aim is to extend Japanese power all the way to the Amur River, the boundary between Manchuria and Russia. The *kanji* can also be read as the Black Dragon Society, which is more fun to use in my dispatches.

The gist of the Black Dragon Society pitch is the need for order based on a proper hierarchy. This is the doctrine of the Eight Corners of the World Under One Roof, the roof being provided by the emperor of Japan, the direct descendent of the Sun God.

October 6, 1932, Tokio - Kodama Yoshio has been given a six-month sentence for his effrontery in the attempt to lobby the emperor in the streets of Tokio. Being an out-of-control patriot is okay as long as the craziness doesn't involve a member of the royal family. That's still going too far, but I wonder how long even that restraint will last.

2

June 2, 1934, Tokio - The demon patriotic buglers were across the street again yesterday, bugling their passionate hearts out at the devil Western journalists. This was the tenth day in a row of non-stop bugling. We've given up trying to calm them down. They're bugling for Japan and have every right to bellow their bugles wherever and whenever they please. Every time we send an emissary to plead for civility, if not a moment's silence, they blow all the louder and even more off-key, if that's possible. We've concluded that we're going to have to move, but we have to discuss this very quietly out of fear the buglers will follow us to our new lodgings. None of us have any doubt that they're bent on following us wherever we might go.

On our way to work yesterday, Bill Howard of the UP put his thumb and forefinger to his mouth and gave them a loud Bronx cheer, and they went nuts, totally haywire. There was no cultural misunderstanding there. A fart is a fart in any language. You'd have thought he had fired a rifle at them, and they responded with a wild round of frenzied, crackpot bugling that had us laughing all the way to the Foreign Ministry.

The buglers are just the latest chapter in the general madness that is gripping the country. The Japanese seem to be competing to see what manner of outrageous and hyperbolic assertions they can dream up. It is nearly impossible for anyone to be too patriotic. To read a Japanese newspaper is to learn how we Westerners are bent on screwing their wives and daughters, and it is our most determined goal to keep the Japanese a backward and second-rate nation. Things have gotten so loony that Ambassador Crew has taken to wearing a pistol, although he says it makes him feel silly. With the rhetoric being what it is, nobody can blame him.

Kodama Yoshio has now risen to become leader of the most frantic and demanding of the nationalist groups, Tenko-kai, the Society for Heavenly Action. Like almost all Japanese, it seems, he is caught up in the grip of the *Hagakure*, the teachings of a samurai turned priest named Yamamoto Tsunetomo (1659–1719), which are being lavishly extolled as *yamato-damashii*, which translates roughly as "the unique spirit of Japan." No claim in the *Hagakure*, no matter how extravagant, is regarded as hyperbole. There are several popular editions being read, but they're all condensations because the original ran to eleven volumes. It seems that Yamamoto himself only wrote the first four volumes of the *Hagakure*, which literally means "Hidden Among the Leaves."

Everybody from the emperor on down seems to be pawing through a copy and quoting Yamamoto with approval. That an entire nation could get so worked up over such obvious nonsense is amazing. I've bought a copy and am struggling through the Japanese. If learning whatever is hidden in the leaves will help me understand the crazed buglers, I'll give it a try, what the hell.

June 11, 1934, Tokio - Kodama Yoshio was on the front pages again yesterday, this time bristling with indignation at the published opinion of a not very well-mannered Dutch diplomat who had the audacity to say that the best-selling *Hagakure* doesn't make sense in places. Kodama said the Dutchman's first error, among many, was in trying to apply Western logic to the *Hagakure*; the *Hagakure* is above absurd Western logic.

Kodama said Yamamoto is always correct, never to be questioned. If he occasionally seems contradictory it is because Yamamoto knows only too well that life is full of contradictions. Yamamoto's notions on death are the spookiest in my opinion:

I discovered that the Way of the Samurai is death. In a fifty-fifty life or death crisis, a samurai *chooses death. There is nothing complicated about dying. Just brace yourself and proceed. Some say that dying without accomplishing one's goals is to die in vain, but that is a calculating, imitation* samurai *ethic of arrogant Osaka merchants. We prefer to live. In a fifty-fifty situation we naturally find an excuse for living on. The correct choice, dying, is nearly impossible. But one who chooses to live after having failed in one's mission will be despised as a coward and a bungler. If one dies after having failed, it is a fanatic's death, but not at all dishonorable; it is the Way of the Samurai. A* samurai *prepares himself for death morning and evening, day in and day out. A* samurai *constantly ready to accept death has mastered the Way of the Samurai, and he may unerringly devote his life to the service of his lord.*

Japan is on a binge of *Hagakure*. Reading that kind of hyperbolic nonsense made me pity the poor Koreans and Chinese caught in the path of the Kwangtung Army.

According to Yamamoto and his modern-day followers, including the impassioned Kodama, the way to start a new day is to imagine your death. This view holds that death from illness is the work of nature, whereas self-destruction has to do with a man's free will. When one chooses death, one chooses free will. Therefore whether one dies being cut down in Manchuria or committing ritual suicide, *hara kiri* or *seppuku*, it makes no difference: Both are honorable.

That an entire nation could buy into this crap boggles my mind. I wonder if any of those buglers last spring were prepared to die by having a bugle jammed up his ass?

August 17, 1934, Tokio - As designated pitchman for the Society for Heavenly Action, Kodama Yoshio was at it again yesterday, this time at a patriotic rally on the grounds of the old Imperial Palace in Kyoto. In addition to his usual blather of proper order and hierarchy and Japan's proper place at the top of it, he exhorted the Japanese to honor the soldier as they once honored the noble samurai and et cetera. He also delivered a long tirade about the value of the *Hagakure*, referring to it as the Japanese bible, proper medicine to a long list of Japanese ills, most of them Western values imported from the white *gaijin*, or hairy devils, that's us. The newspapers today reported all this nonsense at great length and with much enthusiasm.

Kodama quoted with approval Yamamoto's belief in the debilitating effects of what he calls the feminization of the Japanese. According to my edition of the *Hagakure*, Yamamoto first noticed that the male pulse was rapidly becoming the same as in females. This had not always been the case back in the days when men were men and women were women, he said. And how was it that a true man should behave?

There is dignity in assiduity and effort, dignity in serenity, and dignity in closeness of mouth. There is dignity in observing proper etiquette, dignity in behaving always with propriety, and great dignity too in clenched teeth and flashing eyes. A samurai *concentrates on these externally visible qualities at all times and is totally sincere in displaying them.*

Judging from the photographs of him in the newspapers, Kodama himself is bent on displaying nothing but clenched teeth and flashing eyes. What was it Shakespeare wrote?

Yon Cassius has a lean and hungry look. He thinks too much. Such men are dangerous.

I wonder what Bill Shakespeare would have thought about Kodama Yoshio?

October 14, 1934, Tokio - Kodama Yoshio has shown that he is more than clenched teeth and flashing eyes and buckets of manure. He and several of his sidekicks have been arrested for conspiracy to murder Prime Minister Viscount Saito Okato.

4

November 8, 1934, Tokio - Kodama Yoshio is now on trial for planning to assassinate Prime Minister Saito and judging from the coverage in the Japanese press you'd think it was he, not Saito, who was put upon. The heroic Kodama. Regular *samurai*. How he must love it!

There is much talk at the trial about one's *giri*, or loyalty, versus *ninjo*, which is variously translated as one's feelings of humanity, empathy, kindness, or sympathy. Kodama said he was compelled to act both by *giri* and *ninjo*. The Japanese have all sorts of *giri*, depending on the nature of the group. In this case it is Big G patriotic *giri*, loyalty to the emperor, that is involved. Kodama said he could not stand to see the emperor and the Japanese people misled. Kodama was torn by his loyalty to the emperor, who is a direct descendent of the Sun God, and his feeling of *ninjo* for the Japanese people, who will be deprived of their rightful destiny under the policies of men like Saito.

Kodama said that when a man's *ninjo* is violated on this scale, he is obliged to act or surrender all claim to manliness. Someone had to act. Kodama said his own life meant nothing to him. A man without honor is already dead.

Of course, the Japanese newspapers just love this kind of horsepucky and quote Kodama's self-righteous testimony at great, boring length. Although Kodama's role in the dashing action is unclear, he is said to be a man out of Japan's romantic Tokugawa past. A genuine man of action. A *samurai.*

If idiots like Kodama get their way and we find ourselves in a war with these people, we're in for a real struggle, guaranteed.

October 12, 1937, Tokio - My patriotic friend Kodama Yoshio is to be released from Fuchou Penitentiary next week, the day before I am to fly to China to cover the war. There is much excitement in the Japanese press surrounding Kodama's release because the *yakuza,* as the local gangsters are called, are to give him a huge *demukai,* or ceremonial welcoming on his release from prison. Judging from their right-wing rhetoric, these *yakuza* gangs are hardly distinguishable from the numerous patriotic groups that crowd the newspaper columns every day.

The *yakuza* operate according to the *samurai* code of Bushido and view themselves as sort of patriotic outlaws. The word *yakuza* comes from the name of a losing hand at a card game. Full-fledged *yakuza* members have full-body tattoos ending at the neck, the ankles, and at a level on the arm that may be covered by a short-sleeved shirt. When a *yakuza* soldier screws up a job, he is required to surrender one joint of a finger in atonement. These digits are kept pickled in a jar of alcohol—on display at the gang's headquarters.

There are not just scores or hundreds of these gangs in Japan, but literally thousands of them, with super gangs or associations of smaller gangs staking out territory to be milked primarily through extortion. While these are violent crooks, they are part of a curious tradition in Japan, and their presence is regarded with stoicism on the part of the larger public.

The *yakuza* chiefs are called *oyabun*, father, and the followers are called *kobun*, or children. Several famous *oyabuns* have jumped into the competition to see who is most patriotic and ready to give their lives for Japan's glory. These *oyabuns*, citing *samurai* ideals that make a man a man and not a sissy wimp, seem to be welcomed without reservation by everybody concerned, hyperbole being the order of the day.

What fascinates me about the *yakuza* tradition of the *demukai* is that the *oyabun* of a man who nobly serves his time will ordinarily give him a promotion or important assignment. The more outrageous the offense, the more grand the gesture of reward, a message that the ex-convict is unbroken, unrepentant, and unyielding. He was imprisoned, yes. But defeated or chastened? Never!

Kodama Yoshio was ready to sacrifice his life on behalf of *ninjo* and *giri*. He did hard time for his part in the attempt to assassinate a weasel of a prime minister and has become a kind of folk hero because of it. I wonder what manner of extraordinary reward he earned for that.

December 5, 1937, Nanking - From our vantage point on a small hill in the international section, a safety zone, we hope, we watch the Japanese army advancing on the city. The German reporters have somehow come by a large French-made telescope that we've mounted on the wall by the edge of the hotel verandah.

The story from Suzhous is that Japanese soldiers wearing hoods to protect them from the rain simply walked unrecognized past the Chinese sentries who were either sleeping or smoking opium. There is much dry-mouthed joking about whether or not this is any kind of omen for Nanking. We are told that Gen. Tang Sheng-zhi is to defend the city. He told one of his American advisors that he would defend it to the last man. It is all madness.

December 7, 1937, Nanking - Generalissimo Chiang flew the coop today, not a good sign. General Tang has closed and locked the gates to the city as part of his defense. Some American missionaries who witnessed the capture of Suzhou two weeks ago likened the Japanese army to determined ants filing in and out of every bank, shrine, shop, or house and carting off everything inside. They told us their driver found it difficult to use the roads because of all the dead bodies. That story has given rise to the sick joke

that by sealing the population inside Nanking, Tang is simply playing the gracious Chinese host, seeing to it that the Japanese have
a well-stocked city to loot.

December 13, 1937, Nanking - After four days of Chinese confusion
and systematic Japanese bombardment, the rout of General
Tang's army of 100,000 men is complete and Nanking belongs to
the Japanese. The sporadic and haphazard nature of Tang's retreat, if every man for himself can correctly be called a retreat,
was topped by the spectacle of Chinese patriots atop the city's
walls using machine guns to strafe anybody who tried to break
their way out of the locked gates. God knows how many Chinese
were killed by their own soldiers.

The doctors who are living here in the international zone were
out there doing their best to stem the flow of blood. One of them
said two vehicles burst into flames inside a packed seventy-foot-
long tunnel leading to one of the blocked gates. The doctor said
he walked over bodies from one end of the tunnel to the other.

Then, finally, came the triumphant entry of the Japanese into
the city. We took turns watching the event through our French
telescope, not wanting to leave the international section until our
safety was assured. The sober General Masui led the way in an
open-topped car, followed on a prancing white horse by a man I
recognized as Colonel Hashimoto, one of the crazed ultranationalist officers. I'll bet money, marbles, or chalk that he's a real fan
of the *Hagakure*. Probably reads it every night. Colonel Hashimoto, mighty *samurai*.

December 15, 1937, Nanking - The Japanese have installed a gentleman named Wang Ching-wei as the puppet prime minister of
Nanking. Scuttlebutt has it that the Japanese have assigned a cer-

tain Major Kodama as Wang's personal bodyguard. Could this Kodama be Mr. Super Patriot, I wonder? From convict to major in the Japanese army in two months? Naw. Couldn't be. Lots of Kodamas in Japan.

December 17, 1937, Nanking - It turns out that yes, the Major Kodama who is Prime Minister Wang's bodyguard is Kodama Yoshio. The Japanese all said the *yakuza* would see to it that he was rewarded for his sacrifice. Indeed!

December 18, 1937, Nanking - The Japanese apparently regard the Chinese women as existing for their pleasure, and the Japanese commanders, now led by Lt. Gen. Prince Asaka Yasuhiko, who had come by his position by marrying the emperor's aunt, are doing nothing to discourage this attitude. Brutal attacks on females are constant, casual, and unembarrassed; girls, pregnant women, old women—nobody is spared. In a seminary near here two days ago, seventeen Japanese soldiers took turns with one poor Chinese girl in broad daylight. And yesterday afternoon a Japanese soldier committed sodomy on a sixty-year-old woman then slit her grandson's throat when he cried at her suffering. Little bastard. The nerve of him displaying emotion at the sight of his grandmother being sodomized.

And neither are the noble *samurai* satisfied by mere rape. No, no. Their tastes are far more exotic than that. Chinese males have been buried alive, used for bayonet practice, castrated, disemboweled, and deprived of their eyeballs, ears, noses, tongues, hands, and feet—the exact organ or limb depending on the momentary whim of their tormentors.

And yesterday, in some kind of Cecil DeMille spectacle of perversity, the Japanese lined up as many as 20,000 Chinese soldiers on the far side of the Yangzhi River and casually machine-gunned them. We could hear the guns carrying out their grisly task all afternoon. The distant rat-a-tat-tat and the screaming became a macabre chorus that numbed the senses.

If it is open season on both Chinese men and women, it should hardly come as a surprise that nothing in Nanking is beyond the astonishing greed exhibited by the heroic conquerors.

This morning, accompanying a detail of medical doctors to listen to the polite denials of the Japanese Embassy, I saw Kodama Yoshio riding grandly through the streets in an open-topped car followed by an armored truck. I didn't see Prime Minister Wang anywhere near his alleged bodyguard.

December 20, 1937, Nanking - If there is any credence to be lent to rumor—and surely no story is beyond belief in this city—when I saw Major Kodama a couple of days ago, he was in the process of carrying off a most unusual treasure. He had lifted eleven amazing golden dragons, each weighing about five hundred pounds— a total of about 5,500 pounds of gold. Cast in the twelfth century in northwestern China, the dragons, popularly called the alchemist archers of Xhingsui Gap, are said to be the incarnations of martyred soldiers.

Kodama was nothing if not bent on having the archers in his armored truck. Reports say that four guards employed by a Chinese businessman, Yong An, were deprived of their genitals and two more skinned alive during the determined search for the fabled archers. Why Yong stupidly remained in the city with his archers is beyond me, although perhaps he was reluctant to run the gauntlet of fire laid down by Chinese soldiers executing anyone trying to escape the city.

January 5, 1938, Nanking, China - A footnote to all those who have died here in the last two months. The Japanese have murdered more than 200,000 people in cold blood. I know history records that it was Gen. William Tecumseh Sherman who invented total warfare on civilians as well as soldiers in his infamous march on Atlanta, the so-called scorched-earth policy of modern warfare. I bet Sherman would vomit in his grave if he witnessed what I have. If there is any more barbarous capture of a city by an invading army in the history of warfare, I can't think of it.

Judging by an abandoned copy of the December 7 issue of the *Japan Adviser* picked up by a Chinese nurse a couple of days ago, the Japanese regard the capture of Nanking in the spirit of sport. The newspaper's headline said, *Sub-lieutenants in Race to Fell 100 Chinese Running Close Contest.* In keeping with the samurai nonsense, this sport of course was done with swords. One of the competitors, Lieutenant Mukai, said his blade was slightly damaged as a result of cutting a Chinese man in half, helmet and all. Never mind that he had to sharpen his blade, the contest was "fun," he said.

The Chinese commander, Generalissimo Chiang Kai-shek, didn't have to read the gleeful Japanese accounts to know what had happened to Shanghai the previous month. Chiang didn't know what the hell to do about defending Nanking. I get this from Horst Derner, who writes for the German magazine, *Der Spiegel,* and who has the ear of his countryman, the German military advisor General von Falkenhausen. Von Falkenhausen participated in the discussion of what ought to be done about Nanking.

By von Falkenhausen's account, Gen. Li Zogren, a cool head, asserted that the city was worthless strategically and indefensible. The Chinese should declare it an undefended city so the Japanese would have no excuse to slaughter citizens as they had at Tianjin and Shanghai.

Gen. Bai Chongxi seconded this. Von Falkenhausen agreed, and he could see that the other generals felt the same way, but they hemmed and hawed because nobody wanted to look like a quitter. Finally, the inevitable asshole had his turn, the ten percent that make bell-shaped curves possible. This turned out to be Gen. Tang Shengzhi, who turned emotional, saying that the body of Sun Yat Sen lay in a Nanking mausoleum. What kind of message was this to send to the Chinese people? They should stay and fight to the death.

Incredibly, Chiang agreed to this and assigned the defense to Tang. Horst said von Falkenhausen despairs of trying to advise the Chinese. He said that in recounting the fateful meeting, von Falkenhausen got so pissed he damned near cracked his pince-nez.

It's no damn wonder Vinegar Joe Stillwell has developed a reputation for abrasiveness.

A Swiss doctor told me that in his opinion the reason for what happened at Nanking is that the Japanese, isolated for centuries on their home islands, do not have rules for operating outside of their own culture. To the Japanese soldiers, the Chinese are not really people. No difference between wringing the neck of a chicken or a Chinese. The German contingent here has been trying to run an estimate on the number of women who have been raped so far, and have come up with a figure of twenty thousand, which seems like a nice, round figure, although possibly conservative.

Nothing imagined by Dante can compare with the horror of Nanking. The rape of that city, for it is nothing short of that, is so vile as to be unspeakable. Words fail me. I suspect no writer can describe the pain and humiliation suffered by the innocents caught in the path of the Japanese Imperial Army. Who is to be held accountable for this barbarous atrocity? The enlisted men? Noncommissioned officers? Their commanders? Lt. Gen. Prince Asaka Yasuhiko, the commander in chief? Suma Yakijiro, the Japanese general consul in Nanking?

In the middle of the carnage, my friend Kodama has been busy, busy with his truck collecting the booty of the destroyed city. He's apparently emptied the contents of Nanking's banks, not to mention the alchemist archers.

May 12, 1938, Xuzhou - The Chinese never cease to amaze me with their will to survive and ability to get intelligence from Japanese occupied cities. The Kampei-tai is extremely efficient, and judging from what happened at Nanking, no doubt without equal in its brutality, but news somehow still manages to get out and in oftentimes amazing detail. This intelligence is critical to Chiang Kai-shek who, to his credit, seems to be making a genuine effort not to repeat the mistakes he made at Nanking. The Japanese have captured Peking to the northeast and both Nanking and Shanghai to the south, and word (if not common sense) is that they are planning to move from both sides to trap Xuzhou in the middle. If they do that, as Chiang must certainly know, all is lost.

This time Chiang has appointed a first-rate general, Li Zogren, rather than going for a patriotic moron like the ill-fated Tang. I can still remember the distant rat-a-tat-tat of Japanese machine guns mowing down rows of prisoners with their hands tied behind their backs.

And Chiang actually sat down and honest to God talked to two Communist generals, Peng Dehuai and Zhu De. Yes, talked to them! Communists! Chiang Kai-shek! This was such a stunning gesture on his part that those of us in the press corps went out and got drunk with whatever English-speaking Chinese officers we could scrape up. The beer is made out of rice, and is not what we've been used to, but we put it down in quantity nevertheless.

In the middle of the drunkenness, a Chinese intelligence officer named Chan, who knows I have a continuing interest in Kodama, gave me an interesting report from Shanghai. Chan was even more loaded than me, if that's possible, and could have been making half of this up, but I don't think so. It was too detailed to invent on the spot. I think Chan was simply drunk and wanted to show off a little for an American reporter.

Chan said Kodama has established control over the Chinese triad societies in Japanese occupied territory. These secret societies, the Chinese equivalent of the *yakuza* gangs, control the opium trade and prostitution in China, among other activities. Now they are under Kodama's control, which he exercises with the help and assistance, not to mention the muscle, of the Kampei-tai.

Chan said Kodama has formed an alliance with the boss of the Shanghai underworld, Tu Yueh-sheng, also known as Big-Eared Tu, and his younger brother. He started to tell me about a relationship between Kodama and the Tu brothers, then stopped. I waited for a second while he thought about what he was about to say. Much to my frustration, discretion prevailed over the fog of terrible beer. He abruptly changed the subject.

Big-Eared Tu runs the Shanghai waterfront. His brother, dear God, is a general in Chaing Kai-shek's army and a favorite to become his chief of staff. Little wonder that Chan shut his mouth. What makes this especially interesting is that the Kampei-tai is said to be run personally by the aggressive Gen. Prince Higashikuni Toshihiko, commander of Japan's defense force. Higashikuni is Emperor Hirohito's uncle.

8

October 14, 1940, Canton - It appears that my mysterious friend, Kodama Yoshio, having done three years in prison for the conspiracy to murder Prime Minister Saito, was recalled to Japan to have a go at Prime Minister Prince Konoye Fumimaro. The conspiracy, as it has emerged in the Japanese press, was led by Lt. Col. Tsuji Masanobu, the hero of a corps of young Japanese officers itching for more aggressive action in China. What moved the crazies to action was Konoye's plan, reported to them by a patriotic spy in the cabinet, to meet with Franklin Roosevelt. This was to be a move by Konoye to settle Japan's differences with the United States by diplomatic means. The prospect of a graceful, unmanly peace horrified the would-be warriors full of themselves and dreams of conquest.

Japanese newspapers are reporting that not one but two secret organizations of patriots are bent on disrupting the meeting between Konoye and Roosevelt. The Black Dragon Society, perhaps in emulation of Al Capone and the Chicago gangsters, had planned to ride into Tokio with guns blazing and rid the country of sissy compromisers in one bold stroke. Tenko-kai, the Society for Heavenly Action, decided to emulate the Kwantung army's successful blowing up of Marshall Chang in Manchuria. Lt. Col. Tsuji planned the bombing. Kodama Yoshio was to carry it out.

Konoye, who was scheduled to go to the conference by ship, had to travel to the naval base at Yokosuka by train, there being no good highway. It was Kodama's mission to blow up the train as it crossed the Rokuyo Bridge. Unfortunately, word of the plan was leaked to the government, by whom isn't yet clear. Several hours before he was to depart, Konoye retrieved his mistress from her hairdresser's and took her to the home of Count Ito Bunkichi, the son of one of the great figures of the Meiji Restoration. There, without a servant in the house, and with his mistress serving dinner, Konoye sat down to talk with Ambassador Crew, with Eugene Doonan of the American embassy translating.

Despite the fears of the Japanese patriots, I'll frankly be shocked if anything positive comes from talks like this. With all this public bickering among the military, it will likely be impossible for Konoye to count on enough officers to back him up.

November 1, 1940, Canton - This morning word arrived from Japan that owing to passionate nationalist sentiment in their favor, Kodama Yoshio and the other conspirators in the plan to assassinate Prime Minister Prince Konoye will not be tried. Konoye was, after all, a sissy weasel attempting to avoid war with the United States. And besides, the plan was not executed.

But perhaps there is more to it than mere patriotism.

Wu Shiao-peng, an English-speaking Chinese who claimed to be a cousin of my drunken Chinese friend in Xuzhou, turned out to be just as loose-mouthed as his kin. Wu told me off the record that Kampei-tai officers collecting the war booty are calling it the "Golden Lily," after a poem written by the emperor. In this effort, the Kampei-tai's commander, Gen. Prince Higashikuni, is subordinate to Emperor Hirohito's younger brother, Prince Chichibu Yasuhito, who in turn, the Chinese assume, is subordinate to Emperor Hirohito. He said it was inaccurate and dishonest to call it the Golden Lily. The treasure was Hirohito's Gold. Would any rational person expect anything else?

Wu said Chichibu is not recovering from tuberculosis in an estate near Mt. Fuji, as the Japanese would have us believe. Instead, accompanied by his cousin Prince Takeda, he is traveling incognito in territory occupied by Japanese troops, personally coordinating the collection of Hirohito's Gold. Wu added that Chichibu and Higashikuni put the Kampei-tai at Kodama's disposal for intelligence and muscle in the field. They switched his commission from the army to the navy. And they arranged for him to set up Kodama Kikan with a monopoly for supplying wartime materials stolen from China.

All that detail struck me as more than casual rumor. I asked Wu why he was telling me this.

He cocked his head and said, "Because, Mr. van der Elst, the people who lost the gold want the story known. Nobody knows how this war will end, do they?"

"And you're not really Chan's cousin, are you?"

"This is a large country, Mr. van der Elst. Everybody is related to somebody. Your interest in Kodama's activities is well known. You think we Chinese are, what is the English word, 'inscrutable'? When we want to, we Chinese can be quite helpful."

Ah, so that was it. A leak. Was Chan half as tanked as I had thought that night in Xuzhou? Likely not. I learned as a cub reporter that unconfirmed leaks are notoriously self-serving, and should always be viewed with suspicion. Here Chan and Wu's motive seemed fairly clear. They wanted an independent record of the Kampei-tai operation that was collecting wartime booty. Who were they working for? Most likely Chinese bankers and warlords who had lost fortunes and didn't fully trust Chiang to tend to their interests. Those moneyed gentlemen, eyeing the likely winners at war's end, had chosen me as a conduit to the American public.

That Emperor Hirohito should place his brother and uncle in charge of collecting the booty makes sense.

And what about the crazed nationalist and would-be assassin Kodama Yoshio? Will he be returned to his duties in China? My bet is that he will.

9

December 29, 1941, Kumming, China - The news from Pearl Harbor has put an added urgency to Chennault's training sessions with his Chinese pilots, which I am allowed to sit in on. It is Chennault's opinion that while the Japs are disciplined and will remain in their formations "come hell or high water," as he put it, they can be beaten by creative flying, as his own American pilots have shown.

He's resourceful himself, I'll give him that. He's got Chinese soldiers working around the clock repainting the propeller spinners and changing the numbers on the fuselages of the P-40s that Roosevelt sent him. The poor Japs must think he has a proper air force instead of a couple of dozen planes. The British may have spurned the P-40s as being obsolete, but they seem capable of doing the job here.

Chennault is said to have retired from the Army Air Force because of a bad ear that prevented him from flying. If he's hard of hearing, I haven't noticed it in the briefings, and he takes his turn in the cockpit along with everybody else. It's the theory of some of the reporters here that the imaginative Chennault merely faked deafness so as not to have to listen to the bullshit of his superiors, and in the end the Army Air Force used his bogus condition to get rid of him.

The Japs have amassed 70,000 troops at Yueyang, preparing for what Chiang, Stillwell, and Chennault all agree will likely be an assault upon Changsha on the Liuyang River. In preparation for this, Chennault is training his men to provide air cover for Chiang's defenders, after which he will turn his attention to the unprotected Jap freighters supplying their armies in China. If the Japs can't get their stolen copper, steel, and manganese back to their factories in Japan, what good is it? In the officers' mess one night, Chennault was overheard to say that sinking naked freighters with P-40s may not seem very sporting, but there is a certain satisfaction to it if you just remember Pearl Harbor when you swoop down on them and drop your torpedoes.

Coincident to this, Chiang's intelligence people in Shanghai now report that Kodama Yoshio, doing business as Kodama Kikan, has been put in charge of securing and shipping radium, cobalt, nickel, copper, and other strategic materials back to the Imperial Navy Air Force. Kodama Kikan covets industrial diamonds and platinum as well and has its own molybdenum and salt mines.

No opium or heroin moves in occupied south China without Kodama Kikan taking its hit. These activities dovetail nicely with Kodama's good fortune in the military. His commission has been switched from a colonel in the army to a captain in the navy, and he just happens to run Section Eight, the intelligence section of the Japanese General Staff in Shanghai. Kodama Kikan is said to finance the Shanghai office of the Kampei-tai. Such a spectacular rise in the fortunes of Kodama Yoshio.

Chennault's people are beside themselves trying to decide whether or not to bomb freighters that have been painted white with red crosses on them. There seems to be four of these "hospital ships" in all. The Japanese have been announcing their departure times and courses on clear radio. Chennault clearly believes they're bogus, but if he sends one under and turns out to be wrong, the shit would hit the fan big-time. The commanders of the American sub packs are faced with the same dilemma.

What could be so valuable as to warrant the elaborate, if transparent, deception? Hirohito's Gold?

July 15, 1942, Kumming, China - The Japanese have ceased their mysterious runs in bogus "hospital ships." This comes one month after the Japs lost their much vaunted naval superiority at the Battle of Midway. Is there a connection between the two? What could it be?

10

October 20, 1942, Kumming, China - Included in a bundle of news-papers flown in for Chennault and his officers the other day was a paper out of occupied Singapore showing a photograph of the British General Percival surrendering to General Yamashita in the cashier's cage of a bank. The account in the Singapore newspaper said Yamashita, outnumbered three to one, surprised Percival by circling to the rear and attacking through impenetrable jungle rather than confront the British batteries facing the sea. The audacious Yamashita then bluffed the confused Percival into surrendering before dark, when the British scouts were sure to learn the truth. The paper called Yamashita the "Tiger of Malaya."

This was the same photograph—accompanied by an identical story—that was published in a Jap newspaper that has made it to Kumming. The Jap version of Singapore's fall is rather at odds with British accounts published by Indian newspapers saying that a stubborn and courageous Percival, outnumbered three to one, fought nearly to the last man before succumbing to the Japs. The divergence of these stories is amazing, and I wonder which is true.

Chennault, off the record, said he believes the Japs this time. He says the British account has more than a hint of bullshit about it. Smacks of Churchill, he said.

What interests me is not how Singapore fell to the Japs (I agree with Chennault that the Jap version is probably correct) so much as a photograph that was featured in another Japanese newspaper, published nearly ten days after the surrender. This photograph, of a triumphant Yamashita and his officers toasting their victory at a formal banquet, contains that familiar, broad, heavy face of Kodama Yoshio. With him is Lt. Col. Masanobu Tsuji, one of the conspirators with Kodama in the plot to assassinate Prime Minister Konoye. Both were there to clean out the vaults once the surrender was signed, I'll bet.

I hear two more rumors of Japanese pursuing treasure. The Dutch are said to have moved gold from Batavia to the colonial capital of Jakarta in the Dutch East Indies, where it wound up in the hands of the Japanese. I am also told—by a French officer now working with the British—that the French, having stashed its treasure in Hanoi to get it out of the hands of the Germans, had to move it once again. As the Japanese approached the city, they loaded it onto a train, but the Japanese pursued it to the ruins of an ancient temple at the end of the rail line.

Chennault says he believes that his Flying Tigers have sunk close to 50,000 tons of Jap shipping so far this year, and he says that if the weather holds, the remaining couple of months look delicious. He says he wants to sink his turkey on Thanksgiving Day. The same with his Christmas goose.

To me the success of Chennault's Flying Tigers and the growing boldness of American submarines in sinking Japanese shipping leads to an interesting question. I wonder if Kodama has the balls to ship his treasure back to Japan. It's one thing to lose a load of Malayan rubber or Indonesian oil headed to Yokohama and quite another to forfeit the contents of the Singapore banks.

And where is the accumulated treasure of the Jap campaigns in Manchuria and China? If the patriotic army officers and right-wing thugs were exercising their passion in concert, as the reports out of Shanghai suggest, the Chinese treasure could possibly date to the capture of Mukden by the Kwangtung Army in 1931.

Before the war, Prince Chichibu was a patron of the Boy Scout movement in Japan, but the Jap soldiers are not to be confused with Boy Scouts. There is no way, none, that they're not helping themselves to jewels, art, and the contents of banks in captured territory, along with whatever women they fancy. The fate of bullion and currency is interesting, but not as fascinating to me as the eleven alchemist archers of Xhingsui Gap. There is a mysterious, romantic aura about the archers, which I personally saw being spirited away in Nanking—or at least something being spirited away on the day they were stolen. I wonder what happened to them.

When I worked for the *San Francisco Chronicle,* my city editor always said that if a reporter wanted to get some real stories he'd spend all his time having lunch with bankers. He said no matter what a crook did or how many bogus companies and bank accounts he was using to stash his money, one thing he always wanted, guaranteed one hundred percent, was that when the time came to divvy up the take, he would get his share.

There are enclaves of overseas Chinese throughout East and Southeast Asia. Saigon, Singapore, Rangoon, Kuala Lumpur, Jakarta, and Manila all have large Chinese communities. Those Chinese, who have no love for the Japs, have radios and junks everywhere on the South China Sea. There is no way that the Japs, however determined, can fight a war and monitor all the radio traffic and junks. Ever alert for tidbits and snippets of information that will help me figure out the puzzle of Hirohito's Gold, my helpful Chinese friends are saying that the Japanese are not shipping the treasure to the home islands.

Why not, I ask?

Other than Chennault's P-40s and American submarines, they have no idea.

If not Japan, then where?

They don't know that either, except that their contacts in Manila are claiming that Chichibu, using a pseudonym, has established a headquarters there.

Manila?

March 26, 1945, Off the island of Negros, Philippines - Belly full of shit on the shingle, bladder relieved of the bitter swill that serves as coffee, I sit on the deck of a destroyer in the shade of a lifeboat and wait, writing this to pass the time. It is almost nine, light for three hours, so the Japs have to know we're out here. I suffer the sweltering heat and try to stay out of everybody's way. When the Powers That Be deem it safe for pussy journalists to go ashore, I'll take a deep breath and climb aboard an LSD, hoping I don't catch a one-in-a-million stray like the shot that took Ernie Pyle under. I've survived almost ten years of covering this war; now, in the last days, a stray bullet would be my luck.

Behind us is a small island with a low ridge rising in the interior. This is Guimaras Island, I am told, and just beyond that the city of Iloilo on the island of Panay. In front of us and to our left we can see glimpses of corrugated tin and thatched roofs peeking through palm trees and patches of broad-leafed banana plant. This is the village of Pulupandan, south of Bacolod, a sprawl of rooftops lying to our left, over which two columns of black smoke rise high, thinning to gray in the pale blue sky.

Behind the columns of smoke lie the mountains where more men are certain to die before the madness is finished. The Japs, true to their noble code of Bushido, still fancy themselves as *sam-*

urai and will not quit. Manila has fallen and the war is all but concluded, and they are alone; to demonstrate the undying quality of their madness, they're determined to make a show of dying stupidly.

I am no general, but it strikes me that it may be fairly asked of General MacArthur just why he is sending these men here in the first place. I realize I probably don't know the full story, but wouldn't the commonsense decision be to leave these crazy Japs here? They can't be supplied anyway. So what if they occupy Negros for the time being? I suspect that MacArthur wants to be remembered as the Great Liberator of the Philippines and is determined to see the legend-building to the bitter end, the hell with the cost in human lives. I dare not breathe this around the officers here, some of whom are incredible suck-butts. I don't want to blow the opportunity to interview old Dougie the Ego somewhere down the line.

As the first wave of landing craft carrying members of the 185th Regimental Combat Team near the shoreline, we can hear the intermittent crackling of small arms fire.

It appears that only a lack of time last month kept the Japs in Manila from duplicating their barbarous rape of Nanking. Still, they didn't do badly in four days of torturing and raping. Their manly success in murdering 60,000 Filipino civilians in one night ought to earn them a medal from the Emperor. Their coup of burning down a hospital with all the patients inside surely deserves a footnote in the annals of dishonor. And the spirit of the *Hagakure* was wonderfully evident in the incident at St. Paul's College, where more manly Japs machine-gunned the fleeing survivors of 250 civilians who had been herded into a room with bombs planted in the chandeliers. Great sport!

If my G-2 sources have it right, Prince Chichibu spent most of the war in the Philippines, leaving only to escape the carnage of the American retaking of Manila. His main assignment seems to have been the collection and transportation of Hirohito's Gold. Did he stash the treasure in the Philippines? If so, why not in Japan?

I can't figure it, unless there are political machinations at work in Tokio that we won't know about until the war is over. The Jap nationalists were full of themselves when the war started. *Samurai*, they were. Nobody could stop them. In their frame of mind, defeat was out of the question. The prince likely assumed that the Philippines would be Jap territory when the Western powers finally capitulated. Alas, to paraphrase Robbie Burns, the best laid plans o' rats and Japs *aft gang agley*.

But even if Japan were defeated, Emperor Hirohito likely felt he could save his treasure by claiming the Philippines as part of a negotiated settlement. MacArthur's overheated rhetoric to the contrary, Hirohito knows that few Americans feel any special affection for the Filipinos. After the cost of so much blood and treasure, Americans are sick of war. They want closure. How far will President Truman go to avoid the horrific slaughter of American soldiers that will surely be the price of invading the Japanese home islands?

Claiming the Philippines would require the Japs to control at least some Filipino territory; that would account for their tenacious refusal to withdraw badly needed troops from Negros and put them to use in defending the homeland.

Sitting here remembering the faraway autumn of 1937, I wonder what happened to the alchemist archers of Xhingsui Gap. Did Kodama ship them to the Philippines along with the rest of Hirohito's treasure? Where, exactly, did he stash them? In Manila? In the mountains at Baguio, where General Yamashita was holed up before he surrendered? It's hard to imagine Yamashita being part of Chichibu's inside gang of super patriots; for reasons not clear, Tojo didn't like him and shuttled him off to oblivion in Manchuria for most of the war. Only in the final months of the war, when the defense of the Philippines was doomed, did Tojo bring the Tiger of Malaya in to suffer the ignominy of defeat.

March 30, 1945, Bacolod, Negros - The Japs, having given up Bacolod with scarcely a shot, have apparently decided simply to harass us for the time being, this stall giving their main body of troops time to retreat to the northeast.

The Powers That Be gave me the choice of following the 185th north along the coast to Talisay and Silay, or hook to the east then north with the 160th to follow the retreating Japs through the villages of Granada and Conception. Ordinarily the Japs would be expected to make a spirited defense of Silay because of its natural deep harbor to which the Japs made major improvements, but recon says no, the main body of troops is retreating to the mountains. The chances for action being the same in both cases, I flipped a mental coin and picked the 160th.

So now I sit in a makeshift bamboo bar drinking *tuba*, fermented coconut water, or coconut whiskey, as the locals call it. Again I write to pass the time. In the halls of LaSalle College, which the commanding officers are using for their temporary headquarters, mysterious last-minute changes of plan are being made. This is the doughface's enduring burden: Hurry up and wait, hurry up and wait. Much of this palavering and dithering, I assume, has to do with the results of G-2 interrogations of Filipino refugees from Silay and reports from the Filipino resistance. The scuttlebutt from G-2 is that for weeks the Japs have used forced Filipino labor to dig a series of tunnels and pillboxes in the hills at the base of Mt. Silay. This is apparently the refuge to which the Japs are determined to make their last stand in the Visayan Islands in the center of the Philippine archipelago.

12

April 2, 1945, Silay, Negros - The 160th today caught up with the
185th that had taken Silay earlier in the morning. The Japs had
destroyed the bridge across the Guinhalaron River, but it's dry
season and the 185th was able to ford the river about three hundred yards upstream. I guessed wrong as to the action yesterday.
The 185th met some resistance by the Jap defenders of an airstrip
at Silay. All I got to see was a few Japs hustling their asses across
rice paddies and through banana groves. Bang, bang, stall, and
retreat.

About halfway between the villages of Granada and Conception, Company B forced Japs out of a large house on a small bluff
overlooking some rice paddies, the Japs setting it on fire as they
left. The house must have been impressive, given the size of its
foundation, but what was really nutty was the size, not to mention
the mere existence, of a vast, deep swimming pool beside the
house. It was maybe twelve feet deep at one end with both high
and low boards, thirty feet wide, and sixty or seventy feet long—
fed by a small stream at the top end, and with a plug allowing it
to drain toward rice paddies at the foot of the bluff.

This is an island with an amazing discrepancy between the
landowners and peasants, this being a legacy of the Spanish colonists. If this is any indication, wow! Three of us pussy reporters

who were following the 160th went swimming while Company B pursued the Japs across the rice paddies and through a field of sugarcane on the far side.

Although so far most of the action is on the coast, I am told on the QT that I should stick with the 160th. The 160th has been given the job of routing the Japs out of Hill 3155, their main defensive position. This hill is in an area that the Filipinos call the *Patag*, a hardwood forest at the base of Mt. Silay. I checked the maps and found that Hill 3155, which is flanked on the east by the Hinalinan River and on the southwest by the Imbang River, is located a little more than a mile and a half south of the village of Lantawan and a little more than two miles south and slightly west of the larger village of San Juan.

The story unfolded by G-2 corrobrates the reports in Bacolod, namely that the Japs have spent weeks mining and honeycombing Hill 3155 with pillboxes, trenches, and spider holes. The promontory appears innocent enough on the topographical map, until you realize it's made to order for crossing lanes of machine-gun fire directed down on attackers from above.

The NCO who told me about Hill 3155 took me for a ride in a Jeep to have a look at the deep-water harbor just south of town. A spanking new concrete highway built by the Japs to supply their troops serves the harbor, at the mouth of the Guinhaloron River. There is a confusion of shacks and bamboo huts clustered at the end of an impressive wharf that angles to the right, sticking out into the water for maybe a half mile. Judging from the stolid concrete piling put in place by the Japs, they intended to be in Silay awhile.

I stand in the heat and sticky humidity and slap bugs and look at the huge wharf that seems to have been built to accommodate anything: battleships, aircraft carriers, you name it. At my side, Filipino children with beautiful brown eyes and black hair that glistens in the sun jump up and down, yammering, "Joe! Hey, Joe! Chocolate, Joe?"

I squat to describe what I see and sweat drips onto the paper. My hands and arms are slick with sweat. Everything wet.

April 20, 1945, Knob Hill, Negros - The other pussy reporters and I were in the rear eating Spam and eggs this morning when we got more scuttlebutt about the 2,500-yard-long Hill 3155 that the dog-faces are calling Knob Hill, an oblong affair about 100 yards high and 150 yards across. Knob Hill is shaping up to be a real tit-wringer because the Japs have had time to burrow deep into its steep, brushy slopes. The front slope facing the Filipino and American troops rises on a 50-degree climb that changes to a 60-degree slope before the crown. On the reverse side, a 70-degree rise backs off to 60 degrees near the top. The Japs have been digging into island hills and mountains for most of the Pacific war and now are pretty good at it.

Last night Company A and Company B ran into machine-gun fire as they approached the base of the hill. They dug in for the night thinking everything was going to be okay, when suddenly the Japs on the crest began throwing demolition charges and hand grenades down on them, forcing them to withdraw. So this morning members of Company C took their turn in the lead, and they too were pinned by machine-gun fire. The Japs then fell silent and the Company C commander, Lt. John W. Dolan, took the point in an effort to determine the location of the fire. He did this knowing that the experienced Jap gunners would remain silent until he crossed their firing lanes. They crossed the lanes and, sure enough, they shot him dead. This afternoon, General Brush passed word down that henceforth Hill 3155 would be called Dolan Hill.

13

May 11, 1945, Dolan Hill, Negros - While the 185th and the 503rd concentrated on the hills to the rear and sides of Dolan, the 160th Regiment has had to take daily, brutal punishment from the machine guns and grenade throwers operating from caves, pillboxes, and holes rendered invisible by heavy underbrush. General Mac-Arthur is said to be pissed because of the delay in driving the Japs off Negros. Accordingly, General Brush has decided to show the stubborn little fuckers who's boss, because he's ordered heavy aerial bombardment of the hill to shake 'em up just a tad.

May 24, 1945, Knob Hill, Negros - Despite General Brush's edict that Hill 3155 is henceforth to be called Dolan Hill, the dogfaces getting shot at insist on calling it Knob Hill. The honor belongs to the dogfaces, not the generals. While I hate to rob Lieutenant Dolan of his short-lived immortality, I too will call it Knob Hill.

General MacArthur's ire, expressed through air sorties ordered by General Brush, has really been something. It's been zoom, zoom, zoom, boom, boom, boom, day after day over the last two weeks. On May 11 through May 14, Corsairs and Havoc attack bombers pummeled Knob Hill daily with 1,000-pound bombs and 250-pound demolition bombs. Some show! How the Japs could survive that punishment is beyond me, except that they must be burrowed in very deep indeed.

Yesterday, the 160th made its move. In the course of its advance, the 160th killed 129 Japanese and knocked out forty-two pillboxes. Still the Japs fought on. A squad from Company L, led by Staff Sgt. John C. Sjogren was chosen to lead the assault. The first pillbox Sjogren's squad encountered was protected by ten snipers, and although wounded in the action Sjogren got eight of them. He ordered his squad to blast away at the pillbox split while he scrambled up the steep slope and tossed hand grenades inside. Sjogren destroyed nine pillboxes in this manner, once reaching inside and grabbing the barrel of a Jap machine gun while it was still being fired and giving it a yank before he tossed in his grenades. In all, Sjogren killed forty-three Japs, including one in hand-to-hand. His astonishing heroism gave me goosebumps as I wrote an account of the action for AP's client newspapers.

Although there were stragglers and snipers still being driven out this afternoon, the denuded hill was finally deemed free enough of Japs that we pussy reporters were allowed to take a hike in the sweltering heat to see for ourselves what the 160th had been up against all those weeks. I think I'm probably getting a little long in the tooth for this sort of thing. I scrambled around bombed-out holes and trenches slapping bugs and sweating like I had dengue fever.

No wonder the Japs were hard to drive out. Their machine-gunners, flanked by snipers in strategically placed spider holes, had been protected by reinforced concrete pillboxes. These pillboxes were connected by trenches six feet deep.

Two main trenches on either side of the hill followed the contours of the crown; these were connected by a cross-trench. The trench on the backside, facing Jap lines, was honeycombed with a series of tunnels dug three-fourths of the way into the ridge. When General Brush's airplanes had made their many lethal sorties, the Japs had simply retreated to the cool safety of their deep tunnels, and when the bombing was finished, they returned to their machine guns. No uncivilized amount of lives squandered by Douglas MacArthur could have driven them out. It had taken major sacrifice both by the Americans and their hard-fighting Filipino allies. The Filipinos hated the Japanese for what they had done during their occupation and fought them with a vengeance. .

I wanted to explore the deep Jap tunnels that looked like mine shafts probing the interior of the hill. I wasn't the only reporter who wanted to go inside. The possibility of exotic souvenirs was one of the attractions, but we also wanted to give our readers some idea of what life must have been like in there while General Brush's Corsairs and Havocs pounded the exterior of the hill. Unfortunately, we were told no. The Japs had a habit of filling such places with booby traps and the army didn't want to be responsible for reporters blowing themselves up. The tunnels, deemed dangerous, were placed off-limits to all personnel, both military and civilian.

There was nothing else to see, so I just wanted to get off the hill. The smell of decomposing bodies was enough to knock a dog off a gut wagon.

A postscript here: After Hill 3155 was officially renamed Dolan Hill by General Brush, only to be called Knob Hill by the troops— as in the knob of the door to the Jap defenses—I now find that the local Ilongo term for the hill is Pulak Pulakan, which I'm told means something like a hill in the shape of an inverted cup made out of a coconut shell. Pulak Pulakan. I like it. The name has a nice sound. It flows off the tongue.

14

September 12, 1945, above the Pacific - I am sitting here squat-legged getting this story down on paper while it's still fresh in my mind. I managed to scrounge a ride to Hickam Field in Honolulu on a navy C-130 Flying Boxcar, and I'm still up here. It's been a long, cold, noisy flight. A couple of hours ago I was standing by the head massaging my numb butt when I eavesdropped on some dogfaces on their way to be discharged at Ft. Lewis, Washington. They had served together in the 185th Regiment on Negros, and I might have gotten to know them better if I'd chosen to continue up the coast instead of circling inland with the 160th.

There were three of them, Dave, a sleepy-eyed, raw-boned kid from Denver; Larry, curly-headed and quick to laugh, who had grown up on an artichoke farm out of Phoenix, Arizona; and Jay, a schoolteacher's son from Missoula, Montana. After their discharge they were planning to take off to Jay's place in Missoula and go fishing up in the high country. They were going to drive down to Idaho to ride a raft down the Snake River. Jay said a ride on the Snake River whitewater was a no-bullshit guaranteed pisser of the first order.

That's after they all got laid, of course. Jay told his comrades that women in Montana were sufficiently horny and creative to accommodate their various desires. He said the women in the

Bitterroot Mountains had had years with nothing to satisfy their female needs except riding horses bareback. He said their strategy should be to strike immediately while the pussy was still smoking.

They had enlisted in the army three years earlier, floppy-jointed, big-eating teenagers off to fight Japs and Krauts. Now they were grown men wanting to get home as quickly as possible to reclaim a bit of their lost youth, if that was still possible. Shooting the whitewater was to be a celebratory return.

When I got my turn in the head, the plane started pitching so that a good portion of pee wound up on my leg. Disgusted, I shook my piece and stuck it back in my pants. When I stepped out of the head with my leg plastered with warm piss, the dogfaces from the 185th had shifted to war stories, and Jay was telling how he had helped CIC agents from G-2 interrogate Filipinos after they had captured Silay.

He said one of their best witnesses was an informant for the resistance, an old woman who washed clothes for the Japs. The Japs didn't want to screw her and thought she was harmless, so she was allowed to go about pretty much as she pleased. She was present one morning a few weeks earlier when a Jap vessel moored during the night amid much security.

The next morning she went to visit her niece, and when she got back from her niece's to wash Jap clothes, the entire street leading to the wharf was deserted. It was spooky. She said that unknown to her the docking area had been ordered cleared of everyone. Frightened and not knowing what else to do but hide, certainly not wanting to challenge the temper of a Jap soldier, she hid in one of the small houses that were crowded around the entrance to the wharf. Peering through the cracks of a bamboo wall, she witnessed the arrival of a high-powered officer who had apparently flown into Silay by plane. It was part of her job as a spy for the resistance to keep an eye on the comings and goings of Jap officers, and this was the first time she had seen this one, who was much fussed over and deferred to by his subordinates.

She said the big deal officer personally supervised the unloading of eleven heavy, strapped wooden boxes. It was her job to memorize such details for the resistance, so she counted them carefully. The boxes were so heavy that six Jap soldiers had to struggle to carry each one. One was dropped, much to the annoyance of the officer who had arrived by plane. The box split wide open, revealing a golden dragon.

On hearing this, I said, "A dragon?"

Jay looked up at me. "With beautiful little scales and ruby eyes." He said the woman watched as the Japs quickly repaired the box and loaded all eleven onto two trucks that took them away. He said G-2 later learned these trucks made daily trips carrying food and supplies to men digging pillboxes, trenches, and tunnels in the mountains.

"The alchemist archers of Xhingsui Gap," I murmured.

"Say again?"

"It's a long story," I said.

Jay said the CIC agent fixated on the tactical importance of the digging to the exclusion of everything else. He wanted to know exactly where the Japs were digging and for how long. He rolled his eyes and look disgusted when she told him about the golden dragon. Golden dragon, right.

Jay said in his opinion the CIC guy should have listened to her. She was a simple, honest woman and virtually incapable of lying. Why would she have invented a story like that? He said the golden dragon, if the other boxes also contained dragons, were on their way to Dolan Hill, had to be.

All three dogfaces shook their heads vigorously in agreement. Larry from Phoenix said the poor bastards from the 160th really took it in the shorts at that fucking place, and they all nodded their heads. They were all admirers of the crazed Sergeant Sjogren, who was given a battlefield commission and nominated for the Congressional Medal of Honor for his charge uphill against those terrible pillboxes. In the opinion of the dogfaces, if Sjogren didn't get the Congressional Medal of Honor, it would be a clear-cut case of statutory rape.

Hearing all this, I am a little depressed. The alchemist archers of Xhingsui Gap are likely resting in the bowels of Pulak Pulakan. I decide to tell no one the story. In the first place, who would believe me? In the second place, what am I going to do, go back alone to an impoverished tropical country and try to make away with eleven priceless treasures weighing five hundred pounds each? If I had a death wish, maybe. Forget that.

I know where the dragons are. Anybody else trying to retrieve them, including the Japanese, will face the same obstacles as me. No, check that. The Japanese, being roundly hated by the Filipinos for what they did during the occupation, face even more problems. It's unlikely the statues are going anywhere unless the Filipinos blunder onto them. Someday maybe, when the time is right, and I have some help I can trust, I will return to explore the tunnels of Pulak Pulakan. In the meantime, I'll keep my suspicion under my Stetson.

I feel pretty much like the trio of dogfaces from the 185th. I, too, want to return home and reclaim a regular life—if that's possible after all these years. Unlike them, my youth is pretty much shot, but it's not too late to have a family and a regular life, no problem wangling a stateside assignment from the AP, where, I am aware, I am regarded as something of a journalistic legend. Although I have an idea of the final resting place of the golden archers, my story of the Kampei-tai's treasure is not finished. When I get back to Hickam Field, I'll have to hitch a ride back to Tokio to have a chat with Kodama Yoshio, who is cooling his heels in prison awaiting trial as a war criminal.

I've been following this story since 1931. For there to be any kind of closure, I have to sit down face-to-face with Kodama

Yoshio. I want to surprise him with my Japanese. I want look him in the eye and tell him what I saw in Nanking and what I've figured out over the years. After all these years and all the speculation, I want to see how he reacts and what he says. It's unlikely that I'll learn anything of value, but I have to try. If he says anything, of course, it will likely be a bald-faced lie, but even lies can sometimes be clues to the truth.

15

November 3, 1946, Tokio - My colleagues all tell me that if I want to learn more about Kodama's wartime activities, I should talk to an army intelligence operative in Taipei named Col. John K. Singlaub. Scuttlebutt has it that Singlaub and an officer named Ray Cline, both of whom spent most of the war in Korea and China, are tight with Chiang Kai-shek and have examined numerous captured Japanese documents, including firsthand accounts of Kampei-tai looting and collecting of Hirohito's Gold.

A library of clippings is called a morgue by journalists because it contains dead copy. To prepare myself for an interview with Singlaub, I stopped off in Tokio first to find out what was in the morgue that's maintained by a pool of newspapers with reporters covering the occupation. I also wanted to know more about the wartime activities of Kodama's patrons, Prince Chichibu and Gen. Prince Higashikuni.

MacArthur's treatment of the royal family is annoying to most of us reporters. While folks back in the states, having surrendered so many sons and husbands, want Hirohito tarred and feathered, the developing American line seems to be that Emperor Hirohito was somehow a virtual prisoner of the militarists. It could be that MacArthur is afraid his wonderful new Constitution won't stand a chance unless the Japanese people believe it has the emperor's blessing—the royal family being the "focus" and "symbol" of Japanese patriotism. According to this specious argument, the emperor was passive, see, a withdrawn monarch who was sucking his thumb while officers of the Imperial Army, loose cannons, invoked imperial authority to pursue the war on their own.

Like anybody believes any of that horseshit.

Prince Chichibu has emerged reluctantly, from his—*cough, cough*—alleged isolation from the spa where he spent the war recovering from tuberculosis. Right. It's no secret that he was a fanatical nationalist when the war started. Judging from the prewar photographs of him, he was a slender figure, pale, diffident, and not a little aloof as befitting His Imperial Highness. But not inside. Inside Prince Chichibu was a passionate militarist. Another reader of the *Hagakure.* A would-be *samurai.*

Chichibu is being treated with exaggerated if not preposterous respect and deference by MacArthur's officers. Ask a simple question about him and all you get is poor Prince Chichibu this, poor Prince Chichibu that. The most elementary inquiry draws a put-upon look of censure. Like we're so dumb as not to know there is something going on with respect to Chichibu that we should know about, but don't. I amend that. Most of my colleagues don't have any idea what Chichibu was doing. I do. My suspicions are increased when I hear a rumor that confirms the reports of my Chinese confidants. Sometime in the summer of 1942, using a pseudonym, Chichibu established a personal headquarters in Manila. In Manila! Yes!

Prince Higashikuni Toshihiko, Emperor Hirohito's uncle, was among the "big brothers" who attended Peer's School with Hirohito, that being the place where the sons of royalty and nobility were trained for government service. Their classmates included Prince Asaka Yasuhiko, the gentleman who oversaw the rape of Nanking; the Marquis Komatsu Teruhisa, in charge of naval staff studies for the attack on Pearl Harbor; and Prince Konoye Fumimaro, who as prime minister reluctantly led Japan to war with China in 1937. But the Japanese all know those royals were sissies, downright girls compared Higashikuni.

Himself the son of an imperial prince, Higashikuni married a daughter of the Emperor Meiji. After graduating from the Army Academy and the Army War College, he was named chief of military aviation in 1937 and promoted to general in 1939, taking control of the Kampei-tai in the process. Three days after the Japanese attack on Pearl Harbor, he was named the general commander of Japan's defense.

Tojo persuaded Higashikuni to assume the duties of prime minister at the end of the war—this on the grounds that the military would listen to a member of the imperial family. Higashikuni, part of the Jap contingent on the deck of the USS *Missouri* when Japan surrendered, resigned a month later. Although he was among the most fanatic officers of the Japanese high command, he was spared trial as a war criminal because of his royal status. Crushed by having to participate in the surrender, he chose to declare himself a commoner rather than disembowel himself by ritual *seppuku*. If stories circulating in Tokio are true, he's now running a retail shop and plans to become a Buddhist monk.

I think of the French kings, the British monarchs, the Romanovs, the Hapsburgs, and the Spanish royal families that sent Cortez and Pizarro and Ponce de Leon to the New World. Are we to believe that the Japanese royal family is somehow unique in history in not caring a whit about crass fortune? That Douglas MacArthur would feel compelled to suck up to these people and go along with the pretense that they had nothing to do with the war makes me want to puke.

Which leaves two fascinating questions: If more of Hirohito's Gold than the alchemist archers is in the Philippines, exactly where is it? Who will get it now?

I learned that Singlaub was an OSS agent who parachuted be-

hind German lines to help the French resistance prepare for
D-Day. He later parachuted into China to help Chiang Kai-shek's
guerrillas. He was then assigned to Manchuria to help Chiang's
cause. When Chiang retreated to Taiwan, Singlaub followed. One
of his best operatives, Ray Cline, was pals with the generalissimo's
son, Chiang Ching-kuo. What Singlaub didn't learn from Japanese
documents, he obviously knew from talking to Chiang and his
officers. I think my informants are right. I need to talk to Singlaub.

November 5, 1946, Taipei - An officer with the name Singlaub
pinned on his chest preceded me into the Quonset hut that
housed the American G-2, but once inside I was told that Col.
John K. Singlaub was in Manchuria. I was taken to the office of
Maj. Dale Davis, a man with piecing blue eyes who regarded me
as a kind of worm. When I asked what army intelligence had
learned about a Japanese Kampei-tai officer named Kodama
Yoshio, he looked momentarily startled, "What do you know about
Kodama?" I got the feeling he didn't like it that I knew anything
at all about Kodama.

I told him about my experience as a correspondent in Tokio
and on the Chinese mainland in the late 1930s. I said, "An amazing story. An ex-convict with no military training steps out of
prison and is immediately made an army officer in charge of
Kampei-tai units collecting booty ripped off by the Japanese
Imperial Army. By the end of the war, he is a thirty-four-year-old
admiral and the aide to Prime Minister Higashikuni. An admiral!
I bet he can't read a compass. It's my understanding he was working for Prince Chichibu and General Prince Higashikuni from the
moment he was released from prison. And by extension, I take it,
Emperor Hirohito himself."

Davis looked annoyed. "Your 'understanding.' I see. Based on what, if you don't mind telling me?"

"On Chinese intelligence sources who also told me about Kodama Kikan and Kodama's relationship to Big-Eared Tu in Shanghai. Prince Chichibu was not holed up in a health spa. He was in charge of transporting and storing Hirohito's loot that the Japs call the Golden Lily. He moved around using pseudonyms until he established a headquarters in Manila shortly after we blew the fuck out of the Jap navy at Midway."

Davis studied me, sizing me up. It was clear he wondered just what it was I had learned about Kodama.

"Am I right?" I asked.

He tried unsuccessfully to suppress his annoyance at the question. "That's a fascinating theory, Mr. van der Elst, but I'm afraid I don't have the foggiest idea what you or your so-called 'intelligence sources' are talking about. Kodama is in Sugamo Prison awaiting trial for war crimes. Perhaps the International Tribunal will let you see their records. As far as I know, Prince Chichibu spent the war in a spa being treated for tuberculosis just like they say. You know as much as I do about Higashikuni. As I understand it, the emperor had nothing to do with the war. He was duped by the militarists. Sorry that you came all this way for nothing."

Right, I thought. We certainly wouldn't want the truth to skew the results of a tribunal deliberating in Tokio. I once had a cynical city editor tell me that a good journalist never let the truth stand in the way of a good story. Douglas MacArthur should apply for a job with the *New York Post*.

I had better luck learning about the alchemist archers. With the help of Chinese language translators graciously provided me by the State Department, I quickly learned the gist of the story. Court historians of the Emperor Wu Tse in northwestern China recorded that on March 1, 1144, eleven archers saved Wu's empire from the scourge of Mongols by delaying the advance of the three thousand-man army of the marauding Huong Khan through the Han Mountains. For a critical two hours, heroic archers made their stand at a narrow, rock-walled pass, Xhingsui Gap. The invaders were forced to proceed through the gap at no more than double file on foot and single file on horseback. The archers, firing at close range, forced their enemies to climb over the bodies of their dead and dying comrades to continue the advance. In the end the archers yielded, but gave their lives so that the remnants of Wu's army, soundly defeated by Huong's soldiers two days earlier, could successfully withdraw to the well-provisioned safety of the moated capital city of Sangin.

It was widely held that the heroes were turned into benevolent dragons that rose with the mists to live in the Han Mountains on either side of Xhingsui Gap. When gold was discovered near the entrance to Xhingsui Gap a year and a half later, the emperor believed that the dragons had shown the way. The grateful Wu ordered that eleven golden dragons be struck, intending as well that they should guard his throne upon his death.

Wu's talented goldsmiths provided the golden dragons with ruby eyes and gave them meticulously detailed scales and claws. The dragons were just shy of three feet long and weighed about five hundred pounds each. The martyred archers, faithful defenders turned into gold, came to be known as the alchemist archers of Xhingsui Gap.

Wu Tse died in 1178, but the dragons did not accompany him to his tomb as planned. They were stolen and their whereabouts were unknown until 1645, when they were reported as part of the personal treasure of the warlord Chang Yu-yen in northeastern China. There were undocumented reports of their disappearance and reappearance both in the eighteenth and nineteenth centuries.

In 1931, a Nanking businessman, Yong An, acquired the dragons as part of a deal in which he yielded a portion of his monopoly over valuable opium territory. The dragons were in the personal vaults of Yong's eldest son, Yong Zhi-lu, when the Japanese captured Peking in September 1937. Yong, hoping that the Japanese offensive could be blunted, was reluctant to move them from Nanking until absolutely necessary.

When Shanghai fell in mid-November, the elder Yong was in the grip of a recurring bout of malaria, and his son refused to make a decision without his father's clear-headed approval. Relying on exaggerated reports of Chiang Kai-shek's successful blunting of the Japanese advance, the two Yongs postponed moving the alchemist archers to central China until late November, when Japanese troops were approaching the city.

On December 5, in the final hours before Gen. Tan Shengzhi's defense collapsed, the alarmed Yong, sixty-seven years old and sweaty with malaria, attempted to move his family and the priceless dragons out of Nanking. His party was forced to retreat when Chinese troops, ordered to prevent more army units from abandoning their positions, fired on them. Yong was wounded in the neck. His youngest daughter was killed.

16

November 8, 1946 Tokio - I just got started on my reading of the declassified G-2 war crimes files on Kodama Yoshio—declassified meaning they've been edited to remove anything of embarrassment to the United States. Check that, edited to remove anything that might embarrass anybody with the ability to order something classified. The juiciest stuff is always deemed to be a threat to national security.

It didn't take long before I tumbled across a whoopsie-doo reference to another Jap who had earned for himself a gold star on the list of history's all-time motherfuckers. Rear Adm. Iwabuchi Sanji, known in the popular press as the Butcher of Manila, was the commander of the Jap sailors and marines who sacked Manila in its final hours. I was drawn to the story of what happened to Manila because of Prince Chichibu, who was doing the bidding, it had to be assumed, of his brother Emperor Hirohito.

The honorable Iwabuchi-san was among those war criminals listed as being directly subordinate to Kodama. And Iwabuchi's assignment? Woo-hoo! He was in charge of shipping "strategic war materials" from Southeast Asia to Tokio via Manila. My, oh my, how the intelligence bureaucrats do love euphemisms.

I almost ran to the army clerk who only minutes earlier had given me the adulterated Kodama poop that I had to read in the little room reserved for pussy reporters. It turned out the file on Iwabuchi was dog-eared from being read by journalists trying to fit together the pieces of the Manila horror for which Yamashita had been tried. Why did the Japs do what they did to the poor Filipinos in Manila? And why on earth did Iwabuchi let them do it? What was the point? This wasn't the only time such questions had been asked and it wouldn't be the last. Yet when we read of one human being casually gouging out another's eyes or cutting out his tongue, we furrow our brows in puzzlement and bewilderment. For this reason scores of journalists had pawed through Iwabuchi's file.

Iwabuchi's dossier said that Iwabuchi, fifty-three at the time of reported death in the final hours of the horror, was a graduate of the Naval Academy at Etajima. Although uncertain, G-2 believes he spent his early career in the Kampei-tai, which is no doubt where he met Kodama. In March 1942, he was made captain of the battleship *Kirishima*, which he commanded at both Midway and Guadalcanal. The *Kirishima* was among the ships under the command of Vice Admiral Abe that Admiral Yamamoto ordered to destroy Henderson Field on Guadalcanal. Both Abe and Iwabuchi had to scuttle ships in the ensuing naval debacle. Abe was demoted, but Iwabuchi, curiously, was promoted to rear admiral.

In 1944, Iwabuchi was appointed commander of the Japanese naval base in Manila and given the job, under Kodama Yoshio, of moving "strategic materials" on to Tokio. If they truly were strategic, why not ship them directly to Tokio?

In describing Iwabuchi's duties in Manila, the dossier included what amounted to a throwaway paragraph saying that Iwabuchi was rumored to be personally in charge of the digging of an elaborate system of secret tunnels at various sites in Manila. These included Fort Santiago, Fort Bonifacio, and Intramuros as well as various churches, harbor sites, and municipal buildings. The Japs really love their digging, regular little moles, they are. I had seen their handiwork on Negros. In this case the actual digging was said to have been done by Filipino, American, and Australian prisoners of war who were executed when their duties were completed. The report said the purpose of the tunnels remained unknown and their existence was "incompletely confirmed." Incompletely? How incompletely? In fact, "incompletely confirmed" can be liberally translated as "We know the truth but we have our own reasons for not being specific, so no use bugging us with questions."

As the Americans gathered forces for the retaking of Manila in the first days of 1945, General Yamashita withdrew to Baguio in the mountains of central Luzon and, according to his lawyers, ordered all Japanese forces to abandon the city. He ordered Gen. Yokoyama Shizuo to destroy the bridges over the Pasig River, then quit the city. Yokoyama's story is that under the chain of command, he lacked the authority to force Iwabuchi to do anything he didn't want to do. I have several friends who covered Yamashita's "trial" in Manila, that they said was more accurately described as a kangaroo court. They believed Yamashita.

For whatever unfathomable reason, Iwabuchi refused to budge from Manila. He decided to defend the city with his 16,000 marines and sailors, a bizarre decision given the size of the gathering American forces. As MacArthur's First Cavalry and 37th Division neared the city, Iwabuchi retreated across the Pasig, destroying port and military facilities along the way.

As American units entered the city, Iwabuchi's sailors and marines, bent on a suicidal showdown, turned on the city with a vengeance, murdering 60,000 civilians in the next twenty-four hours and raping uncounted women. Iwabuchi himself retreated behind forty-foot-thick stone battlements in the old walled city of Intramuros. And the Americans, who had refrained from using artillery out of consideration of the city's residents, were forced to call in heavy artillery and mortars, destroying the entire inner city and leveling Intramuros.

Iwabuchi retreated from the Legislative Building to the Bureau of Agriculture and Commerce, and although his body was never found, he was "believed to have died" beneath the rubble of the Finance Building when it collapsed under fire on March 3, 1945.

I'm amazed by this. They couldn't find the body under the rubble. Why not? Believed to have died? What about all those rumored tunnels? I think: *Naturally you can't find his body, you dumb shits. Can't you add two and two?* I'm sure there are people in Mac-Arthur's command who know very well how to add two and two, but are leaving it to us to figure the mathematics if we can.

If the raping and bloodshed that went with Iwabuchi's cruel and pointless defense in any way embarrassed the Japs, they had a curious way of expressing it. In the final days of the war, Kodama was given yet another extraordinary promotion, advisor to Prime Minister Higashikuni. Shortly thereafter, the Imperial Navy—in a final gesture of defiance and contempt—gave the Butcher of Manila a posthumous promotion to vice admiral and awarded him the First Order of the Golden Kite.

Why on earth would the Emperor Hirohito detail his brother to stash his booty in Manila? The entire treasure captured by the Japanese Imperial Army? In Manila? No, no, no. That makes no sense whatsoever. It is impossible. Preposterous. Can't be. There has to be more to it than that.

Later that day I got loaded on hot sake with some colleagues who had been trying to piece together the political intrigue on the Japanese home front during the war. We were all hearing the same thing from Japs we could get to talk. Emperor Hirohito, it seems, had been paranoid about the security of his throne for the better part of ten years. This fear, unreasonable as it might sound, stemmed from the military insurrection of February 26, 1936, the ultimate result of differing interpretations of the national polity, *kokutai*. Out of this rebellion came the notion of *kodo*, the "imperial way," in which the emperor, a paragon of moral excellence, was seen as the living embodiment of Japan. In the ten years following Hirohito's enthronement in 1926, a debate raged between a nationalist, militarist faction and constitutionalists. This came to a head in a show trial of Lt. Col. Aizawa Saburo, of the nationalist faction, who had assassinated Maj. Gen. Nagata Tetsuzan, a supporter of constitutional rule. In the course of the trial, members of the army's hard-line faction, seeking to have Hirohito declare a "Showa restoration," mutinied. The insurrectionists, believing that Hirohito was weak and a puppet of his advisors, began murdering all officials they associated with constitutional government, beginning with Saito Makoto, Lord Keeper of the Privy Seal. By February 29, the revolt was put down, but from that moment on Emperor Hirohito was insecure about his throne and fearful that renegade military units might once again get out of control and put someone more to their liking in his place.

The sick irony is that while Emperor Hirohito called the shots during the war against the United States and its allies, he was the whole time fearful not of domestic sissies or any sort of peace faction, but of military commanders even crazier than himself. This was a difficult concept to grasp, but from all accounts it was apparently true.

As the war went from bad to worse after the disaster at Midway, it made sense that Emperor Hirohito, fearing another insurrection by extremists—especially in the event of humiliating defeat— decided that it was safer to keep his treasure out of their reach, as well as that of an invading army.

Okay, I thought, assume it was true that Hirohito regarded the Golden Lily as his personal prerogative, him being a living god and all. No way he would want to share the Big Sushi with the idiots who had once threatened to push him from the throne. Where could he stash it to keep it out of their reach?

To the Japs, all pumped up with the code of Bushido, unconditional surrender was inconceivable. But Hirohito knew the Americans, British, and Australians were less sanguine about sending hundreds of thousands of soldiers and sailors to their death. What territory could the Japs hope to claim in a negotiated settlement? The Dutch East Indies with its oil? No way. Malaya with its tin and rubber? Not likely.

As Chichibu was allegedly setting up shop in Manila a month after Midway, the "hospital" ships ceased their mysterious voyages to Japan. If the emperor regarded Manila as a kind of refrigerator to keep the Big Sushi out of the hands of the militarists who had once threatened his rule, there was a hitch. Hirohito had no idea, none, that his fantasy of negotiated settlement would be flattened in a single pop over Hiroshima. What followed must have been disconcerting in the extreme. Unconditional surrender. No Philippines in a negotiated settlement. Yes, the Big Sushi was safe both from the crazies in the military and from the Americans, but most of it was buried in tunnels in and around Manila.

I had to smile at the thought of the imperial moaning and groaning and gnashing of teeth that must have followed that awful turn of events. The next question was what Emperor Hirohito would do to retrieve the treasure. He surely wouldn't leave all that gold in the Philippines. That ran contrary to human nature, peasant or living god. And the living god still has to figure a way to escape the gallows as a war criminal. Come to think of it, maybe he already has. The emperor is sitting on one hell of a hole card, that's a fact.

17

November 12, 1946, Sugamo Prison, Tokio - Kodama Yoshio was being held as a Class A war criminal, and although I privately felt that nobody of his astonishing wealth and power would in the end be executed for war crimes, I was determined to note and remember as many details of our conversation as I could. I wanted to talk to him while everything was fresh; although the taproots of the truth would linger to influence the future, the details, I knew, would blur with time and the retelling, first becoming footnotes, then forgotten, buried under the accumulated weight of history.

I reviewed the Kodama entries in my journal, which I had been collecting since 1931 together with the nonclassified highlights of G-2's Kodama dossier. I wanted desperately to lay my hands on the full, classified dossier, but I knew that wasn't going to happen.

The anteroom where I waited to speak to Kodama was empty except for one of the most exquisite geishas I had ever seen. She gave me a nod of her delicate head as I walked past, the nape of her neck exposed and sexy. *I wonder which lucky prisoner she's here to visit.*

Someone of power, has to be.

Interviews with non-English-speaking Jap prisoners were normally conducted with the help of an army interpreter, but if Kodama was surprised that I was alone save for the security guard watching the barred window in the door, he didn't show it.

Kodama had the face of a punk or hood. To imagine him as a rear admiral giving advice to the Japanese prime minister was laughable, like casting Lucky Luciano or Dutch Schultz as White House chief of staff. But of course, "Admiral" Kodama had never commanded a ship. He wasn't interested in seamanship and probably couldn't read a chart. His short-cropped black hair was combed back from a straight hairline. His eyebrows, heavy for a Japanese although narrow, were slightly arched. They looked formidable because his eyes, narrow, unrevealing slits, were set very wide apart.

Kodama didn't have much in the way of a chin. But it was his lips and mouth that set him apart. He had very full lips. The upper lip was long, the lower lip downright heavy, bordering on a pout, and his mouth turned down slightly at the ends. His mouth, which dominated his face, seemed permanently set in an ill-suppressed sneer that simultaneously expressed the loathing, contempt, disdain, hatred, and sense of superiority that informed his personality and that dominated his character. It was easy to see why the nationalist crazies selected him as an assassin before the war.

Judging by the forever-hating, never-quit mouth, Kodama was a natural hood. It was also easy to understand why his patron in Japan had chosen him as the guardian of captured treasure. It was clear there was nothing he would not do to further his cause, nothing, which would have been unsettling in any case, but with Kodama Yoshio it was downright spooky.

Kodama was an unapologetic racist, but it was not his eyes that revealed this feeling. His eyes said nothing at all. It was his mouth. His punk's mouth, with its look of superiority, if not downright pugnacity, said clearly that I was dog shit in his opinion, to be endured because I momentarily had the upper hand. His contempt for me was obviously unqualified.

I assumed that this practiced look of disdain, a permanent feature of Kodama's face, came from reading too much *Hagakure*. It struck me that Yamamoto Tsunetomo's crazed philosophy was not one-tenth as sophisticated and difficult to understand as the Japs made it out to be. Fervid followers of the *Hagakure* spent hours trying to make sense out of every alleged subtlety and, judging from the newspaper columns I had read back in Japan, invented nuances where none existed. It was utter nonsense that no Westerner could know what the author was talking about. All Yamamoto said was that if you walked around all the time acting like you were King Shit, then people would treat you like King Shit. Big deal. I knew a kid like him in grade school. He casually tripped me one day while I was racing out to recess, sending me sprawling face first into gravel.

"My name is Wim van der Elst of the Associated Press," I said politely in my best Japanese.

A flicker of surprise momentarily broke his mask. It was widely believed in Japan that no Westerner could learn Japanese. And here I was, a hairy barbarian who spoke it fluently.

"Won't you sit?" I said. I'd be damned if I would give him a Jap bow.

Kodama sat. He put his hands in his lap. He looked mildly out of the barred window, his face betraying no emotion, his scornful, determined lips set tightly.

I said, "You were born in 1911 in Nihonmatsu City. When you were eight, you were sent to live with relatives in Korea."

All of Kodama's many interrogations and debriefings had begun this way. A recitation of date and place of birth, et cetera, said nothing. He had been in prison before. He was not impressed.

I opened my spiral notebook and studied. He waited. His face registered the emotion of a rock, if that.

I flipped to another page. I looked up and grinned. I said, "A truly enlightened *samurai* investigates all possible situations and solutions beforehand so that he will be able to perform brilliantly when the time comes. An enlightened *samurai* settles every detail ahead of time." This was straight from the *Hagakure*.

Which Kodama knew perfectly well. He bowed slightly, an acknowledgment.

I kept talking: "A *samurai* should know his own stature and pursue his discipline with diligence. He should say as little as possible. There is dignity in serenity and closeness of mouth." More *Hagakure*.

Kodama's chair scraped slightly on the floor.

"I followed the advice given in the *Hagakure*. I prepared for this talk in advance."

He started to yawn, and quickly put the heel of his hand to his forehead.

I said, "When you suddenly feel the urge to yawn, stroke your forehead upward toward your scalp. The yawn will subside. If you do not attend carefully to your appearance, you will look ridiculous." I had remembered Yamamoto's recommendation on yawning because it had seemed so absurd.

Kodama finished defeating the yawn and, hardly moving his lips, said, "You speak very good Japanese, and you know the *Hagakure*. I'm impressed, I admit."

I said, "I covered Tokio for ten years before the war in China. I started reading the *Hagakure* in the early thirties, when it was popular in Japan, and you were in the newspapers telling everybody to read it. I'm told that during the war virtually everybody in Japan had a copy. It gave them solace, they say."

Kodama thought about that, then murmured with those extraordinary lips of his. "It's true what you say. Yamamoto Tsunetomo has been quite popular in Japan. For good reason." He pulled at the lobe of one ear. "If we are to be faulted, it is for merely reading the *Hagakure* and not acting upon its sound advice, Mr. van der Elst. Yamamoto calls upon us to be men of action."

"Yes, he does. Speaking of which, in December 1937, I saw you in Nanking on your way from stealing the alchemist archers of Xhingsui Gap. Eleven archers. If, as they say, each archer weighs five hundred pounds, that's almost five thousand pounds of pure gold."

Kodama blinked.

Aha, I thought. *Gotcha, prick.* "That was the same day your troops used machine guns to execute twenty thousand Chinese with their hands tied behind their backs. Would Yamamoto Tsunetomo have approved of that? Did you try your hand behind one of the triggers?" I put both of my hands up as though I were holding a machine gun and yanked them back and forth, pretending to shoot. I held my mouth like I was going to whistle, and put my tongue against the top of my mouth and imitated the sound of a machine gun the way kids do.

The disdainful lips said, "Soldiers get killed in war."

I rolled my eyes. "Unfortunately, those targets weren't all soldiers, were they? Some of them were boys and old men. Takes a mighty *samurai* to gun down boys and old men with their hands tied behind their backs. What is that, 'assiduity' of effort?"

Kodama looked at the guard watching through the window, probably wondering how we pussy Americans ever managed to win the war, burdening ourselves with having to care for prisoners of war. What did I care about the Chinese? I was an American.

I said, "You were released from Fuchou Prison in October 1937 for having plotted the assassination of the prime minister, and by December you were looting Nanking as an army major. That's not bad, I wouldn't think. In October 1940, you went back to Japan as part of a plan to assassinate Prime Minister Prince Konoye because he wanted to avoid war with the United States. You didn't get your navy commission until 1941, but were promoted to rear admiral in six months. You must be a spectacular performer, Kodama-san. The military life agreed with you, did it?"

He said nothing.

I said, "Tattooed gangsters can't commission hoods as admirals. Members of the royal family can. Who better for the emperor's younger brother and uncle to put in charge of collecting the Golden Lily than an ultranationalist who conspired to murder what they considered a timid prime minister?"

I waited. Kodama wasn't about to volunteer anything.

"You needed army rank to direct the Kampei-tai efforts at stealing the treasure, so your patrons in the royal family made you a major. When you needed to transport the treasure, they promoted you to admiral and gave you access to whatever vessels you needed."

Silence.

"Your CIC dossier says you traveled all over Manchuria and China from 1939 through 1941. The CIC people think it's because you were setting up a network of spies, although they also say that with the help of the Kampei-tai you established an opium monopoly in Manchuria and founded Kodama Kikan to coordinate the ravaging of anything of value in China. You eventually made your way from China to all the other countries of your so-called Co-prosperity Sphere. You were in Burma, Thailand, Indochina, Malaya, Singapore, and the Dutch East Indies."

Kodama blinked. More high emotion.

"Early on, Prince Chichibu provided bogus hospital ships for you to move Hirohito's Gold to Japan, but after Midway he established a headquarters in Manila and had you ship it there, hugging the Southeast Asian coastlines."

Kodama cocked his head. "Oh?"

"If the emperor sent the treasure back to the home islands and Japan lost the war, he risked losing it to dissidents or, even worse, to the American army. On the other hand, it was possible to bury

Hirohito's Gold secretly in the Philippines, using disposable Filipinos and American and Australian prisoners of war." I looked him straight on. "Well, Kodama-san?"

"A foolish theory."

"The details about the tunnels under Manila are in reports of Iwabuchi's activities. Dig, dig, dig. One would think you're hybrid moles." I started to tell him about the tunnels I had seen under Pulak Pulakan but thought better of it.

He said nothing.

"In the winter of 1945, with the treasure safely stashed in the Philippines, you returned to Japan to become advisor to Prime Minister Higashikuni. Your only qualification to be an advisor to the prime minister was that you knew the details of the burial of Hirohito's treasure. As the war deteriorated, the two of you connived to give Iwabuchi a fancy medal. For what? For the rape of Manila?" I shook my head. "No, no, no. For having successfully completed his assignment of having prisoners of war dig tunnels under Manila. He stashed at least some of the gold in those tunnels. That's why he executed the prisoners when their work was finished."

"I say again, you have an elaborate imagination, Mr. van der Elst."

"When you arrived in Tokio to join Higashikuni, the poor damn emperor thought he could claim the Philippines in a negotiated settlement. He had no idea that we would flatten Hiroshima with a single bomb on August 6. Hirohito and his brother and uncle must have dropped a load in their collective pants, and not out of shock at what happened to the residents of Hiroshima. No way in hell we were going to negotiate any kind of deal with you at our mercy."

He remained impassive.

"The people in the CIC tell me you're the second richest of the six hundred forty-four war criminals they have in custody.

They base that on the platinum and industrial diamonds you ripped off with the help of the Kampei-tai and Big-Eared Tu. They have no idea of the amount of gold your Kampei-tai units collected for the emperor."

The evil lips moved slightly when I said second richest. *Second richest?* Ah, pride! Kodama was not second anything. He was *first.* The richest.

"The alchemist archers of Xhingsui Gap must really be something." I studied my notes again, then offered Kodama a Chesterfield. He surprised me by accepting. Despite his best attempt to mask his feelings, it was clear he didn't like talking about the archers. He was wondering how much I had figured out.

He said, "To satisfy your curiosity about the archers, Mr. van der Elst, you will find that the golden dragons are stored in a bank vault in Tokio and I assume will be returned to their Chinese owners after the war. Your investigating officers seem to be quite conscientious about these things."

"We both know the archers won't be surfacing in any bank vault." Should I tell him what I heard on the plane ride back to Honolulu? I thought not.

He paused. "You don't believe me?"

I shook my head. "Total nonsense."

"And you think you know where they are?"

My turn to be coy. I folded my notebook, a sign that I was getting ready to leave. "You've got Emperor Hirohito on your side. You know where his gold is stashed. It's in nobody's interest to send you to the gallows, Kodama-san. You're the emperor's bargaining chip."

Kodama said, "They'll be smoking the pipe long after our grandchildren are dead, Mr. van der Elst."

The pipe? "What pipe would that be, Kodama-san?"

Kodama's lips were triumphant. "Good fortune attained with

the encouragement of all is genuine good fortune." Some *Haga-kure* for me.

Kodama certainly wouldn't need the *Hagakure* by way of receiving solace. I wondered if the fix was already in. Very likely. If not, it was at least being negotiated. Had to be. I stood, deciding to give him a bow after all, a gesture of respect to a formidable adversary. "Sayonara, Kodama-san."

He bowed back. "Sayonara, van der Elst-san."

I walked out of the room, leaving Kodama to find manly peace in the *Hagakure*, if peace was there to be found. On the way out, I stepped aside to admit the elegant little geisha I had seen waiting when I came in. What a beauty! I paused and looked back down the hall, eyeing her sweet little rump that moved this way and that under the silk. As she turned to enter the room where Kodama waited, she gave me a shy glance then disappeared.

The guard at the observation window turned his back so that Kodama-san might have some privacy.

November 13, 1946, Tokio - As I finish writing my interview with Kodama, I wonder how much gold was accumulated privately in the two- or three-thousand-year history of Imperial China. Hard experience had taught the Chinese to prefer gold to currency. Gold will not corrode. It is heavy and so easy to hide. It never loses its value. Long before there were civilizations in Europe that were sophisticated enough to even imagine, much less appreciate, the exotic splendors and riches of faraway Cathay, Imperial Chinese families and Chinese warlords were sitting on intoxicating treasure.

What did the Europeans do when the Nazis threatened? Well, if rumors were true, the French moved much of their national treasures to Indochina. The Dutch moved theirs to their colonies in the Dutch East Indies. Even the British turned to an Asian colony, transferring gold to its fortress at Singapore on the southern tip of the Malay Peninsula.

Has any empire in history offered as much treasure as the territories occupied by the Japanese Imperial Army, which, at its zenith in 1943, included Korea, Manchuria, large portions of China, plus Burma, Thailand, French Indochina, Malaya, Singapore, the Dutch East Indies, the Philippines, Borneo, and New Guinea?

There is precious little transparency in Asia. These countries are largely run in secrecy, by the pull of unseen forces. The black mist of corruption, the Japanese call it. Chiang and Douglas MacArthur's G-2 all know perfectly well what Chichibu and his subordinates did during the war and for whom.

They collected the treasure for Emperor Hirohito. Who in the hell else would they be collecting it for if not the direct descendant of the sun? Bud Abbott and Lou Costello? Betty Grable? Ted Williams?

I remember peering into the lip of hell at Nanking. Who will ultimately profit from all that blood and pain?

Will Douglas MacArthur execute the man who supervised the burial of Hirohito's Gold? Not likely.

BOOK TWO

In Remembrance of Yamashita

1

Dr. Tomiko Kobayashi, having had accepted a cup of coffee, settled into the chair opposite Avi Feuer, the Asian affairs editor of the *New York Times*. Feuer, a slouching man in his early sixties, had a pouch, curly gray hair, and a full beard. The screen on his computer switched to the screen saver, a clip from the movie *Casablanca*, with Humphrey Bogart looking morose, smoking a cigarette in his bar.

Feuer listened to Tomi's story with interest. When she finished, he took another sip of coffee and said, "Yamashita's granddaughter, out to clear the good name of the Tiger of Malaya fifty years later. You're a hell of a story in yourself, Dr. Kobayashi. I envy your finding van der Elst's journal, I admit. The historians say the media have all been had by the forces that are. I don't think I've been had. I've just never been able to get it nailed. It's complicated."

"I take it this is still a classified story."

Feuer nodded. "Yes, and for a reason, if you follow the government's logic. The State Department has to deal with Japan, its most important Asian ally. The CIA has the continuing problem of recruiting foreign nationals. If potential spies can't trust the Company to keep its word, the whole system falls apart. Few people outside of historians have anything to gain by the public knowing the whole truth about Hirohito's Gold and the M Fund, if there are such things. Imelda Marcos pretended to let the proverbial cat out of the bag in a newspaper interview a few years ago. Are you familiar with that story?"

"I've read the articles in the *Philippine Daily Inquirer.*"

Feuer paused and poured a cup of coffee for his guest. "Some of what she told had the ring of truth, that's so. But she likely told just enough to serve her purposes."

"Which are?"

Feuer looked surprised. "Imelda Marcos? She's a Filipina. She's defending her family. I'm surprised at you. You look like an intelligent young woman to me. I know you're American, but you're still an Asian. If you could get the whole story of the alleged M Fund, you'd really have something."

Tomi cocked her head. "The M Fund? You want to tell me what that is?"

"I can tell you what the story is supposed to be. At the end of the war, MacArthur's inner circle of advisors, known as the Bataan boys, are said to have created a fund to finance the Police Reserve Force, the predecessor of today's Self-Defense Force, and to finance anti-Communist plots and support American allies in Asia. MacArthur and General Charles Willoughby, head of the G-2, supposedly put together the Yotsuya Fund. They apparently followed that with something called the Keenan Fund, named for the chief prosecutor in the war crimes trials, Joseph B. Keenan."

"And these funds were financed by what?"

"Hirohito's Gold, plus money from sales of confiscated Japanese military stockpiles of industrial diamonds, platinum, gold, and silver that had been plundered in occupied countries; the sales of shares of dissolved *zaibatsu* companies; and accounts of nonconvertible yen derived from the sales in Japan of American aid imports and commodities. Before the end of the occupation they're said to have collapsed the Yotsuya and the Keenan into the M Fund, named after General William Frederic Marquat, another of MacArthur's inner circle. They imagined it as kind of a secret Marshall Plan for Asia. Come to think of it, the M could just as easily stand for MacArthur, money, or Marshall, couldn't it?"

"A name for all seasons."

"Did van der Elst mention the operations of Kodama Kikan in Japanese-occupied China?"

"Yes, he did."

"What do you think happened to those assets? The platinum and diamonds. That's not to mention the gold. Vice President Nixon officially turned over the control of the M Fund to the Japanese in the late 1950s, but the Company was still involved in the enforcement of some of the original agreements, including the one that you've tumbled onto."

"An agreement with Kodama Yoshio."

"If the rumors are correct, more likely with Emperor Hirohito. Kodama is just part of the story, the tip of the clichéd iceberg. What a cast of characters! Emperor Hirohito. Hirohito's younger brother, Prince Chichibu. His uncle, Prince Higashikuni. Douglas MacArthur. Chiang Kai-shek. Japanese politicians. Ferdinand Marcos. Retired generals and CIA officers. I've always thought that they should have stuck with the name Yotsuya Fund. It was both more descriptive and playful."

"Descriptive and playful what way?"

"Yotsuya is the name of a district in Tokyo. But in the context of the fund established by MacArthur and Willoughby, the name is from *Yotsuya Kaidan*, a classic *kabuki* play. In the story, Oiwa elopes with a *ronin*—a masterless *samurai*. She lives a quiet life in the Yotsuya district of Edo, the old name of Tokyo, not knowing that her parents are desperately looking for her, hoping to take her back. Her husband, who becomes powerful in the *yakuza*,

takes an ambitious mistress. In the second part of the story, Oiwa
returns to haunt her husband, but we don't know if she is living
or dead. Is she real? Or is she a ghost? She is. She isn't. To the
Japanese, Yotsuya means something that is mysterious and secretive, plastic, taking many forms and shapes. You see, a perfect
name for a secret fund."

Tomi grinned. "You're right, a far more imaginative name than
the M Fund. Any further recommendations for my research?"

Feuer thought for a moment. "We know that MacArthur's people released Kodama from Sugamo Prison, after which by all accounts he went to work for army intelligence then for the CIA.
All of MacArthur's biographers say no decision of consequence
was made during the occupation without his approval. Surely that
included the unexplained summary release of Kodama and the
other war criminals. I can give you some leads, but many of them
will probably turn out to be dry holes because the Company people have scrubbed all the good stuff. I'm curious. Just how detailed is this journal of yours?"

"It traces Kodama's career from 1931 through the Japanese
incursions in China and through World War II, ending with an
interview with him in Sugamo Prison. Van der Elst spoke fluent
Japanese. He was in China for much of the war and ended up
covering the action in the Philippines."

"I see. Well, good luck, although I doubt you'll get very far, the
vested interest in the status quo being what it is."

"Mrs. Compton also recommended a state department official
named Roddy Baker."

Feuer grinned lazily. "The estimable Roddy Baker! You can talk
to him, but you'll find him tight-lipped. I interviewed him once.
I came away suspecting he was more likely a CIA operative than
a foreign service officer, but I might be wrong."

"Mrs. Compton said he might be able to put me in touch with

a former CIA man who might be of help. An old Asia hand named Kip Smith."

Feuer laughed. "Whistling Smith! Mrs. Compton knows her stuff."

"You know this Smith?"

"I know of him. I'd like to talk to him myself. A word of advice from a sloppy old man who wishes you all the luck in the world. If I were you, I would be extremely careful. I take it you have made a copy of van der Elst's journal and stored it in a safe place."

"I have."

"There are historians, both Americans and Japanese, who are convinced that we journalists have been bought off by the Japan lobby and we lack the courage to rattle the CIA's chains until it yields. Maybe. Maybe not. I'll tell you one thing: I don't believe there is a journalist alive who would not love to break this story wide open if it were true."

"Maybe it is true."

"And maybe you can let in a little sunshine with this journal of yours, I agree. But do not, I say again, do not show it to anybody until you're convinced you can trust him. The other thing is that I'm a Jew, so I don't have a lot of patience with war criminals. But judging from all I've read of your grandfather's trial, I think he got a raw deal. Admiral Iwabuchi was the Butcher of Manila, not General Yamashita. If I understand the larger story correctly, the Cold Warriors who saw this operation through were part of what we used to call the China Lobby, virulently anti-Communist supporters of Generalissimo Chiang who successfully made Mao an international pariah and kept him that way until Richard Nixon made his famous visit in 1972. When you finish, I've got dibs on being the one to tell your story."

2

It was not a happy Japanese threesome on the sixteenth green of Akagi Kiri golf course south of Tokyo. They were not bothered by the weather. It was a clear, sunny day, and Mt. Fuji was splendid in the distance. The fairways at Akagi Kiri were modest in length, although the rough was truly wicked. The sixteenth green, surrounded on three sides by amoebae-shaped sand traps and on a fourth side by a lake, was difficult but not impossible. The lake, surrounded by cattails, was home for a resident flock of mallards, and the iridescent green heads of the drakes were grand as they swam about with their faithful hens.

Suma Obe, a short, wide Japanese dressed in a wide-brimmed Greg Norman white hat, squatted to study the lie of his ball, which was perched precariously on the lip of one of the sand traps. Suma was facing an uphill lie of twenty feet; the ball would tail left in a large loop and hook sharply in the last yard. With the ball about to topple into the sand, proper putting form was impossible. At the least, the challenge required the undivided attention if not extreme concentration on the part of the golfer. But Suma, a former officer in the Japanese Self-Defense Force and now director of the Ministry of Trade and Finance, did not have his mind entirely on golf.

One of the golfers waiting his turn, Kobayashi Katama, CEO of

Saito Industries, an electronics conglomerate, was dressed in Jack Nicklaus gear—his spiked shoes, his light blue slacks, his white knit shirt. His putter, too, was a Jack Nicklaus model.

The third player, Honda Atama, president of the First Bank of Osaka, was Payne Stewart from head to toe. The unlucky Stewart had gone down in a plane crash, but his trademark outfit lived on.

Suma walked up the likely path of his putt, looking for anything that might divert the path of his ball. Studying the green, he adjusted his Greg Norman hat. He ran his fingers down his jaw.

Honda said, "Can you imagine what would happen if the Golden Lily and the M Fund became public knowledge? We'd all have to commit *seppuku*."

Suma made an ambiguous noise in his throat. "The Americans don't want the public to know about the fund any more than we do. They will *never*, I say again *never* allow it to become accepted public knowledge. It's the code of intelligence professionals never to reveal operations that will embarrass an ally. They tell us it's okay for scholars in think tanks to publish their little articles, nobody reads them anyway. Well, okay. Maybe. I know that Director Studeman wrote a letter to the *New York Times* saying the CIA will keep the secret. But it's also clear that we can't have the *Times* and the *Washington Post* asking real questions, and a congressional inquiry is out of the question. Remember what the master Yamamoto tells us, 'Tether even a roasted chicken.' "

"We talk to Roddy Baker?" Honda asked.

"For starters, yes. We do what we have to do, no matter what it takes. We'll send Chiba Wataru. He's a veteran intelligence officer. On top of being my brother-in-law, he's got a level head and will do as he is told. We'll try honey first, then the stick. I'll instruct Chiba to buy a copy of the journal; failing that he'll do whatever is necessary to find out what van der Elst learned."

"If we're to deny its authenticity, we need to know what's in it, I agree," Honda said.

Suma assumed the best stance he could under the circumstances. He took a practice swing at the ball that remained teetering on the edge of a sand trap. Greg Norman, the Great White Shark from Australia, was famous for his nearly impossible, come-from-behind putts.

Suma nodded to the caddie, who removed the flag. Eyeing the green, then the ball, he said, "Our future lies exactly like this. The trick is to correctly read the lie, to anticipate everything that can influence the path of the ball. How is the grass cut? Is it wet or dry? Are we putting uphill or down? Will the ball drift left or right? Then we strike the ball firmly and confidently, better to go too long than too short." Suma gave the ball a measured tap, doing his best to follow Greg Norman's form. All three men watched the white ball pop onto the green and loop uphill toward the hole.

3

Tomi Kobayashi cruised the Bethesda suburb looking for the nearest grocery store or bar near the stone cottage. A stone cottage with a green roof, she had been told. She spotted it, but the number was blocked by shrubbery. She saw an old woman sitting in a wheelchair on an open porch. The woman had knitting in her lap.

Tomi parked her car and got out. She walked to the edge of the porch. "I'm a professor from Washington State University, and I wonder if a man named Roddy Baker lives in that little stone house over there. I can't see the number."

The old woman glanced at the cottage and back at Tomi. "Washington State University?"

"My name is Dr. Tomi Kobayashi."

"That's Roddy's house. He was a Foreign Service officer in the State Department until he took an early retirement. I think it was the State Department."

"That would be him."

"I see him at the library all the time, surrounded by books. That's when he's here. He's almost always gone, traveling somewhere."

"Thank you," Tomi said. She walked across the street and rang the doorbell.

A half minute later a thoughtful-looking tall, bald man in his mid-fifties opened the door.

She said, "I'm Dr. Tomi Kobayashi. I called earlier."

"Ah, General Yamashita's granddaughter! And here you are talking to me with an American accent."

"My grandmother was his Filipina mistress. She immigrated to Hawaii after the war. I'm a Nisei."

"I see." He held the door open for her, led the way to a book-crammed study where he had a pot of coffee waiting. "Coffee?"

"Sure, that would be nice."

As he poured, he said, "How can I help?"

"I've come by a journal written by Wim van der Elst, a reporter for the Associated Press who followed Kodama Yoshio's activities from 1931 to the end of the war. If van der Elst is right, my grandfather had nothing to do with the rape of Manila or alleged Japanese loot. He was tried and convicted by a kangaroo court. Douglas MacArthur knew he was innocent and yet let him be executed." Tomi said this evenly, looking Baker straight on. "If I can run down the full story of Kodama Yoshio and the Golden Lily, I can prove what happened. I won't quit until I learn what happened one way or the other. If my grandfather did what they claim he did, I'll accept it, however reluctantly. If he didn't, I want the record set straight."

"Van der Elst writes about Kodama's activities for the Kampei-tai, I take it."

"And about Prince Chichibu and General Prince Higashikuni. Collecting gold and treasure for Emperor Hirohito."

Baker stepped back, reassessing her. "Hirohito's Gold! So! You said you 'came by' the journal. How was that, if you don't mind my asking?"

"I got it from van der Elst's niece, Mrs. Edie Compton, a seventy-four-year-old cripple living in a nursing home. She has bad eyes and couldn't decipher the van der Elst scrawl. I went through the journal word by word, figuring everything out."

"How did you say you got my name?"

She said, "Mrs. Compton got it from Avi Feuer of the *New York Times*."

"You talked to Feuer, I take it."

Tomi nodded.

Baker refilled his own cup of coffee. "Feuer once interviewed me as part of his research about postwar politics in Japan. I felt flattered, but I couldn't tell him much because of my security oath. Also, World War II was way before my time."

"Mrs. Compton said Feuer told her you might know a former Company man with extraordinary experience in the region, Kip Smith."

"Whistling Smith. Kip is short for Kipling. He is Rudyard Kipling Smith. A few of his old friends used to call him Whistling Smith. He traveled as a wildlife photographer. That's when he learned the bird calls." Baker smiled. "But that's in the past." Baker added cream, real cream to his coffee. "Kip quit the Company to shoot wildlife full time. He does just about any kind of animal. Insects, lizards, whatever. He's got some underwater cameras that cost a bundle."

"This is mostly in Asia, I take it."

"Almost entirely Asia. Birds and crocodiles in Queensland and the Northern Territories. Fish on the Great Barrier Reef. Giant lizards in Indonesia. Orangutans in Borneo. He likes the independence. Turns out he's almost your neighbor. When he's in the United States, you can likely find him at his cabin at Lake Wallowa in northeastern Oregon. That's a little over ninety miles south of Pullman. I checked it on the map after you called."

"Small world," Tomi said. "Feuer said you worked in the State Department. I'm curious. Where was that? In Asia, I take it."

"I had posts all over the world, but my longest assignment was as the political officer at the American Embassy in Tokyo."

"I see. Maybe I should work with you instead of Smith."

Baker shook his head. "I think Kip is probably your best bet for the story of Kodama collecting gold for Emperor Hirohito. He's a former Company operative in the field. He's got personal contacts all over East and Southeast Asia."

"Why is it Smith is no longer with the CIA?"

Baker said, "Kip got interested in his cover as a wildlife photographer, but there's more to it than that. He's complicated. A man of conscience. When you see him, ask him."

"Me?"

"Sure. Why not you? See what he says. The two of you have something in common. His offbeat lifestyle belies his seriousness."

"Offbeat?"

"He refuses to be defined by what he consumes, which is modest. He reads. He believes that life has moral and ethical dimensions—even for generals and politicians. He was an intellectual Company operative, perhaps an anomaly. Or is that an oxymoron like army intelligence? Say, do you mind if I take a look at your journal?"

Tomi hesitated. "I . . . Maybe someday. We'll see."

4

More than ten years after the Rev. Jim Bakker's Praise The Lord teleministry had gone under following his conviction on fraud charges, the faithful continued to believe that he had gotten railroaded by antireligionists in the Justice Department. This loyalty did not escape the attention of Robin and Roberta Fallon. When Robin first suggested the formidable task of emulating the Bakker formula, he and Roberta spent hours reviewing tapes of Jim and Tammy at their best. Fallon was a vain man, but even he had to admit that before their tragic downfall, the Bakkers had been very good indeed.

In the end, the Fallons established an enterprise called Praise Jesus Now—PJN. The Rev. Robin Fallon's first television ministry was a home-taped job broadcast over a public access channel in Athens, Georgia. In their opening PJN telecast, Robin and Roberta Fallon told viewers that theirs was the responsibility to demonstrate by personal example the resolve of Christians everywhere to engage the devil in personal, hand-to-hand combat until he yielded and was defeated once and for all.

Fallon told his new flock that they would together take up the message of love and hope as it was written in the Bible. If folks out there wanted to help the cause, they could dial a toll-free number and use their credit cards to buy an inspirational videotape at a nominal charge of $19.95, plus $4.95 shipping and handling. The Fallons made no mention of the Bakkers. Roberta Fallon avoided the troweled-on makeup and gaudy jewelry the self-righteous liberals and smug atheists found so amusing in Tammy Bakker. Instead, Roberta wore down-home, if slightly odd, hairdos and purple and lavender clothing made of polyester and other forms of processed oil.

Knowing that a signature motif was necessary, the Fallons specialized in showing home movies of their family life: Robin, drooling dog at his side, doing his best to chop firewood; Robin, atop a teetering ladder, busy cleaning the gutters of his roof; a happy Roberta kneading bread dough; Roberta singing a gospel tune as she ironed clothes. After PJN survived the jitters of an uneven start, the audience ratings settled in as steady as a righteous heart, and the Fallons moved their enterprise to Atlanta. Encouraged by the generosity of their followers, Robin and Roberta began looking about for more robust opportunities.

Through a born-again follower associated with Jim Bakker's former entourage, the Reverend Fallon heard that PTL's faithful Brother Vernon Twyman of Tulsa, Oklahoma, had in the mid-1980s been involved with retired Gen. John K. Singlaub, a former CIA officer, in a search for gold and treasure buried in the Philippines by the Japanese in the last days of World War II. Fallon was given to understand through PTL gossip that this treasure, called Yamashita's Gold, was earmarked for the worldwide fight against godless communism. Never-fade-away generals and patriots like Col. Oliver M. North fought the good fight against godless Communists. Christian fundamentalists had always been their natural allies in the fight for a moral universe.

When retired Maj. Gen. Jose Maria Martinez, superintendent of the Philippine Military Academy, was in the United States to visit American friends in Virginia and Maryland, Robin and Roberta invited him to Atlanta for a visit. During Martinez's stay, Fallon let it be known that if ever his modest skills should be found useful to the general, he and his wife would be pleased to participate in the search for Yamashita's Gold. Much to his surprise and delight, several weeks later Martinez sent a letter.

Manila
Feb. 14

Dear Rev. Fallon,

It was quite pleasant visiting you and Roberta. Atlanta is a gorgeous, prosperous city. I can see why you chose it as a base for PJN. As you can see by reading the newspapers, the collapse of the Soviet Empire has by no means eliminated the campaign against Christian decency by terrorists, drug dealers, and purveyors of godlessness. Although they no longer call themselves Communists or Marxists, these people have no concept of a just or moral life. They remain a threat to liberty everywhere.

Ordinarily those invited to participate in various projects involving Yamashita's Gold are specialists of one sort or another. As I told you in Atlanta, the PTL folks you mentioned had engineering and organizational skills that the Delta International people felt were essential. But engineers and technical people are not all that we need at Plymouth Rising, the successor to Delta International. Sometimes the nature of a particular cache requires unusual skills. Although you're not an engineer, Rev. Fallon, your talents just might qualify you and your lovely wife to participate in a project we have in mind.

I'm not free to discuss the details of our tentative plan yet, but I am sending you a brief report on the alchemist archers of Xhingsui Gap so you can see what it is we're after. This is believed to be the last extant stash of the loot collected by the Japanese Imperial Army in the 1930s and 1940s.

I know you and your wife will understand that it is essential that you destroy this correspondence and keep the nature of our discussions entirely to yourselves. As you both know perfectly well, the liberal media are capable of twisting both the facts and our motives in the most outrageous manner conceivable. By necessity this must continue to remain an entirely private and confidential enterprise.

I do hope you find the alchemist dragons of interest. They represent the final chapter in the story of Yamashita's Gold.

Again I thank you for your gracious hospitality and the good time you showed me in Atlanta.

Cordially,
(Signed Jose Maria Martinez)
Maj. Gen. Jose Maria Martinez

5

Rudyard Kipling Smith heard the engine first, when Roddy Baker's rig was still on the parallel ruts that served as a road through the old apple orchard. Kip Smith ran his fingers across his short, silver beard and added wood to the fire. He saw the first flicker of headlights through the cattails of the slough. The headlights swung to the left and right as the rig followed the winding mud road to the riverbank. Smith got his thermos of coffee from his boat.

Baker had said he wanted to go catfishing at night. He hadn't done that since he was a boy. So Smith had gone to Portland to spare Baker the trip to Eastern Oregon. He found a spot on the banks of the Columbia River, far away from the annoying *whoosh, whoosh,* of distant freeway traffic, although the glow of city lights on the clouds above Portland could be seen in the distance.

Baker's rig, a four-wheel-drive Jeep Cherokee, pulled to a stop on a patch of mud packed by tires of fishermen past. The tall, bald man stepped down from the Cherokee wearing a Baltimore Orioles baseball cap plus a nylon windbreaker, blue jeans, and hiking boots. He walked across a clearing littered with cigarette butts, used condoms, beer cans, and broken glass to Smith, who stood behind the fire, cupping his hands to cradle its warmth.

Baker shook Smith's hand, the dancing fire warming their faces. "Hey, Kip, how you doing?"

Smith gripped him around the shoulder and gave a squeeze. "Another covert meeting with Roddy Baker. Two old spooks. Just like old times, eh? *Chilp-chilp-chilp-chilp-chilp-wick-wick.*"

"What was that?"

"A kind of warbler you hear in brushy canyons out here. But I'm no good anymore. Don't practice. Like anything else, you have to practice. Remember those old television ads with Paul Hornung getting into a fancy car with a blonde on each arm? 'Practice, practice, practice,' he said." Smith grinned. "You're looking good, Roddy."

"I saw your kangaroo documentary on the Discovery Channel the other night. Good work."

"Best thing I ever did was to quit the Company. My heart wasn't in it anyway; everybody knew that. You want to plop your butt? I've got our lines in the water."

"Set for the big strike," Baker said.

"That's it. Channel cats, with any luck. I'm using multiple hooks, always the best tactic. Learned that from the Company."

Baker picked a spot on the cottonwood log by the fire and sat, squinting his eyes momentarily at the smoke that drifted up. He shifted his weight and moved to his left on the log, partly because of the smoke and partly because something was poking him in the butt. He rubbed his rear end.

Smith twisted the cap of his thermos. "Coffee?"

"That'd be good, thanks." Baker accepted the plastic cup and took a sip. He shifted again on the log.

Smith said, "If you work at it, you'll find a spot on the log that fits. Don't you just love the air out here? The smell of mud and bugs and dead fish. Smells like work to me. I've sat in one spot for five or six days running, waiting for the perfect shot of crocodiles fucking."

"That's gotta be a thrill." Baker used his rod to weigh the large sinker and hook loaded with worms that dangled from the tip. "Better stand clear, Kip." He glanced at Smith to make sure he was out of the way, then slung the weight out into the darkness, where it landed with a distant *ker-plop* into the Columbia River. He put his rod back on the fork of the stick stuck in the mud and sat down on the log again.

Baker said, "I've had two interesting visits recently, both bearing on your interests. Chiba Wataru wants to talk to you."

"The estimable Chiba! About what?"

"He won't say." Baker squatted by the water and washed the worm goo off his hands. He leaned forward expectantly. The tip of his rod was bouncing up and down.

Smith said, "I believe you've got a little action there, Roddy."

Watching his line, Baker said, "Shall I let him have it?"

"I'd take him."

Baker gave a yank on the line. He had a fish on it briefly, then his line went limp. "Missed!" He began reeling in his line.

"You probably just nicked his lip. Most of these night feeders are pretty determined. They just suck it on down."

The tip of Baker's rod bounced again. "Say, this might be my night." Baker squatted crablike, not taking his eye off the tip of his rod. When he gave it a yank, he had a fish on. He was delighted.

"He's giving you a tussle."

"Fun!" When Baker had the foot-long fish flopping on the sand, he put his foot on its spine.

Smith removed the hook with a piece of wood. "A chub," he said with disgust. He held it up for Baker to see.

"We don't keep chubs, I take it."

"You'd be laughed at. Chubs, suckers, and carp are considered yucko around here. Chubs've got bones. Carp are okay for Siberians. Catfish taste wonderful, but they're not macho fish. Catching macho fish ordinarily takes expensive gear. We're talking the United States here." Smith pitched the fish back into the water.

"Lucky chub to have all those bones." The light of the fire flickered against Baker's face.

"And your second visitor?"

Baker cast his bait into the darkness. "A good-looking female professor from Washington State University, General Yamashita's granddaughter."

"Say again?"

"Dr. Tomi Kobayashi, a Nisei, born in Honolulu. Claims her Filipina grandmother was Yamashita's mistress. Says she's come by a collection of journal entries by an AP correspondent named Wim van der Elst who followed Kodama's career from 1931 to the end of the war."

Smith blinked. "The granddaughter of the Tiger of Malaya?"

"That's what she says, and I have no reason not to believe her." Baker tossed another chunk of wood on the fire. "She started out with the idea of rehabilitating her grandfather's reputation, but now has ambitions of scoring the whole postwar occupation story: the decision to give Kodama and the Sugamo Nineteen a walk, the Yamashita ruse, the Golden Lily and M Fund. The full nine yards, leading right straight to Emperor Hirohito, who we've been repeatedly assured was an innocent dupe."

"She is? Really?"

"She thinks Douglas MacArthur allowed her grandfather, an innocent man, to be executed to appease the Filipinos and she's goddam furious."

"MacArthur did precisely that."

"Judging from her eyes, it looks like she's got a little of the Tiger of Malaya in her."

Smith sat up straight. "All right, Roddy! Yes! You brought me a live one. You know, pal, all those stories about you being an asshole just aren't true. Lies. Nothing but lies! No offense."

Baker laughed. "I thought that would perk you up."

Smith hesitated. "Is she any good, do you think? I mean, she might have a doctoral degree, yes, but can she really think? If she plans on telling this story, she's gotta have some real grit."

"I have no idea. She has an appointment at Washington State University. She managed to find me."

Smith looked out over the darkness of the river, the warmth of the fire flickering against the side of his face.

Smith said, "Chiba-san first, then Dr. Kobayashi. Tell Chiba I'll talk to him in San Ignacio."

"The place in Belize where you fish for snook."

"Neutral turf, and I'll know immediately all strangers in town. Give Dr. Kobayashi directions to my cabin on Lake Wallowa. We'll see if she's got her grandfather's stuff or if she's a pussycat." Smith looked out over the darkness of the river. He murmured softly, "Gina, honey, I'll do my damndest, I swear." He gestured toward Baker's rod. Louder, to Baker, he said, "Say, I believe you've got another one on."

Roddy Baker popped to his feet. "By golly, I believe you're right. We both might have one on."

Both by temperament and experience, the two Japanese gentlemen were strikingly different. The broad-shouldered, graying Chiba Wataru, in his mid-fifties, had been educated in the United States; a veteran intelligence officer assigned to the Foreign Service, he was the brother-in-law of Suma Obe, Minister of Trade and Industry. His subordinate, twenty-seven-year-old Yoshida Akiri, a slender *yakuza kobun*, hard as a whippet and lethal as a cobra, had never been out of Japan. He too spoke English, a rare skill for a *yakuza kobun*, although nowhere near as fluently as Chiba. On the instruction of his *oyabun*, Itoyama Junosuki, and on pain of losing a digit, Yoshida would obey the worldly Chiba as he would Itoyama.

Yoshida had wanted to go to the United States to see what that fabled country was like, but no, the contrary American had chosen San Ignacio, Belize, on the border with Guatemala. Chiba, too, had been more than a little annoyed at the outcome of what had been a simple enough request—that he meet Rudyard Kipling Smith somewhere outside of the United States. When Chiba had made the request, he had had in mind somewhere civilized, London, Paris, or Rome maybe, or Madrid. They could have met in a comfortable hotel and had their talk over a decent meal. But, no. This was Kip Smith, after all. Chiba was philosophical about the turn of events. Yoshida didn't like it one damn bit, although he said nothing.

Their problems had begun at the pathetic airport that served Belize City. Outside the terminal, the gathered taxis were mostly rusting derelict hulks. Chiba did not want to hire a wreck. He wanted a clean, new car with air-conditioning. But he was well traveled for a Japanese and assumed that Belize adhered to the time-honored Third World practice of socking maximum taxes on vehicles. He spotted a late model Nissan that looked clean and well maintained. He headed for it. The driver, a lean black man sporting natty dreads, sat with the doors open in the boiling heat. He perked up when he spotted Chiba, which meant he was calculating the thickness of Chiba's wallet.

The reputation of Japanese preceded them. Everywhere the stereotype was the same. The Japanese were rich. They always traveled in groups. They flew Japan Airlines if at all possible. In foreign countries they traveled in Japanese-owned tour buses. They stayed in Japanese-owned hotels. They ate in Japanese-owned restaurants. They were up-front racists. They wanted nothing but the best. They never asked about the price, a practice they found low class and embarrassing, so they never bargained. Consequently, inflation rose like the surf as a Japanese walked down the street.

Now Chiba and Yoshida rode in air-conditioned silence. The first hour out—from Belize City to the Belizian capital at Belmopan—the narrow, bumpy highway, a real teeth-rattler, was flanked by swamps. After that, the road to Mayan country began to rise through rolling hills and piney ridges. Chiba had not really expected the air-conditioner to work, but, miracles of miracles, it did, and for that he was grateful.

The Nissan had to wait for several minutes on the northern bank of the Macal River before its turn to cross the Hawksworth

Bridge, a rusting, single-lane suspension bridge with a metal grid that made the Nissan's tires rumble like an old propeller-driven bomber in the movies.

At the far end of the bridge, the road looped around a small circle of cement benches that marked the center of the town plaza. An imposing police station with pillared verandas occupied the high ground south of the benches. The police station, once white, was now urine-colored. Opposite the police station, a street down a gentle slope led to the obvious main drag of San Ignacio. It was on this main drag, Burns Street, where Roddy Baker said Chiba would find Eva's. Eva's was impossible to miss, Baker had said. Whistling Smith would be in Eva's for their rendezvous. If he wasn't, then Bob, the owner, would know where he was.

The driver parked the Nissan under a tree by the edge of the circle, and Chiba and Yoshida got out into the stupefying heat. They strolled slowly down the narrow street of clapboard buildings to Burns Street, where they saw Eva's Café opposite a bar or hotel out of which mariachi boomed with ear-splitting decibels.

They stepped inside Eva's, a cozy place with a dozen tables, bulletins and advertisements for tourists, and postcards and clever posters from all over the world. There, sitting among the clientele of bearded and pigtailed backpackers and European expatriates, sat Rudyard Kipling Smith, a tall man in his late forties, with a mustache and ponytail. He was dressed in a short-sleeved shirt, walking shorts, and Birkenstock sandals.

On seeing him, Smith rose and bowed politely. "Chiba-san, it's been a long time."

Chiba bowed in return. "Yes, it has, Kip. You look well. This is my associate, Yoshida-san."

"Kip Smith." They shook.

"Mr. Smith and I—what is the American expression, Kip?"

"We've been around a couple of blocks together."

Chiba and Yoshida looked about Eva's. Three German blondes with backpacks by their feet were eating plates of beans and rice. The girls had hairy armpits and their nipples poked through their T-shirts.

"Have a good trip?" Smith asked.

"The air-conditioner worked. I found it an interesting drive, but I think Yoshida-san would have preferred seeing what the United States was like."

Smith seemed amused at Yoshida, who was obviously finding it impossible not to stare at the Western tits. In Japanese, Smith said, "Great boobs, huh, Yoshida-san?"

Yoshida blinked in surprise at a Westerner being able to speak Japanese. Finding it hard to take his eyes off the chests of the German girls, Yoshida said in passable English that he had learned from an instructor for whom English was a second language, "The air-conditioner worked. There were goats along the way." He struggled with the *R*s in air-conditioner.

Smith switched to English. "You'd probably have a heart attack in Amsterdam. I'm told you have a job for me, Chiba-san."

Chiba looked about, uncomfortable at continuing the conversation in Eva's.

Smith said, "If you'd like, we can walk to *la cantina* down the street. They speak Spanish there. We'll have ourselves some cold Belikens."

"Perhaps that would be better," Chiba said.

Smith rose and put on a floppy hat and sunglasses. They stepped out of Eva's into the blistering sun. Smith said, "So you want to tell me what's up, Chiba-san?"

Chiba flinched at Smith's disconcerting directness. He licked his lips. "We have reason to believe you've had contact with a certain Edie Compton, a woman using the Internet to solicit interest in a journal about Kodama Yoshio written by a Wim van der Elst, an American journalist who covered Japan and the war in Asia for the Associated Press."

"I know of a good place to talk." Saying no more, Smith led the way across the street through wide open doors into La Cantina de Paco, where a Mexican brass band blared from a jukebox inside. He walked straight to the bar where he took a seat on a stool. The stools were all empty. There were six patrons in the bar. Two sat at one table, four at another. Chiba sat beside Smith with Yoshida on his left.

"Tres cervezas. Frio, por favor," Smith said.

They waited while the waitress, a young woman with huge lips covered with bright red lipstick, brought them sweating bottles of Beliken, the Belizian-made beer. Smith took a swig of beer and said mildly, "I've heard rumors about that journal for years, but I'm afraid I have no idea who this Edie Compton is. Sorry that you came all this way for nothing."

Chiba cleared his throat. "I know of people who are interested in the contents of the journal who would be willing to pay, say, one million dollars, for a photocopy of the journal. Mrs. Compton can keep the original if she pleases. No problem."

Smith took a swig of Beliken and sighed. "A million bucks! I would dearly love to lay my hands on that kind of money, Chiba-san, but as it happens, I can't help you."

"Actually, I'm authorized to offer Mrs. Compton more than that if necessary, a substantial sum of money. She should name her price. Perhaps we can come to terms."

"My heavens, that sounds generous, but truly, Chiba-san, I have no idea who this Edie Compton is or how you might be able to get in touch with her. Where was that you were educated? Cal Berkeley was it? Good school, Cal."

"As long as you avoid going into Oakland," Chiba said.

Smith laughed. "You know, Chiba-san, in all the years when I was a spook and you were working out of Japanese embassies and consuls, I can never remember you taking a small potatoes job. Now here you are down here in Belize with your power connections and American education. Nothing down here but beans and rice."

"And from that you deduce?"

Smith shrugged. "Since you didn't get what you were after and you think I somehow know or can get in touch with Mrs. Compton, I probably haven't seen the last of you."

"Same old Kip. Paranoid to the end."

"Straightforward logical deduction. The ambiguity is why I turned to wildlife photography, Chiba-san. Kangaroos fucking are kangaroos fucking. No more, no less."

7

Kawana Katchan, the adopted son of a *yakuza oyabun* in Osaka, also spoke good English. One rumor—that Kawana did not discourage—had it that he was actually Kodama Yoshio's son, the result of a 1946 union in Sugamo Prison between Kodama and a geisha smuggled inside for his comfort and relief. Kawana did not discourage speculation that Kodama the proud papa had watched his progress from afar until the day he died.

Kodama believed that evolution had provided the Japanese with a unique brain, and that this unique brain, plus the unique Japanese imagination, made the Japanese language aesthetically superior to English. But the man who raised Kawana hired a tutor, a young graduate of Duke University, to tutor his adopted son in American English—not realizing he was also picking up a North Carolina accent.

Now Kawana, a broad-shouldered Japanese with shrewd eyes and a heavy-lipped, forceful mouth, emerged from the Marriot Hotel in Cebu City on Cebu, one island east of Negros in the middle of the Philippine archipelago. This was the heart of the Visayan-speaking islands. Kawana hated even for a half minute to leave the refuge of his air-conditioned suite. He jumped quickly into the interior of a dark gray Honda sedan and kicked back, grateful for the new cocoon of coolness, although it seemed to him that in the Philippines it was so hot in an automobile that air-conditioners did no good anyway.

Kawana Katchan had ridden the fifteen miles from Cebu City to Danao so many times that he had the route memorized. Mandaue City, which abutted Cebu City to the immediate north, had a certain charm at first, what with the rusting, almost romantic freighters anchored in the passage between Cebu and Mactan Island. Now Kawana regarded Mandaue City as yet another ugly, impoverished Filipino sprawl.

Kawana knew the ingenious Filipinos could copy virtually anything they set their minds to. It was true that the amazing craftsman at Danao had had their problems when they first set up shop. They had started with a simple, single-barrel shotgun and after a few exploded barrels, they got that down. They then tried their hand at copying a pistol, but their first Smith & Wasaks had a disconcerting tendency to blow up in the shooter's hand.

Wasak was Tagalog, meaning something cheap and disposable. The good-natured, self-deprecating Filipinos said that if a bad guy was coming at you and you tried to shoot him with a Smith & Wasak and it misfired, you simply smacked him in the face with the barrel, threw the gun away, and ran for your life.

The early, exploding Smith & Wasaks were followed by models in which the cylinder didn't turn—the shooter having to fire with his right hand and turn the cylinder with his left. But even that annoying tic had been worked out so that the handsomely blued current models were identical to the originals—except for the telltale Smith & Wasak engraved on the barrel. After the Smith & Wasaks, the gunsmiths, emboldened, perfected an imitation Uzi, the only difference to the untrained eye being the Uzi-DAN engraving—signifying, Danao, the Philippines, instead of the Uzi-IMI of the Israeli-made original.

Of course, none of this was done without the knowledge of the Philippine army. The Durano family, the political dynasty that ran

Danao, was loath to unnecessarily eliminate jobs for Filipino craftsmen. The Danao gunsmiths supported families, after all. Would piety put rice on the tables of these families? So government agents checked the shops occasionally, laying down a few simple rules for staying in business.

If the Filipino gunsmiths at Danao made just one imitation Smith & Wesson without Smith & Wasak on the barrel, then they were out of business. If they made one Uzi without the telltale Uzi-DAN, they were history. If just one Smith & Wasak or Uzi-DAN showed up in the hands of the NPA, then the craftsmen were finished. However, the powers in the government did not wring their hands over people wasted by gangsters in Japan. Kawana was allowed to buy all the weapons he wanted for resale in Japan.

Revolvers and assault rifles were one thing, but now Kawana had offered the Filipino craftsmen a real challenge. He remembered their wide eyes and exclamations of *hijo de puta* when he told them what he had in mind. But they were game. They were Filipinos and had confidence in their ingenuity. Just give us our shot, they said. Get us a sample.

Kawana did. Some gentlemen in Tokyo had access to shoulder-launched Italian Sabatini IV, designed to knock out low-flying aircraft, helicopter gunships, or tanks as required—a star performer in NATO exercises. They loaned him one.

The Filipinos took the Sabatini apart piece by piece to see exactly what it was they needed to copy. In the end they told him they could do it, but they needed help. They needed an electronics technician to help them out with the guidance system. Kawana, equally resourceful, furnished them with a quiet young man from Nagoya who had studied at Cal Tech.

The macadam road wound through gently undulating rises and vales, flanked by banana groves, patches of water lilies, and orchards of coconut palms, the clusters of coconuts at the top looking like large green grapes. They passed the village of Liloan, hardly a stop in the road that surrounded a small white church built in the nineteenth century.

Kawana listened to the radio as he watched the passing scenery. One thing he thought Americans could learn from the Filipinos was their taste in music. Filipinos loved to sing, and they preferred love ballads and songs with lyrics that were understandable. Barry Manilow and Karen Carpenter crooned over Filipino airwaves and Whitney Houston sang her heart out. Kawana hated music that was unintelligible noise; he thought Filipino disc jockeys were very good indeed.

They passed brown goats. They passed a boy pulling a carabao by a ring in its nose. They passed fish ponds poking out into the ocean where the Filipinos raised *bangus,* or milkfish. They passed beach resorts. They passed Cebu Mitsumi, a factory that made parts for boom boxes. They passed over low, bald ridges that had once been forested.

Suddenly, Danao lay before them.

As Filipino towns went, Danao was a neat and tidy place. It was nestled around a gorgeous bay perhaps a half mile wide at its entrance. The bay was unusual because the city fathers had prevented the bay's edge from being overrun by the ubiquitous clutter of *carenderias* and vendor stands. Instead, elegant palms and a strip of grass flanked the picturesque bay. There one might take an early evening walk along the water and enjoy the beauty of the colorful and sleek *bankas* on the water. A tidy little town, it was. Kawana-san never failed to be impressed when he passed over the last gentle hill and Danao City lay before him with its gorgeous, well-maintained little bay. This was just about as sweet as it got in the Third World.

Dr. Tomi Kobayashi followed Roddy Baker's directions to Rudyard Kipling Smith's mountain hideaway in eastern Oregon. She flew to Portland and took a propeller-driven plane east to Pendleton. From Pendleton, she drove a rented Ford southeast through rolling wheat country toward Idaho. A half hour out of Pendleton, she left the wheat behind and ascended a long seven-percent grade of highway carved out of a bald foothill and was soon into the Blue Mountains.

The interstate highway swept through the mountains in long, lazy curves. At La Grande, with the sun setting at her back, Tomi turned northeast on a highway that passed through a beautiful high valley with pine-covered mountains on either side and came at last to Enterprise. She stepped into what she thought was an old red-brick hotel and found herself in a home for the retarded. At last, bone-tired, she settled on a motel that had seen better days. She bought a bottle of wine at a grocery store and sat alone that night, staring out into the darkness. *Am I chasing secrets of the abyss, the cusp of my country's soul? Two countries' souls. Or am I being stupid and melodramatic?*

She awoke early the next morning. She had a cup of coffee and drove to the village of Joseph next to Lake Wallowa, a serene stunner with Alplike snowcapped mountains rising high in the background.

Tomi picked her way among the narrow lanes on the near, town end of the lake, located on high ground behind the water. This was to her right, the east. She eased the Ford down a narrow road matted with pine needles, the cabins on the lake's edge below her and to her left. As she drove slowly down the road toward the water, she spotted what she knew must be Kip Smith's cabin, gray with green trim around the windows and eaves.

He was home, or at least his car was—a cigar-shaped Citroën with a long hood and snubbed-off trunk, a late 1960s model that the driver was able to raise or lower on its eccentric pneumatic suspension system. The only place to park was behind the Citroën and that's what Tomi did, setting the hand brake and stepping out into the cool air to the smell of pine needles.

While Smith's Citroën might not have been the ugliest automobile ever allowed on a public highway, it must have been close. She wondered why on earth anybody would want to own one.

She tried the door. There was no answer, so she went around to the porch in back and made herself at home in a canvas chair, wondering which of the canoes and fishing boats on the water might be Smith's.

In a few minutes, Tomi saw him, a lone figure paddling an aluminum canoe in her direction, the bow cutting an elegant *V* of silvery ripples in the cold mountain water.

When Smith climbed out of the canoe, she saw that he was tall, in his late forties, still slender, thickened imperceptibly, if at all. He had a short, silver beard and long silver hair that he kept in a ponytail. He walked lazily up the hill with a wicker fishing creel on his hip. Before he got to her he called amiably, "I saw you park up there. I got two of 'em. Just right for lunch." He opened the creel and scooped a large trout out of the wet grass inside.

He put the fish back inside and wiped the palm of his hand on his jeans.

"Mr. Baker called you Whistling Smith."

"A nickname from my past." He smiled. "Kip will do just fine. And you must be Dr. Tomiko Kobayashi from Washington State. Roddy said you'd be coming. General Yamashita's granddaughter," he said. "Yamashita rightfully belongs in the company of Irwin Rommel and George Patton as one of the great generals of World War II. Ask the granddaughter of the British general who defended Singapore. I'm honored."

She smiled. "My mother Miki was born in 1946 of a wartime union between General Yamashita and his sixteen-year-old Filipina mistress. She was sent to Hawaii after the war, where she grew up and eventually married my father, an administrator at the University of Hawaii. My sister Miho lives in San Francisco. Call me Tomi, please. Mr. Baker said Kip is short for Kipling. You're Rudyard Kipling Smith."

Smith laughed. "My mother taught literature at Oregon State College. That was before they added a course in literature of the tractor and called it a university. Same thing happened at Washington State University, they say."

Tomi laughed. "Kip is preferable to Rudy, I would think. 'Though I've belted you and flayed you, by the living God that made you, you're a better man than I am, Gunga Din.' "

"My heavens, a woman who knows a little Kipling! What do you say I fry these fish, and we can talk over lunch?"

"Sure," she said, and followed Smith inside his cabin. The cabin had just three rooms, a combination bedroom and living area, a small kitchen, and a toilet. Tomi was so stunned at the astonishing clutter of the main room—a trail led to the single bed—she blinked and stared at the floor and walls.

"Like it or think it's a city dump?"

"Interesting, although I like a little more order. I'm not anal compulsive, mind you, but my heavens!"

Smith looked around, pleased. "I suppose it's not to everyone's taste. I've got Japanese swords, masks from New Guinea, drums from Borneo, antique mahjong sets, Chinese opium pipes, Japanese pottery, name it. Every time I come back, I load up my check-on luggage with stuff. Somewhere under there I've got some jade and scrimshaw that might be worth a few bucks some day."

"Pretty soon there won't be room for you!"

Smith laughed. "It's beginning to look that way. I've been thinking of having the room removed and adding a second floor. Live up top. Fill the bottom."

"Mr. Baker said you have a history."

"A history?"

"A former operative in the field. An Asian hand with contacts all over East and Southeast Asia."

Smith laughed, and smoothed his short beard with his fingers. "I like Southeast Asia the best. Filthy. Corrupt. Dangerous. Pickpockets and scam artists everywhere. Cops and bureaucrats on the take. A maddening place, but it has a certain edge that I like. Roddy tells me you have a correspondent's journal about Kodama Yoshio and Golden Lily."

"Yes, I do."

"And you propose to do what with it?"

"Rehabilitate my grandfather's reputation. He was no war criminal. I also want to tell the truth about Douglas MacArthur's decisions at the end of the war and the involvement of the CIA in our postwar foreign policy. Why did Douglas MacArthur release Kodama and his war criminal friends? Kodama had been in charge of the Kampei-tai units that collected the booty for the emperor. Mac gave Hirohito a walk that might or might not have been justified. I smell quid pro quo. I don't like the odor. In fact, it stinks." Tomi spotted a 5 × 7 framed photograph of a younger Smith and a Southeast Asian woman in the midst of the clutter on top of a bureau of drawers. She picked up the photograph.

"She was my wife," Smith said.

"Very pretty. Was?"

Smith took the picture and sat on the floor, staring at it. "Yes, she was pretty. And a good person, too. I loved her. She used to . . ." Smith looked momentarily embarrassed. "She used to make me a dish of *mongo*—that's the little green bean that grows into bean sprouts—with bits of pork and cabbage and tomato, flavored with onions and garlic, that was of the gods. It was delicious. And . . . Her *pancit* was good, too—that's noodles with bits of pork and shrimp and chicken. And her *adobo,* pork and chicken cooked in vinegar and garlic and onions with a hit of soy sauce until it reduced to almost nothing. Mmmm!" Smith made a clicking sound with his tongue.

"What happened, if you don't mind my asking?"

Smith bit his lip. "Her maiden name was Gina Artes. Sweet Gina. She was a Cebuana. She was murdered in Cebu City in 1985. A terrible thing. Long, long time ago." He clenched his jaw. The memory of his wife obviously ripped at him.

"Who did it?"

Smith gave her back the photograph. "That, Tomi, is a good question. Gina's father was a newspaper editor who insisted on criticizing Ferdinand Marcos in print after he'd been warned to knock it off. I was out of town on a Company job when some assholes showed up to murder him. She happened to be there, too. You ask who did it? Was it the man who pulled the trigger? Well, yes. Was it Marcos's police? The police were responsible, yes. Marcos himself?" Smith shrugged. "No way of knowing. But if you trace the responsibility, you could say that Kodama Yoshio killed her. And beyond that, I'm sorry to say, Douglas MacArthur or even the Central Intelligence Agency."

Tomi's eyes widened. "You hold Douglas MacArthur personally responsible?"

Narrowing his eyes, his voice rising, he said, "They're all accountable for the excess that resulted in my wife's murder. Marcos is a Filipino problem. I refuse to let the Americans involved get away with it. There is no statute of limitation for murder."

"The passage of time doesn't erase their guilt. I agree."

"My wife wasn't the only Filipino casually murdered during the Marcos reign. Nobody knows precisely who was responsible, I'll concede that. Who is ultimately to blame? The man who started the sequence of events? That might be Douglas MacArthur."

After a moment, he reached into the pile at the foot of his bed and retrieved an elegant fan with delicately carved scrimshaw ribs. He unfolded it, revealing a splendid crane on black silk. The crane had a splash of crimson on the top of its head. He handed it to her. "You like this?"

Tomi looked startled.

"What's the matter?"

"I . . . Nothing. She turned it in her hand, admiring it. "It's beautiful."

"Fifteenth century Japanese. Best enjoyed on a languid day with a Singapore sling. It's yours."

She blinked. "Oh, no, please."

Smith said, "It's been under that pile of crap for years. A complete waste. I bought it with somebody like you in mind."

Tomi was nonplussed. "Somebody like me?"

"A woman who can quote Kipling, even if it is one of his most famous lines. And maybe somebody who can help put Gina's death in a more accurate context. Blame, blame, blame. After all these years, I've grown weary of blaming the Marcos family. Marcos, Marcos, Marcos! Marcos did this. Marcos did that. Yadda, yadda, yadda! Bashing Marcos grows tiresome after a while. He was what he was. No saint, that's for sure. If you try to trace down everything he is supposed to have done, you get lost in a swamp of charge and countercharge. I'll leave Marcos's legacy to Filipino politicians and journalists and historians. Let them argue about what he did or did not do, not me. Filipinos get annoyed at know-it-all Americans spouting opinions about Filipino history. Who can blame them?"

Tomi turned the fan in her hand as she listened.

"But as an American, dammit I have a right to know the truth about the occupation-inspired genesis of Marcos's excess. Treasure on the purported scale of Hirohito's Gold has an almost unlimited ability to corrupt. I think the U.S. might correctly bear some of the guilt owing to a decision made by its chief surrogate in the occupation of Japan. Let the Filipinos judge Marcos if they please. But American complicity is *my* legitimate concern. I'm after the corrupting secret that was the treasure collected for the Japanese emperor. Give me Dugout Doug. I need your help to tell the story."

Grinning, Tomi fanned herself. "This wasn't Gina's, was it? I don't think I could accept it if it was."

"Please, take the fan. Consider it a kind of talisman, a gift from a victim to an avenging angel. Fan yourself and the cooling air will be her best wishes. Her way of encouraging you. She was a nice person. If you had known her, you would understand. I was her husband. By the way, Admiral Iwabuchi Sanji was the real butcher of Manila, not your grandfather. I'll tell you that right from the start."

"That was made clear in the trial. Yamashita ordered him to quit the city."

"Given a larger context, maybe there was a reason for the sacking of Manila beyond the Japanese being barbarous shits caught up in the emotion of the moment. The Japanese deny, deny, deny.

Those who know the truth think they have escaped the past. They are beyond judgment. I say no. Not them. Not MacArthur. The case might be circumstantial, but the logic is clear-cut. Let me fix you lunch and we'll talk."

9

Kawana Katchan skipped the usual visit to the shops in Danao, the gunsmiths having all been invited to see the first launch of their sleek little Sabatini-DAN—the celebratory firing set for an isolated clearing in the mountains. He had sent word ahead that the Filipino gunsmiths should be given all the San Miguel and Johnny Walker Black Label they could drink, as well as all the *lechon,* barbecued calf, boiled crab, grilled shrimp, and fried fish they could handle. And no bony little fuckers either. Lapu Lapu. He wanted fruit, too, especially those sweet little Cebu mangoes, and apple bananas, and *lanzones!* The off-yellow *lanzones* came in bunches, like large grapes. To open a *lanzone,* you squeezed one end with your thumb and forefinger. Kawana thought the little sections of the *lanzone* tasted sweeter than a geisha's pussy.

He grinned broadly when the Mitsubishi pulled into a small field filled with old Toyotas, colorful jeepneys, and cars with Filipino-made bodies set on Volkswagen engines, several of them looking like World War II German staff cars. He had promised them all a ten-thousand-peso bonus if the firing went right. With all the San Miguel and Scotch the gunsmiths could drink, plus five hundred U.S. dollars on the line, Kawana knew it would be an entertaining afternoon.

Behind the abandoned bamboo farmhouse that had been

taken over by the caterers, he counted a row of eight pigs being browned over charcoal for lechon. The gunsmiths, babbling in Visayan, sat on folding chairs around two long tables. In front of them, nestled casually in among the San Miguel bottles and plates piled high with *lechon* and crabs were two sleek white missiles—lethal, evil-looking things—each about a yard long, and with stubby fins at the tail. If these were not the highest of high-tech wire-guided missiles, no observer could tell by merely looking at them.

There would be fireworks ahead. Counting the numbers of Filipino craftsmen, Kawana had a momentary pang of regret at offering a ten-thousand-peso bonus. A successful firing of the Sabatini-DAN was going to cost him more than thirty thousand U.S. dollars.

Kawana rarely put in an appearance at Danao, not wanting to inflame whatever local resentment there might be against the Japanese. His craftsmen knew who he was still, and the arrival of the godfather of Kawana-kai was an occasion for much shaking of hands and drinking of San Miguel.

In addition to the missiles, the center of attention at the table was Toto Popong, who had lost two little fingers on his left hand trying out one of the early shotguns. By vote of his fellow workers, Popong was to have the honor of firing the first Sabatini-DAN. Popong munched on pieces of dark mahogany *lechon* skin and drank tall glasses of Johnny Walker to bolster his nerve for the scheduled firing.

All things considered, Kawana thought he'd probably rather fire a shotgun for the first time than a missile designed to knock out a tank or armored personnel carrier. He wondered whether or not Toto Popong was thinking the same thing. He was also curious as to what they proposed to use as targets. They told him they had two test shots planned, one aerial and one surface.

Giovanni, a relative of the superintendent of the shop that had

copied the Sabatini, had arrived by boat from Leyte, bearing a
large pot of his Soup #5 and other Filipino delicacies to bolster
the nerve of both spectators and Toto Popong. Giovanni, whose
regular occupation was a butcher, wore a spanking new white
chef's hat, being thus transformed into Chef Giovanni, much to
the merriment of everyone. His famous Soup #5, an alleged Filipino classic, turned out to contain *carabao* balls, quartered; *carabao*
cock, thinly sliced; *carabao* eyeballs, whole; *carabao* knuckles, or
the animal's Achilles tendon, whacked into gnawable chunks; as
well as chopped onions, carrots, potatoes, green peas, and Chinese *Tongkoi,* among other spices. Giovanni also brought chopped
pork ovaries that had been simmered then marinated in coconut
vinegar, and *putay baboy,* literally pork pussy threaded onto bamboo skewers so as not to destroy their wonderful *putay* shape when
they were cooked over charcoal.

Kawana lowered his spoon into his Soup #5 and came up with
an eyeball, something which, to the best he could recall, he had
never eaten. A *samurai* confronted with an eyeball on a spoon
with foreigners watching? What would Yamamoto advise? Kawana
ate the eyeball slowly, showing no emotion.

Watching this, the Filipinos cheered with gusto. The Japanese
Godfather had a real pair!

Finally, their courage and manliness fortified by Soup #5 and
putay baboy, they all got up, stubbies of San Miguel in hand, and
walked to a nearby clearing occupied by a herd of small brown
goats. They shooed the goats away. What the Danao shop had
chosen for the aerial demonstration was a remote-controlled
model plane that one of the gunsmiths had bought in an expensive specialty shop in Manila, and this man, who had been practicing with the airplane, fired up its tiny gasoline engine and sent
it aloft to the cheering of his colleagues.

Toto Popong, meanwhile, thoroughly in the grip of Scotch,

tried his hand at aiming the tube that contained the missile.

The biplane, a gaudy yellow, flew between two rows of tall, stately coconut palms, did a loop, and flew back their way.

The plane flew right over Popong, who tracked the plane with his missle tube but did not fire.

"Let him have it, Toto!" a gunsmith yelled.

"Do it, Toto!" another cried.

Toto Popong twisted and fell down as the plane passed overhead. He got up, grinning foolishly, as his colleagues cheered him on.

The biplane made another loop and came back for a return pass.

Popong steadied himself, feet wide, knees slightly bent. He was ready this time. He squinted his eyes as he tracked the approaching target.

Again the plane passed overhead and while Popong kept his feet this time, he still did not fire the missile. This brought more cries of *hijo de puta*.

"I'll get it this time. Send it my way," he called to the operator.

The plane approached and the missile—*sssswwwooossshhh*—shot skyward, sailing past the plane. A miss. The plane flew on, undisturbed.

Nevertheless, cheers went up. It was unlikely that the miss was the fault of the missile. Toto Popong was clearly too drunk to hit anything. The gunsmiths of Danao were jubilant. The Sabatini-DAN had worked. A triumph. It had not blown up, costing Popong limb if not life.

The heroic Toto Popong, grinning, barely able to stand, accepted their congratulations and poured himself another Scotch. He had demonstrated *cojones grandes*.

This brought up the question of the Sabatini-DAN's performance as a surface-to-surface weapon. Kawana assumed they had rigged a remote control to an old car, but one of the craftsmen, who had a .22 pistol tucked under his belt, came walking out onto the clearing leading a placid carabao.

The shop superintendent suddenly thrust the second Sabatini-DAN into Kawana's hands. They wanted Kawana Katchan to have the honor of wasting the *carabao*, which was about sixty yards away.

No proper *oyabun* could show a loss of nerve in front of foreigners. Besides, Kawana wanted to fire the missile. It looked fun, and he had been envious of Toto Popong getting to shoot at the model plane.

As he accepted the firing tube, it occurred to him that Popong, by luck of the draw, might have gotten the good missile and he, a dangerously defective Sabatini-Wasak. The missile tube had a simple crosshair sight mounted on the side.

The Filipino with the pistol aimed it at the bull's tail.

Kawana pulled down toward the *carabao*'s stomach and did a practice swing along the anticipated flight.

"Ready?" the Filipino asked, still concentrating on the tail.

"Okay," Kawana said.

He heard the snap of the .22 and the roar of the *carabao* as it shot forward. He swung the tube sharply to his left. The *carabao* flashed behind the crosshair. He touched the launch button.

Sssswwwwooossshhh!

He kept the sight steady on the fleeing target.

The Sabatini-DAN streaked across the meadow, trailing its guiding wire.

Whoooooooooomb! A direct hit.

The gunsmiths of Danao whooped with laughter at the spectacle of the exploding *carabao*. A wild burst of crimson. Heels and hooves. Tongue and tail. Ears and entrails. Every different direction.

The amused Kawana, proud of his marksmanship, yelled, "*Hijo de puta!*"

10

The biscuits were ready. Kip Smith grabbed a potholder and retrieved the pan from the oven. He slid a crisply fried trout onto Tomi Kobayashi's plate. Then came the sauté of morels and sliced wapatoo. When he finished serving, Smith attacked his trout with gusto, hardly glancing up. "There's something very elemental about sitting out there on a mountain lake on a morning like this."

"Roddy Baker says you're good at imitating birds. Whistling Smith, he called you."

Smith laughed. "Congress passed a rule saying Company operatives couldn't pose as journalists. The news organizations wanted foreign governments to trust that their reporters aren't CIA spies. Hard to blame them for that. So I hit on another idea. What if I became a freelance bird expert? Sort of a modern day Audubon with a camera. That's hardly political. That would give me an excuse to cross international borders with parabolic microphones and telephoto lenses. The DCI asked the Senate Intelligence Oversight Committee for approval, and they said yes. To prepare my legend, I started practicing birdcalls off tapes sold by the National Audubon Society. Hence the nickname by a few close friends, Whistling Smith, having a little fun with the Whispering Smith character played by Steve McQueen years ago."

Tomi laughed. "I see."

Smith put his hands to his mouth and gave a low, mellow call.

"A mourning dove. Very good."

"Eventually I branched out and learned to videotape various kinds of animals for television nature programs. I even went so far as to buy diving gear and an underwater camera. A couple of years after my wife's murder, I quit to become a photographer full time. There are people who do wildlife in Africa or North America or wherever. I do Asia. I have numerous contacts and speak fluent Mandarin Chinese, some Cantonese and Visayan, and enough Indonesian, Thai, and Vietnamese to ask directions and read a menu.

"Japanese and Korean?"

"My Japanese is actually pretty good. No Korean. When I was with the Company, I did a lot of urban stuff. Pigeons, rats, cockroaches. But I liked the wilderness better—orangutans and Indonesian lizards. Australian crocodiles. Whatever. I stay away from cities as much as I can."

Tomi took a sample of omelet. "And wherever did you get fresh morels?"

"The morels are just coming out. I lucked out and found these early this morning. When the season gets rolling, a young woman I know in Enterprise ships them off to France for college money. Enterprising, eh?" He grinned.

Tomi speared a slice of *wapatoo* on her fork. "And what is this? This is delicious, too."

"That's a tuber the Indians call *wapatoo*. It's also called arrowhead. They grow in swamps and farm ponds. You can either scoop them up with a garden rake or use your toes. They get as large as golf balls, some of them. They're free and taste good, and didn't kill the Indians, so I figure what the hell."

"They're very good."

"You're not the only one who thinks they're good. They're

prized in parts of Europe and Asia, and the Chinese cultivate them. By the way, the cattail pollen in the biscuits is what gives them that unusual flavor."

"Oh? They're wonderful!" Tomi began buttering another biscuit with interest. "Your friend Mr. Baker also said I should ask you why you prefer living in exile."

Smith laughed. "He did, did he?" Smith stopped and took a sip of coffee. "For essentially the same reason I quit the Company."

"And that would be?"

"The mendacity and stupidity of American politics just drives me wild, so I retreated to Asia. It's true that politics in Asia are even worse than in the U.S., but they don't have anything to do with me. Also America is too clean and comfortable. I like living on the edge."

He stopped and studied her face thoughtfully. "My turn to ask the questions now. You want to tell me how it was that a good-looking woman wound up as a college professor and not on the arm of a brain surgeon or Silicon Valley millionaire?"

Tomi gave him a lazy smile. "My sister Miho wound up on the arm of a Silicon Valley millionaire. I discovered early on that learning is a form of entertainment. It's fun, an end in itself. Carl Sagan once said that if athletes with superior bodies like physical competition, it shouldn't surprise anybody that people with good brains like intellectual competition. I don't see why intellectual fun should be restricted to skinny lasses who wear glasses. I get an elemental pleasure reading a good writer at work. Their words. My voice inside my head. Joint creation."

"Brains and beauty aren't mutually exclusive."

Tomi laughed. "When I was a little girl I used some of my allowance to buy a framed tile at a garage sale." She eyed him. "It had five cranes on it, very light and elegant cranes with an Oriental look about them."

"Cranes?"

"They were on an ivory-colored background. Later, in the library, I saw a photograph of a Japanese bride with cranes on her kimono. I started reading about the meaning of cranes in Asia. I discovered that in China they're symbols of longevity and are depicted carrying the souls of the departed to heaven. The red-crowned crane is found in Japanese paintings, tapestry, and other decorative arts as the symbol of good luck, happiness, long life, and marital bliss. There is a famous Japanese folktale in which a crane transforms itself into a maiden. Cranes flank the emperor's throne in Beijing's Forbidden City."

"It all started with a tile with five cranes. Good story! You know I bought that fan with the crane on it for Gina, and I've seen cranes on paintings and ceramics all over Asia, but it never occurred to me to find out more about what they mean."

"I want to know the truth about what happened after the war because the truth exists. Why shouldn't it be me who finds out what it is? Last I knew, the search for truth is not limited by gender."

Smith laughed. "You want to tell me more about your journal?"

"It was kept by Wim van der Elst, a correspondent for the Associated Press who followed Kodama's career from 1931 to the end of the war. He called Kodama the Great Patriotic Bagman. He believed that Prince Chichibu and Prince Higashikuni, working for Emperor Hirohito, used Kodama and his subordinates, including Adm. Iwabuchi Sanji, to keep the treasure off the home islands and out of the hands of military hard-liners who had staged an insurrection in 1936. Hirohito thought Japan would get the Philippines as part of a negotiated settlement."

"Makes sense. Hirohito didn't know about The Bomb. Did van der Elst cover any of the war in the Philippines?"

"He covered the action on Negros."

"And you say his journal entries mentioned the alchemist archers?"

"I didn't mention any archers."

Smith grinned. "Smart woman. I have a close friend on Negros, Colonel Cading 'Ding' Rodriguez, a sugar planter who is also an officer in *Bawiin mo ang Ginto*, Tagalog for "Take Back the Gold," a Filipino unit charged with recovering assets stolen from the country by the Marcos family." *Bawiin* was pronounced *ba-wi-in*, the two vowels pronounced separately just as Bataan was correctly pronounced *Ba-ta-ahn*, not *Bat-ahn*. "Ding has been telling me for years that the dragons are buried on Negros."

"Van der Elst found out where they were buried. Or thinks he did."

"They're buried in or near a hill named Pulak Pulakan."

Tomi blinked.

"Pulak Pulakan! Ding's right." Smith poured himself another glass of iced tea.

"Will you take me on a canoe ride on the lake? This is like the Alps. Beautiful!"

Smith noticed the change of subject but went along. "I'll use an Indonesian paddle, if you like." He stepped into his living room, dug into the amazing pile, and pulled out an intricately carved paddle. "This is from Bali. They're Hindu on Bali, you know. A conservative culture in some ways. Freethinking in others." He arched an eyebrow and handed her the paddle.

Tomi admired the blade, which was carved with graceful palm trees.

Smith said, "By the way, Ding Rodriguez is precisely the man you want to talk to about Hirohito's Gold and the M Fund. He's a kind of Filipino Javert in pursuit of truth. If you don't mind a trip to Negros, I bet I can sweet-talk Ding into briefing you on what *Bawiin mo ang Ginto* has found out over the years. Amazing stuff. Complement the van der Elst journal."

"You want to take me to Negros?"

"That's where Ding is." He paused, chewing on his lower lip. "If we're going to travel together, I feel compelled to tell you that I think you're an extraordinary woman, good-looking in addition to being smart. This is not just a line, truly. You're really something."

"I . . ."

"Just thought I'd be honest." Quickly, he added, "In case you catch me scoping you on the sly."

"I'm here on behalf of my grandfather, Kip, not to find a man."

He gave her a self-deprecating grin. "I've always found Asian women attractive, which I suppose is why I married one."

"And what is it you find unattractive about European woman?"

"They're okay. There's no accounting for taste. If a man spends years in Asia, he comes to admire Asian women. If I'd spent years in Africa, I'd probably like African women. How about you? You like round-eyed men?"

"How about that canoe ride?"

"You don't like *gaijin*? I'm disappointed."

"*Gaijin* is not a term I use. It means 'hairy barbarian.'"

Smith grinned. "I've been called both. Canoe ride coming right up."

11

The mountains were ordinarily enveloped in a mist during the rainy season. When the clouds parted, sending a rainbow arching over the verdant sugarland far below, Jaime Pineda leaned his M-16 against the base of a tree and sat down to enjoy the view. From this vantage point Pineda could see the huge sugar mill at Victorias, which lay due west, and Silay to the southwest. Cadiz lay on his right, to the northeast. *Haciendedos* with tens of thousands of hectares of sugarland had their cane milled at Victorias. Pineda knew that system well because he had grown up a part of it, hacking cane with a machete.

It was at the mill itself, in a mural above the altar in the Chapel of St. Joseph the Worker, where an enraged Christ glared at the congregation with furious eyes. The chapel of the angry Christ was included in all the tourist guidebooks, years ago having been featured in *Life* magazine, and Pineda knew that it was one of the first places the warlords took their out-of-town guests.

Pineda believed the warlords had made fortunes off Filipinos rendered passive by the priests preaching forgiveness and forbearance. Pineda had been in that chapel and had seen that inspiring mural, and it was clear that if Christ were alive today, his rage would be unrelieved. He would be in the mountains carrying an M-16 along with Jaime Pineda.

Pineda knew that General Martinez must want something very badly indeed to come into NPA territory accompanied only by Pineda's cousin George Villanueva. Pineda would be seconded by the old man, Luis Montoya, who lived in a hut at the end of the NPA's run of pig pits. Pineda had a good idea what this was all about. The American evangelist Robin Fallon was planning a revival in Cadiz, and there had been stories about him wanting to burn candles at Pulak Pulakan for an American war hero. As if Pineda gave a damn about an American war hero. This plus the appearance of a *yakuza* yacht off Cadiz alerted Pineda to the real game. The play was his to call and he knew it.

Saying he needed time alone to think, Pineda volunteered to check the *baboy* pits himself before his rendezvous with his cousin George and General Martinez. And that was true. He did want time to think. The responsibility for playing the NPA hand was his, and he didn't want to mess up.

Pineda could barely see the golf course just outside of the mill—which was a town unto itself—where Pineda and six of his NPA friends, after a night of drinking too much *tuba*, had ambushed a party of planters on the tenth green. They had emerged from the brush, M-16s blazing, and killed three of the planter foursome, including a vice president of Victorias's mill, who was kneeling on the ground studying the lie of his putt. As a legacy of that attack, the caddies at Victorias's golf course took to carrying M-16s in addition to drivers, irons, and putters.

The gap in the clouds closed and Pineda continued on the trail leading to the pit for *baboy talonon*—forest pig—that had been dug under the spreading bows of a forty-foot-tall *katmon* tree, which bore a fist-sized fruit that tasted similar to lemon and that the wild pigs loved. There had once been an NPA campsite near this tree, and the pit, whose sides and bottom were still blackened, had first been used to make charcoal from the slender branches of *ipil ipil* and *madre cacao*, the latter also used as a stalk for black pepper vines.

The ground under the *katmon* had been picked clean of fruit, but there was no *baboy* impaled on the sharpened bamboo stakes at the bottom of the pit. The pit under the *katmon* tree was the sixth of a series of pits that took five days of hard walking to check—with two pits coming on the final leg. Most of the pits were under fruit trees, but some were dug along trails leading to patches of sweet potatoes.

From the empty pit under the *katmon* tree, Pineda headed west, downhill, toward the final pit, dug under a fifteen-foot-tall *batwan* tree, which bore a seedy fruit that turned from green to yellow as it ripened. Filipinos used both the green fruit and the leaves as seasonings.

It was a two-hour hike in the steaming heat to the *batwan* tree. Pineda didn't need landmarks to tell him he was getting close. When he was still about five minutes away, he caught a sniff of an appalling smell up ahead, and he knew from the stench that a pig had fallen on the stakes, probably shortly after the pit was last checked, and so the corpse had a chance to ripen leisurely. Had it not been that he and Luis Montoya were going to feed General Martinez and George Villanueva, Pineda would have given the pit a wide clearance.

Pineda headed straight for the rotting pig, quickening his stride as the stench got stronger. At the same time, he unfastened the woven carryall at his belt.

As he approached the pit, two sated rats scrambled over the edge. When he got there, holding his breath, he quickly lowered himself into the pit with a rope that was tied to the base of the *batwan* tree for that purpose. The *baboy* was ripe in the extreme, with rings of squirming white maggots attending to the flesh where the stakes poked through. Using a stick, Pineda quickly scraped the maggots into the basket and clambered up and out of the pit.

Once on top, breathing once more, he sprinted for clean air, grabbing a fistful of *batwan* leaves for Luis Montoya on his way past the tree.

Luis lived in a *nipa* hut beside a potato patch and a mountain stream, the last stop on the circle of NPA pig traps. Ordinarily whoever saw to the chore stopped by Montoya's to kick back and palaver with the old man, who kept watch on what the Philippine army and the CAGFUs were up to. When Luis had a visitor, he liked to get loaded on *tuba* and do a little talking.

Later, as it began to get dark, Pineda could see smoke drifting out of the hut where Luis lived. He could hear the squawking of Montoya's fighting chickens. He was glad he had collected the maggots.

The old man, with a brown and white goat leaning against his leg, met Pineda outside his hut. "Are you hungry, Jaime?"

"I could eat a little." Pineda flopped his backpack on the floor of the hut. "We'll be having special guests for lunch tomorrow so I brought a treat."

Montoya looked at the squirmers in the basket and grinned. "Nothing's too good for Jaime Pineda's guests, eh?"

Pineda laughed. "They should be fresh enough tomorrow, don't you think? Nobody wants to eat stale maggots."

"We're having corn tonight. I already had the water on. Timed it just right." Montoya dumped a couple of handfuls of cracked corn into a pot of water that he had been boiling above a bed of glowing charcoal.

Montoya said, "You people ought to dig yourself another string of pits. This is what, three times around empty?"

"Three times, I think."

"Of course, I haven't been doing any better with my pits. But I've got some *daludogs* out, though. There's a full moon tonight so the *baboy* will be out foraging. Maybe we'll have some luck. I didn't have any gunpowder so I had to shave some match heads. I was out of gunpowder."

Pineda dug some shells out of his bandoleer. "Here, empty these, Luis."

Later, their bellies full of boiled corn, drunk, they sang love songs in Ilongo, and shortly before they curled up on their mats to sleep, they heard a muffled pop, followed by a crazed screaming in the direction of Montoya's sweet potato patch.

"Got him," Montoya said. "We'll have *baboy talonon* tomorrow."

The pig in the field did not stop screaming.

"You should never use match heads, Luis. They don't do much more than give a pig a headache. Listen to it. *Hijo de puta.*"

The anguished screaming continued.

"Some headache," Montoya said. "I say we've got him."

The pig screamed for nearly an hour before it stopped.

Montoya was jubilant. "He bled to death. We'll be eating *baboy* tomorrow."

The next morning, Pineda and the old man followed the bloody trail of the wild pig until they found a dead sow, minus her tongue and part of her jaw, the result of her having crunched down on an explosive *daludog* nut that Montoya had buried in a sweet potato.

By the time they had lugged the snoutless *baboy* back to Montoya's hut, one of Pineda's lieutenants was there with news. He said Pineda's cousin, George Villanueva, a cadet at the Philippine Military Academy, and another man had checked in at the NPA outpost at the edge of the Patag. They were on their way.

Pineda and the old man, who could hardly believe he was to play host to the superintendent of the Philippine Military Academy, whacked off a large chunk of the *baboy*'s back and ribs. The *baboy* was an *anai*, a sow. They removed its *putay*, and sent the rest of the carcass back to the NPA camp in the tunnels of Pulak Pulakan.

12

Outside the window of the Boeing 747, puffs of white clouds lay spread out against the horizon. As the flight attendant cleared their trays, Kip Smith sipped Bloody Mary mix sans vodka; Tomi Kobayashi poured herself some more ginger ale.

"Good to be getting away from the theater," Kip said.

"The theater?"

"Around-the-clock contrived drama wrought by the twenty-four-hour news cycle. If I'm in the United States too long, I start taking sides and my stomach twists. When I get away from the craziness, I feel better. When you're halfway around the world from the drama, you don't care any more. Out in the provinces of the Philippines, people lie under mosquito nets and listen to crickets."

"Healthier not to care, you think?"

"Have you ever wondered about little itches, Tomi? You get one on your ear. You scratch it. Then one on your scalp. Or on your thigh maybe, or the calf of your leg or your ankle, or sometimes even on the bottom of your foot so you have to take your shoe off and scratch the damn thing before it drives you nuts. All things being equal, your skin shouldn't itch. You're still healthy, but there it is nevertheless. The unanswered questions of the way the Company does many things became little emotional itches for me. Most of these itches had to do with secrets, some decades old, that served no useful purpose. The decisions were made by public figures who are long since dead."

"One of which ended with your wife's murder."

"If I couldn't stand a culture of secrecy, I had an obligation to get out, and so I did."

"I'm curious. *When* exactly did you make the decision? Where were you? What were you doing? Did you have some kind of epiphany?"

Smith thought a moment, then said, "I was in a small town on Mindanao, pretending to be a writer waiting for a new part for my laptop. I was really there waiting to make contact with a Company snitch among the Muslim guerrillas farther south. I fell in with some local cops with big pistols tucked under their belts and spent my afternoons drinking San Miguel with them in a karaoke bar. We got drunk together every day and sang love songs and sentimental ballads. One evening I got back to my hotel, sloshed, and smoked a joint, thinking about the cops and the karaoke and all the fun I had had. I got to thinking about O. J. Simpson, Bill Clinton, and John and Patricia Ramsey in Colorado. In the United States, like it or not, we have separate legal standards for the rich and famous than for ordinary people. Our State Department likewise distinguishes between powerful economies and weak ones. The Japanese control seventy percent of the Asian economy. Japanese corporations pump four to five hundred million dollars a year in lobby money into Congress, a large chunk of that from the M Fund. The truth is, we have one standard of justice for the Japanese and another for the impoverished Filipinos. If Hirohito's Gold had wound up in a larger economy or one populated by Europeans, say Australia, we wouldn't have helped Kodama maintain the myth of Yamashita's Gold. What if the Japanese had succeeded in their advance on Australia and stashed the emperor's loot in Darwin? What would we have done then? You see what I'm saying?"

"You're saying the Filipinos don't count."

"Not to the self-righteous Cold Warriors. Then there's the business about us being a world cop and asserting ourselves as an international moral authority, the champion of human rights and the rest of it. Sometimes we do live up to what we aspire to be, and good for us. All my life I've heard Americans lecture the Germans and the Japanese for ignoring what they did in World War II. Lately the Germans have been facing up to what they did, but Japanese schoolbooks still ignore what the Japanese Imperial Army did. Schoolchildren have no idea what happened. What we did to the Philippines isn't to be compared to the Holocaust or the rape of Nanking, but it sure as hell matters to the Filipinos. You have an itch, too, knowledge that your grandfather was railroaded."

Tomi said, "After all these years, it's not enough to merely prove that my grandfather's reputation was trashed by a grandstanding general. Every time I mention my grandfather's name, people think 'war criminal,' the man who ordered the sacking of Manila and all the pain and misery that went with that decision. But if you read a transcript of the trial, the record is clear. He testified at his trial that he ordered all Japanese troops to withdraw to the mountains. Nobody contradicted that and nobody attempted to prove he said otherwise. The decision to defend Manila and raze Intramuros was clearly Admiral Iwabuchi's and Iwabuchi's alone. Why? That we don't know."

"That, my dear Dr. Kobayashi, is precisely the question you should be asking and which you should know after Ding finishes his briefings."

"He was not tried by officers of equal rank, a long established military tradition. He was not charged with personally participating in acts of rape or torture or murder. Nobody suggested that he ordered or condoned the atrocities or even knew they were taking place. He was found guilty of not controlling his subordinates, even those with whom he was unable to communicate."

"Allowing them to commit acts of barbarity."

"Right again. The charge was based on neither The Hague Convention of 1907 nor the Geneva Red Cross Convention of 1929. In fact, there was no international principle or precedent defining such a crime. *Quod licet jovi non licet bovi,* Kip, 'What is lawful for the victors is not unlawful for the vanquished.' In the Vietnam War, Captain Ernest Medina was acquitted on a similar charge of failing to control his subordinate, Lieutenant William Calley. In 1998, the International Criminal Court made clear that commanding officers 'shall be criminally responsible for crimes by forces under his or her effective command and control.' MacArthur reverted to the practice of ancient Romans when imperial triumph required the strangulation of the vanquished leader. This, mind you, from the general who hid in the lowermost bowels of Corregidor during the Japanese bombardment and who fled for Australia in the night, leaving General Matthew Wainwright to surrender his troops and suffer imprisonment."

"The Filipinos were furious at what had happened to Manila and wanted somebody to pay, so Dougout Doug gave them Yamashita." Smith refilled his plastic glass with Bloody Mary mix.

"Wait, wait, he went further than that. The great general so beloved of well-meaning patriots and the ignorant in the United States ordered the Tiger of Malaya stripped of medals, decorations, and 'other appurtenances of the military profession,' and to be hanged as a private soldier." Tomi's face turned bitter. "And do you know what my grandfather's last words were?"

Smith shook his head. "No idea."

"He said, 'I will pray for the Japanese emperor and the emperor's family and national prosperity. Dear father and mother, I am going to your side. Please educate my children well.' " She leaned close to Smith. "Well, let me tell you, Mr. Smith. I am Yamashita Tomoyuki's granddaughter. I have a doctoral degree from the University of Chicago. You know what I think? I believe General Yamashita, a man of the sword, understood the power of education. I want Douglas MacArthur's family and his many adoring fans to know the truth about their wonderful hero. Let *them* suffer a little pain and humiliation. I personally want to have a hand in stripping MacArthur of all the 'appurtenances' of a national hero. I am a well-educated descendant of Yamashita Tomoyuki, and I say it's tit for tat for our pal Mac." She straightened, her back rigid with determination.

Smith leaned back in admiration. "General Yamashita's daughter rides into battle and takes Douglas MacArthur down with the truth. I like it."

"He was Tomoyuki. My mother named me Tomiko, close as she could get to Tomoyuki. When you compared Yamashita to Rommel, it was not hyperbole. He blitzed the British down the Malay Peninsula in February 1942 and captured Singapore against a force twice as large as his."

"But Tojo was jealous, poor baby."

"Ah, so you know the story. Tojo denied him a hero's welcome in Japan and an audience with the emperor, then immediately isolated him in Manchuria. He was not used again until Tojo was sacked and the Japanese clearly were losing the war."

"I like the spirit!" Smith leaned close to Tomi. "I liked it when you leaned my way. The smell. Mmmmm. You're making me drunk. Warrior woman." He inhaled deeply.

Tomi pretended to be disgusted. "Straighten up and stay focused on what we have to do."

"Easy for you to say. I have to sit beside you on a ten-hour flight to Osaka and another three hours to Manila. I can't stop breathing, for heaven's sake. Give me a break. 'Stay focused on what we have to do.'" He rolled his eyes. "I know what I'd like to do."

"You're a man. No secret what you'd like to do. Shush."

On the last leg of their flight, with Kip Smith sleeping beside her, Dr. Tomi Kobayashi reviewed her notes on Kodama Yoshio's career after he was released from Sugamo Prison. The record was clear—recorded by the army—that the American Counter Intelligence Corps, then under the command of Gen. Charles Willoughby, put war criminal Kodama to work busting labor unions in an effort to dampen their influence in postwar Japan.

In 1949, the newly formed CIA absorbed the army's intelligence network in Japan, whereupon Kodama became a Company operative, leading the *yakuza* gang Meiraki-guma against the labor unions at the Hokutan coal mines. By all accounts, Kodama secretly financed the pro-Western Liberal Party, washing a large amount of unspecified resources through the conservative politician Tsujii Karoku. This bought him political influence that served him for the rest of his life.

Where did Kodama get the money?

The M Fund?

And what was the role of the Central Intelligence Agency, which clearly had a motive in establishing a pro-Western government in Tokyo?

Nineteen-forty eight. The Red Scare was just getting rolling in 1948. The CIA was fighting a cold war in Asia, and blocking the Mao threat in Asia was top priority. In 1950, the United States joined UN troops in fighting a war to stop the Communist North Korea from overrunning democratic South Korea. That same year Sen. Joseph R. McCarthy launched his red-baiting career by claiming to have personal knowledge of two hundred and five known Communists in the State Department. By 1953, the House Committee on un-American Activities began the televised hearings on communism that resulted in the blacklisting of Hollywood writers.

Kodama spent the 1950s forming *yakuza*-dominated patriotic organizations. By the end of the decade he was a *kuromaku* of amazing clout. *Kuromaku*, literally "black curtain" was a behind-the-scenes fixer, a link between the *yakuza* and legitimate businessmen and politicians in Japan. The term was from classic Kabuki theater, in which a wire-puller, hidden behind a black curtain, controls the action onstage.

By 1970, Kodama owned real estate firms, several national newspaper distributors, a national newspaper for sports gamblers, part of a baseball team, a movie company, a shipping line, and several nightclubs in the Ginza. In 1971, a select group of ultranationalists gathered in the posh Okura Hotel in Tokyo. The delegates sang a proposed new Japanese national anthem written by Kodama, the "Song of the Race."

On October 24, 1972, Kodama negotiated what had been long thought to be an impossible alliance between the followers of Inagawa Kakuji, whose gangs dominated Tokyo and Yokohama, and Takoa Kazu, *oyabun* of Yamaguchi-gumi of Kobe, the largest *yakuza* gang in Japan. This amazing truce ended years of bloodshed. Kodama was by then the most powerful *kuramaku* in Japan.

On February 4, 1974, Carl Kotchian, president of Lockheed Aircraft Corporation, appeared before a U.S. Senate Subcommittee on Multinational Corporations. Koch and other executives revealed a secret network of payoffs, commissions, and bribes they paid to do business in Japan. This included seven million dollars to 'consultant' Kodama Yoshio. *Rokkiedo Jiken*—the Lockheed incident—shocked Japan.

"*Kuroi kiri,*" Tomi murmured. She finished reading her notes.

Following Rokkiedo Jiken, a twenty-nine-year-old Japanese actor, Maeno Mitsukasu, dressed as a *kamakazi* pilot, rented a plane and crashed into Kodama's house. Maeno hoped to kill Kodama because he had dishonored Japan and himself and refused to commit *seppuku*. Maeno was one of those who had joined in the singing of "Song of the Race" three years earlier. Kodama retreated from public life and spent his remaining years in seclusion. Over the next decade he had a series of debilitating strokes before he died in 1984 at age seventy-three.

In the passionate days of the Red Scare, she knew, all secrets that helped block Mao were good secrets. Tomi Kobayashi was going into battle against the keepers of secrets as surely as her grandfather had faced British soldiers fifty years earlier. She was Yamashita's granddaughter. She would not quit.

She looked at Kip Smith sleeping beside her. She felt comfortable with him. She liked being with him. He said her odor made him drunk. Surely a line and yet . . . She leaned close to him. She hoped his feeling was genuine. He made her feel giddy.

Tomi looked forward to the action ahead, never mind the danger or the power of their adversaries. She wondered if her grandfather might not have felt the same way as he closed in on the British defenders of Singapore.

13

Luis Montoya wrapped the *baboy* ribs in banana leaves and covered them with charcoal before Jaime Pineda and General Martinez settled down in Montoya's *nipa* hut to talk business. Although he wore rubber thongs—called slippers in the Philippines—old cotton trousers, and a simple, short-sleeved shirt, Brig. Gen. Jose Maria Martinez did not look like a peasant. With his light skin and formidable nose, he was forever a patrician: reserved, soft, and civil—reeking of superiority and demanding respect.

Martinez conveyed his feelings clearly by the way he sat, patiently, spine erect, his face passive, even diffident. All this said: *My family owns thousands of hectares of land, and I am powerful, better than you. You can see that by looking at me. I have never in my life worked with my hands. Other people do that. I do not waste my time with the uneducated, with fools, or with the hot sun. I am wearing this ridiculous getup because I am forced to in order to get what I want.*

Finally, his body language said: *Although you are a murderous zealot, Jaime Pineda, you will not murder me because no matter what you might say, we both know I can do more for you than you can do for me. Any advantage you have over me is momentary. Murder me and you get nothing.*

Beside him, Cadet George Villanueva, looking slightly uncomfortable, adjusted the spectacles on his nose. "Well, how have you been, Jaime?" he said. He glanced quickly at Martinez.

Pineda held the palm of his hand level and waggled his fingers. "Sometimes good. Sometimes not so good. Mostly good. And yourself?"

"Study, study, study. I'm in my fourth year." Mopping his brow with his forearm, Villanueva surveyed the inside of the *nipa* hut.

Pineda said, "It's okay, relax, George. You know I don't have anything against you personally. Maybe someday we'll have a military that respects the people." He glanced at Martinez. "How can I help you, General?"

Martinez said, "Your cousin is doing extremely well at the academy, Mr. Pineda. Are you familiar with the American evangelist Dr. Robin Fallon?"

"The Robin Fallon who's going to do the revival at Cadiz?"

"That's the one. It seems that a member of the reverend's large congregation is the wealthy granddaughter of a certain Lieutenant John W. Dolan, an American officer killed during the taking of Pulak Pulakan in 1945. The daughter is anxious that there should be some tribute to the world disarmament process . . ."

"We would all like peace."

". . . and so has offered to build a new hospital in Cadiz and donate other money here locally, if the Reverend Fallon is allowed to hold a candle-lighting service on Pulak Pulakan for Dolan and the others who were killed in the fighting. Fallon would like to tie this in with his televised evangelical revival in Cadiz."

Pineda burst out laughing. "Robin Fallon is the only one of those *putas* they haven't caught screwing a dog."

"You should hear me out, Mr. Pineda."

Mr. Pineda, was it? Pineda had long wondered when this day would come. The rumors of gold were correct. They were after the archers.

Martinez said, "The Reverend and his followers would of course need access to Pulak Pulakan. They have asked me if it might not be possible to come to some kind of agreeable terms with you in order that they might hold their ceremonies in peace."

"I see. You know I can't make a decision like this independently, General. I have to talk it over with the others."

"I understand that, of course."

"I would want weapons, M-16s."

Martinez said nothing.

"And ammunition."

Martinez nodded, thinking it over.

"And six archers."

Martinez raised an eyebrow as though retrieving the archers had never occurred to him. "Six?"

"Or no deal," Pineda said. "If you want the alchemist archers, you have to give us good reason to double-cross Kawana. As almost everybody on this island must know by now, he's come up with the map. Do you think you can send your people in here on the ruse of a candle-lighting ceremony by an idiot American preacher and simply take over? No, no, no. I'm sitting on the alchemist archers. I name the terms. If you want the golden dragons, you have to beat the Japanese offer, otherwise forget it."

Martinez bit his lip thoughtfully. "It's not good to break up the set of eleven. That reduces the total value to a collector or museum. In addition to which you'd be faced with the chore of fencing them. We'd both be better off to agree on a sum in American dollars."

Pineda said, "A substantial sum, General. Make an offer and I'll consider it. Are you working for Imelda? Or is she pretty much in retirement these days?"

"Mrs. Marcos. Give it up, man. She's history. If it's acceptable to you, we can use George as our go-between."

Pineda said, "George is a good choice. Well, then, shall we eat? The *baboy* ought to be done. What do you say, Luis, are you ready to fix the rest?"

Montoya cut a hole in a husked coconut using a screwing motion with the tip of a cane knife. "Jaime brought me some fresh *uod* yesterday. Why people let perfectly good maggots go to waste has always been beyond me. No uglier eaters in the world than *manok* or *baboy* (chickens or pigs). They'll eat anything. We eat snails all the time. You see any difference?" he asked, looking at the general.

"You're right. There isn't any difference," Martinez said.

"The difference is in your head," Montoya said. "We're also having boiled corn and sweet potatoes. I wanted to be a gracious host."

Martinez glanced at Pineda, saying nothing.

Pineda said, "When you fight with the NPA, you learn what survival is all about. Did they teach you how to prepare maggots at the academy, George?"

"I don't believe they did," Villanueva said.

Pineda said, "This is why you can't beat us, General. If we have to, we're prepared to eat maggots to survive."

When the hole was finished, Montoya washed the still squirming maggots and stuffed them inside the coconut, corking the hole with a plug of wood. Then he wrapped the coconut in banana leaves and dumped it onto a pile of charcoal to cook.

When the maggots were deemed ready about thirty minutes later, Montoya retrieved the coconut from the charcoal and dug the cooked maggots out with a stick. He twisted a leaf into a makeshift press to wring the excess juice from them. He scooped the cooked, dejuiced maggots onto their plates. Pineda and his guests ate with their fingers, Filipino style, seasoning the maggots and corn with pinches of sea salt that Montoya served in a tin dish.

"Mmmmm." Montoya held high a pinch of maggots. "Aren't they delicious? They're delicacies."

Pineda dug right into his maggots. He said, "What do you think, George?"

Cadet Villanueva sampled his maggots. He had the honor of the academy to maintain in the presence of the superintendent. He swallowed solemnly, looking only slightly pale.

Pineda grinned. "And you, General?"

Brig. Gen. Jose Maria Martinez was determined to lay his hands on the golden dragons. He dug with gusto into his portion of hot maggots.

14

A bell rang softly. The seat belt light blinked over their heads. The Cebu Pacific plane was descending to Negros. Tomi Kobayashi and Kip Smith looked down on the tangle of liquid mirrors that were prawn farms reflecting the afternoon sun as the Philippine Airlines airbus approached the runway at Bacolod. In the distance behind the city, the land was green for as far as Tomi could see with what she knew had to be sugarcane.

Smith said, "I take it you know the definition of *kuroi kiri*."

"The black mist."

"We'll be pursuing the answer to that dependable old motive, *'Cui bono?'* In the Latin, 'Who profits?' The Japanese people? The American taxpayer? Individual Japanese and Americans involved in the story? You haven't asked me why *Bawiin mo ang Ginto* hasn't released the results of its investigation if it has learned so much."

"You're right. I should have," Tomi said. "And the answer is?"

Smith said, "Coincidences are rare to nonexistent in the *kuroi kiri*. Do you think the current managers of the M Fund, with all the resources at their disposal, will allow *Bawiin mo ang Ginto* to be truly independent and serve only the interests of the Filipino citizens? Tomi, please! One bumps and feels one's way through the mist, hoping that the shapes are benign. A sharp point can be a thorn or the tip of a descending knife."

Tomi's stomach twisted with anticipation as the plane taxied to a stop. She watched a crew in blue coveralls wheeling stairs toward the forward door. She preceded Kip down the stairs and into the warm bath of humid air. She strode beside him as they headed toward the small terminal with Kip searching the faces for his friend Col. Cading Rodriguez.

Kip suddenly embraced a Filipino and they began calling one another names in the way male friends did.

Ding Rodriguez was about as unlikely looking an intelligence officer as Tomi could imagine—or sugar planter, for that matter. A short, broad Filipino in his mid-forties, Rodriguez wore tattered Adidas running shoes, baggy blue jeans, an Oakland Athletics baseball cap, and a Kentucky Fried Chicken T-shirt stretched over a stout belly. He wore a huge Rolex wristwatch. Or perhaps a fake Rolex wristwatch. On his right hip, hanging rather rakishly, Tomi thought, he carried a .45 automatic.

Rodriguez broke into a wide grin. "You must be Dr. Tomi Kobayashi. I'm Ding Rodriguez." They shook. "Any friend of Kip is a friend of mine. And you are some kind of friend indeed!" He gave her a mock leer and licked his lips. A joker, he was.

Tomi said, "Pleased to meet you, Colonel Rodriguez."

"Call me Ding." He clapped himself on the stomach. "The belly is pure San Miguel. We Filipinos are a poor people, but they say we have the best beer in the world. And our women aren't bad either."

"You should call me Tomi."

Tomi and Smith followed Rodriguez to the line where the bags were being unloaded from a cart. She was aware that an admiring Rodriguez was giving her figure the once-over. She spotted their bags among those piled high on a wagon waiting to be unloaded. "There they are, Kip, on the end there."

Rodriguez helped Smith retrieve the bags. A few minutes later they climbed into Rodriguez's brown and tan Blazer which sat up on great macho, knobby-treaded, go-anywhere tires. Rodriguez fired up the engine; to Tomi's relief, an air-conditioner kicked in.

Rodriguez, who was much given to the high-pitched *meeep* of the Blazer's horn, drove with an assault rifle between his legs. He piloted the Blazer down a bumpy, pot-holed road, tapping the horn—*meeep, meeep*—as he passed a silver jeepney with galloping chromed horses for hood ornaments. Fancy lettering on the side said, *We ride with Jesus Christ.*

Eyeing Tomi, Rodriguez said, "Kip always did like good-looking women."

Smith said, "Quiet, man. What's wrong with you?"

"He does, does he? You want to tell me about that?"

Rodriguez gave her a wry grin. "I've said too much already."

Smith said, "Your former friend, if you keep that up."

"By the way, I have to deliver some glow points for the diesel engine of my boat, then I'll take you to your hotel. I've arranged for your vehicles to be delivered."

"What's that?" Tomi said, staring at the assault rifle. The muzzle was between Rodriguez's feet as he worked the brake and clutch.

"An HK."

"HK?"

"Heckler and Koch, German made. You want to have any respect on Negros, you have to carry a piece. A Heckler and Koch maybe, or an M-16. Isn't that right, Kip?"

"You can't call yourself a proper sugar planter if you don't have bodyguards with assault rifles."

"Kip tells me you're interested in the story of Hirohito's Gold and the M Fund."

"Yes, for a book about postwar American foreign policy in Asia. I want to know who the CIA is protecting by keeping its activities in that period classified and why."

He arched an eyebrow, teasing her. "No interest in the alchemist archers?"

"Well, sure, I guess. Depending. Be foolish not to, I suppose."

Rodriguez laughed. "Kip is what you Americans would likely call an Eagle Scout. He took an oath not to reveal CIA secrets and it gnaws at him. But I didn't take any CIA oath, guaranteed. I will give you a series of briefings on everything *Bawiin mo ang Ginto* has found out, and you can take it from there. You have to understand I'm doing this on my own, without the knowledge or permission of my superiors. You'll have to keep me out of it."

"How about 'sources close to Filipino intelligence?' "

"That will do it. Kip and I want this story made public as much as you do."

Smith said, "You've got that right, pal."

"We'll give you a day to sleep off the jet lag before I give you my first briefing. You tell her what happened to your wife, Kip?"

"I told her."

Rodriguez said, "I knew Gina, by the way. She was a sweetheart. She was one of thousands of people who lost their lives under the Marcos regime." Rodriguez suddenly turned off the road to a weed-infested collection of outriggers on the banks of a wide creek, or diminutive river, that emptied into the ocean. He parked the Blazer and hopped out to deliver the glow points. Then he drove Tomi to the Sugarland Hotel, a small building of coral bricks nestled in among tropical foliage on the road to the airport.

On the way through the lobby of the Sugarland, Smith stopped at a poster touting the Cadiz revival of the famous television evangelist Robin Fallon and his wife Roberta. To Rodriguez, who had come inside to help them with their bags, he said, "Curious, don't you think, Ding?'

"I agree," Rodriguez said.

At the desk, Smith ordered a large room.

Watching him, Tomi cocked her head.

Smith said, "For safety's sake, Tomi. There'll be two beds."

"For safety's sake, sure." Rodriguez arched an eyebrow.

Smith gave him a look. "You be quiet."

The Japanese had recently erected two newer, more expensive hotels on the edge of town, but Tomi was no fan of high-tech sterility. She had been told that the Sugarland was the favorite of veteran travelers to Bacolod, and she understood why. It was clean and airy and modern without being Moonbase Alpha.

After Rodriguez departed, Tomi and Kip lay back on their separate beds to rest and recover from jet lag. Tomi was exhausted, yet she felt giddy with anticipation. It was difficult for her to tell how Kip felt. He was soon fast asleep. Getting sleepier by the minute, she watched him lying there. A good-looking man, he was. She liked him.

15

Jaime Pineda watched from the shade of a *katmon* tree while they dug. It was slow going in the tropical sun. In places like the Philippines digging was done at a leisurely pace. Swing the spade. Rest. Shovel full of dirt. Rest. Swing the spade. Rest. Shovel full of dirt. Rest. Swing the spade. Pineda found it amusing that the alchemist archers of Xhingsui Gap were buried almost directly under a favorite spot for an NPA *baboy* pit. Beneath those squealing, dying pigs lay treasure.

Pineda had heard stories of Yamashita's Gold all his life. His father had been one of those who believed in the existence of the gold. His Uncle Ramon thought Ferdinand Marcos had come by his vast wealth by the simple expedient of stealing from the Filipino people. The tales of buried gold were nonsense, Uncle Ramon said. Tall tales.

One thing that everybody knew that lent credence to his father's belief. During the 1950s and 1960s, Pulak Pulakan was a favorite destination for Japanese war veterans making a pilgrimage to the place where they had made their determined last stand on Negros. The left-wing threat to the Philippine government in those days was not the NPA, which had not yet been born, but the Huks based on Luzon. The guerrillas on Negros were higher up in the mountains and occupied Pulak Pulakan only intermittently.

Not a few of these sentimental Japanese veterans carried with them metal detectors, claiming to be looking for souvenir bayonets and other metal objects. In the tropical world, the landscape changes rapidly. Areas that the Japanese had cleared of brush to give them clear firing lanes at the American and Filipino soldiers attempting to reach the summit of the hill were now overgrown. The off-again, on-again residents of the tunnels had cleared the brush that the Japanese had left in place to obscure the target of American dive bombers. It was no secret among the Filipinos that the guides on these trips, for which the hated Japanese were charged exorbitant rates, were agents of Ferdinand Marcos.

If the stories of gold in Pulak Pulakan were to be believed, the soldiers who had buried the gold had been executed to ensure their silence. Over the years, generations of NPA soldiers had tried their hand with increasingly powerful and efficient metal detectors. No luck.

Now came Kawana Katchan bearing a map and an offer Pineda found hard to resist.

But Kawana wasn't Pineda's only earnest suitor. Gen. Jose Maria Martinez had also paid a gentleman's call. Although Imelda Marcos was said to have eyes and ears everywhere, it was unclear whether Martinez was working for her or not. Like Kawana, Martinez had argued that even if Pineda knew where the archers were located, he could never get them off the island himself. Judging from the size of Martinez's offer for Pineda to double-cross Kawana, the buried dragons meant far more to him than the value of their gold.

Pineda had weighed the competing offers. An Australian had once taught him the game of scissors, paper, and rocks. Scissors beat paper. Rocks beat scissors. Paper beat . . .

Pineda was amused by the fact that the wily Japanese officer who had buried the gold had not chosen any of the tunnels or shafts in Pulak Pulakan, but had stashed the gold higher in the mountains, out of sight from the soldiers digging their fortifications. No fool was he. In pitching his offer, Kawana even told Pineda that Kodama Yoshio was the name of the officer who had supervised the burial. When Kodama died in 1984, he had yet to retrieve his treasure because of NPA occupation of the hill.

Jaime Pineda had never heard of anybody named Kodama. A dead man was history. Pineda did not care about history. He was interested in the here and now. He lived totally in the present, fueled with hatred of the sugar planters and corrupt politicians and oligarchs who kept his countrymen living in poverty.

16

After renting a Nissan sedan for Tomi and a Toyota Landcruiser for himself, Kip Smith left early to run a security check on the area where Col. Cading Rodriguez would give the first of his *Bawiin mo ang Ginto* briefings. When Rodriguez showed up to take Tomi to the briefing, he was wearing a T-shirt featuring what was supposed to be the seal or emblem of the Central Intelligence Agency. The impressive seal looked authentic enough. The CIA seal ought to look like that, if it didn't. The only drawback that Tomi could see was that the T-shirt located the CIA in Arlington, Virginia, rather than Langley.

Tomi said, "I was under the impression the CIA was in Langley. The Pentagon and the National Cemetery are in Arlington."

Rodriguez looked surprised. "Why, I thought you knew! Surely Kip told you. I'm surprised, I truly am."

Tomi was momentarily confused. "Told me what? I don't understand."

"I'm with Filipino intelligence. An oxymoron." Rodriguez burst out laughing.

A few minutes later, they were on their way. Rodriguez tapped his horn—*meeep meeep*—and slowed behind a man on a 150cc Yamaha attempting to transport four trussed pigs. The pigs pulled the bike so low that it seemed to be riding at a sixty-degree angle.

The bottom pig's head nearly banged on the road. In order to serve as a counterweight and to prevent the bike from being flipped over, the driver leaned in the opposite direction, his butt inches off the ground. It was a skilled, nifty performance.

Observing the pigs as he passed them, Ding said, "My relatives."

Tomi's jaw dropped. "Say again?"

"That's my sister there on the bottom," Rodriguez said. Pretending to check the rearview mirror, he squinted his eyes. "No, no. I take that back. She's the one in the middle. My sister always takes the middle."

"Kip said you were having some kind of trouble with your sugar land, Ding. What is that all about?"

Rodriguez held the palm of his hand down and waggled his fingers. "The NPA burned three of my trucks and forty hectares of my cane."

"They what?"

"This was a farm I have in the foothills up north. The owner immigrated to America, and everybody was afraid to touch it, so I was able to lease it. I was doing fine, too, and paying my people more than the minimum, but then the NPA demanded a so-called revolutionary tax, a thousand dollars for each truck and for each one hundred hectares of cane. I spent three years eating maggots in the mountains for the NPA and another three in the stockade on Cebu. Revolutionary tax? Excuse me! I told them what they could do with themselves."

"So they burned your trucks."

"Three of them. Isuzus. Big ten-wheelers. It will cost me a hundred and fifty thousand U.S. to fix them. But I can fix them, and they will be fixed. I'm fixing them right now. I'll be back. Ding Rodriguez may be down temporarily, but never out. Right? There's always a way."

Rodriguez drove a minute in silence, obviously furious. "They only hit the small farms and the ones closest to the mountains.

The large planters all have private armies. Coca-Cola and San Miguel Beer won't pay, so they get hit. We're too small to defend ourselves, so we get hit." He waved his right hand as he talked. "I'll get them, the bastards. Screwballs, they are. They don't know who their enemies are either, until they've tangled with Ding Rodriguez. Screwballs!" Rodriguez shook a clenched fist.

Tomi said, "The Sicilians have an expression, 'Revenge, like lasagna, is best when served cold.' "

Rodriguez brightened. "Best when served cold. That's good!"

"Say, where are these NPA people that they can stay in business with the Philippine army after them? The Philippine army is after them, I take it."

"And the private armies. The government supplies the private armies with weapons, but the planters pay their salaries. Only the largest planters can afford them. The right-wing warlords."

"Well, why can't the army and the warlords with their PCs drive the rebels out of the mountains?"

"There are a lot of reasons. One is that the rebels have friends who tell them when unfriendly people are in the area, and the roads are terrible. You can't do much more than inch along without breaking axles, and they can hear you for miles up there. If you try to get to them by helicopter, they simply disappear into the underbrush."

"Oh-oh."

"The army and the PCs and the rebels have all gotten their hands on the same kind of battle fatigues and now everybody wears the same getup, including soldiers in the regular army. Some have boots. Some don't. They all look alike, so when you're driving in the mountains and you come across some people in fatigues wearing sunglasses and brandishing M-16s, you don't know who they are. They could be anybody: soldier, private army, NPA. They might ask you questions or shoot you, depending on who they are and the mood they're in."

"Does the NPA have a known leader?"

"Jaime Pineda"

"Does he have a headquarters of some kind?"

"He sure does. In a hill called Pulak Pulakan, right down the road from where the screwballs burned my trucks. You can see it from my farm. That's where the Japanese made their last stand on Negros in May 1945. When the NPAs are attacked they use World War II pillboxes and trenches to do what the Japanese did, fire down on people who have to climb a steep brushy hill to get at them. A lot of the Japanese pillboxes were destroyed by American bombers."

"Pulak Pulakan is where the Japanese made their last stand on Negros."

"Yes, it was," Rodriguez said. "Before the NPA took over and before the old farts got too old, the Japanese used to make nostalgic returns to the site. There have always been rumors that the Japanese buried the gold up there, so Marcos always made sure an intelligence officer went along posing as a tour guide. The Japanese tourists almost always drag metal detectors along with them." He went *meeep, meeep* on the horn and slowed to pass a *carabao* pulling a cartload of lumber.

Tomi said, "Did the Japanese veterans ever find anything substantial?"

"I don't think so. They were being watched constantly. Even if they had found something, there is no way on earth they could have gotten it past us Filipinos. That's not happening." Rodriguez broke into laughter. "I razzed Kip about ordering one room, but he had his reasons beyond having a good-looking partner. This is serious business, Tomi, and dangerous. You listen to what he tells you." Rodriguez slowed for some brown goats the size of German shepherds. *Meeep, meeep.*

BOOK THREE

Chiba's Choice

1

Aida's was a covered pavilion housing a dozen or more vendors of *lechon manok*, or broiled chicken. The vendors shared a common space under a roof about forty or fifty yards long and twenty to thirty yards wide. There were no walls. Each vender served two rows of tables, each with a sink and a short counter in the middle. Tomi Kobayashi and Ding Rodriguez walked along the line of vendors, admiring the cooking chicken speared on bamboo shafts.

Tomi peered into the dim interior looking for Rudyard Kipling Smith.

At length, Rodriguez spotted Smith. "*Oy*! There he is. The whistler himself."

Tomi looked surprised.

Rodriguez said, "No, I'm not Jewish, Tomi. *Oy*! is a familiar cry here in the Philippines. It's not a truncated version of the Yiddish *'Oy vey!'* but more likely a corruption of the Spanish *'Ay!'* Another candidate is the Japanese *'Oi!'* which means roughly 'Hey!' "

Arriving at Smith's table, Rodriguez gave his belly a thoughtful pat. "You like *lechon manok*, Tomi?"

"It smells wonderful," she said.

"Then let's order some and we can talk." He stood and led the way to the stand at the head of their table.

Rodriguez placed an order in Ilongo and they started back toward their seats. He stopped at the sink and began washing his hands. "We'll eat Filipino style. That okay with you?"

Tomi didn't understand.

"With our hands," Smith said.

"Ah," she said, and began washing her hands as well.

A few minutes later, the waiter brought them skewers of chicken quarters plus grilled liver and plates heaped with neatly molded mounds of rice. Ding and Smith each laced their rice liberally with a thick yellow fluid that they poured out of a small pitcher. Tomi did the same. Then they took several pinches of sea salt out of a small plate and sprinkled it on the yellow rice. Tomi did likewise.

Using her fingers, Tomi took a pinch of the rice and thought it tasted divine, but she supposed that was mainly because of the salt. "What is that yellow stuff?" she asked.

Rodriguez held up the small pitcher. "This?" He licked some yellow from his fingers. "Chicken fat. Good, huh." Rodriguez paused, watching her. He licked some more fat from his fingers. He laughed again. His belly bounced. "Since you're looking at an historical mystery, I'll give you my *Ginto* briefings as a kind of Filipino Sherlock Holmes, working my way through layers of accumulated lies. There is no existing proof for most of what I'm telling you. Most of the details about the excavation of the gold are reported by a man named Robert Curtis and can be mined from Sterling Seagrave's biography of Ferdinand and Imelda Marcos, which was published in 1987. When I say something is an allegation, it means just that. When we get to the amazing details of Curtis's alleged adventures excavating gold for Marcos, just remember that's all they are.

"I'll start at the end of the war, concentrating on the connection of Hirohito's Gold and what it did to the Philippines because that's been the focus of the inquiries of *Bawiin mo ang Ginto.*

When I'm finished, Kip will brief you on the connection of the M Fund to the CIA and the Liberal Democratic Party."

Tomi said, "We'll be entering the *kuroi kiri.*"

"That's right. A famously paranoid chief of counterintelligence at the Company named James Jesus Angleton called it a wilderness of mirrors. You're confronted with a tape or a document. Is it truth or disinformation? You're confronted with a man with a gun. Friend or foe? You look about and the images are repeated seemingly to infinity. And there are rooms in which the mirrors distort. The fat looks skinny. The skinny looks fat. Stomachs suddenly balloon. Heads become pointed. In such a duplicitous world the truth tends to lose all meaning. Reality has no meaning. The very notion of truth is absurd. There you have it. Two cultures, two metaphors. The Japanese, an outwardly polite and respectful society, well-mannered and well-ordered, feel lost in a black mist of lies and secret deals. The Americans, a boisterous and rambunctious country of hustlers and big dreamers, see a wilderness of deceiving and distorting mirrors."

The line of sight was surprisingly good under the circumstances. Chiba Wataru and Yoshida Akiri were glad that Aida's had no partitions of any kind. In the wretched heat of the Philippines, anything indoors and lacking air-conditioning was stifling. Since most Filipinos could ill afford air-conditioning, a pavilion with a roof only made sense. Mopping the sweat from his forehead, Chiba grimaced. "Did you get that, Yoshida-san?"

Yoshida, who had his shirt off, revealing a torso covered with elaborate, intertwined dragons, punched the replay button on the Sony, and the two men watched the replay on the monitor.

The image of Rodriguez escorting Tomi Kobayashi was clear and sharp. The color was perfect. Yoshida turned a knob clockwise, and they heard Rodriguez exclaim, " 'Oy, there he is. The whistler himself.' "

The sound was clear. Yoshida turned the knob counterclockwise, muting the conversation he was recording.

An effeminate young Filipino, dressed in blue jeans and a white San Miguel Beermen T-shirt and limping badly, passed by their table and dropped a paper bag in front of Rodriguez. "My nephew Donde," Rodriguez said. He retrieved a digital camera from the bag and turned it on. An image of two men popped up in the viewfinder. He gave the camera to Smith.

Smith looked at the image and clenched his jaw. "Figures. I take it Donde was careful?"

Rodriguez nodded. "He's a *bayut* and the limp is from polio. Neither one has anything to do with what's up here." He tapped his temple.

"Mind if I borrow your notepad for a second, Tomi?"

Tomi gave Kip her pad. Smith sat a full minute, thinking. Then he wrote a short note to Rodriguez and handed it to him.

Rodriguez read the note, thought about it for a moment, then said, "Really! That's not a bad idea. You think it might work?"

Smith shrugged and leaned against Tomi, murmuring in her ear. "Two Japanese gentlemen are recording our conversation. It's not to worry. I'll explain later."

Rodriguez put the camera back in the sack.

Smith reached into his daypack and retrieved a tape recorder the size of a deck of cards. "This recorder will tape up to six hours in one setting." He raised his hand and called to a waitress for another round of San Miguel. "Di, Di, another round, please."

Rodriguez said, "You'll notice that Kip and I like our San Miguel. We laugh. We like to admire a passing lady. It is not because we lack *gravitas*. We're friends. Kip grinds his teeth at the mention of Douglas MacArthur. I bristle at the mention of Ferdinand Marcos." Ding looped an arm around Smith's shoulders and gave him a squeeze. "The fat for you. The lean for me. What do you say we give 'em hell, Kip."

Yoshida looked puzzled. "The kid with a limp gave Rodriguez a camera. What was that all about?"

"Looked like a digital camera. It probably contained an image of us getting our gear ready."

"You think so? Yet they're apparently going ahead anyway. I don't understand."

Chiba smiled. "Smith was poking around earlier. Smith and Rodriguez are professionals. No surprise that they would have somebody scan the area for security. Maybe they know we're here but don't care what we do."

"No?"

"I like the American metaphor of a wilderness of mirrors. It's like Smith says. The fat look skinny. The skinny look fat. Nothing is what it seems. Only later, perhaps, will the true shape of their motive become clear."

Ding Rodriguez put down the bone of a chicken leg and licked his fingers. He took a hit of beer and said, "This story is like a great snarl of string, Tomi. You try to untangle the rumors and allegations, and you can see the truth for a little bit, then it disappears into the confusion of circumstance and dubious claims. But if you're patient and take it apart story by story, report by report, allegation by amazing allegation, assertion by astonishing assertion, you'll see that it might very well be all connected. It's taken *Bawiin mo ang Ginto* years to get it sorted out, but I think they're close to getting it right even if they don't want it made public."

"And the strings go where?"

Smith burst out laughing.

Rodriguez said, "To the wallet, of course. To lovers of power. *Oy!* That's where this kind of story always leads, doesn't it? But I suppose that doesn't say much. From one point of view it's all understandable enough, a case of American foreign policy that developed a Cold War mentality and momentum that was impossible to challenge. Over the years there have been scores of thieves and would-be thieves, con men, dreamers, drifters, high rollers, fixers, and hangers-on involved in this sorry tale. But before I continue I have to tell you that in the end it's all based on the premise that Imelda Marcos was telling the truth."

"Huh?"

"Marcos-baiting has long been popular sport both in the Philippines and internationally. We're all familiar with the stories of Mrs. Marcos's alleged five thousand pairs of shoes. The assumption has been that Marcos's story about finding Japanese gold was an excuse to justify his great wealth that he more likely got from ripping off the Philippine national treasury, stealing money from international loans made to the Philippine government, and so on. He might have done all that. He might have done some of it. He might not have done any of it. I don't know. None of that is at issue here.

"Eventually I will tell you about Robert Curtis's alleged adventures recovering gold for Marcos. I say alleged. He claims to have documentary proof. He says he kept tapes, notes, and copies of contracts. He says he gave them to the U.S. government. Where are they now?

"I will begin with Mrs. Marcos's claim that I will assert, for sake of argument, was true. In 1998, Imelda told Christine Herrera of the *Philippine Daily Inquirer* that when President Ferdinand Marcos declared martial law on September 21, 1972, he planned to terminate corporate parity rights in 1974, forcing foreign owners of Filipino corporations to yield sixty percent of ownership to citizens of the Philippines. Foreign capital was needed to boost the Philippine economy, but to Filipino nationalists Marcos's decision sounded reasonable enough. Why shouldn't Filipinos own Filipino corporations?

"The real reason for the move, Imelda said, was that Ferdinand wanted to buy controlling shares of blue chip Filipino corporations for himself. He proceeded to do just that, secretly, through cronies, using dummy corporations. Where did Ferdinand get the money to buy everything in the Philippines worth owning? Imelda claimed he used the proceeds from the sale of four thousand tons of gold that he had recovered from the storied hoard buried in the Philippines by the retreating Japanese Gen. Yamashita Tomayuki.

"Imelda told Ms. Herrera that after Cory Aquino's Yellow Revolution in 1986, the cronies pretended that Marcos's shares were their own. When Ferdinand died in exile in Hawaii in 1989, his friends who had washed his money continued doing business as though the shares were legitimately theirs. In Imelda's view, the controlling shares—in corporations ranging from the San Miguel brewery and the Philippine Long Distance Telephone Company and Philippine Airlines—correctly belonged to the Marcos family. The Marcoses who were victims of this alleged fraud included Imelda, her son Ferdinand "Bong Bong" Marcos, and her daughter Imee. The family wanted its property back.

"Mrs. Marcos's story in the *Inquirer* was pooh-poohed both because people love to hate and mimic her and because none of her husband's former cronies were about to return anything to the Marcos family for any reason. But what we are doing here, because it fits with what happened to Hirohito and Kodama Yoshio in occupied Japan, is to take Imelda at her word. It is foolishness to let caricatures or the sport of hating her get in the way of learning the truth. The truth is more important than the enjoyment of ridicule. After a while Marcos-bashing gets boring." Rodriguez pretended to yawn. "It's an unfashionable position, I know, but in defense of the Marcoses, there is nothing illegal about digging up and selling gold that the Japanese buried on Filipino soil. If that's where the Marcoses got their great wealth, or at least some of it, they did nothing wrong. No court has ever proven otherwise.

"We assert that Imelda *did* tell the truth, or at least enough of it to warrant pursuing it further. We'll take her at her word. But the question remains: how much truth did she really give us," Smith said.

"We humbly beg her indulgence. Maybe we can prove her case for her!" Rodriguez grinned ruefully.

Smith said, "We bear no ill will to those who wound up with shares of Filipino corporations they bought with Marcos money. We have no idea of what Ferdinand Marcos did with his gold money, if he had any. We don't have a dog in that fight. Our goal is limited to the genesis of it all in Japan. *Post hoc, ergo hoc.* After it, because of it. We would like to do more, but modesty prevents us." Smith gave a cheerful wave to an imaginary Imelda Marcos. "Begging your pardon, Mrs. Marcos. We do hope you understand. But we *are* doing this much for free."

Rodriguez added quickly, "As it stands now this story is not proven. It is largely conjecture: *what might have happened.* To claim otherwise is wrong and invites critics to whack us over the head."

Smith added quickly, "The silence is the first thing you hear in this story, Tomi. The omissions of history sometimes make the most noise."

Tomi looked puzzled. "Hear the silence?"

"The Japanese Imperial Army was notoriously rapacious. They ravaged the Koreans, Chinese, Thais, Malays, and Indonesians, taking everything of value. Look at the stories of stolen art and treasure by the SS in Europe. That was a huge controversy after the war. But what about the activities of the Kampei-tai? In postwar Tokyo there was an odd silence, no accounting whatever. The British general surrendered to the Japanese in a Singapore bank. In the photograph of the surrender, we can see the barred windows of the tellers in the background. What happened to the contents of that bank and others? Even Herbert Bix in his authoritative biography declined to get bogged down in speculation that Hirohito was as obsessed with treasure and personal enrichment as with military conquest and the glory of Nippon. It's hard to blame Bix for that. Or maybe there was nothing to report. To Asians the silence has always been thundering."

In the weeks before his assassination, Prime Minister Nakamura met several times with Chiba Wataru to discuss what should be done about 'Edie Compton,' who was using the Internet to solicit interest in the van der Elst manuscript. Chiba had done numerous personal chores for Nakamura over the years. The prime minister respected his education and judgement, but he approached the core of his doubts hesitantly and obliquely because Chiba was Suma Obe's son-in-law.

After Nakamura warmed to the subject, he admitted, however circuitously, that he felt ambiguous about what should be done about the larger story of the Golden Lily and the M Fund. To let the story be revealed or continue to suppress it? He was troubled both by the consequences of acting and what would happen if he did nothing.

Rodriguez stopped, letting Tomi digest what it was he had just said, then continued. "Why the silence on the subject? It's truly amazing if you think about it. The American objective at the war trials beginning in 1946 was to appease cries for justice and revenge by punishing the right-wing nationalists and militarists who were responsible for prosecuting the war. You know the broad outlines of the American postwar objectives—you're an expert on the subject—but in this context they bear repeating. For the decade following the surrender in Japan, American foreign policy in Asia was dominated by an obsession with Mao Tse Tung, was it not?"

"Obsession is an understatement," Tomi said. "We didn't recognize the mainland government until 1972."

"The American State Department was determined to halt the expansion of communism in Asia at all costs. To do that the

United States felt it had to support Generalissimo Chiang Kai-shek on Taiwan, and somehow guide Japan out of the ashes with democratic institutions acceptable to the United States. To block an attempt by Communists to insert their presence in a weakened postwar Japan, MacArthur turned to his natural allies in Japan. And those were, Tomi?"

"Right-wing Japanese," Tomi said. "The very people who led Japan into the war. No small irony there. The general shape of that is well-known."

"Including war criminals," Rodriguez added. "What do you think, Kip, start the gold stories?"

A week before a bullet took him under, Nakamura asked Chiba how he would feel with instructions to make a decision in the field, on his own, based on his reading of the likely outcome of the threat to the greater good of the Japanese people. Chiba had an American education and so had a broader understanding of the known history of the period. Nakamura trusted him.

Traditionally, a Japanese commander gave his subordinate a specific mission. He was expected to carry it out.

At Berkeley, Chiba had read Alfred T. Mahan's The Influence of Sea Power Upon History *and was aware that Mahan attributed the success of the British fleet against the French to the fact that British captains were trained to make decisions in the heat of battle. While winds shifted and formations were broken, the French commanders were obliged to watch the flagship for instructions as to what to do next. It was said to be a strength of the American officers in the Pacific that they were resourceful and creative, adjusting their tactics against the Japanese Imperial Army to fit the circumstances.*

Chiba told the prime minister that he would feel uncomfortable with such authority. Surely this was not a decision to be entrusted to one man.

Rodriguez sighed. "Before we get into the first reports of gold, Tomi, you need to understand something about the culture of the Philippines. We are a country with eighty-six languages and more than seven thousand islands at low tide. I say a country, actually there's Manila and everywhere else. We are poor. We are nominal Catholics, but highly superstitious. We are also credulous. This is a country of wild rumors and stories. We have 'psychic surgeons' and repeated appearances of the Virgin Mary. And where there are rumors of gold and widespread credulity there are bound to be hustlers and con men of every stripe. This is one reason it has been easy for Western reporters to discount the stories of gold. But there are so many of them, and in such detail, that taken together they ought to make any sober observer wonder. Even paranoids sometime have enemies, do they not?

"We at *Bawiin mo ang Ginto* discount the first two reports of gold, but they're of interest because they date the origins of the linking of the gold with your grandfather. Severino Garcia Santa Romana, an OSS officer and Japanese-speaking Filipino, allegedly interrogated Yamashita's personal driver, Maj. Kashii Kijomi, who claimed to have witnessed two large excavations in his duties. These were in the mountains of central Luzon. We don't know how much gold was recovered from these sites, if any, or where it went. We discount the Santa Romana story for three reasons. We're unsure of his ultimate loyalty. The locations are wrong. And the sites were allegedly excavated before Kodama's release from Sugamo Prison.

"As you will eventually learn, Robert Curtis, ultimately the chief source of most of these details, claimed there were a total of one hundred seventy-two sites in the Philippines containing treasure. These two sites in the mountains of Luzon are the only ones associated with your grandfather, but enough for Filipinos hearing the inevitable stories to associate the gold with his name. The phrase 'Yamashita's Gold' became part of a canard of disinformation to divert attention from Prince Chichibu and Emperor Hirohito. Dead men can't talk."

Tomi's face tightened. "Bad enough to call General Yamashita a war criminal because Iwabuchi ignored his orders, but to add perverse barbarity and sheer greed to the list of bogus charges is too damn much."

"You already know the sequence of events. On December 23, 1948, MacArthur's people hanged former Prime Minister Tojo and six other Class A war criminals, including four military officers. Next day they released Kodama Yoshio and eighteen other Class A war criminals from Sugamo Prison. A month later, Kodama returned to the *yakuza* underworld as an operative of the Counterintelligence Corps, the CIC, which was the operational wing of Willoughby's G-2. We know he helped bust labor unions, which were believed to be the vanguard of Japanese Communists. What else he did is uncertain."

"You think Hirohito bought himself a walk with the Golden Lily. The supreme commander of allied powers made a deal under the table."

Rodriguez said, "You need to appreciate the circumstances. In 1948, Douglas MacArthur and the American State Department knew Mao was going to drive Chiang off the mainland. They wanted to halt the spread of communism in Asia, but needed more money than the U.S. Congress was willing to give them after the huge expense of the war. Remember, this is Asia. We don't believe that MacArthur's people used shares of Hirohito's Gold to finance armies or national governments, but rather to assure the continued support of pro-American military officers and politicians."

Tomi grinned. "The black mist descends."

"From the moment MacArthur and his subordinates rescued

Kodama and his friends from the gallows and created the Yotsuya fund, the law of unintended consequences took over."

The night before he was shot, Nakamura called Chiba in once more and said he had come to a decision. He ordered Chiba to run down "Edie Compton" and find out what was in the van der Elst journal. He should try to buy it first, but failing that, he should do whatever he felt was necessary to find out what was in it.

Nakamura said the decision of whether or not to kill Compton was Chiba's alone. He was a lover of country just as Nakamura was. He should balance the requirements of giri *and* ninjo. *The prime minister was confident he would act wisely.*

The stunned Chiba bowed to Nakamura and agreed to carry out his wishes. The decision was to be Chiba's. Chiba's choice.

Rodriguez said, "The truth about Ferdinand Marcos is one of the keys to everything that followed. When Douglas MacArthur made his unnecessary and costly return to the Philippines to salve his wounded ego, he had two hundred fifty thousand Filipino guerrillas to help him, but they were broken into regional, sometimes competing factions.

"At the beginning of the war, Marcos supported the Americans, but he quickly jumped sides. Ferdinand's story was that in January 1942, he had been forced to be the houseboy for Nakahama Akira, the chief of the Kampei-tai in Manila. What the guerrillas also knew was that for a total of eight months in 1943 and in the spring of 1944, Ferdinand had been treated for blackwater fever at Camp O'Donnel, a high-security hospital ordinarily reserved for Japanese officers only and off-limits to Filipinos without the support of the Kampei-tai. After his second visit, Ferdinand was the guest of Nakahama at Fort Santiago. He formed an organization of thieves and profiteers that he called *Ang Mga Maharlika*—Noble

Studs. He later claimed the studs were guerrillas working against the Japanese. There seems little doubt that they were profiteers who sold scrap metal to the Japanese. American army investigators later said it was a 'buy and sell' organization working in the Pangasinan province, not a guerrilla organization.

"The largest guerrilla force on Luzon, the U.S. Army Forces of the Philippines, Northern Luzon, was commanded by an American, Col. Russell W. Volckmann, who had disobeyed MacArthur's orders to surrender at Corregidor and instead joined the Filipino resistance in the mountains. In the winter of 1944, one of Volckmann's subordinates, Captain Ray Hunt, allegedly arrested Ferdinand Marcos's father, Mariano, as a Japanese collaborator and propagandist. Accompanied by a Japanese bodyguard, Mariano had gone from village to village in Northern Luzon making pro-Japanese speeches. Under interrogation, Mariano is said to have fingered Ferdinand as the Filipino who had introduced him to the Kampei-tai. In mid-April, according to one story, the guerrillas executed Mariano. Maybe they did, maybe they didn't. Ferdinand later claimed that the Japanese executed him. His fate is not germane to our argument."

Several weeks after Nakamura's death, Suma Obe ordered Chiba to ignore any instructions he might have received from the late prime minister with regard to "Edie Compton" and the van der Elst journal. An American college professor had now read the journal. Col. Cading Rodriguez of Bawiin mo ang Ginto *and the renegade American Kip Smith would brief her on the Golden Lily and the M Fund on the Philippine island of Negros.*

Chiba, assisted by a yakuza kobun, *was to monitor the briefings. When they were finished, he was to murder the professor, Dr. Tomi Kobayashi, in addition to Rodriguez and Smith. Kobayashi, he added, was the granddaughter of Yamashita Tomoyuki and so was highly motivated to learn the complete truth.*

Chiba felt torn. He felt he still owed giri *to the prime minister, who had told him to decide for himself what should be done. Yet honor now required that he obey Suma, whose instructions were explicit: find out what was in the van der Elst journal, then murder Dr. Kobayashi, Kip Smith, and Ding Rodriguez.*

"On October 9, 1944, Hunt issued orders for Ferdinand's arrest on charges of treason," Rodriguez continued. "When Volckmann's headquarters learned that Ferdinand was in custody, Lieutenant Colonel Arthur Murphy of the G-2 section radioed instructions to execute him, too. When he learned what had happened, Marcos's friends Venancio Duque and Tony Quirino gathered affidavits and pulled every string possible, and managed to get Marcos a reprieve."

"I take it I can check U.S. Army records on this."

"Yes, you can. There seems little doubt that Marcos was wheeling and dealing and doing whatever was necessary to turn a peso off the Japanese occupation. But his claims to be a war hero are contradicted by previously missing U.S. Army records uncovered in the national archives by the historian Alfred McCoy, author of the classic *The Politics of Heroin in Southeast Asia.* McCoy turned them over to reporters of the *New York Times* and the *Washington Post.*

Rodriguez rolled his eyes in disgust. "In fact, Marcos's war history has been so twisted by Marcos partisans and critics that there is no separating fact from fantasy, American army records or not. Are the most heinous allegations true? We don't know. Since he was never convicted as a war criminal we have to presume him innocent. He likely did work for both the Japanese and the Americans. A lot of Filipinos did. Hard to judge them at this late date."

Smith said, "We don't have a dog in that fight."

"For our purposes only two things matter. One, Marcos apparently did have contacts among the Japanese who occupied Luzon.

Two, Filipinos identified as having helped save his hide from the guerrillas pop up again later when the American war crimes investigator Minoru Fukumitsu investigated claims of 'Yamashita's Gold.' "

Smith said, "The Marcos family has always taken the sensible position recommended by the Arab proverb, 'The dogs bark, but the caravan moves on.' "

Rodriguez stopped and wrote a short note that he handed to Smith.

> *In a matter unrelated to our briefings, I have sources telling me that we've got all kinds of action at Cadiz on the northern tip of the island. The American evangelists Rev. Robin Fallon and his wife are holding a revival in Cadiz, and a yakuza oyabun named Katchan Kawana has a huge yacht anchored there.*

Smith read the note and arched an eyebrow. "Tomi and I will take a look around."

As Tomi and Smith left Aida's and walked toward his Toyota Land Cruiser, she said, "You said two Japanese gentlemen were recording Ding's briefing. What Japanese gentlemen?"

"Chiba Wataru, a Japanese intelligence operative accompanied by what is likely a *yakuza kobun* named Yoshida. Chiba's brother-in-law, the Japanese Minister of Finance, is said to be one of the fund managers."

Tomi looked stunned. "What?"

"They want to know what is in van der Elst's journal. Chiba-san and I are old acquaintances, as it happens. A long story."

"And we did nothing. Apparently plan to do nothing. Why, for heaven's sake?"

Smith unlocked the door to the passenger's side of the Land Cruiser. "If we try to run, they might try to kill us. Better to let them listen and for the moment postpone the question of getting off the island. If the three of us know the whole story, maybe one of us will escape and find a way to make it public."

Tomi's mouth dropped.

"I warned you this is dangerous business. If you want me to put you on a plane back to the United States, I can do that. Your call."

2

It was always difficult to get face time with the president of the United States in an official social gathering, but Suma Obe was the man in charge of the powerful Ministry of Industry and Finance, known to most Westerners by its initials, MITI. Until the contentious factions in the Liberal Democratic party decided who should replace the fallen Nakamura-san, Suma was the most powerful man in Japan. Never mind that his father, Suma Yakijiro, was governor general of Nanking during the infamous rape. The winners wrote the history. Who was to say how much of the so-called rape was the truth and how much blasphemous slander.

Suma circled the room drinking Wild Turkey whiskey out of respect to his American guests, knowing that in time the president's aides and the other Japanese would politely withdraw to give them time alone. The Americans, he knew, called this valuable "face time."

Japanese policy was in the main conducted by bureaucrats and the heads of Japanese banks and corporations. Here was the tail that wagged the dog of Nippon. In the view of Americans and European economists and businessmen, MITI was the most obstinate, powerful, contrary public institution in Japan. Superior to presumed equals among agencies of the Japanese government, MITI contrived to keep Western banks from doing business in

Japan and Western corporations from selling their products there—going to extremes to prevent an outsider from making so much as a single yen in Japan. At the same time, MITI bureaucrats had amazing skill at negotiating rules allowing Japanese corporations to dump CD players, television sets, electronic gadgetry, and automobiles on the American market with nary a squawk of protest from Congress.

How the Japanese managed this extraordinary feat was a political mystery only to the naïve.

The president had made the trip to Asia ostensibly to consult with his allies about the troublesome North Koreans, the blustering government in Beijing, and the ailing economies of Southeast Asia. Then, too, there were the troublesome MITI trade practices that resulted in whopping American trade deficits.

But Suma knew that it was unlikely that North Koreans, Southeast Asians, and trade deficits were uppermost on the president's mind. The president faced re-election in two years, and a sensible politician, whether he lived in the White House or was in charge of MITI, did what he had to do to retain power. The myth of public service was frosting on the cake of personal ambition.

At length, both Japanese and American politicians and officials parted respectfully, allowing Suma to be alone with the president, a charming Southerner with handsome silver hair that a couple of years earlier had been a pedestrian brown. Suma assumed this cosmetic change was an attempt to make the president look more mature and presumably more responsible.

Suma exchanged bows with the president, and they shook hands. "So good to see you again, Suma-san."

"And you, Mr. President." Suma spoke excellent English, having worked hard to overcome those troublesome *R*s and *L*s.

"I'm very pleased that your economy is perking again, Suma-san." The president might have added that Japan would have done far better if MITI had allowed foreign competition to give the beleaguered Japanese consumer a break, but didn't.

Suma thought the president's Southern accent was charming. "And you're doing well, too, Mr. President. I see where you're scoring remarkable positives in the polls."

The president smiled broadly. "Well, those polls are something else again, I can tell you, Suma-san. There seems to be some kind of political gravity at work. What goes up must come down. The trick is to have the polls up on the first Tuesday in November of an election year. All other polls are irrelevant. Good for the pundits and talking heads on the tube, but other than that they aren't worth squat and everybody knows it."

"Perhaps we could be of some assistance in that regard. Friends support friends in time of need."

The president blinked. "Oh? How would that be?"

"Perhaps we could make a small contribution to your campaign."

The president looked concerned. "Well, thank you for your concern, Suma-san, but as you know, contributions from foreigners are illegal in the United States. I couldn't have any part of that. But I appreciate you for your offer, nevertheless. It's nice to know one has friends who are willing to pitch in and help out."

Suma cleared his throat. "Well, I'm sure there are ways to move the money judiciously, if we use our imagination. I was thinking of a contribution in the order of seven figures."

The president patted his stomach. "You know, I'm getting mighty hungry, Suma-san. I dearly love sushi and those tempura fried shrimp you folks make over here. What do you say we join the others at the buffet table?"

Suma bowed. "That sounds good, Mr. President."

Just like that, the deal was concluded. The president had scored a one-million-dollar campaign contribution in return for not asking Suma a single embarrassing question about one-way Japanese trade practices. In such a political exchange, the quid pro quo was never specified or written down. Who got what was simply understood.

As they headed for the buffet table, Suma's able assistant caught his eye. "If you'll excuse me for a moment, Mr. President, I have to attend to some business."

"You hurry up now, Suma-san. I see a whole lot of sushi and tempura on that table. Looks mighty good."

Suma bowed and quietly strolled to the waiting assistant, who said, "A call from Chiba-san, sir."

Suma took the cell phone. "Yes."

Chiba said, "We've begun taping. No problem."

"Keep me informed if you have any snags."

Suma punched the off button with his thumb and joined the president at the buffet table. The president, looking pleased that his trip to Japan had been so productive, was munching contentedly on a shrimp. Suma thought American politicians were just about the best deal on the world market. When you had the M Fund at your disposal, you could buy incumbents by the bagful. It went without saying that a president cost more than a speaker of the House did, just as a Senate minority leader was more expensive than a freshman senator from Montana. Buy cheap, get cheap.

3

As part of the first step in finding out what was going on at Cadiz, Kip Smith gave Tomi Kobayashi the assignment of wangling an appointment with the colorful, pistol-packing lady mayor of the fishing village. Passing herself off as a *Los Angeles Times* reporter, Tomi was to learn more about the planned revival by the Rev. Robin Fallon and his wife, Roberta. Smith gave her a plastic press card for the *Los Angeles Times*, complete with her photograph.

She studied the card, looking amazed. "Where on earth did you get this?"

"I've got a spook kit that lets me make whatever kind of ID I want. I'll go separately as a photographer for either *Time* or *Newsweek*, depending."

"Depending on what?"

He grinned. "On whether or not I spot any *Time* or *Newsweek* photographers. If there's a *Time* guy here, or woman, begging your pardon, and they challenge me, I'll whip out my *Newsweek* card and say the Filipinos got the magazines mixed up. If there's a *Newsweek* man here, I have a *U.S. News & World Report* card for a backup."

"A photographer for all seasons. Why would American evangelists be involved in a search for the archers?"

Smith cocked his head. "Preachers like gold, same as everybody else. But better to let Ding give you the complete answer to your question in his briefings. I'll tell you now that the principal non-Japanese and Filipino players in the search for Hirohito's Gold have been CIA officers, right-wing generals, and Christian anti-Communists. When a famous evangelist appears on Negros at the same time as Kawana, it makes Ding and I wonder. Maybe it's just a coincidence. Maybe not."

"In any event, we check it out."

"Correct. All you have to do is follow the road through Bacolod and keep going north until you come to the end of the island. You can't miss it."

Tomi had heard enough you-just-won't-believe-it stories of crazed traffic in the Philippines, with people packed into jeepneys and clinging to sidecar-bearing bicycles and 150-cc motorcycles, that she was determined to proceed cautiously, thank you.

She slowed to pass the Burgos Market in central Bacolod, passed a plaza with an aged cathedral to one side, then headed north along a narrow cement road. The beer and soft drink industries appeared to be engaged in a bizarre competition to see who could get the most signs up. The companies had obviously provided free signs to the owner of whatever lean-to that aspired to being a shop, and so there were San Miguel, Coca-Cola, Pepsi-Cola, and RC signs everywhere advertising such makeshift thatched-roofed bamboo establishments as Carlito's Store, Elita's Sari Sari, and the Five Sisters Store. Manila Beer and Carlsberg Beer had so few signs as to be pathetic competitors.

A recent interest in prawn farming was evidenced by newer billboards advertising prawn feed and chemicals to clean the water in the ponds. Tomi couldn't see many of the farms because they were hidden behind bunkerlike concrete containing dikes. The prawn farms quickly gave way to sugar land, often separated by rows of elegant coconut palms. Tomi, beeping her horn, passed an aged, rusting Isuzu truck heaped high with cane. Did they load the Isuzu that high every trip? How on earth did the Isuzu's frame stand up under that kind of weight?

Passing a *carabao* pulling a cartload of wood, she drove through the village of Talisay and then Silay, the ramshackle center of which included the inhabited and uninhabited ruins of what must have once been grand administrative offices for the Spanish colonialists. Magnificent white columns that had once spoken to an optimistic if not grandiose future, were now filthy, broken, and in some cases supported no roof at all, and some of the decaying ruins had gutted interiors. Goats browsed among weeds in one. Was this a form of architectural cemetery, a testament to the arrogance of colonialists past?

She eased her way past the traffic in front of the Silay market. Had the Japanese occupied these buildings in World War II? Were they in grand condition then, or already rotten from disrepair?

Victorias and Manapla were next after Silay. As she approached Cadiz, she passed the Filipino version of an antebellum cotton mansion; splendid white, it was, with pillar and portal to boot. A warlord? A congressman or senator?

She came at length to Cadiz. A cement road had recently been poured on the outskirts of town, but the luxury of smoothness quickly gave way to potholes, chuck holes, and mud walls which Tomi negotiated as carefully as she could, but it was impossible to spare the Nissan a horrible pounding of its suspension system. She wondered how on earth their vehicles survived that kind of beating.

The road passed by *nipa* huts with thatched roofs mixed in with tiny boxes with rusting, corrugated, galvanized iron roofs—the architecture of poverty that Tomi thought was similar to that she had seen in the rural South, or the black districts of many Southern and Midwestern cities, with tarpaper as well as galvanized iron roofs as the signature. Tomi couldn't imagine a more unlikely place to hold an evangelical revival, and yet she could understand why, living in conditions like this, Filipinos would be attracted to the notion of a better deal in an afterlife.

As Tomi had seen in Latin America, each house had a fence. The poorer houses, some barely visible though banana leaves and broad-leafed foliage, had perfectly serviceable bamboo fences, the points of which looked formidable to her. The more ambitious residences were surrounded by concrete block fences topped with shards of glass, the green of broken 7-Up bottles being the color of choice, although Tomi saw a few fences topped with the dark amber of San Miguel bottles. She thought surely by now any self-respecting Filipino thief must know how to go right over those shards of glass. She wondered if having an expensive, shard-studded fence of concrete blocks might be a form of show, an indication of status, suggesting that one had something to steal.

The city hall was unexpectedly modern, a two-story building overlooking a handsome plaza with well-tended flowers and neatly tiled walkways. To one side of this park there stood a globe perhaps twelve feet in diameter, a touch that Tomi admired. She loved globes and atlases.

She walked through the heavy glass door entrance and found herself in a large, wood-paneled portico or foyer entering into offices straight ahead. It was evident that the offices of Her Honor the Mayor were situated on the second floor, somewhere behind the balcony overlooking the foyer.

Tomi took a chance and went up the stairs to the left. The second floor was abuzz with people, including several Westerners. The white men wore suits and ties and the woman high heels and perhaps a trifle too much makeup. Tomi wondered if wearing a Western suit in that weather might not be symptomatic of an odd form of masochism, or perhaps it was self-punishment as a way of thanking the Lord for his many bounties.

In the confusion that seemed to be taking place outside the

office of the pistol-packing mayor herself, a plump Filipina with an erect posture and a huge behind spotted Tomi. "Excuse me, and you are with?" the woman asked, adding quickly, "I'm Elsa Sablada, an assistant to the mayor."

Tomi felt uncomfortable with lying. "My name is Tomi Kobayashi. I'm a reporter with the *Los Angeles Times*. I'm here to cover the revival, and I may want to make an appointment with the mayor in the next few days." She dug out her bogus *Los Angeles Times* press card.

"Well, you're just in time, aren't you? These are Praise Jesus Now people, and the mayor is just getting ready to take them on a tour of the proposed site of the televised revival. I'm sure she wouldn't mind if you tagged along. No problem."

"I'd like that very much. Thank you."

"Just let me know when you want the appointment."

A slender Filipina with bangs and large eyes emerged from the mayor's office followed by even more freshly scrubbed white people. The woman, dressed in blue jeans and wearing a shirt with the tails out, was obviously the pistol-packing mayor, although no pistol was in sight. Tomi thought it must be in her handbag.

Beaming and gesturing instructions in Ilongo to her assistants, the mayor strode down the stairs leading to the ground, interrupted halfway there by the woman who had talked to Tomi.

Smiling, the mayor looked Tomi's way and beckoned with her hand. "Sure, come on along," she called. "Welcome."

"I'll follow in my car. Thank you very much."

Having lucked out, Tomi accepted a photocopy of a street map of Cadiz from the mayor's assistant, and joined the PJN advancemen as they filed down the stairs and spilled out into the foyer. She followed them outside past the globe to the curb, where the cars waited to take them to whatever site it was that the advance men for PJN had selected for Fallon's big show.

As she fell in behind the motorcade of four cars, Tomi studied her map of the town. The main part of Cadiz was confined inside a half-mile-long rectangle with the Visayan Sea on the left and the Guimaron River on the right. The Guimaron took a ninety-degree turn to the left for a two-hundred-yard run to the ocean, providing the effective end of the rectangle.

Cadiz was a fishing village, and it turned out that the docks, located along the river at the end of the rectangle, were where the motorcade was headed.

The mayor's lead car stopped at the harbor and the occupants of the motorcade got out to admire the colorful and romantic *bankas*, the snarls of nets being untangled, and silver fish hardly more than an inch and a half long being spread out on tables to dry.

The outriggered *bankas* were truly wonderful, painted green and yellow and red and white. The Filipinos liked their boats the way they did their jeepneys, as bright and colorful as possible. There were *bankas* on the ocean side and river side as well as sailboats dead ahead. This was a super panavision, picture-postcard, wraparound Filipino fishing dock.

And just behind these *bankas*, in the center of the *U* formed by the Guimaron River and the ocean, was an empty field of dirt with patches of short grass. At the edge of the field, tens of thousands of inch-long silver fish were spread out to dry on long tables. Three men in the field gestured to the left and right. The visitors in the motorcade, having taken in the vista of beautiful *bankas*, headed for the gesturing men.

Tomi got out of her car and went to join them. One of the men in the field had a video camera that he panned right, then left, along the boats. She suddenly understood the choice of Cadiz for the revival site, if not the connection with the alchemist archers.

The Rev. Robin Fallon was famous for his dramatic striding to and fro as he ministered the Lord's gospel. If they moved the fish-drying tables out of the way, *voilà*, the harbor at Cadiz was shaped like a giant stage, the field being surrounded by colorful, outriggered fishing boats on three sides.

Tomi eavesdropped on the crew-cut man who was talking to the mayor:

". . . end Fallon was also moved by a letter from Mrs. Bessie Case Flanders, of Orlando, Florida, whose grandfather, Lieutenant John W. Dolan, was killed on the morning of April 20, 1945, at Hill 3155, which General Brush renamed Dolan Hill in his honor. Lieutenant Dolan was posthumously awarded the Silver Star Oak Leaf Cluster for his bravery.

"Of course, it is Mrs. Flander's bequest in the name of her grandfather that makes this revival possible. We know a ceremony like this is unusual, but the Reverend Fallon feels it's good to move our services out of artificial environments whenever we have the chance. Get out here under the sun and stars and show the Heavenly Father in all His glory."

The mayor was amazed. "You want to light candles at Pulak Pulakan? Do you know about Pulak Pulakan? Have you done any research at all?" When the mayor turned, Tomi saw that she had an automatic pistol tucked into the small of her back, the grip concealed by her shirttails.

"Oh, yes, we've done our research." The man with the crew cut was buoyant. "It was a terrible battle, we know that. Nearly two thousand American boys lost their lives there. The candles will most certainly be for them as well as Lieutenant Dolan."

When Tomi got back into her car to return to Bacolod to meet Smith and Rodriguez, she saw the sleek white yacht that Ding had mentioned, anchored offshore beyond a dredge that was removing silt from the channel leading to the river. It had *Giri* painted on its bow both in English and what looked like bold, red strokes of a giant Japanese *kanji* brush.

Striding back to her car for the drive back to Bacolod, she

remembered the old movie in which a wide-eyed hat check girl, upon seeing the size of Mae West's diamond ring, had exclaimed, "Oh, my goodness!"

Mae West gave her a lazy half smile and drawled, "Honey, goodness ain't got nothin' to do with it."

Tomi Kobayashi was confident that goodness also had nothing to do with the success of whoever owned the *Giri*.

4

Kip Smith parked his Land Cruiser, curious about the sleek white yacht anchored beyond the dredge that was deepening the channel to the mouth of the Guimaron River, where the Cadiz fishermen anchored their colorful pumpboats. How would he get a closer look at the *Giri*?

Smith wore his full photographer's regalia—lenses and paraphernalia hanging from his multipocketed vest. The Company had sent him to a school in Rochester to help him develop his legend, and over the years he had become a skilled and artful photographer. He had both video and still-camera lenses necessary for shooting from extreme distances, and he was good at waiting patiently for that just-right shot—a snake swallowing a rat, a concerned crocodile guarding its young.

Smith wasn't bashful about firing away, following whim and his imagination. Shoot enough pictures, he knew, and there were bound to be a few that were professional quality.

Smith's stomach began to growl. He settled in at a ramshackle café in the row of shacks along the Guimaron. The café was empty save for two fishermen having San Miguels. He ordered a bottle of San Miguel and a plate of fried fish and rice and watched the dockside activity as he ate.

A boat arrived with a modest catch. A crowd of giggling schoolchildren in blue uniforms with white blouses and shirts boldly crammed themselves onto an undersized, tipsy boat and were ferried across the river. Three hundred yards offshore of the river's mouth, the dredge scooped up the accumulated silt.

Smith finished his fish and was working on a second bottle of San Miguel when the first of several cars and jeepneys showed up bearing what appeared to be local newspaper and radio reporters. The reporters, toting recorders, cameras, and notepads, were escorted to the water where boats waited to take them to the dredge.

Smith said to the two fishermen, "Excuse me, but I'm curious about the reporters going to the dredge, do you know what that's all about?"

Both fishermen grinned. One of them said, "Senator Enrique is going to show them the many wonders of government in action."

The other fisherman said, "They managed to wait until the silt had completely filled the channel. We haven't been able to get out of here at low tide for years."

The first said, "Should have been dredged twenty years ago."

Smith, looking at the dredge relative to the yacht, said, "I'm a photographer for an American magazine. Do you suppose I could con my way aboard?"

"Just join the others," said the first fishermen.

"Thank you, I think I will," Smith said. He collected his gear. With cameras dangling from both shoulders, and with a Seattle Mariners baseball cap to protect his nose from the sun, he picked his way down rickety wooden stairs to the water where the shuttle boats tied up. He spotted a young man who was obviously in charge of ferrying the reporters, and said, "A couple of fishermen up there say you're holding some kind of press conference on that dredge out there. I'm a photographer for *Time* magazine, and I was wondering if I might join in. Never know what might come of it."

The young man flashed perfect white teeth. "Of course. Hop aboard. We should have another load in a couple of minutes." As he said this, three more Filipino journalists arrived: a photographer, a long-haired reporter with a pad sticking from his hip pocket, and a Filipina with her hair cut in bangs. She was so cute Smith had to prevent himself from groaning out loud. Smith introduced himself as they were helped aboard a *banka* for the trip to the dredge.

The boat's captain started the engine, and they were off— *karachug-kong-kong, karachug-kong-kong, karachug-kong-kong.* Smith wondered if the pistons might be traveling sideways or whether he could hear loose ball bearings tumbling around in the crankcase like baseballs in a clothes dryer.

The young woman, GeeGee Mendoza, took it upon herself to be Smith's guide, which was acceptable to him. GeeGee represented something with the initials COBRA-SAN, which she explained was an association of journalists on Negros. "The purpose is to more efficiently take advantage of envelopmental journalism," she said.

"Envelopmental journalism?"

GeeGee was a tease. She narrowed her eyes and pretended to be secretively passing out wads of bills from a wallet. "Used to be a politician had to make a whole lot of little payments to stay in business. Now he stuffs one big envelope, and we all share." She beamed. "See? Far more efficient this way."

"All right." Smith beamed. The Filipinos had a self-deprecating sense of humor that Smith liked. Philippine Airlines advertised the archipelago as Asia with a smile, and in that they were accurate. They were the liveliest people with the biggest smiles in Asia, and Smith admired them greatly.

She said, "Today we're going to listen to Senator Buddy Enrique take undeserved credit for dredging the river channel, something that should have been done years ago. He'll claim to have personally saved the economy of Cadiz. Verbal bilge. He's got the brains of a fish, if that."

"They say we have senators in Washington who have to be watered once a week," Smith said. "Their administrative assistants put them by a window so they'll get plenty of sun."

"But Enrique's quite generous at his press conferences," GeeGee added quickly. "There'll be buckets of crabs, and all the San Miguel we can handle, which is why so many of us showed up. The food makes up for there not being a real story."

"I see. Where does he get his money?"

GeeGee laughed. "Foolish man. Graft and corruption, where else? And he has a huge spread of sugar land outside of Silay."

As the shuttle boat drew near the dredge, Smith kept an eye on the sleek yacht, the *Giri*. A few minutes later, the shuttle was idling—*karachug-kong-kong, karachug-kong-kong*—alongside the dredge and Smith followed GeeGee Mendoza up a ladder onto the dredge, which was crawling with people.

On the bridge, Smith saw a man he assumed was Senator Enrique solicitously shaking hands with well-wishers. Looking dapper in Columbia blue trousers and a complementary blue shirt, Enrique was accompanied by a tall, handsome, light-complexioned Filipino who was a gentleman of consequence, judging by the deference given him and his posture, at once imperious and aloof, yet somehow grandfatherly. The light-complexioned Filipino in turn seemed to be attended by a serious-faced young man in glasses, who nodded gravely at every comment of the older man.

Smith joined GeeGee and her companions as they watched a huge crane swing a metal claw into the water and emerge with several cubic yards of silt, which the operator dumped—*kaaa-splooooooosh!*—into the bottom of the boat's open hold, sending forth a mushroom of brown water.

The startled visitors jumped back at the impressive plume of water, and the iron claw, trailing muddied water, emerged from the hold empty.

The operator swung the claw back into the sea and then it was up and over the hold again, *kaaa-sploooooosh!*

GeeGee told Smith they would be eating in a few minutes, after which Buddy Enrique would have his press conference. She said, "The crabs and San Miguel come first. The idea is to buy us off by feeding us before the propaganda. We know how that works. We have to have strong stomachs, or we'll all be sick from pretending to be interested in what he has to say."

As GeeGee had predicted, there were goodies galore: tubs of crabs; tubs of fried fish; and tubs of Coca-Cola and 7-Up and San Miguel smothered in cracked ice. There were also huge bowls of rice and crates of bananas.

The payoff was worth the ride out, Smith had to admit. Although he had just eaten, he couldn't resist going for a couple of crabs and a San Miguel. While GeeGee was led astray by her colleagues, he found a smidgen of shade on deck and squatted to pick the crabs apart and consider the *Giri*. As he sucked on a crab leg, he noticed GeeGee talking to the grave young man with Senator Enrique and his aristocratic-appearing companion.

At the urging of one of Enrique's hostesses, Smith had himself a couple more crabs and another San Miguel, and then it was time for the press conference.

Smith joined GeeGee on the bridge where Enrique, standing beside his mysterious companion, held forth on the blessings of the expensive dredging project: ". . . solemn promise I made to the voters when I ran for office. It's been a long, difficult struggle."

Smith listened to Enrique explain how much it cost per day to lease the dredge, how much the crane operator got paid, how many times each day the dredge had to put out to sea to dump the silt, how deep the new channel would be, and how long it would last before it had to be dredged again.

Smith noted that the distinguished-looking gentleman with the senator appeared to be more interested in the *Giri* than in the mechanics of dredging. So was Smith, and he slipped quietly away from GeeGee Mendoza and her sated colleagues, who now had to pay for the crabs and beer by pretending to be interested in what Enrique had to say. A so-so deal, in Smith's opinion.

He retreated to his shady nook and fitted his Nikon with a 300-millimeter lens and quietly began shooting pictures of the *Giri* on the off chance there was something of interest on her deserted decks.

Later, as he and GeeGee waited for their turn on a shuttle to shore, Smith asked her who Enrique's handsome companion was.

"That's General Jose Maria Martinez, the superintendent of the Philippine Military Academy. He's supposed to be a Marcos loyalist. I went to school with George Villanueva, the younger man you might have seen me talking to. He's a fourth-year cadet at the academy. I think he's had a crush on me for years."

"He's got good taste in women, I'll give him that."

GeeGee blushed. "Well, thank you, but he's not my type. Too gung ho and military academy rah-rah. George is Jaime Pineda's cousin. You've heard about Jaime, I take it."

"The NPA leader? His cousin? Really?"

"Grew up with him. This is an enclosed community of Ilongo-speakers, an amazing web of personal connections. We speak Ilongo on Panay, and here on Negros Occidental, but on the other side of the island, Negros Oriental, they speak Visayan."

Smith knew all that, but he said, "One language on the eastern side. Another on the western side."

"That's right. Everybody thinks Martinez is a Marcos loyalist, but he's more likely loyal to whoever is in power." GeeGee rolled her eyeballs skyward.

"I noticed that he seemed more interested in the *Giri* than in the senator's speechifying. Do you know who owns the *Giri*?"

GeeGee said, "They say it belongs to Kawana Katchan, a *yakuza* godfather who runs guns from Danao to Japan and controls most of the sex trade in Manila. He also owns most of those prawn farms you saw on the way from Bacolod."

"You suppose that's why General Martinez brought your cadet admirer along for the ride? A little surveillance to have a look at the evil Kawana for himself."

GeeGee glanced back at the sleek powerboat. "That's probably the reason why, come to think of it. I saw George taking pictures of that boat a few minutes ago."

5

Tomi, Smith, and Rodriguez went for a leisurely walk down the street from Rodriguez's compound. With a balmy breeze blowing at their backs and rippling waves in the tropical grasses, they strolled past tethered goats on their left and grazing *carabao* on their right.

Smith said, "I think your hunch is right, Ding. We've got a Japanese *oyabun* who likely has Kodama's map. We've got General Jose Maria Martinez accompanied by a cadet from the Philippine Military Academy who is Jaime Pineda's cousin. We've got Robin and Roberta Fallon getting ready to pitch God's tent. Hard to believe the Fallons give a damn about a fallen war hero from fifty years ago, much less saving the souls of Filipinos who don't have a pot to piss in."

A piece of paper blew past them.

Rodriguez said, "They're after the archers, no question."

"If Kawana has the map. He made first contact."

"The way I see it."

Smith said, "The problem for the Japanese has always been how to get the archers out of NPA territory and off the island. What would Katchan have to offer Pineda to get his cooperation, aside from bucks up front?"

Rodriguez thought a moment, then said, "A butcher friend of

mine recently made Soup Number Five for a party of Danao gunsmiths at the test firing of a copy of an Italian wire-guided missile.
A Sabatini. He said one of the Filipino gunsmiths missed a model
airplane but Kawana himself exploded a *carabao*. I might have
been skeptical except that the butcher's story was confirmed by
my wife's third cousin, Toto Popong, the guy who missed the
plane. He was drunk, he said, paralyzed by fear that it was a *wasak*
that would explode when he pulled the trigger. What possible use
would a *yakuza* gang have for a wire-guided missile? They kill one
another with Smith & Wasaks, but a missile? What use?"

"Jaime Pineda would just love to be able to knock down a few
helicopter gunships," Smith said.

"What are you thinking?"

"Even if we do get to the bottom of Hirohito's Gold and the
M Fund and find a decent publisher, we'll still be up against a
wall of entrenched self-interest. The Japan lobby protects its powerful clients. The State Department doesn't want to embarrass its
main Asian ally. The Central Intelligence Agency doesn't want to
break the faith with Japanese nationals it worked with. It truly is
hard for a reporter who has pooh-poohed a story for years to
admit he was wrong."

"Or she," Tomi said.

"Or she, begging your pardon. Few Americans give a damn
about Yamashita's good name. Almost nobody gives a damn if an
innocent Filipina was casually murdered nineteen years ago. To
believe that the truth will turn the trick is naïve. Money talks.
Everything else is bullshit."

Tomi said, "You're saying if we could lay our hands on the
alchemist archers we might at least have a chance."

"I'd donate my share on justice for my wife in a heartbeat."

Tomi cocked her head, studying him. "And I'd spend mine on
letting the public know the truth about my grandfather."

Rodriguez said, "To get the truth out, count me in."

They stopped to allow a young man to lead a *carabao* across the road.

Smith said, "If I make this sound, what do you think of?" He puckered up his mouth and went, *"Cheeeep, cheeeep, cheep-cheep, cheeeep, cheeeep."*

"A chicken," Tomi said.

"Threatening?"

"Harmless," Rodriguez added.

"Ahh, but if you were in Australia and had a nest of babies or a clutch of golden eggs, you wouldn't be deceived. That's the mating call of the black-shouldered kite. You can learn a lot about tactics by watching animals. They use the basics of stealth, speed, camouflage, deception, superior hearing or eyesight, size, poison, whatever—all the primal means of survival. We Homo sapiens have our wonderful cortex."

"And the tactics of the black-shouldered kite?" Rodriguez asked.

"It's a patient, crafty kind of bird that floats silently above the grasslands watching for mice, lizards, or grasshoppers, but it will eat almost anything, including the catch of buzzards or hawks. It drops soundlessly down from the wind like a phantom, snatches its prey, then is gone again quicker than the batting of an eye." Smith gave a languid flip of his fingers. "There are just us three little chickies. A Filipino with a belly. A one-hundred-pound Nisei female. An oddball who does birdcalls. *Cheeeep, cheeeep, cheep-cheep, cheeeep, cheeeep.* We're no threat at all to a tough-as-nails *yakuza oyabun* or a general as crafty and treacherous as Martinez. Right? Unless we're black-shouldered kites."

6

Colonel Cading Rodriguez held the second *Bawiin mo ang Ginto* briefing in Sonny's, a broad, deserted, open-air bar above the street in downtown Bacolod. It was a lazy, indolent, sweaty day. They were attended by a single Filipina waitress dressed in a black skirt and white blouse and watched by the bartender, another Filipina similarly dressed.

As they talked, they ate fish balls and squid balls sold by a vendor on the street below, with Smith giving the waitress twenty pesos, about fifty U.S. cents, for each trip down the stairs to the vendor. By Filipino standards that was a generous tip and the waitress, eager for the next trip down the stairs, kept a careful eye on Smith. The vendor, an aging Filipina, would ordinarily have kept her cart on the move, but she knew she had customers watching her from Sonny's, so she stayed put. The balls were made of ground fish or squid mixed with garlic and flour and deep-fried. Smith and Kobayashi dipped them in a thin, tangy, orange-colored sauce. After a hesitant sample, Tomi found she liked them.

Smith put a fresh cartridge into his tape recorder. Kobayashi got her notepad ready. They had hot fish balls. They had cold bottles of San Miguel. They were ready.

————

Chiba Wataru observed Yoshida tending to the details of recording the conversation in Sonny's. As he watched Yoshida, Chiba thought about the eighteenth-century story of the forty-seven ronin. *This tale, which resonated* giri *and* ninjo, *was known by every Japanese schoolchild.*

Every year the Shogun Tsunayoshi in Edo sent gifts to the Emperor in Kyoto and received gifts in return. In 1701 the Shogun sent greedy and conceited Kira-Kozukenosuke Yoshinaka to Harima Province to receive gifts. When Lord Asano Takuminokami Naganori offered what Kira thought were improper gifts, Kira became abusive and insulting.

After suffering abuse and humiliation for two months, Asano drew a sword on Kira, wounding him slightly. The Shogun ordered Asano to commit seppuku, *but treated Kira like a hero.*

When a samurai *lord committed* seppuku, *the Shogun confiscated his castle, disinherited his family, and disbanded his* samurai *retainers. Should Asano's* samurai *peacefully surrender the castle? Should they murder Kira to restore their Lord's honor? Or should they respect the law and peacefully surrender? Oishi Kuranosuke, a councilor to Asano, tried and failed to get the family reestablished under Asano's younger brother, who ordered Oishi and the other fifty-nine loyal* samurai *to turn over the castle. They fled, vowing revenge on Kira out of* giri *to Lord Asano.*

Oishi sent thirteen of the samurai *home to their families. He and the other forty-six spent two years trying to run down Kira. On December 14, 1702, they attacked his mansion in Edo, killing his sixty-one armed guards without losses of their own. They found Kira hiding in an outhouse and beheaded him. Oishi informed the Magistrate of Edo what he and his* ronin *had done and they waited for whatever punishment the Shogun deemed appropriate.*

The Shogun was impressed by their loyalty in redeeming their lord's honor, nevertheless he ordered them to commit seppuku. *In an act of magnificent sacrifice, they did just that on February 4, 1703.*

Each year thousands of Japanese were moved to tears and excitement as the ritual suicide of the forty-seven ronin *was celebrated in a play called* Chusingura. *Even more visited the gravesite of Oishi's forty-six* ronin *followers at Sengaku-ji Temple to pay homage and loyalty to the* samurai *and their dedication to the code of Bushido.*

Chiba had both seen Chusingura and visited Sengaku-ji and had never failed to be moved. On this most important of assignments, Chiba Wataru was aware that he now carried the burden of Japanese history and tradition.

Rodriguez took another hit of beer. "The emperor, thinking the Japanese would keep the Philippines as part of a negotiated settlement, ordered Chichibu to set up headquarters in Manila. Chichibu was aware that treasure ships arriving weekly would attract attention so he had an engineer named Nakasone construct a tunnel from the piers to the warehouses at MacArthur's old headquarters in Fort McKinley. The next question was where to hide the Big Sushi. Chichibu knew that American bombers would likely spare churches and historic sites, many of them four hundred years old. That was where he would begin. As an added precaution, he housed American and Australian prisoners of war in the churches and historic sites and announced that fact on clear radio.

"In late 1944, the Japanese cruiser *Nachii* went under as it left Manila Bay. It was a curious sinking because the Americans didn't do it. There were no survivors among the one thousand Japanese seamen aboard. We now know that as the Japanese realized their cause was clearly lost, and with no time to bury the most recently arrived portions of Hirohito's Gold, Prince Chichibu ordered it placed aboard thirteen vessels. Admiral Iwabuchi Sanjii sank some, including the *Nachii*, in Manila Bay. Iwabuchi had two minisubs remaining at his disposal. Others were scuttled in other locations in the archipelago. Their crews were killed so there would be no survivors who knew the coordinates of the sunken vessels. Note and remember the Butcher of Manila and the cruiser *Nachii*."

—————

Watching his subordinate at work, Chiba said, "Yoshida-san, I know you've been told to follow my instructions and keep your mouth shut. But we've got a long way to go before we get to the end of this. I'm interested in what you think about the story they're telling the woman."

Yoshida looked incredulous. "Sir? My opinion?"

"After we hear them out, we're going to kill them anyway, so where's the harm? Speak up, Yoshida-san. I want you to tell me what you think."

"Me?" Yoshida seemed to regard expressing his opinion to a superior as a bewildering concept.

Rodriguez said, "When Kodama left Manila for Tokyo in late 1944 to become an advisor to Prime Minister Prince Higashikuni, he knew it was a matter of time before Japan lost the war. The Japanese might surrender to MacArthur, but for Kodama the war would never be finished. The emperor's younger brother had safely buried Hirohito's Gold, but unfortunately on Filipino soil. The lily was so well buried that retrieving it would require major excavations—in some cases under public buildings in Manila. President Manuel Roxas died in April 1948, and Elpido Quirino was elected president a few months later. Remember Elpido from the war."

Kobayashi checked her notes. "He and his brother Tony helped free Marcos."

"And Venancio Duque. There you go. If we are to believe Marcos's story, and we rarely if ever should, he claimed some years later to have had his first encounter with part of Hirohito's Gold in the spring of 1945. He encountered twenty Japanese soldiers on a patrol in Kayapa, in the mountains of Nueva Vizcaya on Luzon. He followed the patrol north toward the rice terraces at Ifuegao, where he picked off a straggler who was lagging behind because his pack was too heavy. Marcos said a bullet struck him in the back as he bent to pick up the dead man's pack, but he held onto it anyway and it contained three gold bars. The back wound was superficial. *Oy!*"

Tomi said, "Lucky Ferdinand."

"Marcos had to have some way of explaining the gold bars he waved around all the time. Ferdinand and Imelda had so much money and power that nobody ever challenged their stories. The business about the superficial back wound is a bit like movie cowboys all the time getting grazed on the scalp. What do you think, Kip, another round?"

"Sounds good to me," Smith said.

Rodriguez waved his hand at the barkeep.

"In 1950, Marcos had law offices both in Baguio and Ilocos Norte. He said later that he was called upon to settle a claim by some Filipino laborers who had been hired by two veterans of the Japanese army to dig a large pit in the mountains. They found gold at the bottom of the pit, but the two Japanese were so greedy that they refused to pay the workers for their labor."

Smith burst out laughing.

"Marcos always made his stories slightly improbable so they didn't sound like lies. Who would believe that the Japanese could be so stupid? The story had to be true. That was Marcos's little gambit. He told stories so outrageous and bizarre that his listeners believed he was telling the truth." Ding Rodriguez held up his finger. "And it is possible, however remotely, that he *was* telling the truth. You judge."

Rodriguez pursed his mouth, considering how to continue. "If the Japanese buried Hirohito's Gold in and around Manila, somebody had to have made maps. I think we can safely assume that." Rodriguez took another hit of San Miguel. "We'll begin with what is alleged to be Marcos's story of Paul Jiga and Benjamin Balmores."

"And the truth?"

Rodriguez cocked his head. "The truth? What Kip and I are trying to do is prove that Imelda Marcos's claim was true, so these stories or rumors, or whatever, are germane, but may or may not be true. This is primarily Marcos's explanation of Jiga and Balmores as reported by Robert Curtis, who will be a recurring figure in this story. But more on him later. Most of his story is found buried in bits and pieces throughout Sterling Seagrave's 1987 biography of the Marcoses, *The Marcos Dynasty.* Curtis later used his experience as the basis of a novel that he wrote under a pseudonym and peddled on the internet. Both Kip and I think his story has the ring of truth."

"In the main, we believe him," Smith added. "And his story as reported by Seagrave, not in his novel, which neither Ding nor I have read."

Rodriguez looked amused. "I agree with Kip. True in the main. As reported in Seagrave's biography, not in Curtis's novel. And we should add that Marcos's relationship to Jiga and Balmores dates to the early 1950s."

Yoshida looked disgusted. "They're telling us that Prince Chichibu buried the Golden Lily? Impossible! What could Prince Chichibu and Prince Higashikuni possibly have to do with any of this? Why hasn't anybody mentioned this in Japan? I've never heard it. It's total nonsense. Rubbish!"

Chiba shifted in his seat. "You think so?"

"Prince Chichibu was Emperor Hirohito's younger brother. He would never have had anything to do with the Golden Lily without Hirohito's knowledge. Everybody knows the emperor was an innocent manipulated by the Japanese army. Ambitious officers deliberately kept the emperor in the dark. If the emperor had been involved in planning the war and had received good advice, we would have won. Fools lost the war. That's been well established."

Chiba shrugged. "It's possible Smith and Rodriguez are just trying to deceive us, I agree."

Yoshida fell silent. Then he added, "I'm sorry, sir. It's just that I cannot abide such slander against the emperor of Japan."

"No, no, Yoshida-san. No reason to apologize for being a patriot and loving your country. We both owe giri *to the Japanese people and the memory of our honorable ancestors."*

Rodriguez dipped a squid ball in the sauce and popped it into his mouth. "Marcos's story was that Leopoldo 'Paul' Jiga was born in Manila of a Japanese father and a Filipina mother. He was twenty-three years old when the war started. The Japanese put his father to work as a translator in occupied Manila. They put Paul to work as a houseboy and valet to General Yamashita, who was in charge of burying the Japanese booty in both onshore and offshore sites. Jiga told Marcos that the Americans and Filipinos who buried the Golden Lily in pits and tunnels were shot to keep the locations secret. Those who buried the gold at offshore sites were shot and left for the sharks. Jiga also told Marcos that he witnessed the sinking of the *Nachii*, in which all hands went down.

"Ben Balmores was also a dual national. During the war, the Japanese employed him as a translator and spy. Marcos said Balmores confirmed Jiga's story that the Japanese dug miles of tunnels around Fort Santiago, housing their slave labor in a Spanish dungeon there. When a detail of POWs buried part of the treasure in one of the tunnels, they were sealed inside and left to die. Balmores told Marcos he was disgusted and made almost physically ill by memories of seeing thousands of POWs beheaded or buried alive.

"This is Marcos's story as told to Curtis."

"Correct. This is Curtis's account. Jiga and Balmores supposedly told the amazed Marcos that some of the gold was trucked into the mountains and buried in caves or tunnels in the mountains near the Benguet gold mines in Baguio. Other gold was buried in deep pits in areas outside Manila. Jiga and Balmores said they had witnessed twelve hundred Australians and Americans buried alive after they had dug two treasure chambers deep underground at Teresa just outside Manila. And, finally, the Japanese bored holes in coral reefs, stashed gold inside, then capped the holes with concrete and coral."

"They told all this to Ferdinand Marcos? Why?"

"Good question. Anyway, that was Marcos's story for years." Rodriguez added quickly, "Says Curtis."

"Says Curtis."

"Kip and I want to be careful with our story. If we assert too much without documentary proof, we erode our credibility. That's your basic Conspiracy Theory 101."

"But I say again, Ding and I believe Curtis," Smith added quickly. "We think it's at the heart of Mrs. Marcos's claim that her husband had access to gold buried by the Japanese. How much gold and under what circumstances is another matter."

Rodriguez said, "Jiga and Balmores also showed Marcos their maps."

Tomi blinked. "Maps? What maps? They had maps to the gold?"

"According to Curtis, they had one hundred seventy-two maps, thirty-four detailing water locations and one hundred thirty-eight describing land sites. If we are to believe Marcos as reported by Curtis, Jiga and Balmores told him the maps were kept in Manila until General Yamashita began his withdrawal to Baguio. After he got to Baguio, Yamashita knew he couldn't defend that either, and ordered a withdrawal higher in the mountains. He made his last stand at a place called the Kiangan Pocket. Yamashita was in charge of moving seventy thousand troops high in the mountains, and in the confusion at his headquarters, nobody was paying any attention to the maps. So the opportunists Jiga and Balmores nipped off with them, the rascals."

"What?" Tomi said. "The maps to Hirohito's Gold. Isn't that a bit easy? Those maps would have been valuable in the extreme."

"You're thinking that Yamashita would have slept with them under his pillow."

Rodriguez shrugged. "Anyway, that's allegedly Marcos's version of Jiga and Balmores."

Tomi looked confused. "I don't understand. Why didn't Ferdinand and his pals just go dig up the gold?"

"There were complications. Gold is so dense it hardly takes up any space. The Japanese buried it so deep that if a thief was off a few inches one way or the other, he'd miss it entirely. Accurate maps were essential. Unfortunately the maps Jiga and Balmores showed Marcos used an archiac Japanese dialect to explain the significance of the human bones that were buried to give directions—crisscrossed femurs and so on. Also, the Japanese placed booby traps to foil amateurs—everything from sand traps to one-thousand-pound bombs. What logical question should be answered at this point?"

Tomi thought a moment. "I don't know, but it's hard to believe the Japanese who buried that much gold would simply shrug their shoulders and let two subordinates and a Filipino politician recover the treasure."

"Exactly. For twenty years Jiga and Balmores showed Marcos only enough maps to ensure his cooperation. For their part, they lived ordinary lives in Manila. They were logically following the orders of the wartime hierarchy that led to Emperor Hirohito, the man for whom the Golden Lily was originally collected."

Tomi furrowed her brows. "And who was to get the split after Hirohito's Gold was recovered? How was it to be divided?"

Rodriguez said, "Good questions, Tomi. For the moment it's best to stick to the chronology. The story is complicated enough without jumping back and forth. You need to hear the story of Fukumitsu. Then the whole truth about Jiga and Balmores. And finally about Marcos's efforts to wash incredible amounts of gold through the international market. You'll learn about *Shi Pa* when we get to Executive X."

"*Shi Pa* being?"

"The gentlemen who allegedly split the gold."

"Including Emperor Hirohito?"

Rodriguez said nothing.

"Kip?"

"We think most likely," Smith said.

7

Smith decided on some breakfast while he waited for the Praise Jesus Now crew to begin preparing for the construction of the PJN revival stage. The Filipinos did not have specific foods for different meals in the manner of bacon and eggs or cereal for breakfast, a sandwich for lunch, and meat and potatoes for supper. For them it was maybe garlic-fried rice and an egg for breakfast, but ordinarily they ate the same foods any time of day.

Smith headed for his favorite *carenderia* to have a San Miguel and a bowl of *pochero*, hearty soup made from *carabao* hocks. There he saw a familiar face sitting alone with a San Miguel looking out at a *banka* gliding into the mouth of the Guimaron River.

Smith circled behind Roddy Baker and studied the offerings of the day, taking the lids off the aluminum pots to have a look inside. The rice noodles looked good. He studied the *pochero*, which looked long on cabbage and water and short on *carabao* hock. The *pancit*, a kind of noodle, was long on cabbage but it contained bits of *manok* and *baboy*.

"Some *pancit* and rice please, and a San Miguel." Smith watched her scoop some *pancit* and a mound of rice onto a plastic plate. He took his plate and cold bottle of beer and without saying anything plopped down at the table with Baker.

"Yo, Roddy," he said, grinning.

Roddy Baker blinked, then looked quickly left and right.

"It's cool. I'm alone," Smith said.

Baker took a quick, nervous swig of beer. He said, "Kip Fucking Smith! I haven't seen you for years. What in the hell are you doing here? Practicing bird calls?"

Smith sampled some of the *pancit*. It was good, but Smith found it hard to adjust to the Filipino custom of eating the food at room temperature. Of course, a *carenderia* was food for the people. The proprietor cooked big pots of food, put a lid on them, and set them on display. If a Westerner wanted hot food, he had to eat at the right time. "Shooting pictures of wild pigs," he said, his mouth full of *pancit*.

"What?"

"For the *National Geographic*."

Baker looked dubious. "Where is that?"

"The *National Geographic*? Their editorial offices are back in the U.S."

"Jesus! Moron! Not the location of the magazine. Where are you going to shoot wild pigs?"

Smith gestured with his head. "Up there."

Baker took another swig. "Where up there?"

"In the Patag."

"Bullshit. There's NPA up there. You want to have a Nikon shoved up your ass?"

"Had to split half my *National Geographic* fee with a gentleman named Jaime Pineda, but I'll still do okay. And how about you? What have you been doing lately?"

Baker scowled. "My brother and I sell sailboats out of Fort Myers, Florida. A sailboat with a weighted keel is getting so pricey they're hard to move. Outriggers are far cheaper to build than weighted keels. *Bankas* are beautiful. And they go fast. Just right for the Gulf of Mexico. Our idea is to have them built for us here in the Philippines and import them to the United States."

"Their ancestors settled the Pacific islands in *bankas*. The locals call them pumpboats, did you know that?"

"Pumpboats?"

"The more prosperous fishermen add a motor to their *bankas* to get them home if there's no wind. They ordinarily use the same Briggs and Stratton two-cycle gasoline engine that's used to pump water from one rice paddy to the next, hence the term *pumpboat*. Each village has developed identifying quirks on a single basic model. At sea they can tell if a *banka* in the distance belongs to a friend or acquaintance or is from another town."

"I've pretty much got my heart set on a model designed by a man in Bacolod, but I thought I'd check out the Cadiz boats just in case."

"I see," Smith said. "And which do you like best?"

Baker said, "They're both colorful, but I like the bow of the Bacolod model best. It's slightly more curved. Elegant is the word."

Smith took a hit of San Miguel and gestured with the bottle to the sea off the mouth of the Guimaron. "Who do you suppose owns that fancy yacht out there?"

Baker looked out at the *Giri*. "Good question. I've been wondering that myself."

"They tell me the *Giri* belongs to a *yakuza oyabun* named Kawana Katchan. Any truth to that, do you suppose?"

"That's what I heard, too."

Smith lowered his voice to a barely audible murmur. "Ding and I heard rumors that Prime Minister Nakamura was killed because he was having second thoughts about keeping the lid on the M Fund secret. Then the M Fund managers send Chiba Wataru to Belize to try to buy a copy of van der Elst's journal. It was you who sent him to me, Roddy. And who should be eavesdropping on us yesterday in Bacolod? Why, the very same Chiba and his *yakuza* sidekick."

"Oh?"

"I wouldn't sell it to them so they're gleaning what they can by taping us with a parabolic, after which God knows what they've been told to do. And here you are, too. Small world. You were always a desk man, Roddy. You should have stayed behind the desk. Dumb letting me run into you like this. An elementary blunder."

Baker cleared his throat.

"I've always heard that the M Fund managers had Kodama's archer maps. Now Kawana obviously has them. How did he get them? As payment for assassinating Nakamura?" Smith waited for an answer. "You know, Roddy, I've known you for twenty years, during which time you constantly bitched about the secret of Hirohito's Gold and the M Fund. Not good to keep it under our institutional Stetson, you said. You were convincing as hell, I admit. I believed you. I thought you were a friend. But that was all a ruse, wasn't it? You're part of the horseshit loop. The only question is for whom are you working. The Company or the M Fund managers. Or is it both?"

Looking embarrassed, Baker checked his watch. "I've got a flight out of here in three hours. Back to Maryland for me. This heat! And the bugs!"

8

It was closing in on 10:30 P.M. in Manila, and Roberta Fallon, already in the bathroom for more than two hours, showed no signs of emerging. The Rev. Robin Fallon and his guest had long since become bored with small talk, and resentment at the wait was eroding the high spirits on which the two men had begun the evening. A television set with the sound or mute was showing CNN International.

Fallon and Maj. Gen. Jose Maria Martinez, dressed in dark slacks and white *barong Tagalogs*—loose-fitting Filipino shirts—sat on the couch, inwardly furious at the narcissistic Roberta, but outwardly patient. Martinez, the silver-haired superintendent of the Philippine Military Academy, wondered about the discipline of American wives, but said nothing. If American women were all like Roberta Fallon, Martinez was thankful he was Filipino. Of course he could go for an American mistress. He liked that white skin and those big rumps and bumpers.

Fallon glanced at his wristwatch and bunched his face in dismay. "You know women," he said.

Martinez chuckled. Yes, the patronizing chuckle said, Martinez knew women.

"Goodness. Goodness," Fallon said. This, too, was directed at the absurd length of time they had been kept waiting, but judging by Fallon's strangely hypnotic eyes, you'd have thought he was Christ, willing to wait forever on a woman, if necessary, without complaining or condemning. He watched a woman giving a report of the weather in Asia. Her mouth moved soundlessly. Up popped a clip of a sandstorm in China.

Martinez broke a silence that had grown uncomfortable. "I understand you and Jim Bakker were longtime friends, Reverend. Poor man."

Fallon thought Bakker was a posturing little moron who looked like an overweight chipmunk. He said, "Oh, my goodness sakes, yes, Jim Bakker and me go way back. Heavens! Nobody was more surprised at what happened to Jim and Tammy than Roberta and me." Fallon looked bitter. "It was the dang liberals and kikes that did it, you know. They run the television business, and the newspapers aren't much better. They wanted to show the evangelical movement who was boss, a straight railroad all the way. The gol' darndest hatchet job you ever saw."

Martinez, wondering if Fallon would say "manure" if his mouth was full of it, said, "A railroad job is the picture I got from reading the newspapers, but of course I didn't know the details."

Fallon pumped his head up and down in agreement. "They was good people, the Bakkers, but they didn't know padoodle about keeping books, not padoodle. Of course when you're Jim and Tammy Bakker, it doesn't take a whole lot to nail you. You know, they say you can't squeeze blood out of a turnip. Well, I'm not sure that's true in the case of the IRS. If they want to provide an example bad enough, they can just about pin anybody they choose. Doesn't matter a padoodle who you are. And the media people just flat made stuff up about the Bakkers, printed fiction as fact, and nobody could call them on it. My gracious heavens! But old Jim has made a remarkable comeback, you have to give it to him."

Fallon looked out on the night-lights of Manila and the traffic on Roxas Boulevard, which flanked Manila Bay. At times like this he wished he were anything but a reverend. The devil ran amok in Manila, he had been told. He wondered what it must be like to take a walk out there where the music thumped and naked little Filipinas danced on bar tops. He'd heard all kinds of stories. He could not go for a stroll in the wild streets. He was forever stuck in sterile hotels. All he could do was dream about those beautiful, lithe, hard bodies and lope his goat in the toilet.

The Rev. Robin Fallon's part in the plan conceived by Martinez was for him to stage an evangelical revival on the island of Negros. The inevitable catch was that news of the arrival would precede the approach to the rebel leader Jaime Pineda. The generals reasoned that if Pineda thought they were working together, he'd jerk them around forever.

An evangelical revival took weeks of planning to stage properly, and after the arrangements were locked into place it was impossible to withdraw gracefully. A cancellation would be terrible PR. Fallon would risk all manner of callous allegations when he returned to the United States. Given his druthers, Fallon would have left the worthless Filipino pesos to the sweating Jimmy Swaggart as a form of charity, but this was different. This time he was going for a nick of the alchemist archers. The choice was clear. No guts, no glory. As Robin had told Roberta, "Sometimes you just have to suck up your collection plates and go for it." And he did. He'd scheduled an evangelical revival on Negros, overhead be damned.

"Surely, we can come to some kind of arrangement with him," Fallon said.

"Him?" Martinez said.

"Pineda. My heavens, there should be plenty of gold for everyone."

"You know about the NPA," Martinez said. "But I agree, Reverend, there must be a way."

"Lordy," Fallon said. Fallon was annoyed by the prospect of

holding a revival that lost money. He wondered if there were enough pesos on the island of Negros to pay for the ghastly expense of setting up his evangelical big top.

The two men fell silent again. On CNN, a South African springbok raced over the goal of the New Zealand All Black. In proper rugby fashion, he touched the ball on the pitch.

Suddenly, Roberta Fallon made her entrance from the bathroom. "Well, are you handsome gentlemen ready?"

Roberta had never had an opportunity to travel before PJN, although she had always wanted to. Unfortunately, she knew almost nothing about tropical humidity. She had arranged her red hair in a retro version of the 1960s beehive, and she wore a plum-colored knit dress molded to her breasts and rump—guaranteed to entomb her in the heat on the way to the air-conditioned restaurant.

Seeing the expressions on the two men's faces—even the Reverend Fallon looked mortal in his distress—she looked surprised. She blinked. Her mouth opened slightly. She said, "Oh, I'm so sorry. Did I keep you boys waiting?"

"Oh, heavens, no," Fallon said. He rose, as did the general.

Martinez sneezed softly.

Robin said, "My heavens! God bless, Brother Martinez."

"We're not late, are we? I bet our host won't be on time either." Robin stuck out her foot. "I bought a new pair of shoes for tonight." She turned her foot. "They've got a little heel." She looked suddenly alarmed. "You don't think they're too much, do you?"

"They're just fine, darling," Robin said.

Roberta calmed. She had wanted to meet Imelda Marcos, who was rich and famous and had a large collection of shoes, but Martinez said Ms. Marcos was traveling in Europe. Instead, Martinez arranged for Roberta to meet a Filipina actress whom Roberta had never heard of. Still, show business was show business, whether televangelism or the movies, and Roberta allowed as how it might be fun to meet a colleague. She checked out her feet in the full-length mirror. "Black pumps are always a safe choice. Maybe she'll like to talk shoes. You think she will, General Martinez? You men are always business, business, business. We women like to talk shoes."

Glancing at the television set, she saw that former President Bill Clinton was being interviewed. She looked offended. "Him again. Carrying on in the Oval Office with that fat girl! With her . . . Using her . . . saying *that* wasn't sex! *Ugh!*" She made a face. "And then the rape charge! Biting that woman on the mouth. 'Better get some ice on that lip.' Putting on his sunglasses, Mr. Cool. Who could make up a story like that? Does anybody truly think she was lying? My word!"

9

The next morning, Tomi Kobayashi, bearing another request for the mayor's office, drove back to Cadiz to meet Kip Smith. Tomi passed Filipino workers who were busy hammering and pounding on the platform where the Rev. Robin Fallon would hold his revival. She inquired at the mayor's office, where she found Elsa Sablada, the mayor's assistant, whom she'd met the previous day.

"You're the reporter from the *Los Angles Times.*"

"Tomi Kobayashi. Yes."

"How can I help you today?"

"I was wondering if it would be possible to get somebody to drive me to the Patag to see what Pulak Pulakan looks like. The Patag is behind Silay, which I passed on my way here from Bacolod, is that right?"

Sablada nodded. "After the Reverend Fallon's revival here Sunday morning, PJN will take people to Pulak Pulakan to light candles for Lieutenant John W. Dolan, who was killed there in 1945. The ceremony will be televised back to the United States by satellite. The Reverend Fallon received a donation from Dolan's granddaughter."

"I know. I was just hoping to see the hill in advance for some details for my story. All the people in the U.S. will see is Robin Fallon pacing back and forth in front of worshipful Christians."

Sablada looked sympathetic but shook her head "no." "I'm sorry, but that would require permission of the NPA, which would have to be negotiated through go-betweens. It might be done, but it would take time. We would have to arrange the necessary contacts."

"I take it NPA wallets would have to be fattened."

Sablada smiled. "Well, there's that. Even if we got that far, you would risk being kidnapped, depending on the whim of Jaime Pineda."

"Shoot!"

Sablada said, "You missed the season's big media event in Cadiz yesterday. After you left, a Filipino senator held a press conference aboard the dredge that was cleaning the river channel."

"Oh, well. I'll take a look around and get some details for my revival story."

"If I can be of any help, just let me know."

Tomi took a stroll near the string of shacks along the riverbank where the fishermen moored their elegant pumpboats. She walked to an interesting mound running back thirty or forty feet from the water's edge. The mound looked somehow artificial, and she realized it was an immense accumulation of packed dirt and garbage.

She walked to the top of the mound. On the other side, Kip Smith, with his back to her, stood calmly relieving himself while he whistled "The Battle Hymn of the Republic." He was wearing a multipocketed photographer's vest from which dangled cameras, lenses, gadgets, and high-tech doodads.

Tomi started to turn away but thought, *To hell with it.* There was something about Smith urinating while whistling that she found amusing. She imagined that the slight hollow Smith had found was a favorite peeing spot for the fishermen and wondered if Smith might not be standing on a carpet of urine crystals.

Suppressing a giggle, she called, "Hey, down there. Whistling man."

Still peeing, Smith jumped, startled, and glanced back over his shoulder. Seeing her, he grinned broadly. "Oops!"

"Caught in the act."

"I was examining a hybrid cucumber. A handsome specimen, raised by hand. Would you like to see it?"

"I believe I'll pass, thanks."

He looked disappointed. "Figgers." He stuffed his organ into his pants and zipped his fly.

Tomi said, "Miho said I should hang out in the faculty club at Washington State if I wanted to meet an interesting man."

"And?"

"She was probably right." Tomi looked around. "Can you imagine being a woman and having to find a place to relieve yourself?"

Smith started up the gentle slope of the mound. He did a crazed bird laugh. *He-ha-ha-ha-haa-haaah-haaah.*

"And what kind of bird was that?"

"A laughing gull. The herring gull has a good laugh, too." *Yuk-yuk-yuk-yuk-yuk-yuckle-yuckle.*

Startled, she looked around.

He laughed, "Don't worry, nobody is paying any attention to us."

"You want to tell me what you are supposed to be doing? Shooting fruit bats?"

"Wild pigs. I've been using my *Time* magazine card. This revival may be more fun than shooting the bushtit—*tsit-tsit-tsit-tsit-clenk-clenk.*" Smith looked skyward. "Maybe I'll shoot a prize-winner with the sunrise reflecting off the Reverend Fallon's irises and mountains in the rear. Did you ask the lady with the plump butt about the yacht?" He swung a Nikon off his shoulder and dropped to one knee to focus on the *Giri.* Smith clipped a larger lens onto his camera. "This little town is like Tombstone on the eve of the OK Corral." He snapped off three quick shots.

"The yacht being loaded with, what was that, 'spring' for the water trade?"

Smith adjusted the lens speed. "Unlikely he's got Japayuki aboard. Uzi-DANs most likely, or Smith & Wasaks."

"Smith & Wessons?"

He snapped two more frames and without looking up, said, "No, I mean just what I said, Smith & Wasaks. Say, you don't mind giving me a lift back to Bacolod, do you?"

"Sure," she said. "How did you get out here?"

"Took a jeepney. Decided to leave my Land Cruiser at the hotel today."

"Really?"

"What's good enough for the Filipinos is good enough for me. Living in the United States is like a rat living in a stainless-steel cage. No texture. No natural smells. People sweat and let secret farts on jeepneys."

As they were walking back to Tomi Kobayashi's rented Nissan, Tomi was unaware that Smith—having for the moment forgotten about the dubious pleasures of living in the Third World—was covertly giving her rear end an admiring scope.

She said, "Well, what do you think?"

"Nice. I like that side-to-side action."

"I'm thrilled that you approve," she said dryly.

Smith glanced out at the yacht. "I think we've got it right. They're gathering here to have a go at the archers."

They were at her car. Tomi began unlocking the doors. "You want to drive? This traffic and the potholes on this road drive me crazy."

Smith snagged the keys.

Tomi slipped into the passenger's seat. "You want to tell me more about Chiba Wataru? Surely, there's nobody listening in out here."

Smith frowned. "He's working for the managers of the M Fund. Beyond that it gets complicated." He glanced at his wristwatch. "We better get going if we're going to get to Winston Monzon's in time for our next briefing." He opened the door for Tomi and strolled around to the driver's side.

Smith put the Nissan into gear and headed back toward Bacolod, handling the pot holes and hazards with aplomb, hand ready for the horn, foot prepared for the brakes. The first corner out of town he braked hard for a skinny yellowish brown dog that had strayed onto the road. The dog, frozen with fear, looked up, wild-eyed and confused.

10

By Western resort standards, Winston Monzon's wasn't much of a beach resort—a thatched bamboo bar and kitchen on stilts stuck out over the mud. The beach itself was a dirty gray color. And such modest tide as there was at five degrees north longitude was out, leaving a vast expanse of mud spread before them. A sprinkling of women and young girls, thigh-deep in muck, searched for clams with their toes.

They could see graceful *bankas* out at sea sailing in a fitful breeze.

As usual, Kip Smith and Rodriguez drank stubbies of San Miguel. Their snack this time was Spanish peanuts cooked in garlic oil.

When the tape recorder was set and Tomi's notebook ready, Rodriguez took a hit of San Miguel and said, "The estimable Minoru Fukumitsu made his dubious contribution to the story while the Korean War was in full swing. His 'investigation' is the key to the ruse of Yamashita's Gold that's held over the years. I'm putting his surname last because he was an American."

Rodriguez swabbed the sweat from his forehead with the back of his arm. "Fukumitsu was a war crimes investigator. He arrived in Manila in 1953 to negotiate the release of two hundred Japanese prisoners of war still in Filipino stockades facing death sentences or life imprisonment. Fukumitsu was charged with talking to the prisoners and to people who had interrogated them. Tell me, Tomi, what agency of the United States government had a logical, abiding reason for collecting all that data?"

"The Central Intelligence Agency."

"Which was formed in 1947. Information about the activities of the Japanese prisoners during the war was invaluable in establishing networks for collecting intelligence about China. I submit that the man who interrogated those prisoners either worked for or with the CIA. If he didn't, the people in Langley were derelict in their duty. Agree or disagree, Tomi?"

Tomi thought a moment. "I agree. At least I think I do."

Rodriguez said, "It's imperative to understand the spirit of the times in which MacArthur made his deal with Hirohito, and what was happening in the United States six years later when Fukumitsu was sent to Manila."

"Given the war and the Red Scare, I agree that in 1953 it was easy to justify the continuing operation, if there was one."

Smith interrupted. "If anybody had objected to the operation on ethical grounds, he would have been branded a Communist sympathizer, if not a Communist, and his career destroyed. Simple as that. This isn't the only example of the lengths Cold Warriors were willing to go to fight the good fight. Also keep in mind, Tomi, that the longer a covert operation is allowed to continue, the more difficult it is to halt."

Yoshida slapped a bug on his neck. "They call this a 'beach resort'? This is no beach. This is a mud flat. Yuck! And to call it a 'resort'? Spare me. And the heat! Too much."

Chiba smiled. "Patience, Yoshida-san."

"Sir, I . . ." Yoshida fell silent.

"You have something on your mind, Yoshida-san. Go ahead."

"We listen to their scurrilous story, which is so filled with inaccuracies that it's obscene—"

Chiba interrupted. "Some inaccuracies, Yoshida-san."

Yoshida opened his mouth to speak but closed it, saying nothing.

Chiba said, "A lot of this is hard to accept, I agree. Is it possible, do you think, that the Central Intelligence Agency contrived to manipulate Japanese politics at the end of the war? They had motive, as these two are pointing out. They hated the Communists and feared Communist manipulation of the new Japanese democracy."

"I think, sir . . ." Yoshida fell silent.

"You think what, Yoshida-san? Speak up."

"I think the 'facts' are irrelevant. We're here to prevent the shame and humiliation of the royal family and the Japanese people."

"Okay now, here we get into the first reports of gold uncovered in the Philippines that pass our minimum standards of credibility. The amounts sound impossible. Some of them maybe are. We're still checking them out and so should you. I hesitate to give them to you because they're red meat for skeptics. Never mind that the SS plunder in Europe was known to be in the billions. Our critics will seize on the more bizarre assertions of gold and yell, 'Aha, see! I told you! Couldn't be! Impossible! This is nonsense!' If a single account turns out to be hyperbole or worse, they'll claim our entire story is bogus. To even mention the numbers is like giving the naysayers a megaphone and saying, 'Here, ridicule us. Say our entire story is a fantasy.' Prove it, prove it, prove it. Well, I'm going to give them to you anyway."

"With that caveat."

"Exactly. That there was a Golden Lily seems certain. We have no reports of Japanese booty being recovered in Japan, or for that matter in any other Asian country that they occupied. Only the Philippines. Even our most vehement critics might be forced to concede that where there is glitter, there conceivably could be gold. That's why, for the sake of argument, we're taking Imelda Marcos at her word. Her husband *could* have recovered gold stolen by the Japanese. How much there was is another matter, and we won't get into the truly bizarre amounts until my third or fourth briefing. Listen, shake your head if you will, but please bear with us."

"I'll be patient," Tomi said.

Rodriguez paused, thinking about his story. Then he said, "Earlier some of the prisoners had told interrogators about buried treasure they were calling Yamashita's Gold. Fukumitsu worked out a deal with President Quirino so he could get to the bottom of the stories. Check back through your notes. Who do you suppose, besides Marcos or Tony Quirino, might have been assigned to accompany Fukumitsu on that detail?"

"Mmmmm." Kobayashi flipped back through her notepad. "Venancio Duque?"

"That's right. The man who prevented the guerrillas from executing Ferdinand as a spy. Fukumitsu and Duque said they interviewed more than three hundred people. They paid a visit to the National Archives in Washington. The Japanese government was said to have given them secret documents. And while they were in Tokyo, they interviewed former members of Yamashita's staff."

"My grandfather's staff?"

"Better to have the 'rumors' identified with him than risk untoward attention being drawn toward Kodama and the deal between MacArthur and the emperor."

"I see," Tomi said.

"Of course, General Yamashita did not toss the loot into hastily dug foxholes during his retreat from Baguio to Kiangan Pocket. In fact, the Japanese buried most of Hirohito's Gold in Manila and just outside Manila and in sealed-up caves and tunnels in the mountains and holes bored in coral reefs. Fukumitsu and Duque came up with an alleged map and set off to find out whether the rumors were fact or fiction. Where do you suppose they dug?"

"Not any place close to Manila, I bet."

"There you go. Assisted by Venancio Duque, Fukumitsu supervised several excavations along the route between Baguio and Kiangan Pocket in Central Luzon and found nothing." Rodriguez grinned. "After a definitive investigation of the matter, Fukumitsu said, he had concluded that Yamashita's Gold was rumor. Thus was born the official story of Yamashita's Gold, the treasure that officially did not exist. It was a myth. After conducting his 'investigation,' Fukumitsu quit his job as a war crimes investigator and emigrated to Japan, where he became a successful businessman."

"With Kodama's able assistance."

"Makes sense that he went to work for Kodama, yes. The truth is, we don't know if Kodama was his patron. We only have circumstance to go on."

Staring into the eyepiece of the camera, Yoshida said, "What about this Fukumitsu, sir? Was there such a person?"

"I believe so, yes."

"An American."

"As I understand it. An American of Japanese ancestry."

"Working for the Central Intelligence Agency?"

"At that point, most likely," Chiba said.

"And working for Kodama-san, as well?"

Chiba nodded. "It appears so. Emperor Hirohito, too, if this story is to be believed."

"So the American and the Filipino are cleverly mixing in a tidbit of truth here and there amid their lies about Kodama Yoshio and the emperor."

"That's one way of looking at it." Chiba, deep in thought, began rocking gently back and forth.

Yoshida spit angrily. "They see the Kampei-tai under every rock. The greedy, self-serving emperor manipulating everything from afar. Pah!" He spit again.

Rodriguez said, "Fukumitsu's story admits of only two logical possibilities, Tomi. One, Fukumitsu and Marcos's friends duped the gullible and incompetent Central Intelligence Agency and the State Department. CIA operatives were ignorant of the gold and how it might have got there. Do you believe that?"

She hesitated.

"Could have happened. Or two, the Americans carried out their anti-Communist policy in Asia indifferent to the consequences to innocent people. They weren't about to acknowledge the existence of either Hirohito's Gold or the M Fund. The U.S. doesn't want to admit that the ruling party in Japan was essentially its creation." He stopped.

Tomi waited.

Rodriguez said, "There are no other conclusions to be drawn. If you can come up with one, Tomi, please, I'm willing to listen. They were either fools or spies and diplomats doing their Cold War duty. Not much in the way of tweenies that I can deduce. The red herring established by Fukumitsu was essential to the CIA's gambit."

Smith removed the insulating wrap from his empty beer bottle. He raised his arm and signaled to the waitress, "*Duha*, Di. You want another, Tomi?"

Tomi said, "Sure, why not?"

"Make that *tulo*, Di." Then, softly, Smith added, "Conscience is what separates us from dogs."

Yoshida frowned. "So we listen to whatever Smith and Rodriguez tell the woman, then eliminate all three. Surely they recorded their story elsewhere before talking to the woman—in a safe deposit box or somewhere. An elementary fail-safe. What is the point in our listening to all this maligning of Emperor Hirohito? I don't understand."

Chiba thought about that for a moment. "What you say is true, Yoshida-san. It's entirely logical that they have it recorded elsewhere. That's precisely why we're hearing them out."

"Sir?"

"If we know in some detail what the Filipinos have found out and what the van der Elst journal contains, we can better prepare to deal with the story if it pops up elsewhere. If we're to protect the emperor's reputation, we need to know what their charges are likely to be."

Rodriguez took a swig of San Miguel. "After Ferdinand Marcos was elected president of the Philippines in 1965, there were repeated rumors in the gold markets in Hong Kong, Sydney, and London of clandestine sales of gold from the Philippines. There were stories of ten metric tons in a single transaction, more than the known gold reserves of the Filipino government. In London, these were known as Marcos's 'Black Eagle' deals, the term *Black Eagle* referring to two-point-five billion dollars in gold and currency that vanished from the Reichbank in Berlin just before the end of World War II. By 1968, Marcos was reported to be the richest man in Asia.

"In 1971, a Filipino named Rogelio Roxas somehow came by a map that he said showed a treasure site. He said he took a metal detector to an abandoned shaft of the Benguet gold mines near Baguio and checked it out inch by inch. After seven months of effort, he and some friends reached a cave littered with skeletons and a single crate containing a twenty-eight-inch-tall golden Buddha that weighed two thousand pounds, plus eighteen gold bars measuring one inch high, two inches wide, and three inches long. Roxas said he couldn't explore the site any further because the old mine started caving in."

Tomi sat back. "Whoops, what happened?"

Rodriguez grinned. "Others who had access to the map later said Roxas had found the Buddha, yes, but not at Benguet. He found it buried under a flagpole in the quadrangle of a former Japanese military compound, a site clearly marked on the map. Roxas was swamped with offers to buy the Buddha, including one by Ferdinand Marcos's mother, Josepha. He refused to sell. At two A.M. one morning, Marcos's brother-in-law, Marcelino Barba, accompanied by two soldiers and bearing a warrant from Josepha's brother-in-law, Judge Pio Marcos, confiscated the Buddha."

"Wait, wait, wait. What on earth was Roxas doing with a two-thousand-pound gold anything in his home?"

Rodriguez shrugged. "Good question. After two weeks of controversy following Marcelino Barba's confiscation of the golden Buddha, a judge in Baguio ordered the military to turn over the statue. Ten days later Barba produced a brass statue. Marcos allegedly kept the brass Buddha in his study in Malacanang Palace, evidence for his critics, 'See here, Roxas was a liar. It was a brass Buddha, not a gold one.' "

Tomi shook her head.

Rodriguez said, "In May 1971, the Philippine Senate opened an investigation of the Buddha affair, infuriating Marcos, who called it politically motivated. Finally, in August, Roxas decided to tell his story on television. He was about to step before the cameras at a political rally at Plaza Miranda in Manila when Marcos agents attacked the gathering with bombs and hand grenades, killing nine and injuring ninety-six, including eight candidates for the Philippine Senate."

Tomi, scribbling a note, shook her head.

Rodriguez said, "On September 17, 1972, President Marcos, citing the continued threat of Communist rebels, declared martial law in the Philippines. The next month, Kodama arranged his famous treaty between the *yakuza* gangs run by Inagawa Kakuji and Takao Kazuo, earning *giri* from both sides. Both Inagawa-kai and Yamagumi-guchi controlled Manila's Ermita sex district for several years, running sex clubs, massage parlors, bars, and travel agencies. In December, Kodama ceded Ermita to his young protégé Kawana Katchan, who turned Manila into a world-class whorehouse, competing with Bangkok for sex tourists in Asia. The next year, Marcos awarded all rights to explore coral reefs in the Philippines to Kodama's friend and confidant, Machii Hisayuki, a Korean-born Japanese also known as the Ginza Tiger. Then came an, uh, snag."

Tomi raised an eyebrow. "A snag?"

"On February 4, 1974, the president of the Lockheed Aircraft Corporation appeared before a committee of the U.S. Senate and revealed a system of payoffs and bribes that American corporations paid to do business in Japan."

Yoshida said, "Kodama was a genius. A genius! Nobody but he could have negotiated the treaty between Inagawa-kai and Yamagumi-guchi. His mistake in the Lockheed scandal was getting involved with Americans."

"It appears that way," Chiba said.

"Accepting a bribe was nothing, the way business is done. And although the Americans would deny it, I bet plenty of it takes place in the United States. They might call it by another name, but it's still bribery. The tragedy was that Kodama embarrassed himself by allowing the bribery to become public. A bribe kept secret is no bribe at all. Worse, he allowed himself to be embarrassed by American idiots."

"Easy for conniving fools to make him out to be an evil genius," Chiba said.

Yoshida nodded vigorously. "The way I see it."

Chiba ran the palm of his hand down his jaw. "I take it you don't think his wartime activities in any way involved the royal family."

Yoshida straightened. "If Kodama Yoshio did wartime errands for the royal family, it was an act of patriotic duty. The facts are clear on the issue of the war. Emperor Hirohito was deceived. To suggest otherwise is a treacherous, treasonous lie."

Rodriguez said, "Immediately after the Lockheed scandal embarrassed Kodama, the ambitious Marcos terminated parity rights in the Philippines so that Filipino nationals would be required to own sixty percent of Filipino corporations. If we're to believe Imelda, he used cronies to secretly buy controlling interest in the most powerful and profitable Filipino corporations. The allegations multiply. By 1978 he was said to have a personal fortune of five billion dollars. Marcos allegedly controlled a tobacco monopoly in the Philippines. He allegedly received a cut from import licenses. He was supposed to have confiscated land from hill tribes and resold it to multinational corporations. He is asserted to have stolen money from the Philippine national treasury, and diverted loans to the Philippines from the International Monetary Fund, and money paid by the United States for its leases of land occupied by the navy at Subic Bay and the air force at Clark Air Force Base. It must be said that the Marcoses have consistently denied all these charges and have never been found guilty in a court of law."

Rodriguez slapped his belly. "So maybe their fortune did come from Japanese gold, or most of it. That there was a Golden Lily, we have no doubt. We think at least some of it was buried in the Philippines. Imelda later said it was. We think she was probably right. She said her husband used it to secretly buy shares of Filipino corporations. We have no idea about that."

Smith said, "Like I said before, we don't have a dog in that fight."

Watching Yoshida at his labors, Chiba said, "Tell me, Yoshida-san, what do you make of Ferdinand Marcos?"

"These people are right about one thing. Marcos was a liar of epic

proportions. Everybody knows that. Look at what he did to his own people. Stealing from them. Taking their property. Shame on the Americans for giving him refuge."

Rodriguez said, "The world's supply of legitimate gold, or white gold, in the 1970s was about fifteen hundred pounds a year and was controlled by a London cartel of dealers with some competition from Switzerland and the United States. The London Five as they were called, included Samuel Montagu, Sharps Pixley, Moccata and Goldsmid, Rothschild's, and Johnson Matthey.

"The Philippines officially then mined less than two hundred tons of gold a year, two-thirds of this going abroad in unrefined copper ore. The gold refined from this copper, sold back to the Philippine Central Bank on paper, remained physically in the gold pools of London, Zurich, New York, or Tokyo. Marcos's front men allegedly bought Benguet Consolidated gold mines, but Benguet's known reserves were too small to fence the Kampei-tai gold. Also, metallurgists were able to trace the origins of gold, a form of 'fingerprint.' Is a given tranch of gold white, or legitimate? Or is it black gold, that is, stolen or otherwise illegitimate? Big problem."

"So one would think."

Smith said, "Here is where we get into the heart of Robert Curtis's story. We haven't talked to him personally. We have gleaned all this from secondary sources that have long been available to any curious and determined reader. In the main, we believe him. We think his story is the best direct evidence we have that Mrs. Marcos's 1998 claims are true."

Rodriguez said, "With that caveat, I'll continue. Ferdinand Marcos later said he met Robert Curtis through the president of Costa Rica when both were in Cancun at a conference for developing nations. The undocumented story is that Curtis, a former member of the 82nd Airborne, worked in banking and for Kaiser Aluminum. He dropped all that when he discovered an outcropping of platinum and turned his attention entirely to metallurgy and treasure hunting. He eventually owned four plants to process the ore of his various finds. And he was said to have perfected two wonderful systems, one that would increase the percentage of gold refined from copper ore, and the second enabling him to melt 'black' gold and recast it in bars containing any known metallurgical fingerprint of 'white' or legitimate gold."

"Ah, technology rears its benevolent head."

Rodriguez said, "Curtis allegedly had one personality tic that was unknown to Marcos. Over his years of chasing treasure, Curtis claims, he became paranoid about the possibility of betrayal. By his own account, he had turned into a tape recorder nut, taping all his telephone conversations. When he traveled, he took a matchbox recorder with him, secretly taping all face-to-face meetings. Or maybe he didn't. Maybe it was a con man's ruse." Rodriguez paused, looking amused. "Now we get into some fun stuff. Although Ferdinand Marcos had access to the maps of the treasure given to him by Jiga and Balmores, he had read about a Swedish psychic, Olof Jonsson, living in Chicago, who had allegedly found several treasures. There were popular books written about his exploits."

Tomi looked astonished. "The president of the Philippines consulting a psychic?"

"Marcos allegedly invited Jonsson to Malacanang Palace, after which Jonsson introduced Marcos to a Wisconsin businessman. From Malacanang, the businessman called Curtis in Reno, Nevada. Then he made several trips to Nevada, telling Curtis that Marcos had already retrieved several hundred million dollars worth of bullion and other treasures including Rogelo Roxas's golden Buddha. On behalf of Marcos, the businessman allegedly worked out a deal whereby Curtis would set up his gold laundering system in the Philippines under the ownership of Benguet

Consolidated, so that the treasure could be recast and sold as Philippines gold. Curtis would be a member of the secret Leber Group established to retrieve the treasure."

"Leber Group."

"*Rebel* spelled backwards. Marcos supposedly chose the code name Charlie for himself. If this is all true, Marcos's friend General Fabian Ver, code-named Jimmy, was in charge of operations. Curtis claims he was to have received up to two billion dollars."

"You say Robert Curtis kept immaculate records and taped his telephone calls?"

Rodriguez said, "That's what he later said. Much of this was published in the *Las Vegas Sun* in 1978. Nobody believed him. A teller of tall tales. Maybe he was lying. He allegedly taped everything, remember. And look at all that detail! What you think, Kip? Another round?"

"Sounds good to me. And some of those peanuts." Smith signalled to the waitress. "Di! Di!"

Yoshida said, "There's something here that I don't understand, sir."

"Go ahead."

"If Curtis's adventures in Manila with Marcos were reported in American newspapers in 1978, why didn't this blow up in our faces then?"

Chiba rolled his eyes. "Because it was reported in the Las Vegas Sun."

"So?"

Chiba said, "It wasn't reported by the New York Times or Washington Post."

Yoshida looked confused.

"Suppose a story like this had broken in a newspaper on Okinawa, Yoshida-san. Would we in Japan have believed it?"

Yoshida looked disbelieving. "On Okinawa?"

"How about Asahi Shimbum?"

"I would have believed it then. No question."

Chiba grinned. "There you go."

Rodriguez said, "Although Marcos was allegedly sitting on a fortune himself, he got Curtis to agree to pay the living expenses of both Jonsson and the Wisconsin businessman, in addition to the cost of moving Curtis's equipment to Manila from the United States. Curtis was to get the exclusive right to refine gold from the Philippines, both the Japanese gold and that mined at Benguet. In March 1975, Robert Curtis allegedly flew to Manila with Johnsson and the Wisconsin businessman to meet Marcos and his Leber colleagues. Incidentally, he claimed that at the time he was three hundred and seventy-five thousand dollars in debt to the John Birch Society."

"Taping his conversations as he went."

"So he alleges. Correct. But when Curtis arrived in Manila, he read in the newspapers that Marcos was negotiating with Johnson Matthey to build the refinery that had been promised to him. Ver told him not to worry, Johnson Matthey had bought Philippine gold for years; when its officers arrived in town saying they wanted to build a refinery in the Philippines, Marcos pretended to encourage them. That was all there was to it. He had no control over newspaper gossip."

Smith said, "Never let it be said that Ferdinand Marcos was a lousy host."

Rodriguez slapped his belly. "What a piece of work he was. Curtis's story is that he met with the rest of Leber Group, including General Ver and a Filipino colonel who was in charge of security for Imelda Marcos, plus one of Marcos's trusted gophers and Paul Jiga and Ben Balmores. Both Jiga and Balmores had stuck by their agreement to live modest lives. Jiga worked for the Philippine Refining Company that made toothpaste and shampoo. Balmores was retired."

"Are you going to tell me the real story of Jiga and Balmores?"

"Patience. Patience. What's real and not real is difficult to know. A guest at Malacanang Palace, Curtis claims that he was shown the treasure maps then taken to burial sites at Fort Bonifacio and Fort Santiago. He was taken to sites at Christ the King Church, at San Sebastian Church, at San Augustin Church, and in the old walled city of Intromuros. He was taken to a site near a railroad and to the estate of Don Paco Ortigas. And finally, he was taken to the barrio of Teresa, thirty miles from Manila.

"After he toured the burial sites, Marcos and Ver allegedly took him to Marcos's beach estate at Marviles, on the Bataan peninsula opposite Corregidor. At Marviles, Curtis claims he saw a room stacked with gold from floor to ceiling, perhaps as much as sixty million dollars worth, and Ver told him there were more rooms of gold. These ingots, with both Chinese and Japanese characters stamped on them, were cast in a variety of sizes and shapes characteristic of gold cast in Asia."

"Surely that can't be so."

Rodriguez shrugged. "Good story though, don't you think? Concrete. Lots of details. Specific places. Marcos allegedly showed him the golden Buddha he had stolen from Rogelo Roxas in 1971. After seeing the treasure, Curtis claimed that he and Marcos got down to business, with Marcos insisting that the paper trail had to be perfect so that the gold could be marketed 'white' in the gold pools of London and Zurich."

"Are you serious?"

Rodriguez said, "The Leber Group had several options for the recasting. They could cast some in the standard twelve-point-five kilo bars known on the world market as Good London Delivery. They could cast some in the book-shaped ingots marked AAA that were common in Australia. They could cast some in the Sumatra Lloyd ingots such as those that were taken to Australia from the Dutch East Indies in World War II. And they could cast some in the odd shapes found in New Guinea and isolated Australian mines.

"Having seen the gold, Curtis says, he agreed to dismantle his two furnaces and other equipment in Reno and, under cover of Benguet Consolidated, have it shipped to Manila. After consulting with Jiga and Balmores, it was agreed that the search would begin in three places: the property of Don Paco Ortegas, the village of Teresa, and the sunken cruiser *Nachii.* The very first would be the *Nachii.*"

11

The sun set at just about 6 A.M. as it did around the world that close to the equator. Kipling Smith, waiting for total darkness, killed two more hours drinking San Miguel and eating marinated pig's intestines in a diminutive bamboo bar frequented by Cadiz fishermen.

After that Smith went back to the dilapidated hotel room he had rented for the night and began assembling his gear: tanks, masks, flippers, electronic tail, plastic explosives, detonating remotes, Hinkley tape. He packed the equipment into a nylon bag, smiling to himself, the old vet was back in action. He got a kick out of shooting pictures of crocodiles and twenty-foot-long Anaconda snakes in Australia, but it was true, he had to admit—even better were the adrenaline rushes of danger he had known in his Company days.

He slung the gear into his rented Toyota and cruised the street on the ocean side of the peninsula. He parked on a side street just short of the fishing docks and got out, slinging the duffel bag over his shoulder. He walked to the seaward end of the line of colorful outriggered boats and found a private spot behind a shack that was locked for the night; there he removed the scuba gear from the duffel bag, undressed, and put his clothes in the bag that he hid by the base of the shack. He packed the electronic tail, the Hinkley tape, and the plastic explosives in the waterproof bag.

He stood momentarily naked with a warm breeze caressing his balls. Then he pulled on his swim trunks, donned his mask and oxygen tank and snapped a waterproof pouch around his waist. He kept his flippers in his hand because the tide was out, and he had to walk nearly thirty yards with warm, yucky mud oozing between his toes.

When he reached water deep enough for him to swim, he took a look at the lights of the *Giri*. He was ready. He took a deep breath to calm his nerves, turned onto his back, and began swimming at a leisurely pace. The water was warm, and the sky was clear, and the stars high above were beautiful.

After a couple of hundred yards, Smith rolled over for a check. He was nearing Kawana's yacht. He slipped under the surface and swam steadily toward the *Giri* for a few minutes, then resurfaced again.

He heard music coming from the boat. The sound drifted lazily across the warm water. Ah, party time. He was curious about the music, but he couldn't afford the exposure. He mentally adjusted his course and slipped quickly below again.

In a few minutes, he saw the shadow of the anchored boat looming ahead.

He angled deeper and came up directly under the hull that he followed to the bow, where he surfaced again. Above him, Englebert Humperdinck sang:

Cuando, cuando, cuannn-dddo.
Oh, my darling tell me when.

Then some men laughed and a girl giggled. Kawana was relaxed on the eve of action. Party time!

Party time was perfect for Smith's purpose. He had a job ahead of him, and he immediately set about his task. He hauled the pouch of gear to the surface and pulled the tab that inflated a flotation ring. The inflation apparatus was supposed to be soundless, but wasn't entirely. Smith was grateful for the music on deck.

He fastened the flotation ring to the hull with a suction cup anchor and retrieved the waterproof tailing device. He slipped on a pair of rubber gloves and slipped underwater again, heading for the stern.

He crawled under the screws and searched until he found just the right spot. The rear deck of the stern had an eight-inch overhang with storm lights at the corners. On deck, Kay Starr sang:

O-ho, the-uh, whe-heel of forr-hor-tune
Goesss spinninggg round.

Smith peeled back the Hinkley strip and carefully locked the tailer into place on the underside of the overhang next to the hull.

The rubber gloves had nothing to do with fingerprints. They were a precaution that had to be taken with work that involved Hinkley adhesive, so named for Warren Hinkley, the 3M research scientist who had developed it for the Company. Hinkley adhesive—super glue that fastened as well as screws, bolts, or rivets—worked in the air or underwater. If a person's skin came into contact with Hinkley's best, the epidermis came away the loser.

Smith knew Kawana wouldn't be taking Filipina sweeties on any gold run, and since Smith didn't mind wasting a few *yakuza* hoods, he had brought six charges of plastic explosives where one charge, correctly placed, would have sunk a boat far larger than this one.

The plastic charges—equipped with pull-tab Hinkley strips—were oval-shaped, scarcely thicker than a magazine, and streamlined on the edges so as not to produce any noticeable drag on the hull. Smith took his time fastening them in place on the deepest part of the hull. Using a one-sixteenth-inch-wide electrical version of Brother Hinkley's wonderful tape, Smith connected the charges into a single circuit that he fastened to the detonator, anchored beside the tailing device.

He surfaced.

Where are the clowns?
Bring in the clowns.

He dove again working quickly but carefully, thinking: *Down here, Judy, you've got a clown under the stern. A moron with Hinkley tape.*

Confident that everything was in place, he surfaced again and swam forward to retrieve the gear tethered to the underside of the bow.

A female began screaming directly above him.

He looked up to see the upper half of a nude Filipina hanging over the deck rail. Her eyes were closed tightly, and her face was bunched with pain. She was being slammed rhythmically from behind. Her black hair—close to two feet long—hung limply toward the water and undulated each time her thighs were rammed against the rail.

Bam, bam, bam.

Smith winced at the beating she was taking.

A hand grabbed her by her hair and yanked back.

Her body hurtled over the rail. She hit the water with a splat.

Smith retreated to the shadows under the hull. He watched the girl, unable to do anything to help her. The music switched to the Fantastics.

Time to remember, the kind of September
When love was mellow, and oh, so tender.

A rope ladder flopped into the water.

Men laughed on the deck. A man speaking English with an accent that was both Tarheel and Japanese, said, "Well, climb up on the damned thing. You ain't drowned, and you ain't hurt. We've hardly got started. The night's young. Come on now, get that little brown butt moving."

"If I were you, little darling, I'd do what the man says," said another man with an American accident. Roddy Baker.

Smith's mouth momentarily dropped.

As the girl climbed the ladder, sniffling, Smith saw that she was truly beautiful—a grand flower for a Japanese Godfather.

The man said, "Ain't no free lunch around here, girl."

"Got some big old sausages, though," Baker said.

When the Filipina was on deck and the rope ladder pulled up, Smith stowed his gear in his bag and slipped under the water again. As he headed for shore, he passed under the hull to admire his handiwork, grinning with near adolescent enthusiasm.

He had done his best to set the explosives artfully, that is, in such a manner as to scuttle the boat in seconds. Smith had pride of craft. When he wired a boat, it was wired properly. When it was time to punch the *Adios, samurai* button, the boat was guaranteed on its way to the bottom.

When Smith sent the *Giri* under, dammit, he wanted it under right then—with shocked and surprised looks on the faces of the drowning crew members—not later, giving Kawana a chance to float away in a lifeboat like a Japanese Darth Vader.

Smith could now follow the *Giri* from over the horizon if he had to, and he could pull Kawana's plug from as far away as thirty miles.

After witnessing Kawana's treatment of the Filipina, Smith hoped most fervently that he would get a chance to test his craftsmanship. The idea of deep-sixing a jerk like Kawana when he least expected it was Kip Smith's idea of wonderful, if possibly sick sport. Was this how Admiral Yamamoto felt as he had planned the ambush of Pearl Harbor?

Sure it was, and Kip Smith was going to get his rocks off anticipating the results just as those long ago treacherous bastards had dumped their nuts as they swooped down over Pearl Harbor on that lazy Sunday morning of December 7, 1941.

Above him, he heard a muffled pop.

The corpse of Roddy Baker, the desk officer who was, unfortunately, inexperienced in the field, landed—*splash*—directly in front of him. Roddy looked at him with lifeless eyes. He had a bullet hole in his forehead. His body turned in the water. Smith saw a huge hole where Roddy's brains had made an unexpected, hurried exit.

12

Kawana Katchan sat in the shade of the parasol mounted on the stern of his yacht. He had run out of Kirin and so now had to drink San Miguel while one of the crew made a run to Bacolod for proper Japanese beer. Kawana thought San Miguel tasted like water, but it was better than the American Budweiser. The heat and the humidity were beyond imagination this close to the equator. Weak beer and a climate like a Turkish bath. No wonder the Filipinos didn't have an economy. How could anybody work in this latitude? It was impossible.

Kawana's steward called out to him.

"*Hai*!" Kawana answered, and held up his empty bottle.

The steward gave him another plus a fresh, frosted glass.

Kawana filled the glass, thinking about how much fun it had been to waste the conniving fool, Roddy Baker.

Kawana did his best to follow Kodama Yoshio's advice in dealing with Americans. Kodama had regarded Americans as fools who were wary of Asians, but at the same time so gullible it was nothing short of amazing. They were always grinning and laughing. Such idiots! And they had no idea how to lie. They were all emotion. And talk about transparent! On top of all that, they believed that if they stuck by MacArthur's deal with Emperor Hirohito then the Japanese would, too. Kodama had believed this elemental naïveté was the single greatest exploitable weakness of Americans.

Don't be afraid of Americans, Kodama had said. Lying to them is as easy as breathing. In the case of MacArthur, at least, that appeared to be true. Pretend to be turned. Pretend to work for them. By way of proving his assessment of American character, Kodama had wonderful stories about how he had talked his way out of Sugamo Prison, with, yes, a little help from a special friend in a very high place, and how he had thereafter screwed MacArthur and Willoughby and their subordinates with impunity. The self-important Douglas MacArthur, a fatuous moron, somehow thought he was above being fleeced. And Willoughby was maximum dumb. An easy mark, as well. Emperor Hirohito and Kodama Yoshio outsmarted them both.

Roddy Baker had been Kawana's CIA control for years, and if Suma was to be believed, an M Fund mole at the same time. Kawana had never liked the confusion.

Suma swapped the map to the archers for the Tanaka assassination, after which he sent Baker to allegedly help Kawana retrieve them. Kawana found it hard to believe that Suma would part with the map without conniving to steal them for himself. Kawana had earned the map, fair and square.

If Suma Obe wanted the archers, let him try to take them.

13

In the distant past—and in some archaic cultures still—witch doctors, shamans, medicine men, fakirs, and healers of one sort or another worked the faithful into trances with rattles, drums, and primitive flutes. Those had evolved into pump organs in numerous Christian churches. Choirs had largely replaced the colorful writhing and barking and shouting in tongues.

The Rev. Robin Fallon wanted the assembled believers properly locked into an ecstatic trance before the solemn call to give money. To that end, he commissioned the Yamaha Company to design and build a special electric organ for Praise Jesus Now, one that he could take with him on his traveling revivals. The amazing organ cost the faithful $1.5 million dollars. Yamaha delivered an organ from which thundered a bass chord that, as it were, rumbled and reverberated straight from the heavens. The modular sections of the organ could be disassembled and reassembled for transport on the C-130.

Before Robin and Roberta Fallon took their places before the cameras, yards of cable had to be connected and dozens of microphones and cameras adjusted. Owing to PJN's famous organ and the fanfare and hype over Fallon's meticulously and dramatically staged revivals, there were those lovers of things mechanical and electrical who gathered to watch the sound engineers and cameramen assemble the complicated equipment. Filipinos were no different, and a crowd gathered to watch the high-tech action.

By 10 A.M. the field behind the fishing docks was abuzz with activity. The PJN setup crew had the limelight, not Fallon. The technicians were aware they were being watched and loved it. This was their time to show off, and there was not a little arrogance and pride in their strides. Both males and females brandished the badges of their trade, fancy leather belts from which hung an impressive array of wire strippers, snips, and screwdrivers.

At first, the technicians, as if to demonstrate their storied efficiency, bustled about as they might have in Milwaukee, but that pace was far too fast for the tropics. The amused Kip Smith, alert for a little kid or old woman who might make a good shot, watched the frenzied, sweaty activity from the shade of a food shack by the dock. He wondered what the Filipino spectators must think of the crazed Americans moving that quickly, their white skin frying in the heat.

The crew's first chore was to fasten together the numbered aluminum supports for the stage—the sections of plywood upon which Fallon would later share his intimate conversations with Jesus. The workers started screwing and bolting the braces together at a brisk, nearly Germanic pace, but as the morning wore on and the sun rose higher, Smith suspected this duty was not going exactly as planned.

Moons of sweat began forming under the worker's armpits. Their efficient stride slowed a bit, and Smith suspected that the tools fastened to their belts felt heavier and heavier as the chore progressed. The sun got higher and hotter, and the relative humidity matched it degree by degree and then some.

Smith could hardly keep from laughing out loud when a half dozen of them squatted in the shade of an Isuzu truck looking frantic and wild-eyed, squeegeeing perspiration from their foreheads as they tried to fashion makeshift sweatbands with trembling fingers.

At eleven o'clock, the plywood sections of the stage were in place, and crewmen driving forklifts hauled the first of the modular sections of the PJN organ up a foldout aluminum ramp and onto the stage.

A few minutes later, a black limousine pulled to a stop at the edge of the field, and there was a commotion among the gathered spectators.

Robin Fallon stepped out, followed by his lovely Roberta, who bore a small bouquet of white flowers. Robin wore dark slacks and a lacy, white *barong Tagalog*, an airy Filipino dress shirt worn with the tails out so the air could circulate. Roberta, her long red hair wound up in coils and balanced on her head like a furry bowl of fruit salad, wore purple slacks of processed oil and a matching lavender blouse.

Smith knew a real picture when he saw one. He sprang into action, striding boldly toward the sainted Fallons, who strolled toward the stage. Here was a just-folks preacher chosen by God to spread the word of the gospel no matter where it took him. The Filipino onlookers inched closer for a better look at the anointed couple.

Smith whipped out his bogus press card and called. "Reverend Fallon, Kip Smith. Here for *Time* magazine."

Fallon seemed to glow with joy, although the truth was he despised reporters and photographers from nonreligious publications, believing them to be godless swine out to nail him. *Time* magazine was not a creepy little rag bent on cheap shots. Fallon yearned to one day score a *Time* cover, and was sensible enough to know that was a long-range project requiring years of image building.

He pumped Smith's hand with energy. "Well, by golly, Mr.

Smith, how are you? This is my wife Roberta. Honey, Mr. Smith is from *Time* magazine."

"*Time* magazine?" Roberta Fallon beamed.

Smith looked modest. "I do hope you won't mind my running around shooting film all weekend. You know, I was in Los Angeles a couple of years ago and shot some pictures of you and General Glenn at that conference on family values. Fine man, General Glenn."

"You know the general?"

"Oh, no, sir. I don't know him personally or anything like that. I was one of a couple of dozen photographers firing away at him. An impressive man. He refused to yield an inch to the Communists." Smith watched Fallon's eyes.

Fallon bunched his face in agreement. "An American patriot."

"I was talking to a reporter from the *Los Angeles Times*, Tomi Kobayashi, and she told me she has an appointment to interview you tomorrow on a farm. That sounds like a wonderful place for some good pictures. I was wondering if it would be okay by you if I hitched a ride with her. The more shots I take, the better chance I have to score something that'll impress the photo editor."

"Goodness, Mr. Smith, you just come right on along with Ms. Kobayashi and shoot all the pictures you want. If Roberta or I can be of any help at all, why you just let us know. Aren't these just beautiful people? Jeepers creepers! Why, they're living in a gol-durned paradise. Paradise!"

"I just hope it isn't this hot the day you hike into the mountains for the candle burning."

Fallon looked unconcerned. "They tell me it cools off quickly here once the sun goes down, and shucks, Mr. Smith, even we Christians have enough sense to take our durned time on a walk like that. Heavens to Betsy, isn't this heat something?"

"Well, thank you, Reverend, I sincerely appreciate your help."

Fallon said, "They tell me they're about to test the organ. Gee whillickers, you mustn't leave until you've heard the organ, Mr. Smith."

A technician on the stage punched a single key of the instrument.

Mmmmmwwwwwwhhhhhaaaaaabbbbb!

The ground seemed to literally shudder beneath Smith's feet. He grinned at the sensation.

Fallon looked pleased. "You haven't seen anything yet, Mr. Smith. He's just getting started."

Roberta said, "Better brace yourself, Mr. Smith."

MmmmmMMMMMWWWWWWHHHHHAAAAABBBBBBbbbbb!

Vibrating from the sound, Smith laughed out loud. "You do have yourself an organ, Reverend!"

Fallon called to the man at the instrument, waving up up with his hand. "Vincent, you want to take it a step higher."

MMMMMMMMMMWWWWWWWWWWWHHHHHHHHHHAA AAAAAAAABBBBBBBBBB!

The amazed Smith said, "Surely, bounty must be at hand with an organ like that, Reverend Fallon."

Fallon said, "You've got that right, Mr. Smith. Bounty is almost certainly at hand. This is what the Bible promises, and the Bible is God's word. By golly, isn't it amazing what they can do with technical things these days?"

"I see by the papers where *carabao* are going to carry both your water and your gear into the candle lighting. That sounds pretty low-tech to me."

"God put water buffalo on this good earth to plow and carry things, Mr. Smith. They tell me that a person can load a half ton on one of those carts, and the water buffalo will plod along thinking it's had the day off."

Vincent said, "Hello-oh-oh-oh, Reverend-end-end-end Fallon-on-on-on! Hello-oh-oh-oh, Roberta-ta-ta-ta. Praise-se-se-se Jesus-sus-sus-sus. Now-ow-ow-ow!"

"Now he's getting it," Fallon said. "He'll tune the echo out, and he'll have it. Isn't that organ and sound system something, Mr. Smith? Sunday is going to be some kind of day, eh, Mr. Smith? A revival followed by a trek to Pulak Pulakan to light candles for an American hero. Yes, sir, I do look forward to it. The wonderful bounties of the Lord. My goodness gracious!"

14

The Praise Jesus Now people gave Tomi Kobayashi instructions on how to get to the farm near Granada for her scheduled interview with Robin Fallon, and judging from the details of the annotated map, PJN was nothing if not efficient. An endnote recommended that Tomi hire a driver with a four-wheel-drive vehicle.

On the day of the scheduled third M Fund briefing at the beach resort, Kip Smith drove Tomi to her interview. With Smith piloting a Toyota four-wheeler and Tomi manning the PJN map and instructions, they turned east onto Burgos Avenue in Bacolod, and Smith drove past Ding Rodriguez's house and an outpost of the Philippine Army and a San Miguel beer plant.

Tomi read the PJN map and instructions. "Van der Elst was with the American 185th Infantry Regiment that passed through here. He mentions fighting at a large house with a swimming pool. Has to be the same place."

Following the instructions, Smith slowed for the village of Granada, then turned left—north—on a bumpy gravel road toward the village of Conception. He braked to a stop for a herd of brown goats that stood in the road, obstinately certain of their right of way. He waited patiently as two young men shooed the goats across the road.

Tomi said, "Don't you think goats are cute? They look like big dogs."

"Ah, the noble goat," Smith said. The goats passed, and he put the Toyota into gear again.

Smith drove past two teams of young men playing basketball on packed earth with a rim and crude backboard nailed to a tree, then crossed over a small stream and was quickly into sugar country, with cane rising high on both sides of the car. The foothills of the mountains rose ahead in the distance.

He turned left onto two parallel trails for wheels that were chopped up and crisscrossed by gullies, potholes, washouts, and cave-ins. The Toyota, all four knobbies digging steadily into the mud, lurched wildly from side to side.

Tomi held on with both hands, her torso whipped this way and that as Smith, seemingly unaffected and certainly undeterred by the outrageous road, kept his foot on the accelerator. The Land Cruiser slid to the right, perilously close to the ditch. Smith was barely able to stop it. He eased forward. Having survived one treacherous slide, he slowed for another, even bigger washout. A monster. "Holy Mama! Look at this one!"

Tomi could hardly believe it. "Do we have to turn back?"

Smith looked surprised. "At this?" He eased the vehicle down the near slope of the washout.

Tomi, eyeing the pit, wondered if Smith might not be defeated by the chasm. She didn't look forward to walking the rest of the way in the withering heat.

Smith said, "I'm not going to do anything if I think you're going to get hurt, but you better hold on."

"Holding on."

Smith glanced at her, looking worried. "I mean really hold on. On second thought, maybe you better get out and wait for me on the other side." He gave her hand a squeeze.

She frowned and got out.

Smith bit his lower lip and aimed the Toyota up the muddy slope of the far side of the hole and gunned the engine. The Toyota slid to the left and to the right and to the left again, then climbed out of the pit. "See there, no problem." Smith grinned in triumph.

Tomi climbed back in. "Good work!"

Smith eased the Toyota farther down the parallel ruts. "Are you sure this is the right road?"

"A note here says to watch for the pit."

"That was a pit. No doubt of that."

They exited the cane field and started up into the mountains. Smith said, "By the way, those are pepper plants there on our left." He was referring to a large field with rows of slender trees about six feet tall.

"Pepper?'

"You can't see them from this distance, but the peppers grow in small bunches, like tiny grapes, from vines that are curved around those trees."

At length, Smith slowed for a gate. He got out and opened the gate and drove through, stopping to close the gate behind him. In another hundred yards they came to several Land Cruisers that had ferried the PJN advance party to the site. Smith and Tomi were both astonished at what lay beyond the vehicles.

A splendid swimming pool on a bluff overlooked several acres of rice paddies. At the end of the pool, which was perhaps twenty feet wide and sixty feet long, an elegant, sophisticated bamboo house, a mansion by bamboo house standards, also overlooked the rice paddies. A small stream at the top fed the swimming pool. The water ran through a bed of charcoal before it emptied into the pool that was drained by a plug at the lower end.

They got out of the Toyota. In his photographer's vest, with two Nikons dangling impressively from his shoulders, Smith escorted Tomi toward the swimming pool. Within seconds several Filipina PJN volunteers assisting the hosts for the day, wearing their prettiest dresses, were upon them.

Smith and Tomi were told the Fallons would be a few minutes late. They were invited to sit at a white metal table under a huge, spreading mango tree at one end of the pool, and were served wonderful *lanzones*, looking like large, off-yellow grapes, and slices of green guava with salt, and tall glasses of fresh coconut water. Smith attacked the *lanzones* with relish, peeling back the skin with his thumbnail, and slugged the coconut water down with abandon. Tomi, who puckered her mouth at the first sip, thought the coconut water, while it sounded exotic and romantic, must surely be an acquired taste.

Several sets of the white tables and chairs had been assembled under the mango tree, and to one side a longer table awaited the arrival of the food being prepared inside the large bamboo house. A *baboy* was being cooked over a bed of charcoal to one side of the pool. A middle-aged Filipino turned the pig by hand over the glowing bed of coals. He used a paintbrush to periodically swab its skin. The skin had already reached a rich, beautiful mahogany color, a sign that it was ready to serve.

Tomi studied the map and said, "This says Japanese officers were holed up here, and the Americans had to drive them north toward Conception."

A few minutes later they heard the distant *whop-whop-whop* of an approaching helicopter. Robin and Roberta Fallon were arriving. The Filipina hostesses scurried to the buffet table and to the house to retrieve the food for serving.

The helicopter settled onto a field behind the grove of guava trees. The blades came to a stop and a few minutes later Tomi and Smith heard voices and laughter as the Fallon party strolled down a path toward the house and swimming pool.

Robin Fallon wore a *polo barong*, as he had the day before. Roberta Fallon wore a broad-brimmed hat and a loose, flowing, flowered dress. The bamboo house was far enough up in the foothills that a cooling breeze stirred, furling the scarlet azalea blossoms at the bottom of Roberta's skirts.

Fallon beamed when he saw Smith and Tomi, striding forward with his hand extended. "Why, for heaven's sakes, how are you, Mr. Smith? Isn't this a lovely day? Isn't this just wonderful? And this must be Ms. Kobayashi of the *Los Angeles Times*. How do you do?"

Tomi said, "I'm doing fine. Very pleased to meet you, Reverend Fallon."

"Did you have a nice ride out? The country looked just beautiful from our helicopter."

"It was a real ride," Tomi said.

"If you folks will excuse us for a few minutes, we'll meet the good people who prepared God's bounty for us. We're told that among other delicacies we'll be served a fish named, what was that, hon?"

"Lapu lapu, I think it was, darling."

"No better fish in all of God's oceans, they say. And then maybe we can have our talk, Ms. Kobayashi."

"Lapu Lapu was the man who killed Ferdinand Magellan, who was busy spreading the word of the Lord," Smith said.

Fallon blinked. "Say, I bet these good folks could rustle up a couple of San Miguels or a little Filipino rum for you two. I told our lovely hosts that you might not be such, uh, committed Christians as ourselves." Fallon grinned impishly and winked. "We all get to heaven in our separate ways, eh, Mr. Smith?"

"That was very thoughtful of you, Reverend. I'd like a rum with a little twist of *kalamansi* if they have it, certainly," Smith said.

Indeed their hosts did have rum on hand, or at least quickly rustled some up, and Smith and Tomi were soon sipping Tanduay dark on cracked ice. They watched while Robin and Roberta,

carrying tall glasses of mango juice, were introduced to the gathering of followers with much sincere pumping of hands, polite
laughter, and earnest exclamations of "Praise Jesus."

After the introductions, the Fallons and the gathering of about
a dozen PJN admirers, those with wealth and position, filed past
the gorgeous buffet. The table was spread with lapu lapu and
lechon, rice, fish soup with hunks of green papaya, eggs that had
been cured in tidal mud, several kinds of vegetables, and *lechon
manok.*

When the meal was finished and the clutter cleared, the Fallons
joined Tomi at the table under the spreading mango for their
interview. As they talked, Smith circled this way and that, wasting
film with one of his Nikons, the camera making a satisfying *ka-
snap* with each shot. He listened to Tomi's questions, waiting for
just the right moment to flip a lure from his mental tackle out
there on the uncertain waters of suspicion and paranoia. This had
to be a finessed delivery, rather like lofting a bass plug in that just
right place, inches from entangling weeds and sunken logs. Then
he would have to retrieve it correctly, giving it a lifelike, irresistible
motion.

Tomi asked Fallon how it was, other than the urging of Mrs.
Bessie Case Flanders, of Orlando, Florida, that he had decided to
hold a revival in the Philippines.

"We do it because of the people up there." Fallon motioned
toward the mountains. "They're not giving up and neither are
we."

"The Communists, you're talking about. The New People's
Army."

"Oh, for goodness sakes, yes, Ms. Kobayashi. My heavens to
Betsy, we're Christian soldiers. Surely you've heard that old hymn,
'Onward Christian Soldiers,' ' . . . and with the Cross of Jesus,
marching as to war.' You know, the boys who fought on this island
forty years ago knew what evil was, and they confronted it head-

on. Our debt to them hasn't ceased just because fifty years have passed. No sir, by George."

Fallon paused for Tomi to complete a note. "We Christians don't shrink from calling ourselves soldiers. No, ma'am, by golly. Gracious me, we're fully prepared to fight. The GIs fought the Japanese with bullets. We fight the devil with discipline, and danged if we'll give up. That's what this candle lighting is all about, Ms. Kobayashi, a recognition of the honorable, mutual sacrifice for the greater good which is God's will. We want to show the world what we Christians are made of."

Tomi said, "So generals and preachers are natural allies then?"

Fallon grinned. "Oh my, that's a loaded question. You're the dickens, you are, Ms. Kobayashi, but I'm not afraid of honesty. The fact is I think the most ardent and committed Christians are annoyed by the casual criticism of professional soldiers that we often find these days."

"I see."

"Both generals and preachers are comfortable with the idea of rank and place, Ms. Kobayashi, and we both respect authority and the need for personal discipline and honor. We both seek peace in our ways, and like military men we seek order, not chaos. That may seem inconsistent with Christian values, but if you think about it a moment, it isn't. Not at all."

Smith flipped the well-used and dependable bald-faced lie in front of his fish. "Tomi, this morning the Reverend Fallon said he and General Holden Glenn are good friends. Does he also know General Martinez?" *Ka-snap*, he shot another frame—the deft retrieval.

"I . . ." Robin cleared his throat.

Ka-snap, ka-snap.

Roberta perked up. "It was General Glenn who introduced us to General Martinez, the head of the Philippine Military Academy.

In fact, we had a wonderful dinner in Manila last week with General Martinez—"

Robin shot her a reproving glance.

Roberta straightened her seat and sniffed. "General Martinez is a good friend of, of . . . who was that nice man, Robin?"

"General Singlaub," Robin said. He couldn't restrain himself. He, too, liked to drop names.

"General Singlaub was a hero!" Roberta said, thrilled. "They say he parachuted into France in advance of D-Day, and he was once commander of all the forces in Korea. And when he was in China and Manchuria during the war he learned about the activities of that man Koda . . ."

Fish on!

"Roberta!" Robin said mildly, his voice rising.

Roberta smoothed her skirts and smiled happily. She liked to talk. And it was fun having her picture taken by a photographer from *Time* magazine.

Ka-snap, ka-snap.

15

A sudden squall, said to be the southwestern edge of a typhoon racing across Luzon to the north, buffeted the palm trees lazily to and fro. Kip Smith and Tomi Kobayashi waited in Smith's rented Toyota Land Cruiser parked beside an abandoned *nipa* hut a quarter of a mile down the road from Ding Rodriguez's residence at the edge of Bacolod. Behind them a tethered *carabao* grazed contentedly in the wind. Next to the *nipa* hut, a battered sugar truck was parked in front of Ding Rodriguez's offices, where security-guarded vehicles awaited repair in open sheds.

Rodriguez's house had a high, steeply pitched roof that gave it an almost chaletlike appearance. A security wall, topped with the ubiquitous shards of 7-Up and San Miguel glass, likewise surrounded the chalet and its compound. Smith and Tomi ordinarily would have been unable to see anything other than the top of a regular, open-sided work shed of some kind, but Rodriguez's security guards, rather less disciplined than marines guarding an embassy or the Secret Service protecting the president, had left the swinging gates wide open. A swimming pool was to one side of the house. A smaller building with a conical roof and a covered lanai faced the swimming pool.

It was 6 P.M. and the sun was an orange orb slipping beneath the mountains to the west. Bacolod was a little over ten degrees north longitude, close enough to the equator that the sun rose and set at 6 A.M. and 6 P.M., plus or minus ten minutes depending on the time of year.

Watching the setting sun, Smith was pleased. "Dark in a few minutes. We'll be okay." He adjusted the recorder hooked up to the microphones that Ding Rodriguez had placed under the table where he and Martinez would be talking. "The lanai there by the pool is where Ding and his friends drink beer and have *marienda* and bullshit until late at night. I've spent many an hour on that lanai."

Tomi said, "I don't understand. Why on earth would General Martinez be visiting Ding?"

"General Martinez believes everybody has a price." Smith said.

"Ding doesn't?"

"Perhaps the general isn't as good a judge of character as he thinks. In his experience, everybody who learns the truth about Hirohito's Gold is immediately altered in a fundamental way. It is as if mere knowledge of the existence of the gold is transforming. All qualities such as conscience, soul, and heart are rendered moot. The fantasy overwhelms everything. Nobody has seen it in his self-interest to reveal the truth except Robert Curtis and nobody believed him."

"What if Martinez doesn't show?"

"He might not," Smith said.

"And if he doesn't?"

"We'll have sat here in the wind for nothing. Won't be the first time for me. Patience, patience."

"God, will you look at those palm trees? Isn't this wind something?" Tomi opened a package of dried mangoes. "Here, want some of these? They're delicious."

Smith helped himself to a slice of mango. "Mmmmm. You're right." He quickly grabbed two more slices.

A bare light bulb behind Ding Rodriguez highlighted a spot on the white wall, and in the middle of that spot—choice because the light attracted all manner of gnats and bugs—a small green lizard called a *ti-ti* (tee-tee) on some islands and a *to-to* (toh-toh) on others waited patiently for its supper. Rodriguez poured himself and General Martinez another measure of Johnny Walker Black Label.

On the wall the *to-to*'s tongue shot out, nailing a passing gnat.

"He's here on the island passing himself off as a photographer for *Time* magazine. He's with a woman who is allegedly a reporter for the *Los Angeles Times*," Martinez said.

"I know. I've had a couple of beers with him."

"You have?"

Rodriguez rolled his eyes. "He was trying to find out what I know, of course. I've known him for years. But I've got brains enough to come in out of the rain. He didn't say anything about *Time* magazine. He used to be with the Company, and now he's a wildlife photographer."

"What did he tell you he was doing here?"

"He says a cable television producer wants him to shoot a documentary about wild *baboy*. To do that, he says, he has to negotiate with the NPA. He wanted to know if I could arrange a meeting with Jaime Pineda."

"You believe him?"

Ding slapped his belly. "Do I believe horses can sing and whales can fly? Not if he told somebody he's with *Time* magazine. Who did he tell that to?"

"The Fallons. His old friend Roddy Baker is here, too. Baker has been on the yacht with Kawana. We know that."

"How? How do you know that?"

Martinez said nothing.

"Watching the yacht from the dredge. Smart," Rodriguez said.

"Unlikely that Baker and Smith are here on holiday."

Martinez said, "Is the woman working with Smith, do you think?"

Rodriguez shrugged. "The woman? I have no idea. I know the Americans have gotten carried away with women's lib, but this can be dangerous business in the end. The Americans have got female combat pilots."

"I met Smith once about ten years ago," Martinez said. "He used to be married to a Cebuana, did you know that? I liked him. Any American who has taken the time to learn both Visayan and Tagalog."

Rodriguez said, "He had to do that for the CIA. He speaks a little Mandarin and Cantonese, too."

"He knows where the bodies are buried."

"But not necessarily the archers," Rodriguez said. "To say that the archers are buried somewhere in Pulak Pulakan isn't enough. We both know the NPA had been using metal detectors on the floors and walls of those tunnels for years. Why haven't they found them before now?"

"He and Baker are after them, no question. Kawana knows where they are. They're either watching Kawana or working with him."

"One or the other," Rodriguez said.

"If you should get any funny ideas, just remember, I can beat any deal he can make, guaranteed."

Rodriguez looked offended. "You don't trust me?"

Martinez said, "I wouldn't trust my own mother with the archers."

The lizard waited.

Another bug passed by.

The *to-to*'s tongue shot out again. Another bug devoured. The *to-to* had that old bug magic. Americans thought the *to-to*'s call sounded like *fuck you*. Before Filipino nationalists sent them packing, American sailors at Subic Bay and airmen at Clark Air Force Base had famously called it the Fuck You lizard.

The lizard called, *Fuck you. Fuck you.*

Rodriguez, observing the lizard, said, "That spot beneath the light is prime real estate."

Martinez said, "The bugs like the light."

A second lizard entered the edge of the light and hesitated.

The *to-to* in the center, seeing this, attacked the interloper, which retreated quickly into the barren shadows. The *to-to* in the shadows envied the big lizard's prized light.

A third *to-to* tried his luck, but he, too, was driven away.

The big lizard, having driven away his competition, returned to the warming glow of the light. His tongue shot out. Another bug. More protein. Victory. *Fuck you. Fuck you.*

Rodriguez said, "You know, a person can learn a lot by watching a *to-to*. Ever think of that?"

"Oh?"

A brown rat emerged from the shadows and stood looking up at Rodriguez, then, just as quietly as he had appeared, he was gone.

Rodriguez, observing this, poured them both some more scotch, then stood. "Time for Bengal tiger," he said.

Martinez furrowed his brows. "What's Bengal tiger?"

"A game. Just as instructive as watching *to-to*s eat bugs, you'll see. I'll be right back." Rodriguez went into his house and a few minutes later came back with a bowl of cooked rice and a .22 automatic pistol with a silencer on the end. He sat down, took a sip of whiskey, and said, "At night the *illaga* (ill-ah-*gah*, rats, singular and plural) come in from the cane fields and hang around the compound looking for a scrap of food that might have been left on the ground. What we do is sprinkle some rice on the ground here like this." He leaned over the rail at the edge of the lanai and tossed some rice onto the ground at the edge of the grass. "*Ilaga* love rice. We wait them out and take turns with the pistol. When you miss an *ilaga*, you lose a life. Lose three lives and you lose the game." He gave the pistol to Martinez.

Martinez weighed the pistol in his hand. He turned his chair so he could get a better angle on the rice.

Rodriguez said, "We can talk if we want. They know we're up here. They're under us right now, foraging around."

No sooner had he said that than a rat emerged from the darkness, eyeing the rice. Martinez wheeled and fired. The rat disappeared.

Rodriguez laughed. "*Hijo de puta!*"

"I missed. One life gone," Martinez said. He was dismayed. "How did I miss? He was right there. Right in front of me. How could I do that?" He gave the pistol to Rodriguez, who sighted down the barrel at the ground.

Another *ilaga* emerged from the shadows. It hesitated, testing the air with its nose.

"Take him," Martinez whispered.

Rodriguez waited.

"Shoot the little fucker."

Rodriguez was calm.

The rat moved forward, closer to the rice.

"Now, Ding!"

Rodriguez licked his lips.

"Do it."

The *ilaga*, more confident, looked around and took one more step toward the rice.

The pistol snapped. The rat was pinned to the ground with a .22 slug in its spine directly between its shoulders.

"Good shooting, Ding."

Rodriguez grinned crookedly. "The secret is not to wheel and deal with your pistol. It's too dark to see clearly. You pick a spot in front of the rice where the *ilaga* has to go if he wants to eat, and you wait. When the white spot of rice in front of your sight disappears, you pull the trigger."

"Hey! Very good."

"It's why we have to be careful with this gold business, General."

Martinez said, "We don't want to step in front of somebody's gun sights, I agree."

"Which brings us back to the question of Kip Smith. The guy's smart. He worries me."

Martinez looked scornful. "Kip Smith doesn't know squat. He only thinks he does."

"He's a professional, just like you. Just because he takes pictures of animals doesn't mean he's forgotten everything he's ever learned."

Martinez said, "The question is not whether Whistling Smith is going to get in the way, but rather if your boat can do the job."

"It can," Rodriguez said.

"It has to be able to carry the weight and have both speed and range."

"Walang problema."

Martinez rolled his eyes. "No problem! Where have I heard that before? The other question is whether or not you can forego the Filipino pleasure of screwing me over when my back is turned."

Rodriguez poured them another round of whiskey. "You think I'd do something like that?"

Martinez studied him, saying nothing.

Rodriguez took another hit of whiskey. "What do you take me for? *Hijo de puta!*"

Tomi Kobayashi, listening to this through the microphone Ding Rodriguez had planted under his table, and watching through binoculars from Kip Smith's Toyota Land Cruiser, was incredulous. "What's going on here?"

Smith ran his fingertips down his jaw. "Like I said, Martinez is of the opinion that everybody is on the take if the price is right, but he doesn't want to deal Ding in on anything. He just wants Ding to think he might deal him in."

"And Ding?"

"Ding thinks Martinez is a greedy *botakal*."

"*Botakal?*"

"Visayan for boar hog. Ding has contacts all over the island, including in the NPA, which is why General Martinez is sucking up to him. Ding's sources tell him that Martinez and Pineda met in the mountains for a pow wow about a week ago. That had to be about the archers."

Tomi looked puzzled. "I thought Pineda was a Marxist and a leader of the New People's Army. How on earth did the superintendent of the Philippine Military Academy pull that off?"

"One of Pineda's cousins is a cadet."

"I see. Do they propose taking the archers off the island by Ding's boat?"

Smith said, "Good question."

"I don't understand. Martinez just asked him again if it's large and fast enough."

"Martinez could be setting him up. Maybe he wants to use Ding's boat for a decoy. You ever think of that?"

Tomi blinked. "What a complicated, treacherous world you lived in. No wonder you quit."

16

The Big Veg in Bacolod was yet another tropical bar open to the sidewalk. The entrance was adorned with a plastic reproduction of an enormous deformed banana grown on Negros, a fruit of such unusual proportions as to resemble nothing less than a huge penis, although the likeness was left to the imagination of the patrons of the bar. The idea of the reproductions was that of the son of the owner, who attended the Massachusetts Institute of Technology. The son's American girlfriend, an artist, had hit upon the idea of making copies of record or unusual vegetables—huge watermelons, cobs of corn, and so on. She made a mold of the fruit or vegetable and from the mold made a plastic duplicate that she then painted in the likeness of the original. The son, no fool, talked his father into decorating his Bacolod bar with reproductions of tropical vegetables—mangoes, papayas, bananas, *lanzones*, *durians*, and the rest.

The girlfriend made a visit to Bacolod, and the result was intertwined carrots that resembled copulating humans. A gnarled potato that looked like W. C. Fields. A pair of drooping papayas resembled nothing so much as a pair of exquisite, orange breasts, replete with nippled ends. A deformed *durian* that looked like Bart Simpson.

Tomi Kobayashi settled in with Kipling Smith and Ding Rodriguez. She had been told the story of the origins of the vegetables earlier, but now she looked around with amusement at the decor. Not all the fruits and vegetables were tropical in origin—the girl-friend had obviously brought some unusual reproductions with her from the United States.

Lazy ceiling fans stirred the listless tropical air. Smith ordered squid balls and three bottles of San Miguel beer, and Tomi was ready for the briefing.

Tomi punched the start button of the recorder.

Rodriguez dipped a squid ball into some sauce and ate it, savoring the flavor. "Let's see, where were we in Hirohito's Gold briefing?"

Tomi checked her notes. "Kodama has been destroyed by the Lockheed scandal. Marcos is feeling independent. If Imelda is right, Marcos rescinded parity rights so he could secretly buy Filipino corporations with the gold. If Robert Curtis is right, Marcos found an American who could wash it. Curtis allegedly saw the gold for himself and agreed to ship his gear to the Philippines. They were ready to excavate. President Marcos issued a presidential decree requiring his personal approval of all salvage operations in Philippine waters."

Chiba put down his bottle of San Miguel. He peeled the label off with his thumbnail and without looking up said, "I would like to talk to you about giri, Yoshida-san."

"Sir?"

"Giri to your oyabun. Giri to the emperor. Giri to the Japanese people. I want you to put them in order for me. Which is the most important. Which the least."

"A hard question."

"There are no right and wrong answers. I understand that."

Yoshida took a deep breath. "Giri to the Japanese people. Giri to the emperor. Giri to my oyabun."

"In that order. First to last."

"Yes, although I must tell you I find it impossible to believe that the emperor or my oyabun *would ever ask me to do anything that is not in the interest of the Japanese people. They put the Japanese people ahead of themselves. People say we* yakuza *are criminals, but the truth is we are patriots first, criminals second. I could easily reverse the order with no harm to the Japanese people. The American and Filipino seem to think it was terrible that Kodama-san had friends among the* yakuza. *How horrible! Well, let me tell you something, Kodama was a patriotic Japanese all his life. What he did, he did out of love for Japan and the Japanese people and respect for the emperor. He did not act out of small greed or because he wanted material things. I deny it. He was a patriot and a great man despite his failing in the Lockheed incident."*

"How about the prime minister? What if I included the prime minister in the list, or a member of his cabinet? How would they fit in your ranking of giri?"

"The prime minister might put himself before the Japanese people. A cabinet minister would not hesitate to put himself first. We all know about kuroi kiri. *But there is a huge difference between a politician and a* yakuza oyabun *or the emperor. The latter are genuine patriots. An emperor is Japan. He is a paragon. It is inconceivable that he would put selfish personal interests before his subjects. That is why this tale of theirs makes no sense whatever. Such treachery by the emperor is by definition impossible."*

"By mid-April, Leber Group was ready. Curtis's story is that the psychic Olof Jonsson, Jiga, Balmores, and the Wisconsin businessman boarded a Philippine navy patrol boat loaded with General Ver's security men, and they were off. They spent several hours exploring the area where Jiga and Balmores said the cruiser *Nachii* had gone down. No luck. They were about to quit when the psychic found the sunken cruiser. Ver's divers attached buoys to both bow and stern."

Smith took a swig of San Miguel. "This is the part I like. Only in the Philippines!"

Rodriguez grinned. "When they went back the next day, the buoys were gone, and the sun set before they could find the *Nachii*. They discovered silver coins on a barge the *Nachii* was towing, hardly evidence that the warship was on its way to Japan. On the third day they placed new buoys, and Ver promised tight security; there would be no more problems with the buoys. They went back to Manila. When they returned three days later with divers, the new buoys were gone. Rather than play hide and seek with whoever was messing with their buoys, they shifted their attention to the land site at Teresa II, described on Japanese maps as containing treasure worth seven hundred seventy-seven billion yen in 1944 currency."

"How much is that in U.S. dollars?" Tomi asked.

Rodriguez shrugged. "I don't have any idea. You'll have to look the figure up and adjust for inflation and the rest of it. This session is about the digging. The bizarre numbers will come up later."

"Got it."

"Before I continue, I should tell you that Ver allegedly told Curtis they had to postpone the recovery of the sunken vessels because the Japanese wanted to recover the bodies of the sailors for a proper burial in Japan. They were really after the gold. They couldn't retrieve a cache under the Fort Santiago site, because the Spanish fort was a major tourist attraction and the head of the National Historical Society objected to its being closed for 'restoration.' They couldn't retrieve any of Hirohito's Gold from a site four hundred yards from the St. Augustin Church because the Catholic priests would object. Finally, they turned to a site thirty-eight miles south of Manila, three miles from the village of Teresa.

"After Curtis and his companions successfully located the

Teresa II site, General Ver chose a construction company owned by one of Marcos's golfing pals. The workers were told that the purpose of the excavation was to retrieve soil samples to test for a proposed subdivision. Members of Leber were told that leaks of information could be fatal. Work began in mid-May.

"Curtis's story is that on Jiga's map, the top of the tunnel was ninety feet from the surface. This stash of Hirohito's Gold was allegedly loaded onto twenty-three trucks sealed in the tunnel. The maps said eight one-thousand-pound bombs were rigged to explode in the tunnel, some attached to the trucks. Crews of twenty dug around the clock. They averaged three feet a day, passing through layers of charcoal and glass and uncovering arm bones and hand bones arranged in patterns.

"In the first week of June, Ver's men replaced them. On June 8, eighty feet down, Ver's workers pierced a tunnel and were stiffened and sickened by methane gas from decomposing bodies trapped underground for thirty years. When the gas had dissipated, they kept digging, wearing gas masks. As the maps indicated, they found a level of burned charcoal, a level of bamboo, then crisscrossed boards, then bones, then the fender of a truck, and then, under the fender, the metal tip of something.

"The Filipino colonel guarding the operation vanished. He returned a few minutes later with a truck full of troops loyal to Marcos. They took over guarding the site. As the Leber Group pondered what to do about the booby trap, Jack Anderson was telling American readers about Marcos digging for Yamashita's Gold at a site just outside Teresa. Marcos, furious about the leak, shut down the digging on July 6. The psychic Olof Jonsson, having an intuition of danger, flew out of town the next morning.

"Meanwhile, Curtis says, he was reading in Filipino newspapers that President Marcos had awarded Johnson Matthey an exclusive contract to refine gold mined at Benguet. Since Curtis had gone to great expense to ship his processing equipment, he was furious.

He went to see Ver, claiming that he had been double-crossed. Ver told him that it was too late to stop the shipment and attempted to calm him down by offering him a week in Baguio, which is high in the mountains and cool.

"Curtis had been studying the Japanese maps of Jiga and Balmores when he had his conversation with Ver. He realized that Ferdinand Marcos had just stolen his gold processing equipment, leaving him three hundred seventy-five thousand dollars in hock to the John Birch Society. Marcos never planned to deal Curtis in on anything. He was a congenital thief masquerading as a head of state. All he wanted was Curtis's reprocessing system.

"Curtis tucked the maps into a briefcase and on July 10, 1975, boarded an airplane and flew back to the United States. At first, nobody had the courage to tell Marcos that Curtis had made off with the maps. When he did find out, Marcos was furious. He set about to discredit Curtis, calling him a liar and a criminal."

Rodriguez burst out laughing. "Robert Curtis successfully stole the Japanese maps to one hundred seventy-two sites where Hirohito's Gold was buried. Unfortunately Curtis made off with something else of value: the truth about Paul Jiga and Benjamin Balmores. All this, I say, if we are to believe Curtis. Did he invent all that material? It's possible, but detail of that quality is amazing. It is difficult for anybody with a reasonably open mind to casually blow it off."

Yoshida had his gear in place. "Sir, I have a question."

"Ask it, Yoshida-san. Go ahead."

Making little attempt to mask his irritability, he said, "I know these two are liars, sir, but can you tell me why on earth Smith would recruit a woman to help him out. Yes, yes, I know women are all 'liberated' in America. They're firemen and soldiers and the rest of it. But we know the truth, don't we? What can a woman really do in a case like this? Can you name one female historian of note, just one?"

Chiba pursed his lips. "Barbara Tuchman."

Yoshida frowned. He had never heard of her.

Mildly, Chiba said, "If I might be so bold, Yoshida-san, I would suggest the wise course is never to underestimate the power of a determined woman."

Yoshida smiled. "Good that we Japanese keep them in their place." He looked thoughtful, then added, "Although this Kobayashi woman is different in one essential way. I'll concede that."

"And that would be?"

"Yes, I know she was born in the United States. Japanese is her second language. She is one-fourth Filipino. Nevertheless, she is the granddaughter of a Japanese general whom she believes was wrongly convicted of war crimes. She is embarrassed and shamed by a wrong done to her ancestor, and she wants to recover his honor. She has giri *to Yamashita. For that reason she is formidable."*

Chiba grimaced. "Just because their languages don't contain a word precisely the same as giri *doesn't mean Westerners or other Asians don't understand the concept. You're right, Dr. Kobayashi owes* giri *to her grandfather. But Smith owes* giri *to his murdered wife, and Rodriguez owes* giri *to his suffering countrymen. On this mission, they are all three* ronin, *Yoshida-san. Masterless* samurai. *You are right when you say she is formidable. So are her companions."*

Rodriguez said, "Who were Jiga and Balmores and how did they really come by the maps? Had General Yamashita just left them lying around for them to grab and make off like Arabs in the night? In fact, Benjamin Balmores, troubled by his wartime past, allegedly told Curtis a secret he had been bearing with him for thirty years.

"Curtis says Balmores told him Prince Chichibu was examining a major burial site outside the town of Bambang in Nueva Vizcaya province in early 1942, when his houseboy died of a fever. The houseboy's duties included doing the officers' laundry, polishing their boots, and keeping their gear clean. Chichibu's aide de camp returned with a replacement, fourteen-year-old Benjamin Balmores, who remained with the prince for the duration of the war. He saw the burial sites, but was not allowed to enter them.

"Balmores said that Major Nakasone, the Japanese officer in charge of constructing the tunnels, interviewed Leopoldo Jiga, then twenty-eight, because he had the same last name as one of Nakasone's military instructors, who had become a minor diplomat in the Japanese Embassy in the Philippines. It turned out that Jiga's mother was the diplomat's common-law wife. Since Jiga spoke both Tagalog and Ilocano in addition to fluent Japanese, Nakasone assigned him to his staff. Chichibu later commissioned him as a sub-lieutenant in the Imperial Army and sent him to school in Japan. When Jiga returned to the Philippines, Chichibu promoted him to captain and put him in charge of inventorying and burying the Golden Lily.

"Balmores said that by war's end, he and Jiga were commanders in the Japanese navy, directly subordinate to Rear Admiral Iwabuchi Sanji, Rear Admiral Kodama Yoshio, and Prince Chichibu."

Tomi said, "That was the order of command then. Jiga and Balmores subordinate to Nakasone. Nakasone subordinate to Iwabuchi. Iwabuchi subordinate to Kodama. Kodama subordinate to Higashikuni and Chichibu."

"Correct. And beyond Chichibu, if we are to believe Curtis's account, it is fair to conclude, Emperor Hirohito. Jiga and Nakasone supervised the digging of the tunnels to bury the gold. It was Chichibu, acting on behalf of Hirohito, who ordered Japanese marines to bury the POWs alive to eliminate witnesses—including twelve hundred Australians and Americans in Teresa. Your grandfather, Yamashita Tomayuki, was out of the loop. After his stunning victory in Singapore, Tojo exiled him to Manchuria, where he remained until near the end of the war when Tojo assigned him the doomed defense of Manila. Yamashita was executed to pacify enraged Filipinos then used as a red herring to divert attention from Iwabuchi and Kodama. And of course to protect Prince Chichibu and his brother, Emperor Hirohito. Yamashita's Gold? Bull. It was Hirohito's Gold."

Yoshida shook his head in disgust. "Rodriguez and Smith never give up trying to blame Emperor Hirohito. They're like anti-Japanese robots with their circuits stuck in a loop. Chichibu, Chichibu, Chichibu. Hirohito, Hirohito, Hirohito. You know what I dislike most about this assignment?"

Chiba dug at his crotch. "Tell me."

"I hate it that we have to wait to kill these people. It will be a distinct pleasure, believe me."

Chiba sighed. "Patience."

"And you know what else?"

"What's that?"

"On the subject of giri. Giri *is what holds Japan together.* Giri *to one's husband or parents.* Giri *to one's company.* Giri *to the emperor. It strikes me that the only institution in the United States that understands* giri *is the Central Intelligence Agency. If there is any truth to this story, and I don't concede that there is, the CIA has maintained* giri *to the agreement between MacArthur and the emperor,* giri *to Kodama and* giri *to the other patriotic so-called 'war criminals' who helped the United States when the Americans needed help. This man Smith used to work for the CIA, and now he seeks to betray their secrets. And yet, he is not without honor."*

"If you think about it, Yoshida-san, that places him somewhat in the position of one of the forty-seven samurai, *doesn't it? Which* giri *does he follow? That owed to the CIA, which swore him to secrecy? Or that owed to his wife, who was murdered as a consequence of the CIA's secret operations?"*

"If our theory of Hirohito's Gold buried in the Philippines is correct, at the end of the war the emperor faced a terrible problem of how to retrieve his treasure from the Philippines. There are two possible solutions. One, Kodama covertly sponsored a wartime collaborator who would be susceptible to extortion. Two, while Marcos was not a wartime collaborator, strictly speaking, he was open to a little dealing. Either case would explain why we don't get reports of excavations in the 1950s. The first excavations didn't occur until after Marcos took power.

"Remember, I told you that Marcos gave exclusive offshore mineral exploration rights to a *yakuza oyabun* named Machii Hisayuki. Well, Machii, who was born in Korea, where Kodama had grown up, was Kodama's longtime comrade. He was called the 'Tiger of the Ginza' because of his widespread Ginza property. South Korean President Park Chung-hee gave him the profitable concession to operate the ferry between Pusan and Shimoanaseki, the closest points between South Korea and Japan. Then there's Sasakawa Ryoichi, a close friend of Kodama's since the 1930s."

"Mentioned in van der Elst's journal."

"Correct. In 1971, Sasakawa proposed to turn the Filipino island of Lubong into an exclusive World Safari Club whereby wealthy Japanese could hunt wild boar then retreat to air-conditioned quarters to enjoy 'private companions,' that is to say, young Filipinas. In the excitement of the moment, Sasakawa told reporters how he and Marcos had been pals long before Marcos became president. He wasn't lying about that. He did time with Kodama in Sugamo Prison and was released along with Kodama in the Hirohito deal. The Lubong proposal fell through, partly because of the objections of the Catholic Church, but it's instructive nevertheless. Marcos did favors for Kodama's cronies because he had no choice."

Rodriguez rested his hand on his belly, thinking for a moment before he continued. "It has been easier for Filipino nationalists to believe that they unhappily elected a grotesque thief as president than to accept the awful likelihood that the Japanese emperor had connived to help place a wartime collaborator in Malacanang so that his people could retrieve the treasure they had buried on Filipino soil. We Filipinos are a talented, intelligent people, Tomi. We're poor but proud. Better to believe that Yamashita's Gold was a myth than to admit that."

"What did Marcos do to get the maps back?"

Rodriguez grinned. "Curtis was too smart not have hidden the maps where they'd never be found. Kill Curtis, lose the maps forever. Marcos was on a real hook. For one thing, the Japanese ultimately in charge of recovering Hirohito's Gold must have been furious. Marcos couldn't kill Jiga and Balmores for letting Robert Curtis run off with the maps because they had supervised the burial of the treasure. If he killed them, he would have lost all connection to the treasure. The only thing left was to call Curtis and plead his case, which he did. Once he got the maps back, he could kill Curtis."

"All this if Curtis's version of the story is correct."

"Exactly right. It has the ring of truth. Is it true? Not true?" Rodriguez shrugged. "Marcos told Curtis he had publicly called him a liar and a thief for political reasons. He had to divert attention from the gold. He said he assumed Curtis was too politically sophisticated to get all bent out of shape. Curtis should have understood what was happening. If Marcos admitted to the existence of the gold, he'd have the original owners of the gold on him like a bad smell. But the suspicious Curtis remained cool to his entreaties. As Marcos made more calls, he began to get quarrelsome and impatient. Dammit, he wanted those maps!"

"Just quarrelsome and impatient?" Tomi asked, looking amused.

"One pissed off son of a bitch!" Smith said.

Rodriguez laughed. "He wasn't the only one who was feeling out of sorts. Curtis's story is that the John Birchers, reading Marcos's denial of the existence of the gold in the newspapers, sued him, alleging that he had borrowed three hundred seventy-five thousand dollars from them under false pretenses.

"Curtis's story is that he decided the best way to protect himself and fend off the lawsuit by the John Birch Society was to go public. He claims he took more than two thousand pages of documents, including receipts, letters, and waybills and three hundred hours of taped conversations to the office of Senator Paul Laxalt of Nevada, who was then head of the Senate Intelligence Committee. The material was allegedly reviewed by Laxalt's aide, Robert Hall, and later by members of the Intelligence Committee. Curtis says he also took it to the State Department."

Smith said, "If that's all true, it fell into the abyss of secrecy surrounding the establishment and maintenance of the M Fund. We can only look at the detail and wonder."

Rodriguez said, "You're an historian, Tomi. This is not writ in stone. Maybe Curtis was a pathological liar and a con artist. You know how to follow a paper trail. Curtis also told his story to writers for the *Philippine News* in San Francisco, to Brian Greenspun, an editor of the *Las Vegas Sun*, and to columnist Jack Anderson, where they were published simultaneously. Despite the documents and tapes nobody believed him. Curtis's story broke in the *Las Vegas Sun*, not the *New York Times* or the *Washington Post*. Jack Anderson had taken over Drew Pearson's political gossip column 'Washington Merry Go Around,' hardly a definitive source of the truth."

Tomi shook her head.

Rodriguez said, "If Curtis had placed a simple telephone call to the *Times* and given them his tapes and documents, he would likely have brought to the surface the entire story of the Golden Lily. In late June 1978, three Filipino exiles in San Francisco reportedly spotted General Fabian Ver and three companions there. The exiles had worked for the *Philippine News* and so knew Robert Curtis. They believed Ver's companions were colonels in the Philippine army. They quickly contacted Curtis and told him to beware. Curtis immediately adopted a new identity and went underground, taking his maps with him.

"Although Curtis had his maps, Marcos now had Curtis's reprocessing equipment. He could now recast Teresa II gold into Good London Delivery, Australian AAA book-shaped ingots, Sumatra Lloyd, or the three-and-three-quarter-ounce gold bars that Johnson Matthey marketed in India and the Arabian Gulf. When the International Monetary Fund changed its rules to allow government central banks to buy gold directly from private sources, Marcos issued a decree putting the government, that is himself, in charge of all gold transactions in the Philippines. This enabled him to wash the Golden Lily through the Philippine Central Bank before he sold it on the world markets. Comes now the Nugan-Hand Bank. You want to take over the story, Kip?"

Yoshida shook his head in disgust. "All this American talk about the wonders of democracy. If this man Curtis kept all these documents and taped his conversations, then turned them over to a committee of the United States Senate that was supposed to oversee the intelligence service plus gave them to newspapers, how come nothing came of it? Are you telling me this is how American democracy works? All their posturing and high-minded lecturing to the rest of the world."

"They are a bit self-righteous, I'll give you that," Chiba said.

Yoshida clenched his jaw. "Yes, we Japanese have our kuramaku. *Yes, we have* kuroi kiri. *Our way of doing business could possibly be improved, I'll concede that. Onions cost so much because they change hands five times before they make it into a bowl of noodles. But look at the record of the Americans in this instance. Are they any better?"*

"Good point."

"These three are clearly deluded. We do a favor to put them out of their misery."

"Have you killed before, Yoshida-san? I take it you have."

"Eighteen times." Yoshida said this with some pride. "I'm good at it, and I do what my oyabun *tells me."*

"Which is why you were given this assignment."

"I think so," Yoshida said. *"Also I'm loyal. I say again, I do what my* oyabun *tells me to do. I owe him* giri.*"*

Smith said, "The Nugan-Hand Bank was established during the Vietnam War to give wealthy Asians an alternative to the uncertain security of banks in Laos, Cambodia, and Vietnam. Headquartered in the Cayman Islands to maintain its secrecy, Nugan-Hand was later used to wash money for the Shah of Iran. A former director of Central Intelligence was legal counsel for Nugan-Hand. A retired admiral, formerly in charge of plans and policy for the U.S. Pacific Command, headed the Washington office. A retired general, once an aide to DCI Allen Dulles and later a staff member of the National Security Council, was in charge of the Honolulu branch.

"Beginning in the mid-1970s, Ferdinand Marcos became a valued customer of Nugan-Hand, and in 1978 the bank opened a Manila branch headed by a retired general who was a former assistant to the Joint Chiefs of Staff for counterinsurgency. Shortly thereafter, Nugan-Hand allegedly began flying shipments of Teresa II gold from Clark Air Force base to the American deep black security base at Pine Gap, near Alice Springs in the Australian outback. The gold was trucked out and sold on world markets as AAA ingots."

"How do you know this?"

"We don't, for sure," Smith said. "It's easy to assert that the CIA did this or the CIA did that, but almost impossible to prove it. That's why they're at the heart of so many conspiracy theories. Shortly after the alleged Pine Gap flights in 1979, one of the bank's principals, Frank Nugent, was found dead behind the wheel of his Mercedes near Sydney. He had a bullet hole in his head and a rifle on the seat beside him. His partner, Michael Hand, simply vanished. In the ensuing scandal, the bank collapsed; its deposits included three and a half million dollars credited to Marcos's sister, Elizabeth Marcos Rocka."

"Again proving nothing."

"Correct. The details about the Nugan-Hand Bank surfaced in a Honolulu fraud trial in 1981. Ron Rewald testified that at a polo club in Hawaii he met a Filipino banker who was a CIA conduit for Filipino black money flowing into the United States. He said the banker helped transfer gold to the U.S. for Mrs. Rocka. Did Rewald perjure himself? Possibly. But chalk it up as more circumstantial evidence backing Mrs. Marcos's story."

Rodriguez said, "We are told that in 1981, the Philippine Central Bank put three hundred thousand ounces of 'excess locally derived gold reserves' on the market in a scheme whereby British, American, and German banks leased the gold for three to six months. The leasing banks transported the gold and paid Marcos a one-percent investment fee. A retired soldier of fortune told the Federal Witness Protection Program that Bankers Trust–Zurich sent him to Manila to fly out fifty tons of gold in an operation headed by an officer of Marcos's security command. The deal fell through at the last minute because of a quarrel over the terms of the sale, but the pilot saw the gold, which had Chinese and Japanese markings.

Smith said, "The only way to make sense out of all this is to sort through the coincidences chronologically, step-by-step. In 1982, intelligence operatives allegedly working out of the National Security Council were busy collecting covert money to support the Nicaraguan Contras. The anti-Communist good fight. In that year Colonel Oliver M. North borrowed millions from the sultan of Brunei, a deal marked by a screw-up in which the money went astray because the sultan was given the wrong numbers for the Swiss bank account. What was the ostensible mission of the World Anti-Communist League?"

"To fight communism." Tomi said.

"In 1982, General John K. Singlaub was president of the World Anti-Communist League. This is the same Singlaub who was an intelligence officer during the war and in place in East Asia when the deal was struck with Hirohito."

Smith said, "He was close to Chiang Kai-shek. His friend Cline, a pal of Chiang's son, was made Company station chief in Taipei in 1958 and four years later returned to Langley to become a deputy director. Singlaub was deputy director of CIA activities in South Korea when Kodama worked for the Company in the early 1950s. He rose to command the American forces in South Korea until President Carter sacked him for publically opposing proposed troop cuts."

Rodriguez said, "The sponsors of the World Anti-Communist League included Kodama Yoshio, Sasakawa Ryiochi, Park Chunghee of South Korea, President Sukarno of Indonesia, Chiang, and Marcos, who regularly attended league meetings. In the late 1970s, Marcos supplied false end-user certificates to mask the real destination of illicit weapons. In 1983, he began supplying certificates masking weapons sent to the Contras. A Filipino arms dealer later produced documents showing that General Fabian Ver received a five-percent commission on a one-hundred-million-dollar deal in 1983. There's more to that tangle, but I'll return to my main story.

"We have allegations that Ferdinand Marcos had two deals flop in the winter and spring of 1983. In the first, Filipino army officers tried unsuccessfully to get the head of the American Express Private Bank in Hong Kong to broker fifty tons of gold. In the second, a California firm is said to have contacted R. B. Wilson of Kerr & Associates in Sydney with a proposal to move sixty metric tons each week for five years, for a total of four thousand tons of gold. The gold was to have been moved with the assistance of Mitsubishi Bank in Las Vegas."

Yoshida said, "If this story is true—assume for the moment that it is—you'll note the stamp of American greed is all over it. All those American generals and intelligence officers running branches of the CIA's bank. With those huge sums of money being moved about in secret, are you trying to tell me that a few coins here and there didn't make their way into the pockets of those esteemed patriotic gentlemen? Ultimately the American tax-payers paid for all this. What assurance did they have that it was being run honestly? None." Yoshida spit on the ground.

"I see your point, Yoshida-san."

"And the Americans accuse us Japanese of being secretive and greedy!" Yoshida spat again. "I said before that the CIA is the only American institution that understands giri. *Perhaps their* giri *is not to the Japanese they might have worked with after the war, but to their right to establish and maintain money-laundering rackets in secret. They tried to justify the maintenance of their own bank as necessary for their fight against communism, but was it only that?"*

"Good point," Chiba said.

"Now they justify their secrets by saying it's because they owe giri *to Kodama and the others. Such liars they are. Pah!"*

Rodriguez said, "A Filipino whose wife was the niece of a guard at Malacanang was allegedly involved in still another gold deal. Although the Filipino didn't tape his telephone conversations, he kept careful records, later producing correspondence, telexes, and copies of contracts to prove his role in selling part of Hirohito's Gold to a consortium of buyers in Australia, the U.K., and the U.S. The Filipino's story is that he agreed to broker the sale of sixty metric tons of gold ingots a week for two years—a total sale of fifteen thousand six hundred metric tons through both Hong Kong and American banks."

Tomi leaned forward. "I'm listening, Ding."

"The Filipino alleged that in May 1983, Marcos's people

trucked sixty tons of gold to Clark Air Force Base at Angeles City, Luzon, where U.S. transport planes flew it to Hong Kong. This routine was repeated weekly until August, when Ninoy Aquino was assassinated on the tarmac of Manila Airport."

Rodriguez said, "Here we come to Executive X, who allegedly came away with signed documents to prove his allegations. X is said to have been an executive vice president of a large American defense contractor. A friend of X, a retired air force colonel, had traveled to the Philippines for years and had become friendly with a number of senior Filipino army officers. On this officer's recommendation, in May 1983 X flew to Manila, where Marcos showed him a vault containing a tranche of one hundred metric tons of gold, properly hallmarked and packed for international trading.

"Marcos asked X if he would like to broker delivery of two tranches of bullion to London. The first deal was for thirty-eight thousand metric tons of twelve-point-five-kilo Good London Delivery, then worth three hundred eighty billion U.S. dollars. The second was for a slightly smaller tranch of thirty-seven thousand metric tons of twelve-point-five-kilo ingots. This was just shy of the total amount of gold estimated to have been legitimately mined throughout history."

"Oops!" Tomi said.

"Marcos was a big talker. Are those bizarre numbers accurate? Probably not. We believe he did have a hoard of gold. How much is the question. In relating this story later, X allegedly showed contracts bearing Marcos's signature. Ordinarily the buyers would purchase gold certificates representing the value of the bullion, but in this case Marcos wanted to sell Philippine Central Bank Treasury notes in U.S. dollar denominations, which the buyers could then swap for gold certificates—a transaction for which X claims Marcos wanted to charge one percent. If the bankers agreed to that, not only would Marcos have earned an extra cut, he could later claim to have issued the bank notes in exchange for foreign loans."

"But the buyers didn't agree."

Rodriguez shook his head. "Nobody believed the gold had been mined at Benguet. Executive X claimed Marcos made it clear he was not the single seller; the gold belonged to a pool or consortium of some sort. X pressed him for specifics. Finally, Marcos allegedly told him that it was being divided among anti-Communist friends of the United States. In the contract, unnamed VIPS and GRLS were listed as the owners. The rest was to be divided among Asian GRLS who were listed as 'intermediaries/beneficiaries.' The intermediaries/beneficiaries were to be paid at accounts designated by Marcos, who was to receive one percent. VIPS stood for Very Important Persons, but X wasn't sure what GRLS meant. X asked Marcos. Marcos said generals. X asked how many VIPS and generals?

"Marcos said, *'Shi Pa.'* X asked what *'shi pa'* meant. Marcos said, 'It's what they call themselves. Chinese for one hundred.' X said, 'One hundred VIPS and generals?' Marcos said, 'No, not a hundred, but a lot.' 'Where are they from?' X asked. 'Twelve countries,' Marcos said.

"X turned down the deal. He later tried to float the story to an American journalist with a national reputation for honesty, but the journalist laughed at him. Couldn't be true."

Smith interrupted. "What is wrong about this story is that Marcos had his Chinese numbers wrong. *Shi Pa* is not one hundred. It is eighteen, which is more like the number of GRLS and VIPS splitting the lily, making X's story far more credible. *Shi,* the number ten, is pronounced *shur. Pa*, number eight, is pronounced *bah.* The mistake of calling *Shi Pa* one hundred has been incorrectly passed on in accounts of Executive X's encounter with Marcos. By the way, the gentlemen of *Shi Pa* went so far as to form an organization to give themselves a reason to have periodic public meetings. Come on, Tomi, you already know who that likely was."

"The Asian Anti-Communist League, which became the World Anti-Communist League."

"Eventually guided by whom?"

"The OSS operative John K. Singlaub, confidant of Chiang Kai-shek and his son."

Ding said, "*We at Bawiin mo ang Ginto* think Douglas MacArthur's bargain with Emperor Hirohito let Hirohito keep his crown plus roughly twenty percent of the booty. The rest was split among the remaining members of *Shi Pa.* Hirohito regarded the Golden Lily as his perquisite as the emperor. In the end he used it to get the best possible deal for himself. Dumb, he wasn't."

Yoshida said, "Let me get this straight. They're saying that after our defeat at Midway that Emperor Hirohito had his younger brother bury the Golden Lily in the Philippines to keep it out of the hands of Imperial Army officers he distrusted. And after the surrender, he lied to the Japanese people about his role in the war, then secretly accepted a share of the loot in a deal with Douglas MacArthur."

"Yes, that's what they're saying. Seems pretty clear-cut."

"They lie!"

Chiba shrugged.

Yoshida clenched his teeth with rage. After a minute, he calmed down and said, "There are clearly two ways of looking at all this."

"Oh? Tell me, Yoshida-san."

"Rodriguez and Smith are saying this was all a plot to help Japan fight Communists after the war and to bribe anti-Communist allies of the United States. But could it not have also been a conspiracy by some renegade CIA agents working with Chiang Kai-shek and some worthless Koreans and overseas Chinese to rob Japan of what it had honestly captured in battle?"

"If you adjust the logic only slightly, I agree. That's what you get."

"You talk about mirrors. What you see in the mirror depends on how close you stand to the glass. And at what angle do you see the reflection? Smith and Rodriguez see what they wish to see. I see Chinese ripping off the Japanese with American CIA operatives taking their cut, all of which they justify in the holy name of fighting the Communists. Pah!"

Chiba smiled. "Reality in the manner of 'Rashoman.' Kurosawa-san would agree entirely."

"Sorry, sir."

"No, no. Many of your points are well taken, Yoshida-san. I said I wanted to know your opinion. I still do."

Smith said, "The Asian Anti-Communist League was supported by Chiang Kai-shek and his son, by anti-Communist Koreans, and by Kodama Yoshio. It was the invention of Paul Helliwell, who co-ordinated financial support for anti-Communist armies and governments throughout Asia. Kodama continued working for the CIA after it was formed in 1947. When Mao pushed Chiang off the mainland in 1949, Helliwell established Sea Supply Corporation and Air America to supply the anti-Communist operations throughout Asia, including the opium armies in Thailand.

"If what Executive X said is true, what he saw was an M Fund contract, a legal smoking gun. If so, Marcos was not the principal. He washed Hirohito's Gold for a percentage. The beneficiaries of the treasure were Emperor Hirohito and Asian strongmen, allies of the United States. *Shi Pa*, eighteen, is a believable number. Of course we may cheerfully discount all this if we believe that Robert Curtis, the Filipino whose niece worked for the Marcoses, plus Executive X and the all the bankers approached to wash gold all forged contracts and invented detailed stories confirming one single truth." Smith held up the palms of his hands. "Does anybody believe that's likely? Hello!"

17

Kip Smith followed Ding Rodriguez's Blazer out of Bacolod on the road to the airport until Rodriguez crossed over a river perhaps a hundred feet wide and took an immediate hard right. Smith slowed his Land Cruiser as he passed a turnoff that wound downhill toward the river and ended in the yard of what looked like a dilapidated boat building or repair operation.

Rodriguez parked his Blazer by the rotting carcass of what had once been an outriggered fishing boat. There were *bankas* in various states of repair both in the water and on the shore. The derelict boats on the shore—narrow hulls with their outriggers removed—faced this way and that like jackstraws, amid weeds and jumbled piles of lumber.

Smith continued on the highway for a hundred yards and parked his Land Cruiser on a wide spot just off the road.

Few people could keep up with Smith on a sidewalk in Berlin or London or New York. In temperate climates Smith was a crisp, brisk walker, setting forth with long strides, negotiating anonymous crowds according to custom—with nary a "Howdy" or "Good evening" or a tip of the head.

Smith retrieved a shoulder bag and a battered walking stick from the trunk and set off in the direction of the boatyard. He assumed his Tropical World, heat-and-humidity walk, slow and lazy. Lethargic. Only tourists and morons walked fast in those parts of the world where the hot air hung limpid and heavy. Hurry for what? To do what? To go where? Fast walking was not only dumb, but also boorish and perhaps even a little offensive. When one walked in the tropics, one acknowledged other strollers with a nod and whatever was the local greeting.

Smith sauntered lazily down the short, winding road, into the parking area of packed mud amid a thicket of weeds. A once splendid but now faded and peeling sign, hung crookedly on the side of a small, open-windowed building, informed Smith that he had entered the domain of the Bacolod Yacht Club. The clubhouse had a porch that faced the water. Two skinny dogs slept on the porch, and an old man sat whittling.

Directly in front of this porch, Ding Rodriguez stood on a two-board catwalk on the side of the narrow cabin of one of the most unusual boats Smith had ever seen. The *Lapu Lapu*, painted a splendid black and red, was a sixty-foot-long, powered version of a *banka*.

Smith made his way along a narrow catwalk and hopped onto the *Lapu Lapu*. He tight-roped his way from the outrigger up to the brace on the boat's slender hull. "This is it?"

"The mighty *Lapu Lapu*. What do you think? Up to the job?"

Smith peered inside the narrow cabin. Then he pulled up the lid to the rear hatch and peered down at the engine. "What have you got powering this thing, Ding?"

"Two hundred horsepower diesel."

"Hot boat! Good for you." That Smith admired the boat was clear from the expression on his face. He did not have to own something himself to appreciate it. He could be an enthusiast if he wanted, and when he did, his face showed it.

"I designed it myself," Rodriguez said.

"You've got no drag at all. You must just skip across the water."

"It moves right along."

"Got any range?"

"Depends on how many tanks you want to add," Rodriguez said. "We need to talk."

"I agree." Rodriguez, stretching his arms for balance, walked back across the outrigger's brace to the catwalk. Then he hopped onto shore and headed for the clubhouse with Smith following him. When he got to the clubhouse porch, the whittler and one dog had abandoned the shade. The remaining dog seemed unconcerned that he would be stepped on. He was too tired and hot to look up. He dug at his gut with one paw, an indifferent attempt to rid himself of a bothersome flea.

Smith glanced through the open window inside the clubhouse that was a clutter of boards and mahogany shavings on a bare floor. He flopped onto a bench on the porch just below the window. Rodriguez sat on a rickety chair. A slight breeze stirred, then they were left with the heat.

Smith said, "I went with Tomi for her interview with the Fallons yesterday before our meeting in the Big Veg. Roberta Fallon loves to drop names, and she allowed as how she and Robin recently had dinner in Manila with guess who?"

"You don't have to be Columbo to follow the links, Kip. Martinez was with Leber, then Nippon Star, then Delta International, and now Plymouth Rising. No way he's going to let us ferry the archers off the island on the *Lapu Lapu*. That's bullfeathers."

"He wants to paralyze us with gold fever so he can keep an eye on us," Smith said.

"What do we do now?" Rodriguez asked.

"We keep our eye on the rice and wait."

18

On the afternoon of their short flight to Cebu for a briefing in Our Place, Ding Rodriguez took Kip Smith and Tomi Kobayashi for a reconaissance trip to the area of Sen. Buddy Enrique's sugar plantation, located less than two miles from the edge of the Patag. The Patag, at the base of Mt. Silay, was one of the largest uncut stands of tropical hardwoods left in the Philippines. In fact, it was officially the Patag National Park, although its flora and fauna went undescribed in travel books. No Filipino family went there for a Sunday picnic. The Patag had for some years been under the control of the New People's Army, and the presence of strangers in the park—whether kings, potentates, or Robin Fallon—was by permission of the NPA.

Rodriguez, *meep, meep, meeping* his horn, and niftily dodging animals, potholes, and people, drove east toward the mountains and the Patag on a road flanking the winding Malogo River.

As he drove, he explained that Enrique, who owned more than 13,000 hectares—2.47 acres equaled one hectare—was one of the most powerful planters on the island. Enrique existed so close to the Patag by virtue of his private army.

"Private armies." Rodriguez's mouth tightened. "The NPA leaves planters like Enrique alone for fear of being hit themselves, and so the little guys wind up paying tax on their land and trucks.

If it weren't for his helicopters and private army, the NPA'd be on Enrique like a bad smell. They can hit and run if they're being pursued on the ground—"

"But not when they're being followed overhead by helicopters," Tomi said.

Rodriguez grimaced. "Only Enrique doesn't own the helicopters himself. That's the racket. They belong to the Philippine government, on loan to the CAGFUs. The government arms and equips the CAGFUs, but the planters pay their salaries. Who do you think they're loyal to, Tomi? Someone like Enrique, who pays their salaries, or the little guy next door who could use some help? You tell me."

"Enrique."

"Of course. Why else would a warlord want to be a senator?"

Smith said, "I take it the superintendent of the Philippine Military Academy is an old pal of Senator Enrique."

"Old pals. Maybe even related."

Smith said, "I think we need to stop well short of the plantation. Is it possible to circle through this cane for a quick look and then retreat?"

Rodriguez looked alarmed at the suggestion. He swerved to avoid a pothole. "We'll roast in there! And the bugs!"

Tomi appeared anxious as well. "What on earth are you talking about, Kip? Can you imagine the heat?"

Smith shrugged. "You two can go back to Bacolod for an afternoon movie if you want, but I'm the one who has to figure the action. All I want is a quick look-see, and we can come right back out. If I can help it, I don't want to be seen nosing around. When we're finished we can spend the afternoon drinking San Miguel."

Tomi sighed. She was game, but no enthusiast. "Well then, let's get hiking."

Rodriguez pulled the Blazer onto a side lane and turned off the key. "Enrique's place is just down the road."

"How far?" Smith asked.

"About three quarters of a mile. All we have to do is stay parallel to the road and out of sight."

They stepped out of the Blazer into the sweltering heat, Smith wearing a photographer's vest and a small Nikon slung over one shoulder.

They set off into the cane field until they couldn't see the road. Rodriguez took a sharp left and continued parallel to the road. Smith hadn't gotten twenty feet into the stifling, buggy, humid hot box of sugarcane when he wished he'd paid more attention to Ding Rodriguez.

In front of him, Tomi, sputtering, took a cobweb in her mouth. "*Aaaaaahhhhhh!*"

"We haven't even started," Rodriguez said.

They trudged through the cane, growing hotter with each determined step, knowing that the road and relief from the heat lay not fifty yards away. After forty minutes of effort, they came upon a single strand of wire at the edge of Buddy Enrique's plantation.

"Connects the perimeter of bug lights," Rodriguez said. "Turn them on at night, and it's snap, crackle, and pop."

Enrique himself lived in what looked like an American ranch-style house that sat on a low hill, surrounded by a sprawling, rich green lawn that might have been part of a well-tended golf course. At the edge of the lawn, a flag waved atop a stick in the middle of an immaculate putting green.

Smith said, "A little pitch-and-putt action, I see."

"He likes his golf," Rodriguez said.

In addition to the putting green, the lawn had elegant white chairs and benches under tropical shade trees. At the edge of the lawn, Senator Enrique had a private fishing pond with a spiffy rowboat tied up at a neat little dock. His domestic help lived in four tiny houses at the edge of the cleared area.

There was an orchard of some kind at the end of the farm opposite Enrique's house.

"What's that?" Smith gestured toward the orchard.

"*Kalamansi* or *lemoncitos*," Rodriguez said.

In the center of the farm, between the *kalamansi* and the house, there was a large outbuilding, and in front of the outbuilding, five helicopters sat on an oil-stained concrete pad.

Smith said, "Let me see if I have this straight, Ding. Several hundred PJN faithful will be driven by four-wheel-drive vehicles past this ranch on a primitive road to an area near the Patag National Park. There, accompanied by *carabaos* pulling carts of water and gear, they'll hike in the dark for two hours on a trail cut by the NPA until they come to Pulak Pulakan, where Fallon will pray for peace and light candles for Lieutenant Dolan. They then will walk back out to the park and go home in a dramatic procession bearing candles. Is that right? Is that what they say the plan is?"

"That's correct," Rodriguez said.

Smith looked thoughtful. "Lots of possibilities. Well, shall we go back before we're spotted by ill-tempered private soldiers?"

If the way in had been bad, returning was even worse. Both the heat and humidity seemed to rise by the second. Smith looked like somebody had poured a bucket of water on him. He paused for another breather.

Behind him, Rodriguez muttered, *"Hijo de puta!"*

Smith said, "I thought you Filipinos were used to this heat."

Rodriguez looked at him with glazed eyes.

Tomi stared at the ground, her legs spread wide, hands braced on her knees. "God!"

Smith thought Tomi was dangerously wobbly. The last thing they needed was to suffer heat stroke on the eve of the big day. Smith didn't want to miss his chance to pull the plug on General

Martinez's ambition. "Are you going to make it, Tomi? Are you all right?"

Tomi looked at him, breathing heavily. "I'll be okay."

"You want to turn back? Easy to do."

She looked grim, but grateful for his concern. "We push on. I'll keep up."

Smith considered the road and glanced back in the direction of Enrique's plantation. If they weren't far enough away and something went wrong and they blew their shot at the gold, then that was that. They were trapped in a monstrous, impossible combination of heat and humidity. Smith was finding it increasingly difficult to handle the heat himself. Under the circumstances, there wasn't much else he could do. He glanced at the suffering Tomi. "Screw it. We'll take a chance," he said.

Without waiting for objections, Smith made a right-angle turn and strode, head down, plowing through cane and cobwebs toward the road and sweet release.

A few minutes later they pitched forward out of the oven of sugarcane, rejoicing as a barely detectable but blessed breeze stirred along the road and the cooling air washed across their sweaty bodies.

Rodriguez threw off his shirt.

Tomi unbuttoned her sweat-drenched blouse, holding her arms wide to catch the air on her ribs and sodden bra. She fell to her knees in the widening sliver of shade at the edge of the cane. "Air-conditioning! It's air-conditioning! Nature's own."

The shirtless Smith dropped his walking shorts around his ankles to let the air circulate through his boxer shorts. Ahhhh, it felt soooooo good.

They heard the engine of a vehicle coming from the direction of the Patag.

"Crap!" Smith yanked his pants back up and Tomi started buttoning her blouse. Smith considered the options. "Back to the cane or do we take a chance?"

Tomi said, "I think I risk croaking if I have to back into that field again in this heat. It's too hot to breathe in there."

"Ding?"

"I agree with Tomi. We stay on the road."

"Okay then, you do the talking, Ding. If they look okay, we'll see if we can hitch a ride back. What's your line?"

"I'm your guide."

"And you, Tomi?"

"I met you in Cadiz. You're shooting the revival and candle lighting for *Time*."

"If they're NPA or some other kind of bad asses and something's wrong, or if I should call either one of you Clyde, I want you to drop the ground. There'll be rat-a-tat-tat and boom-boom."

With that, a Toyota Land Cruiser appeared around the bend, traveling fast and trailing a plume of red dust.

Rodriguez waved his thumb. The Toyota slowed.

When Smith saw who was inside, he relaxed.

As Rodriguez stepped to talk to a broad-faced Asian who was driving, Smith stepped around to the passenger's side. "GeeGee! GeeGee Mendoza!" He felt the cool air spill out as the cute little GeeGee rolled down her window. Air-conditioning!

"Mr. Smith! What are you doing out here?"

"I needed a framing shot for my Robin Fallon spread. I figured a cane field with the Patag and Mt. Silay in the background. I got good sun and no clouds, but this heat got to us all, I'm afraid."

GeeGee said, "Mr. Norita Yasanuri, this is Mr. Kip Smith of *Time* magazine. I met him at a press conference on the dredge off Cadiz."

Smith stuck his hand through the window and shook hands with the Japanese. "Pleased to meet you, Norita-san."

In a Carolina accent, Norita said, "Y'all look plumb tuckered, Mr. Smith. Could you use a lift back to your rig?"

"Could we ever, thank you," Smith said.

As Smith and his companions scrambled into the backseat, GeeGee said, "Norita-san owns several of those prawn farms you may have seen along the highway, Mr. Smith. He's thinking of buying some sugar land as well."

With the windows rolled back up, Norita put the Toyota into gear and turned on the air-conditioner, which was as heaven to the passengers on the rear seat.

Smith said, "I kept looking for just the right angle for my shot and didn't realize how far we'd gone. You thinking of buying sugar land out this way, Norita-san?"

"Miss Mendoza says the land gets cheaper the closer you get to the mountains."

"Of couse, you have to factor a tax to the NPA into the cost of doing business," Rodriguez said.

"There is that, true. But Miss Mendoza says if I pay my help well, I won't have any problem. The land's so cheap I can afford to pay them a living wage. I sell most of my prawns to the Japanese, and if they're in a buying mood I do okay, but when the economy went sour, so did my market. Everybody eats sugar, good times and bad!"

Smith said, "I love your good old boy accent, Norita-san. Where did you ever learn to talk like that?"

Norita laughed. "Americans always wonder about that. My father was a visiting professor at the University of North Carolina at Chapel Hill. I wanted to try my hand at living like Americans live. I wanted an American experience, so I joined a fraternity."

"A fraternity?"

"A Japanese counted as a minority, and I was good for the house GPA."

"I see."

"I studied English poets, and my fraternity brothers drank beer."

"And you wound up with a North Carolina accent."

"I've had Americans say I sound like a Japanese redneck." Norita grinned broadly. "The same thing would happen to you if you learned Japanese on Okinawa. If you took your Japanese to Tokyo, people would know immediately where you learned to speak."

Smith said, "Here's our vehicle coming up on the left. You teach English to your Japanese friends, Norita-san?"

Norita slowed to a stop to let them out. "Y'all have a good day now, hear?"

Minutes later Kip Smith and his companions were back in Ding Rodriguez's Blazer and on their way to Silay, luxuriating in the air-conditioning. They rode without talking at first, as their bodies continued to recover from the exertion in the sun.

Smith broke the silence. "Ding, this is the road you'd take if you were going to see Jaime Pineda, correct?"

"Yes, it is," Rodriguez said.

"What can you tell me about that little COBRA-SAN reporter, GeeGee Mendoza."

"She's a left-winger, but not crazy."

"Left enough to be able to talk to Jaime Pineda if she wanted."

"Oh, sure, no problem. If GeeGee wants to talk to Jaime, she talks to Jaime."

Smith said, "If I were to come barrel-assing down the road from the Patag with a load of hot goods that I wanted to put on a fast boat as quickly as possible, where would I go?"

Rodriguez said, "It's almost a straight shot from the Patag to the concrete piers the Japanese built for their deep-water wharf at Silay. It's got a dock, but the bay is filled with silt. You'd have to ferry them to deep water with *bankas*."

"No problem doing that?"

"None that I can see." Rodriguez checked his Rolex. "We better hustle if we're going to make the flight to Cebu."

Our Place was Kipling Smith's favorite expat bar in Asia. This was not because it was "best" in any objective sense or according to the ratings in guidebooks, although it got decent marks from *Lonely Planet*. It was rather because of the mix of friends that Smith had made there over the years. An expatriate anthropology professor at the University of San Carlos was six hours older than Smith was. An expatriate mumbler, an intellectual, gave his companions extended, rambling lectures on the history of military tactics. A Filipino who taught architecture at San Carlos had gone carousing with Smith on several memorial occasions. Collectively, these were members of Smith's Cebu *barcada*. In the Visayan language, called Cebuano on Cebu, a *barcada* was used in the singular, one's friend, or in the plural, one's close circle of friends.

Located on a second floor at the corner of Sanciangko and Palaez streets, Our Place was one block toward the mountainous spine of the island of Cebu from the teeming Colon Street—the heart of downtown Cebu City. Owned by the storied Wes Mills, a retired army master sergeant, and his Filipina wife, the bar was American country-and-western with an international touch. The owner spoke fluent German dating from his days in the army, and his menu was strong on German dishes. These included *wiener schnitzel*, bratwurst and knockwurst and other German sausages made to order by Filipino butchers, and hot potato salad. American travelers and expats could order an American hamburger, potato salad, or a bowl of chili.

The walls of Our Place were covered with Bavarian travel posters, plaques commemorating the visits of various vessels, and a painting on black velvet, of dogs playing poker. The San Miguel was stored in a red Coca-Cola refrigerator above which was a painting of John Wayne. It was widely held by Smith's Cebu *barcada* that Wayne's grimace was owing to cowboy constipation, not any attempt to intimidate bad guys. A half dozen large, languid fans on the high ceiling pushed the humid air over the customers. When the owner was in, the house boom box played country-and-western music. When he was out, the Filipinas who ran the cash register and waited tables played love ballads.

Smith was relieved that none of his *barcada* were in. He and his two companions settled into a table at a Spanish window overlooking Palaez Street, the route in which Filipina coeds in jeans and white T-shirts walked to the University of San Carlos, thus making it the favorite table for Smith's *barcada*. Smith took them to the coveted window seat, which he did not always score when his friends were gathered.

On Smith's recommendation, they had a lunch of garlic steak with German potato salad, after which Smith and Rodriguez had their usual bottles of San Miguel. Tomi readied her notepad and tape recorder.

Rodriguez eyed a pair of University of San Carlos coeds on the sidewalk below them.

Yoshida finished the adjustments on his camera. "I can't figure why they would choose a place like this when they obviously could afford a more comfortable place with air-conditioning."

Chiba sucked air between his teeth. "An American like Smith would ask you why Japanese travelers hole up in the Plaza Hotel on top of the hill and have everything brought to us. Why don't we come down and join in with the other expats and adventurers?"

"It's the language," Yoshida said. "The language barrier. And we're more at home with Japanese. That's understandable."

'East is east and west is west and never the twain shall meet, is that it, Yoshida-san?"

"We are more comfortable with our own, that's true."

"But they might have a point, if one thinks about it. We don't give them a chance to know us. Why do you suppose we so assiduously copy their fashions?"

" 'We.' Don't include me in that. I don't want to be like Americans in any way whatever."

"Curious how that works. Did you know, Yoshida-san, that although the Americans denied all forms of titles and other trappings of royalty when they rebelled against George III, they have maintained an unusual fascination with the royal families of other nations over the years, our own included."

"Sir? Is that true?"

"At war's end, the American public wanted revenge taken out on Hirohito's hide. But they were quite willing, possibly even relieved, to accept Douglas MacArthur's assurance that the emperor had been duped and kept in ignorance by his advisors and officers of the Imperial Army."

"The emperor was innocent," Yoshida said quickly. "We know that for a fact. It couldn't be otherwise. Striking a deal with Douglas MacArthur? Impossible. I deny it!"

"Easy, Yoshida-san. I am not suggesting he was guilty, only that the American reverence for kings and royalty is unusual for a country that has none itself. The unquestioning respect most Americans have for the emperor has been most helpful in protecting his reputation over the years."

Rodriguez said, "Now come the really wild allegations of gold. In May 1983, an employee of a Belgian bank in Luxembourg allegedly helped process a contract for the sale of four-point-two million gold ingots from the Philippine Central Bank. These were twelve-point-five-kilo ingots—more than one-point-six billion ounces. The one-hundred-twenty-four-billion-dollar sale of the first tranche of seven hundred nineteen thousand forty-five ingots had already been approved, so the story goes, with the Belgian bank acting as correspondent between the seller and the buyers, members of the London gold pool. The buyers had requested a letter from Marcos giving them immunity from seizure, investigation, or arrest. If the story is true, the memorandum of agreement was written on paper containing the letterhead of President Ferdinand Marcos and was signed by Konsehala Candelarin V. Santiago, Marcos's executive secretary."

"But we don't know if it's true."

"At this late date, no. The story is that the Belgian wanted to know if the documents were genuine so he took them to the American Embassy. The Americans took the documents and studied them, later returning them with the stamp of the vice consul certifying them as authentic.

"Three years later, reporters for the *Philippines Free Press* in San Francisco, not having any idea of what had happened in Luxembourg, claimed to have gotten their hands on a contract by the Mercantile Insurance Company, dated February 4, 1983, and signed by the vice president of Mercantile. This contract, addressed to a firm in Nassau, insured the shipment from Manila to London of seven hundred nineteen thousand forty-five standard twelve-point-five-kilo ingots, Good London Delivery."

Tomi said, "Precisely the same number as the first tranche of ingots in the deal cleared by the Belgian bank."

"There you go," Rodriguez said. "Some, if not most, of Hirohito's Gold was shipped from Manila to Johnson Matthey in London between 1970 and 1983. In 1984, rumors surfaced in London that Johnson Matthey was in some kind of trouble. There were suggestions that improper loans had been made and banking procedures were maybe too flexible, and this was no small matter: Johnson Matthey handled seven-point-five percent of the world market for gold and fifteen percent of the London trade. Like French wine and American baseball, the image of the London gold pool had to be kept pure. A firestorm of rumor threatened the pool and its treasured power."

Rodriguez's beer was empty. So was Smith's. Rodriguez waved his hand at a waitress. "*Duha*, Di!" He waited for their beer to be delivered before he continued. "In September 1984, the Bank of England and the other four members of the pool met secretly one weekend and on the following Monday the Bank of England took over Johnson Matthey. They sacked eight Johnson Matthey executives, then said nothing serious was the matter. There were some documents missing, they said, but on the whole everything was shipshape. The rumors then turned on allegations that substantial amounts of gold had been smuggled into Johnson Matthey vaults for which the seller, in this case Ferdinand Marcos, had not paid the fifteen percent British value-added tax."

Smith looked impressed. "Marcos apparently stiffed everybody he came across from Curtis to the British government. You have to admire him in a coarse sort of way. On his terms, he was a kind of genius."

Rodriguez pretended to pray to the heavens. "In 1986, after two years of fighting charges and countercharges, during which Prime Minister Margaret Thacher's ministers remained tight-lipped, the British government put Johnson Matthey up for sale. Mase-Westpac, an Australian syndicate of mining, bullion, and banking concerns, bought Johnson Matthey and changed its name to Minorities Finance. Despite all that had happened, nobody believed Robert Curtis. Or pretended not to. Impossible.

Nobody believed the stories of banks approached to launder gold. Couldn't have happened. Executive X's story never saw print. A likely story. You think these are all lies?" Rodriguez burst out laughing.

Yoshida regarded the latest turn of events with disbelief. "Kawana-san? Here to retrieve the alchemist archers?"

"He has a map showing where the golden dragons are buried and has been bargaining with local guerrillas who occupy the area. Suma-san had an operative detailed to monitor the recovery, but he is now missing. We're not sure why."

"Do you know the missing operative, sir?"

"He was Suma-san's mole in the CIA. Or at least we think he was our mole. Maybe the Americans doubled him. Or maybe he was loyal only to himself or a bank account in Switzerland or the Cayman Islands. Hard to tell. In any event, you and I are now detailed to take his place. We've been given Kawana's radio frequency and a cell phone number, and he has ours. If he requires our assistance, we are to give it, identifying ourselves as Banzai One. If we are not needed, we stay out of the way."

Yoshida said, "Kodama-san is said to have had some beautiful photographs taken of the golden dragons. Have you seen them, sir?"

"Yes, I have," Chiba said. "They're extraordinary—in full color, unusual for the period. The dragons are covered with tiny, exquisitely rendered scales, and they have rubies for eyes. They're the basis of Kawana's duplicate dragons."

"Sir?"

"Which gives him the ability to deceive that his erstwhile competitors lack. Which dragons are real? Which are bogus? Only he knows."

Yoshida cocked his head. "Very clever. Sir, I have a question . . . I . . ." Yoshida closed his mouth.

Chiba laughed. "Don't worry. Do you do really think Suma-san will allow Kawana to keep Emperor Hirohito's gift to Kodama Yoshio? No, no, no, Yoshida-san. Suma's patrol boats will relieve Kawana of the archers when he nears the Japanese coast."

Rodriguez said, "This chapter is about a generous, but perhaps naive first lady. Tell me, Tomi, why do you suppose the United States spirited Ferdinand Marcos safely out of Manila when he was surrounded there in Malacanang Palace? If justice had been served, they would have left him there, right? Maybe the Filipinos would have strung him from his heels like the Italians did to Mussolini. But no. The Americans rescued him. Why? That's fun."

"Fun in what way?"

"In a sick kind of way, I suppose, depending on your politics and loyalties. In late 1977, remember, Robert Curtis took his tapes and documents to the chief aide of the chairman of the Senate Intelligence Committee."

"Senator Paul Laxalt of Nevada. Friends of the Reagans."

Rodriguez said, "Correct. A close friend of the Reagans. Are we to believe that Laxalt, knowing that the Reagans were also friends of the Marcoses, never mentioned the topic of Hirohito's Gold to his friend the president?

"Perhaps yes. To protect him. He couldn't be blamed for what he didn't know."

"That's possible. I agree. The Reagans might not have known. Now then, Tomi, pop to the weekend in February 1986. Malacanang palace was surrounded by Cory Aquino's supporters."

"The Yellow Revolution."

"Correct. On a Saturday night Marcos had a barge tied up at the palace quay on the Pasig River. That night and the next day, Marcos is said to have had a barge loaded with bullion from the Philippine Central Bank and with Japanese gold that he had stored in vaults under a warehouse. The next night the barge was taken downstream to Manila Bay, and the gold was loaded onto the presidential yacht, *Ang Pangulo*, which set sail for Hong Kong."

"Marcos got it out of there."

Rodriguez said, "Marcos certainly wasn't going to leave the Philippines without the gold. At 5 A.M., Monday morning, 6 P.M. Monday night in Manila, the State Department convinced President Reagan to issue a statement saying Marcos should resign. Well, Tomi, you can imagine. That night the poor old Filipino traitor and thief was feeling downright lonely and blue. He was losing the country that Japanese mobsters had bought for him and which had been his toy for twenty years, and he wasn't keen on giving it up. So at 1 A.M. Manila time on Tuesday—that's 2 P.M. Monday in Washington—he phoned a member of the United States Senate, to see if he could get a little help. Who did he phone?"

"Paul Laxalt?"

Rodriguez looked amused. "Laxalt later said Ferdinand had a cockeyed scheme in mind whereby American helicopters would fly the Marcoses to Ilocos in northern Luzon, where they would rally their troops and retake the country. Later, Imelda got on the phone. Want to hazard a guess as to whom she called?"

"Don't have the foggiest."

"Nancy Reagan. Nancy called back and said under the circumstances of a popular revolution, it would be impossible for her husband to intervene on behalf of President Marcos and repeated the State Department's offer of refuge in the United States."

Smith made loud sucking sounds with his mouth. "Keep in mind that even under the circumstances of being forced out of office, Marcos still had a little leverage of his own. If these combinations of allegations and assertions are largely true, he knew enough to blow the whistle on Hirohito's Gold."

Taking a swig of San Miguel, Yoshida said, "When we met Mr. Smith in Belize, I couldn't help noting that you two knew one another. Quite well, it seemed. I was wondering: Does this have any bearing on his allowing us to tape everything he and the Filipino are telling the young woman? Why would he do that? I still don't understand."

Chiba thought for a moment. "I do know him, that's so. Quite well as it happens. Shortly after he quit his job as a CIA operative—that wasn't too long after his wife was murdered—we got drunk together in Kuala Lumpur and he told me why."

"And that was?"

"He said he was tired of bearing the burden."

"The burden?" Yoshida furrowed his eyebrows.

"Of maintaining secrets he believes are morally wrong and unnecessary. He knows we're here. And he knows he and his friends are at our mercy. I think he imagines himself as the rector of December."

"Sir?"

"He is reminding me that the memory of what happened in occupied Japan and Cold War Asia is dimming fast. In time, it will be lost entirely."

Yoshida clearly did not understand why Smith would care so passionately.

"He is foremost an American patriot. He seeks confession and absolution for the mutual sins of our two countries. He is wrong, of course. Misguided." Chiba stared into the night.

After a while, he added, "Smith may be impatient with us Japanese, Yoshida-san, but he does not hate us. He is not our enemy. On the contrary, he admires the best in us. He respects our intelligence and discipline, our aesthetics, and the many blessings of our adherence to tradition. By making it as easy as possible to hear his case, he is asking for my help. He pleads with me to let his story be made public, after which historians may winnow the truth from the lies and inaccuracies."

"Sir?"

"It could be that he and Rodriguez are betting that I'm so weak and debilitated by my American education that I will ignore my giri and help them, make public the facts surrounding Yamashita's fate and his wife's murder—not to mention how all that happened to the Philippines was

*done by that swine Ferdinand Marcos. They forget that I am not an
American. I am Japanese and will remain that way until I join my ancestors."*

"We're almost to the end of my briefing, Tomi. After Marcos was
deposed, the Leber Group allegedly reformed itself as Nippon
Star, a legal entity, allegedly listed as Phoenix Exploration Service
Ltd., London, and registered in Liberia, where laws of incorpo-
ration allow principals to hide their identity. There were two secondary companies associated with Nippon Star. One company was
owned by an Oklahoman who was a friend of the televangelists
Jim and Tammy Bakker, and a financial backer of the Praise The
Lord church of the PTL television broadcast network."

Smith said, "You wondered how the Fallons came to be involved in all this. There you have it, the Christian, anti-Communist
connection."

Rodriguez said, "A second company was the Phoenix Overseas
Project, allegedly owned by General John K. Singlaub, who had
offices in Phoenix, Arizona.

Tomi's jaw dropped. "Oh, no. Singlaub again!"

Rodriguez guffawed. "But hey, the gold was only a myth, right?
Didn't exist. The first post-Marcos attempt to retrieve the gold
was based on Paul Jiga's memory. An engineer from Georgia had
developed a laser device to find buried gold. Jiga led him to a
reef in Calatagan Bay, seventy miles southwest of Manila, where
the Japanese allegedly used forced labor to bury the gold after
which the shaft was booby-trapped and capped with concrete. But
without a detailed map, the effort was frustrated. Two Nippon Star
representatives finally found Curtis, who was still holed up under
an assumed name. They wanted to look at the maps. Curtis said
he refused. Then he was allegedly approached by the same member of the John Birch Society who was now with Nippon Star. He

said the lawsuit would be forgiven. He said General Singlaub wanted to use the money to set up an endowment to fight communism around the world."

Smith held up his hand. "Context, Tomi! Context! Here is where the story, if it is true, comes full circle."

Rodriguez continued, "Curtis claims to have told him no. No maps. For weeks, the man called him repeatedly. Each time Curtis said no. Then, he claimed, a retired general, a former member of the National Security Council, called him from the Pentagon office that he was still using. The general told Curtis it was his patriotic duty to help Singlaub fight communism. At last, Curtis relented. Still recording his conversations, he flew to Hong Kong where he was offered a seat on the board of directors of the endowment that included some powerful Filipinos and retired American generals.

"When Nippon Star swung into action, it had as many as ten excavations going at once. Rather than being low profile, as the Leber Group had been, Nippon Star's workers were guarded by flashy security troops with automatic rifles. Newspapers in Manila began reporting the digging as though it was a spectator sport. Curtis soon had enough. He threatened to take off with his maps again unless the eager generals butted out. The generals did as they were told, and Curtis, claiming to have remained out of sight, directed a team of workers digging under Fort Santiago."

"They wanted that gold for the Contras?"

"And maybe a share for themselves, do you suppose?" Rodriguez clapped his belly. "Suffice it to say that over the years, such caches of Hirohito's Gold as there were to recover were in fact excavated and split among the generals and VIPS of *Shi Pa*. One of the last remaining stashes was the alchemist archers of Xhingsui Gap, Emperor Hirohito's gift to Kodama."

Rodriguez looked down through the Spanish window, momentarily distracted by some Filipinas walking up the sidewalk toward the University of San Carlos, dressed in blue jeans and white T-shirts. He groaned softly. "Isn't life grand?"

Yoshida said, "Sir, you tell me you have not forgotten your giri. *You will not abandon it. I accept that. But if I am to do my duty, I am obliged to ask a straightforward, but disconcerting question. I asked it once. I ask it again, respectfully."*

"Ask, Yoshida-san."

"Why, if you were not testing the logic of the story, did you seek the opinion of a yakuza kobun *on the case being made by Smith and Rodriguez? What I think is irrelevant to our mission."*

Chiba looked thoughtful. "You're a yakuza kobun, *a patriot. I was curious as to how you saw it. No harm in that. My instructions are to hear the full course of their lies and wait until the business of the alchemist archers is settled, then kill them—an objective clearly in the best interest of everybody concerned. What you think has no bearing whatsoever on my duty. I have my orders."*

"I apologize for seeming to doubt you, sir."

"You asked the question because you're under instructions to kill me if you think I'm having a change of heart." Chiba watched Yoshida. "I understand that and accept it."

Yoshida's mouth dropped. "Sir, I . . ."

Chiba smiled. "Rest assured that I remain committed to my instructions. I will not be responsible for Japan's humiliation or the embarrassment of the royal family."

Yoshida seemed clearly relieved. "I hope we get to kill them, not Kawana or one of Martinez's people."

BOOK FOUR

Ceremonies

1

The Rev. Robin Fallon insisted on walking up front with Gen. Jose Maria Martinez and their guides, a slender NPA named Danilo and his brother Rudy. Behind Danilo and Rudy, the mute, suffering Roberta, all dressed up in her Banana Republic safari outfit, rode atop a water buffalo being pulled by Felix, a gentle, broad, curly-haired Filipino. Beside and behind them trudged PJN photographers, plus cameramen and reporters from the national English-language dailies, the *Philippine Daily Inquirer*, the *Manila Times*, the *Philippine Star*, and the *Manila Bulletin*, and representatives of Manila's four television stations ABS-CBN-3, GMA-7, RPN-9, and BBC-13. The BBC was the Bureau Broadcasting Corporation, not the British Broadcasting Corporation. Fallon was disappointed that the *Time* magazine photographer Kip Smith had failed to show. Fallon had entertained a brief fantasy of having his picture in *Time* leading Filipino Christians up the storied Pulak Pulakan to honor the fallen hero, Lt. John W. Dolan.

Robin had seen a road entering the cane fields that led in the direction of Pulak Pulakan. He had been told that the road effectively ended at the far end of the sugarcane, but he thought that was just talk by Filipinos exaggerating the difficulties that lay ahead. He had envisioned a crude road of some sort. If the NPA made their headquarters in Pulak Pulakan, did they not have to bring in supplies? That meant some kind of vehicle and at least a pair of parallel ruts for the tires.

In his wildest nightmare Robin had never dreamed that he was being told the literal truth. Looking back at the line of thirteen *carabao* behind him, plodding under heavy packs, and the three hundred Filipino faithful back of them, he concluded that these people were not just God-fearing, but perhaps a trifle touched. He had gotten them all worked up at the revival in Cadiz, yes, but why on earth, knowing of the bugs and heat that lay ahead, had they chosen to actually follow him to Pulak Pulakan? To light candles for dead soldiers? He was amazed. But whenever he began to doubt what General Martinez had gotten him into, he had only to think of the golden dragons that lay ahead.

And poor Roberta. She had imagined a hot, sweaty walk, but perhaps something more in the line of strolling down the street to buy a sno-cone at a 7-Eleven in Atlanta on an August afternoon. Roberta had started out on foot. The party had proceeded no more than fifty yards past the end of the sugarcane, with the mountains rising before them, when she was soaked with sweat. Wanting to look her best for the photographers, she had perhaps overdone her makeup. The result was that her face was streaked with running mascara, foundation, lipstick, and rouge that collected in the wrinkles at the corners of her eyes and mouth and ran down her neck, exaggerating her age and making her look like a Halloween celebrant. When she mopped the sweat and slapped the bugs, it got even worse. Her eyes were glazed from the heat and the realization that in preparing for the candle lighting she had made a dreadful miscalculation.

Seeing the terrible deterioration of his wife, who seemed to be aging by the minute, Robin decided to put her astride a *carabao*. The first *carabao* carried medical supplies that were part of the deal with Jaime Pineda. The second *carabao* carried drinking water for the pilgrims. They unloaded the medical supplies and divided them among those on foot. They hoisted Roberta atop the *carabao*, which assumed its new load without blinking. A water buffalo did not have the smooth gait of a Tennessee walking horse. Sitting atop the *carabao*, her legs spread across the immense back of the plodding beast, Roberta—doing her best to look game—held onto a rope with both hands. It was an inelegant ride; she lurched back and forth with each stride. She had planned on being able to show videotape of their adventure to their viewers back home, but now this. This was impossible. Holding on for all she was worth, she imagined people waiting at grocery store checkout stands in the United States being amused at her on the front page of the *National Inquirer*, sitting atop a water buffalo with her face a swamp of sweat and makeup.

Roberta rode in a cloud of flies, mosquitoes, and other tropical bugs that seemed to have singled her out for special torment. Her ankles, the backs of her hands, her neck and face were all targets of opportunity for their stingers, suckers, and eager beaks. Back and forth, back and forth, she waved at her face, but to little avail. They danced and hopped about in the humid air, mocking her. She did not know whether to scream or weep, but every time she felt she could go no farther, she thought about the alchemist archers and was consoled.

The *carabao*'s only defense against the flies was a tail caked with manure. Some of this manure was dried. The most recent to be evacuated from the animal's bowels resembled greenish-brown lava and had a gluey consistency. Roberta had received several disgusting swats across the legs of her Banana Republic safari trousers. Each time the tail landed, she flinched. Yeeee! The noxious odor of warm excrement wafted up. Felix, a calm man by nature, was clearly worried about his charge and glanced back periodically at the suffering Roberta.

Felix gave his lead rope to his brother Rudy and retrieved a plastic bottle of water from the pack of the *carabao* following Mrs. Fallon's and handed it up to her. "Maybe a drink would help, ma'am."

Roberta hesitated. The bottle cap was unscrewed. She had heard stories of bad water being poured into empty containers, and even of alleged pure spring water being taken from the grossest sources. Nevertheless, she took a modest sip. "Thank you, Felix. You're very kind," she said. The water tasted awful. A spike of anxiety coursed through her stomach.

Up front, Robin did his best not to show weakness in front of Martinez. But Martinez was a Filipino. Although he led the good life as superintendent of the Philippine Military Academy, he was no stranger to the heat. Growing up in the heat, he had adjusted to it.

Robin was beside himself. He had put up not only with flies, but with mosquitoes that rose up in invisible swarms. These were not macho mosquitoes like those he had seen in the United States. They were tiny and seemed not to buzz at all. They just landed quietly, planted their greedy beaks, and filled up with no warning to their victims. The itching was just as terrible as that inflicted by odious buzzers in Alaska or Minnesota.

Slapping them at an increasing rate, Robin realized that the sweat pouring down his face had long since washed off the disgusting insect repellant that he had smeared on his skin. There was no way to remove the sheen of sweat from his face. His handkerchief was soaked. Roberta having done the shopping for the trip, Robin was wearing an expensive, short-sleeved Banana Republic tropical shirt. His forearms glistened with sweat. He stopped. The bugs were impossible, maddening. He did his best to clean his face with his sodden handkerchief. He applied a new coat of insect repellant.

Martinez looked concerned. "Will you be okay, Reverend?"

"We've come this far, we'll make it," Robin murmured. He glanced back. "The Lord is testing us."

"My goodness, yes, he certainly is," Roberta said. "But these kind gentlemen are taking care of me. The water is delicious. Perhaps you should have some water, Robin."

Felix retrieved the bottle of water for Robin, who had the same reservations as Roberta, but drank it anyway. It tasted like warm pee. "Fresh water! A bounty of the Lord. Truly delicious," he said. "Thank you, Felix."

The tail of the *carabao* landed a plop of goo on Roberta's leg. "Yeeeeee!" She sat up straight, mouth open, fighting back tears.

"Keep the faith, darling," Robin said.

Felix grabbed a stick. "Would you like me to take care of that for you, ma'am?" Felix asked.

"Please," Roberta said.

Felix scraped the goo from her leg, but the warm dung had soaked through the cotton and her Banana Republic trousers were plastered to her leg. Roberta looked momentarily on the edge of vomiting, but restrained herself.

"Perhaps we should rest," Martinez said.

"Yes, that might be good," Robin said. He squatted on the trail. Mosquitoes, flies, and bugs quickly descended on him. He slapped the side of his face. He smacked his forehead. He spanked the back of his hand. "Perhaps we should just push on," he said.

"Whatever you think, Reverend," Martinez said.

"This is more trying than I had imagined," Robin said.

"Yes, it is warm," Martinez said. He turned his head so that the Reverend Fallon could not see the hint of a smile at the corner of his mouth.

The setting sun was an orange sliver as they arrived at the foot of Pulak Pulakan. The Rev. Robin Fallon was exhausted. His Banana Republic outfit was soaked with sweat. He smelled like a goat. His face was covered with insect bites. He burned everywhere—on his arms and the backs of his hands, on his neck and face, and on his ankles. On top of that he had developed a burning rash between his buttocks. He was on fire down there. The itching was the devil's torment. He fought off the urge to dig in there with his fingers and give himself some relief. But he dared not in front of the Filipinos. A famous minister of the Lord did not dig frantically at his butt.

Pulak Pulakan remained to be scaled for the lighting of candles. It was difficult for the Fallons to conceive of soldiers having to fight in this heat, much less struggle up the brushy slope with Japanese firing down on them with machine guns.

Roberta, too, was on fire from the bites and smelled like a sewer from repeated swipes of the *carabao*'s sodden tail. Although Felix had cleaned her legs repeatedly with his manure stick, her lower trouser legs were a slime of *carabao* dung. "The bugs, the bugs. I can hardly stand it," she murmured to her husband. "Whatever have we gotten ourselves into?"

"Perhaps it will cool off now that the sun is going down. This is what they don't show you in the movies. Think of it as an adventure, darling."

"Movies? Adventure? Do you see the bites on my face and legs? Why didn't somebody advise me to bring a change of clothing?"

"When we get back you can take a nice bath," Robin said. "Just lie back in the tub and remember. It will be like none of this ever happened." He lowered his voice. "We get one of the archers, remember. Perhaps if you had more faith in the Lord. He is by our side. He is with us. Speak to Him, Roberta."

Roberta gave him an impatient look. "You know you have a way of getting carried away with the sound of your voice. Just make this as quick as possible, and let's get out of here."

Robin smacked a mosquito on his forehead. "You don't have to worry about that."

George Villanueva, who had been sent ahead, met them at the foot of a trail that wound up the steep hillside.

"Everything ready, George?" Martinez asked.

Eyeing the worshippers strung out behind Martinez and the bedraggled Fallons, Villanueva said, "They've cleared out a space on top for the candle lighting. We'll take the *carabao* on a trail that leads to the back of the hill."

Martinez said to Robin, "Danilo will lead you and Mrs. Fallon and your party up the trail to the top for your ceremony. Cadet Villanueva and I will lead the *carabao* around the base of the hill to do what has to be done. I'm afraid you'll have to hike up the hill, Mrs. Fallon."

Roberta knew that Martinez meant taking the *carabaos* around to the side of Pulak Pulakan. Her spirits soared. "We've come this far. Let's do what has to be done."

With that they began climbing the winding trail leading up the slopes of Pulak Pulakan, where in the spring of 1945 machine guns chattered and wounded men cried out.

It seemed somehow cooler on the top of Pulak Pulakan. Having heard stories about the honeycomb of tunnels dug by the Japanese, the Rev. Robin Fallon was naturally curious. But the top of the hill was overgrown with tropical undergrowth that was the NPA's shield against the prying eyes of military helicopters. Fallon had no doubt that the tunnels were there, but he could not see them. The spot cleared by the NPA for the ceremony was hardly larger than his living room back in Atlanta.

The Japanese godfather also had the map necessary to unearth the alchemist archers, but Gen. Jose Maria Martinez knew what was required to score the golden dragons for himself. Martinez had assured Fallon that everything in the Philippines was for sale, including loyalty and principles. Judging from the bribes necessary to arrange his revival in Cadiz, Fallon believed him. The

Filipinos who would suffer the most were residents of Negros Occidental. These were Ilongo speakers. Martinez, being from southern Luzon, spoke Tagalog. Did he care what happened to Ilongo speakers?

Robin Fallon was pleased to be working with such a professional as General Martinez.

Now Fallon looked out on the flickering candles. "Dear Lord, we are gathered on this hilltop that was consecrated more than fifty years ago by the blood of young American and Filipino soldiers. We light these candles so that the world will remember and honor the memory of Lieutenant. John W. Dolan, one of many young Americans and Filipinos who surrendered their lives on the treacherous slopes of this hill. Their families sacrificed their brave sons in the name of a greater good so that we might be free to live and worship as we please. We God-fearing Christians know what will lead the world to prosperity. Christian faith! Life righteously lived! When pressed, we will fight the good and honorable fight. But we will never forget those who made the ultimate sacrifice on our behalf. Make no mistake, ours is part of the never-ending struggle against the abject, barbarous greed of small, pathetic people seeking the so-called good life. The good life does not lie in gold or treasure, it lies in living one's life according to the gospel of the Lord . . ."

2

The night had cooled somewhat, and although Robin and Roberta Fallon were still burning from the insects that had tormented them on their journey into Pulak Pulakan, the trip back seemed far more pleasant. They had endured the worst of it. The brushy hills were an exotic gloom silhouetted against the starry sky. Perched atop the plodding *carabao*, Roberta reminded herself that each passing minute brought her closer to the end of her long day of suffering. Each lurching step forward was one step closer to a cold bottle of Coca-Cola and air-conditioning. Behind her, strapped one each atop the backs of plodding *carabaos*, were the alchemist archers of Xhingsui Gap.

The more Roberta thought about it, the more she concluded that her abject misery, far from being an embarrassment, was a wonderful testament to her Christian courage and determination. As she rode, Roberta imagined the stories she could tell while their followers watched the PJN tape of their ordeal. This wasn't pretend suffering that everybody knew was hyperbole. This was the real thing, genuine misery, taped as it happened, proof that she was not a quitter. She stuck with it, enduring heat, bugs, and a sodden *carabao* tail so that candles might be lit for Lt. John W. Dolan and all the brave young American and Filipino soldiers who had died on her behalf.

When she wasn't dreaming of the glory of her televised ordeal, Roberta imagined herself in the bathtub, soaking the poisons from her skin while admiring the golden dragon that General Martinez had promised. Of course, there remained the business of shipping the dragon to Atlanta without paying a barbarous duty to the U.S. government. But that didn't strike Robin or Roberta as an insurmountable task. The PJN equipment had to be returned to American soil, did it not? What crass customs officer would spend an undue amount of time disassembling an organ of touring evangelists? They were famous Christians with a devoted following that would not take kindly to their being jerked around by petit bureaucrats.

Her mind thus occupied, time passed.

At length they came to the road through the cane field that led to Sen. Buddy Enrique's farm. There awaited the passenger vehicles the Filipinos called jeepneys, turned so that they faced the farm. The gentle Felix helped Roberta to the ground where she stood on uncertain legs.

Robin put his arm around her. "Courage," he murmured. "It won't be long now."

"We did it. We did it. We did it," she said.

In the pale light, General Martinez gave them a victorious thumbs up before he supervised the removal of the heavy boxes atop the *carabaos*, and watched over them as the Filipino laborers loaded them one by one into the huge jeepney, known as a chariot. Finally, they were ready to go. Together with Martinez they got into the chariot and they were on their way. Although she was jerked and yanked as the jeepney slammed across the ruts and potholes, Roberta was jubilant. This was the most memorable day in her life. She would never forget it. And not only that, she and Robin had it on videotape.

And after all the stories she had heard, it was such a pleasure dealing with General Martinez. And as befitted his rank and position, Martinez was truly a gentleman. He lifted Roberta's faith in humankind.

The surprise came when they exited the cane field.

There heavily armed Filipino bandits waited.

Roberta glanced at Martinez. What had gone wrong? Surely the experienced Martinez had anticipated this? But from the stricken look on Martinez's face, it was clear that he had not. Martinez stood looking uncertain when a bandit bearing an assault rifle hopped aboard the rear of the jeepney. There was no doubting what he was after.

Chiba Wataru and Yoshida Akiri got out of the taxi. After paying too much for the ride, Chiba and Yoshida waited for the driver to unload the trunk, which was stuffed with heavy canvas duffel bags.

Yoshida slung one of the duffel bags over his shoulder. The driver took the second, wobbling under the weight. Chiba took a third, lighter bag. Yoshida and the driver followed Chiba down the sidewalk to the *Sugarland Princess*, which sat tethered to the dock. The *Sugarland Princess* was so clean and new that it might well have been moored quayside at Yokohama or Kobe.

Yoshida and the driver relieved themselves of their burdens. Chiba dropped his also and hopped lightly aboard the vessel, where a broad-shouldered Filipino met him with a nice smile.

Chiba bowed to the old man. "Ahh, Mr. Canizares. Are we ready?"

Canizares, still beaming, said, "We are not ready, sir."

Chiba's eyes widened. "No? What's the matter?"

"We have to replace a bearing." The smile never left Canizares's face.

"What?"

"No problem. I've sent my nephew Dodong to get another one. We'll get it fixed in no time at all." Canizares said this while still smiling.

"No problem? No time at all? How long is 'no time at all'?"

"A day. Maybe two. It depends on whether or not Dodong has to go to Cebu or Manila to get the right bearing. Not such a good choice in Bacolod. We could try Iloilo, but I doubt we'd find it there."

"A day or two."

"But maybe he'll be lucky. Maybe sooner."

Chiba clenched his jaws. "I chose this boat because it looks new."

"New body. Old motor."

Chiba ran his tongue over his teeth. "We need a boat very badly, Mr. Canizares. Can you recommend another one? One that works."

Canizares, who had never stopped grinning, said, "Oh, sure. No problem. My cousin Bong has a very good boat. Works perfect."

"Your cousin Bong?"

"A good man, sir. Very good."

Aboard the *Lapu Lapu*, Ding Rodriguez answered his cell phone. After listening for a minute, he hung up, looking pleased. "That was my cousin Antonio. He scared Chiba off the *Sugarland Princess*. Told them he had a bad bearing." Rodriguez blew air out between puffed cheeks. "Close call. With the *Sugarland Princess* on our tail, we'd have been toast."

"What will Chiba do now?" Tomi asked.

"My cousin recommended another boat."

"And that would be?"

"*Nita's Baboy.*"

Smith, glancing at Tomi, said, "Translated, 'Nita's Pig.' And who does *Nita's Baboy* belong to?"

"Another cousin, Bong Alburro. No problem staying ahead of

Nita's Baboy." Rodriguez glanced at his watch. "Four o'clock, we'd better push off."

With Kip Smith and Tomi Kobayashi peering over his shoulders, Ding Rodriguez piloted the *Lapu Lapu* from its berth at the Bacolod Yacht Club at four o'clock. Because of the extra tanks of diesel fuel, the narrow hull of the *Lapu Lapu*, ordinarily kept high in the water by its sleek outriggers, rode lower in the sea than usual, yet when Rodriguez goosed the diesel, the boat fairly jumped forward.

Chiba and Yoshida hired two young Filipinos to lug their heavy duffel bags to *Nita's Baboy*, tethered a block away from the *Sugarland Princess*. Yoshida, looking grave, took the lighter bag. Chiba chewed on his lower lip as they walked.

When Chiba saw *Nita's Baboy*, he groaned aloud. Yoshida looked stricken. The vessel, if it could accurately be called that, looked like a floating dump. Such paint as remained on its hull was faded and peeling. The rotting deck was littered with broken boxes, rusted machinery, and a snarl of ropes. Although it floated, it clearly listed to port.

Yoshida glanced at Chiba.

Chiba and Yoshida both expected a young man. What they got was a skinny Filipino in his early sixties dressed in cut-off blue jeans and a sweat-stained Pure Foods Hot Dogs T-shirt. The wiry, wizened Captain Bong looked both fit and cheerful.

"Yes, sirs. Can I help you?"

Hesitating, Chiba said, "A gentleman named Antonio Canizares said your boat might be for hire."

Bong said, "My cousin. A very good man. Yes, it is for hire."

Chewing on his lip, Chiba said, "We need a boat that runs well."

Bong looked around at the deck. "You will please pardon the litter. We were just getting ready to clean her up. She might not look the best, but the motor in *Nita's Baboy* is almost new. A Komatsu diesel. Japanese. Very good."

Chiba looked up and down the dock. Looking out to sea, he saw the *Lapu Lapu* passing by. Quickly, he said, "We'll take it."

Rodriguez took the *Lapu Lapu* well out into the Guimaras Strait before turning north at a leisurely pace, the big engine running an effortless *ka-rob-ob-ob-ob* at the lower end of its capacity. They could see glimpses of tin and thatched roofs tucked in among banana trees and palms on the shoreline.

They passed Talisay and slowed as they neared Silay. Rodriguez turned toward shore and idled momentarily at a series of heavy concrete supports that had once supported a four-hundred-yard pier that took a dogleg right at the end. In the gathering dusk, the piers, some yet erect, others tilting at odd angles, took on the appearance of ghostlike hulks marching single file into the water.

Rodriguez said, "Silay was a major Japanese port during the war. They had an airstrip about a half mile from here, just across the road from Bacolod to Cadiz. Over the years it filled up with silt just like the harbor at Cadiz did before they dredged it."

Chiba Wataru gripped the rusting rail so tightly that his knuckles turned white. Beside him, Yoshida said, "This is impossible, sir."

Chiba, tracking the *Lapu Lapu* with his binoculars, said, "We do our best and hope for the best, Yoshida-san."

The engine of *Nita's Baboy* made a horrific noise. It was like the diesel was a clothes dryer tumbling rocks. The engine clattered and banged in a positive din. *Batta-batta, whack, whack, bonk-bonk! Batta-batta, whack, whack, bonk-bonk!*

"I bet they can hear this in Tokyo," Yoshida said.

Chiba mopped the sweat from his forehead with his forearm. "Easily that, I'm sure."

Yoshida said nothing.

"Perhaps the sound doesn't carry well in this tropical air. I can still see the *Lapu Lapu* dead ahead. For the moment that's all that matters." To Bong, he shouted, "You said this engine is almost new. If I might ask, how old is it?"

Cheerfully Bong said, "Oh, I don't know. Eighteen or twenty years. Something like that. I know a friend who has an engine just like it that lasted thirty years. You Japanese know how to build an engine that lasts. You're famous for it, you know. We get most of our used diesels from, Japan."

Batta-batta, whack, whack, bonk-bonk! Batta-batta, whack, whack, bonk-bonk!

Ding Rodriguez anchored the *Lapu Lapu* off a brushy promontory called Calubcub Point. It was 6 P.M. and the sun was setting over the Guimaras Strait, setting streaky clouds aflame with reds and oranges.

The Praise Jesus Now schedule for lighting candles called for worshippers to board PJN buses in Bacolod, Talisay, Silay, and Cadiz, and to arrive at the Patag National Park at 3:30 P.M. with the trek to Pulak Pulakan to begin thirty minutes later. PJN estimated that the head of the procession would arrive at Pulak Pulakan at six. The trek back would begin at eight.

When the *Lapu Lapu* was safely anchored, Smith checked Rodriguez's charts. The *Giri* would make its first appearance as a green dot on the screen of Smith's tailing device when the vessel passed Tomonton Point, five miles north of Calubcub Point. He poured himself a cup of coffee and kicked back on the bridge to watch the sun set over the Guimaras Strait. "You suppose Wim van der Elst felt something like this while he waited to go ashore with the GI dogfaces in 1945? Tomi, did you read *The Naked and the Dead*? Marines waiting to go ashore the next day. Remember that simple line that spoke volumes, 'The night before, they could not sleep.' Was that it? Something like that."

Tomi said, "Will this really work, Kip?"

Smith changed the angle of his sprawl. "Look at it this way, if it doesn't work, we'll enjoy a nice sunset well out of harm's way and drink too much San Miguel. People have suffered worse fates. There's one thing I can guarantee: It will or will not work depending on whether it does or does not work."

"A logician!" Rodriguez said.

Smith helped himself to some more coffee. "I have to admit, I didn't have the action figured until we hitched our ride with GeeGee Mendoza and the Japanese guy."

Rodriguez said, "Norita, the prawn farm man."

Smith shook his head no. "He might own some prawn farms, but his name is Kawana Katchan, not Norita."

"What? Kawana? How do you know that?" Tomi asked.

"From his Carolina accent. I'm betting he was most likely on his way back from a final talk with Jaime Pineda. Ding, do you want to tell the professor how Kawana smuggles his weapons to Japan?"

"He puts them in packages of frozen prawns."

"Ding's sources tell him General Martinez worked a deal with Jaime Pineda calling for Jaime to send decoy statues out to flush Kawana, but Kawana trumped Martinez's offer."

Tomi gave him a sly grin. "Let me guess. He offered him Sabatini-DANS to knock down the gunships of the Filipino army."

Smith said, "Jaime will send the real statues out first, not the fakes, which is his agreement with Martinez. Kawana's *koren* will snatch the archers and truck them to the *Giri*. By the time Martinez figures it out, if he does, the *Giri* will be halfway to Japan."

"But the *Giri* is still sitting off Cadiz last we knew."

"Too risky to load them in Cadiz," Rodriguez said. "This is the only other place with a dock that can handle boxes that heavy."

Tomi said, "What I don't understand, Ding, is how come General Martinez has been talking to you?"

"Martinez knows that I have too many sources for him to keep this scam secret. They know about my friendship with Kip. He wanted me to think I was part of his plan, hoping Kip and I would try to hijack the archers from Kawana's people. Well, they were right. Fun, huh?"

Smith said, "Kawana is probably sitting out there sipping sake and chewing on whale blubber or whatever a *yakuza* godfather does on the eve of a triumphant score." He fell momentarily silent, then said, "Waiting like this always makes you start to wonder. Never fails. You wait and nothing happens, and then your guts begin to grind. You begin retracing the logic to see where you might have screwed up." Smith looked mildly at Tomi and sucked air between his teeth. "Time passes and the worrying gets worse. It can't be helped, but it doesn't do any good either."

At quarter to eleven, the green light on the screen began to move, catching them all by surprise even after the waiting and the expectation. The light moved, somehow lethally silent, and that was it, no hoo-hoo or boom-boom crescendo of timpani.

"We float in the air and watch like a black-shouldered kite," Smith said, watching the green light.

Smith and his companions gathered around the small screen of the monitor, watching the light. As it brightened to an intense green, they saw the sleek silhouette of the *Giri* on the water, easing through the darkness without night-lights.

Rodriguez said, "Remember the other night when I played Bengal Tiger with Martinez?"

"This is our rat," Smith said.

"The best way to shoot the rat is to pick a spot and be patient. A tactic that's a little different from your black-shouldered kite, but not a whole lot. We have to be patient, smarter than the rat at the start, and smarter than the rat at the finish."

They watched as the green dot began to pale slightly, then it held steady as the *Giri* anchored offshore of the old Japanese piers at Silay, where in the spring of 1945 the Filipina woman saw Japanese soldiers drop a heavy box revealing a golden dragon inside.

On the *Giri*, Kawana Katchan took the cell phone call from his subordinates, looking satisfied. All was going as planned. He lit another cigarette, took a deep drag, and kicked back, letting the smoke curl out of his nostrils into the warm night. The trucks were on their way.

Kodama had called the Philippines Treasure Islands as a joke because of *Treasure Island*, a famous novel written by an Englishman named Robert Louis Stevenson and said to be widely read by British and American schoolchildren.

Kodama used to tell amazing stories of the lying, treacherous Ferdinand Marcos, whom he likened to a puppet in the form of an obedient reptile. When he was a young *kobun* in his late twenties, Kawana had been with Kodama and his colleagues in a Ginza nightclub one night—all of them totally pissed on Johnny Walker—when Kodama had first likened Marcos's broad face to that of a turtle. Marcos had heavy-lidded, turtle eyes, Kodama said. When Marcos lied, he blinked like a turtle. His mouth was eager to snap at proffered meat. He did not chew; he ripped. He did not swallow; he gulped. But for all his bravado in stealing his countrymen's property, he was a docile coward when it came to dealing with the Japanese in charge of retrieving Hirohito's Gold.

That night on the Ginza they had all laughed louder and louder as the amused Kodama continued with his description of Ferdinand the turtle. Kodama claimed that when Marcos received an order from Tokyo, his legs and head would tentatively emerge from his shell and he would look about, uncertain, but eager to please. Then Kodama had mimicked him, peering left and right, calculating the dangers. He said Marcos had courage only when dealing with his countrymen and then used thugs or soldiers. He said Marcos regarded his countrymen as human bugs who existed solely to satisfy his personal appetite.

No Japanese would have betrayed his country like the conniving Marcos had done to the Philippines during the war. A Japanese would have committed *seppuku* first. It was impossible for Kodama or any of his subordinates who dealt with Marcos to have any respect for him. Sasakawa Ryoichi had some especially good stories. When Sasakawa told Marcos he was to help him establish a World Safari Club on Lubong Island, Marcos had been so eager to participate, it was pathetic. No honorable Japanese would have cheerfully volunteered to pimp for foreigners, selling the daughters of his countrymen. Marcos was devoid of any sense of *ninjo*. The concepts of honor and civility and conscience escaped him. The traitorous Filipino turtle would do anything.

But when Marcos began passing himself off as a war hero, Kodama and his Japanese associates were appalled. Lying about his treachery was one thing. Pretending to be a war hero was pathetic. And the Americans, who knew better, went along with it!

If Kawana had any worries as he waited, it was about the former CIA agent Kip Smith, who had thrown in with Col. Cading Rodriguez, the Negros representative of *Bawiin mo ang Ginto*. Kawana didn't like having to anticipate Smith and Rodriguez. Smith was one of what the American spooks disdainfully called a "boy scout," meaning that he was afflicted by what Kawana thought was a genetic anomaly—he was afflicted by what Westerners called "conscience."

If Ferdinand Marcos was an example of how awful a Filipino could be, Ding Rodriguez was a product of the Filipino culture at its best. He was genuinely doing his best on behalf of the Philippines. Kawana was perplexed by such maddening honesty.

He found it disconcerting that after having outsmarted the conniving Martinez, he had to deal with an American sorehead and an honest Filipino who understood both *giri* and *ninjo*.

What were Smith and Rodriguez doing now? Where were they? Smith appeared not to have recognized Kawana when the Filipina sweetie GeeGee Mendoza had driven him back from his meeting with Jaime Pineda. But what if he had? Smith and Rodriguez almost certainly were out there planning something. What? What did they have in mind?

Kawana's cell phone rang. He picked it up and listened to the male voice. He murmured his agreement into the receiver then disconnected the phone. He picked up his night binoculars. The trucks had arrived. He watched as his men unloaded the first of the boxes. They struggled under the weight as they lugged it to the water and put it on a *banka*.

Watching, Kawana looked pleased. He took another satisfying drag on his cigarette. In a few minutes Kawana would get to run his fingers over the scales of a solid gold dragon weighing five hundred pounds. Kawana would own the alchemist archers of Xhingsui Gap. Emperor Hirohito's gift to Kodama, the symbolic power of the archers, would be his.

Kawana Katchan was destined to replace the legendary Kodama Yoshio as the most powerful *kuramaku* in Japan. He stood triumphantly and punched the night air with his fist. *"Hai! Hai! Hai!"* (Yes! Yes! Yes!)

4

Slapping night bugs, Kip Smith and Ding Rodriguez took turns with Smith's night binoculars watching the loading of boxes onto *bankas* that ferried their cargo out to the *Giri*. The boxes were about a yard long but very heavy, judging from the effort it took to transfer them from *bankas* to the *Giri*. Tomi passed the time taking notes on her laptop computer, a fancy Toshiba with a crisp color monitor.

Smith grinned in the darkness. "Everything's okay now, isn't it? Everybody's happy. Kawana has the dragons. Robin and Roberta think they've lost the dragons. Martinez thinks he has them."

"If you two have got it figured right," Tomi said.

"A worrier to the bitter end, eh? You're right, we've got a long way to go. We'll give him a nice lead before we crank up. We don't want to crowd him, and there's no sense wasting diesel."

"This is it?" Smith said. He gave Rodriguez the binoculars.

"What's happening?" Tomi asked.

"He's got 'em all loaded. He's just starting his engine."

"Where's he heading?"

"We'll know in a minute." Smith took the glasses. "We follow the light, remember, not the boat. If we can see him, he can see us. We'll keep everything dark. No lights."

They waited for nearly twenty minutes, watching the green light grow dimmer, until Smith said, "Okay, gentlemen. We follow the fish and go for Plan A. You want to crank her up, Ding?"

Rodriguez turned on his diesel—*ka-rob-ob-ob-ob.* They waited while Rodriguez's winch pulled in the anchor.

Tomi looked annoyed. "Is it too much for you two hustlers to tell me what your Plan A is all about?"

Rodriguez said, "Tell her, Kip?"

"I don't think she can tell anyone from here."

Rodriguez said, "Kawana has two ways to go home. He can go north around the tip of Panay and through the Sibuyan Sea and the Verde Island Passage between Mindoro and Luzon. That will take him along the west coast of Luzon to the chain of small Filipino islands that lead north to Taiwan. From there he can negotiate the Nansei Shoio archipelago northeast to Japan. He likely used the reverse of that route when he came here, pulling in at Manila to talk to his *koren,* who recruit girls for the sex trade. But with the possibility of Martinez's people looking for him, he likely won't want to pass by Manila on his way back. Kip and I are betting he'll go east through the Visayans and track the Pacific coast of Luzon."

Smith said, "We follow him and sink the *Giri.*"

Tomi looked alarmed. "Say again?"

"The best place to bury the archers is on the bottom of the ocean. As long as we know the coordinates and nobody else does. We lay low for awhile and go back later with scuba gear. If Kawana is faster than we are, we catch him when he stops to top off his diesel. We don't want competition when we retrieve the archers. Too many fishermen in *bankas* in these waters. The trick is to take him under with no Filipino witnesses. We don't want competition for the salvage."

"Just sink him. *No problema,*" Tomi said. "How do you propose to do that?"

Smith dug into his daypack and retrieved a small black transceiver. "I just punch this little button right here and detonate the charge I planted on the *Giri*. Kawana's boat, crew, and beloved archers will be underwater in minutes."

Kawana made his intentions clear immediately. The *Giri* proceeded east along the northern tip of Negros.

"Which way is he going?" Tomi asked.

Rodriguez studied the monitor of his tracker. "East. I know the most about the Sibuyan and Visayan Seas. I'll take the first shift," Rodriguez said.

Tomi watched Smith studying the horizon to the aft with his binoculars. "What are you looking back there for? The *Giri* is in front of us."

Smith shrugged. "Just curious."

"Curious about what?"

He put down the binoculars. "General paranoia."

Captain Bong seemed cheerfully indifferent to the horrific racket of his marine diesel, which seemed to grow in intensity with each passing minute. *Nita's Baboy* plunged confidently through the waves.

Batta-batta, whack, whack, bonk-bonk! Batta-batta, whack, whack, bonk-bonk!

Yoshida was clearly worried. "I am wondering, sir, how . . ."

Chiba completed the sentence. "How long before that engine blows up?"

Yoshida cleared his throat.

Batta-batta, whack, whack, bonk-bonk! Batta-batta, whack, whack, bonk-bonk!

"I share your concern."

"Captain Bong is supposed to be a cousin of Captain Canizares. They say everybody knows everybody else on this island. You don't suppose they could be in league with, uh . . ." He licked his lips.

"With Colonel Rodriguez. Yes, that thought did occur to me.

When we first looked at the *Sugarland Princess*, Canizares said his engine was in perfect order. At the last minute, he suddenly needs a part. Impossible dealing with these people. Impossible!"

The diesel suddenly took a turn for the worse. *BATTA-BATTA, WHACK, WHACK, BONK-BONK! BATTA-BATTA, WHACK, WHACK, BONK-BONK!*

With a sudden edge, Chiba said, "Get me the chart, will you, Yoshida-san."

Taking care not to trip on the clutter, Yoshida retrieved a water-proofed chart from the smallest of their three bags. He spread the chart on the deck, and the two men squatted, examining it with a flashlight.

At the helm, Captain Bong, apparently oblivious to the torment of his Japanese passengers, began singing in falsetto Whitney Houston's song, " 'Give me one moment in time!' "

Yoshida said, "I think we should kill this Captain Bong before the night is finished."

Chiba, with his finger on the map, said, "I quite agree, Yoshida-san."

BATTA-BATTA, WHACK, WHACK, BONK-BONK! BATTA-BATTA, WHACK, WHACK, BONK-BONK!

" 'Give me one moment in time . . .' "

"He hates us, sir."

"He seems to," Chiba said quietly, his face twisted with fury.

From the helm, Bong said happily, "We Filipinos love to sing. You gentlemen like to sing?"

The *Giri*, still proceeding east, entered the Tanon Strait that ran between Negros Oriental and Cebu. Rodriguez said, "Just as we figured. He's headed for the Surigao Strait and the Philippine Sea, planning to return north along the east coast of Samar and Luzon."

"Can you catch him, Ding?" Smith said.

Rodriguez cranked up the diesel of the *Lapu Lapu*, but the truth became clear almost immediately. The *Lapu Lapu* was as fast as the *Giri*, but not faster. Rodriguez looked disconsolate. "I thought I could run him down, I really did. Hard to believe I can't."

"Not to worry. We'll eventually catch him." Smith said.

Rodriguez said, "We'll just bide our time and take him under off the coast of Samar. What do you think, Kip, four-hour shifts? I'll teach Tomi the ropes first shift."

"Sounds good to me. Tomi?"

"Teach me what I have to know," Tomi said.

On Rodriguez's shift, with Smith taking a catnap, the *Giri* crossed the Tanon Strait, then passed between the northern tip of Cebu and the smaller Bangtayon Island, and turned southeast into the Camotes Sea with Cebu to the west and Leyte to the east.

On Tomi's shift, with Smith watching to make sure she was doing okay, the *Giri* passed between the small Camotes Islands between Cebu and Leyte and negotiated the Canigao Channel between Bohol to the west and the southern tip of Leyte. They followed the *Giri* south just off the shore of Cebu.

Chiba and Yoshida got out their radio on the bow of *Nita's Baboy*, as far away from the hammering and clattering of the engine as they could. The coast of Cebu was less than a hundred yards off their starboard.

Chiba adjusted the radio to the right frequency. "We've got scramblers and descramblers at both ends, so it doesn't make any difference who might be listening in." He thumbed a button and spoke into the radio. "Kawana-san, this is Banzai One. Our instructions are to escort you safely to international waters."

BATTA-BATTA, WHACK, WHACK, BONK-BONK! BATTA-BATTA, WHACK, WHACK, BONK-BONK!

"Am I in danger, Banzai One?"

"No immediate danger. You are being followed. We're well back of your tail, but we are experiencing engine difficulties. We need to put in somewhere so I can order a fit replacement vessel from our consul in Cebu."

Chiba waited several seconds. "Do you hear me, Kawana-san? I say again, 'Do you hear me?' "

He waited six or eight more seconds.

BATTA-BATTA, WHACK, WHACK, BONK-BONK! BATTA-BATTA, WHACK, WHACK, BONK-BONK!

"Where did you say you were? What's that racket I hear?"

At the helm, Captain Bong switched to Pat Boone. " 'A white sport coat, and a pink carnation. I'm all dressed up for the dance.' "

"It's the engine of this vessel coming apart, Kawana-san. That's why we have to put in. We have to do it quickly."

"Say again? I can't hear you."

BATTA-BATTA, WHACK, WHACK, BONK-BONK! BATTA-BATTA, WHACK, WHACK, BONK-BONK!

Chiba shouted, "I SAID, IT'S THE ENGINE OF THIS VESSEL COMING APART!"

"We will put in at Danao. I have friends there. Thank you, Banzai One, whoever you are."

Bong did a fair Elvis. " 'Don't be cruel, to a heart that's true.' "

"This is one time I pull rank. I'll be the one to kill him," Chiba said.

Yoshida's shoulders slumped.

BATTA-BATTA, WHACK, WHACK, BONK-BONK! BATTA-BATTA, WHACK, WHACK, BONK-BONK!

The vessel turned suddenly seaward. Chiba looked back at the helm. No Bong. Where was the singing old man? "Grab the helm, Yoshida-san." Chiba shined his flashlight across but did not see anything.

At the helm, Yoshida said, "What now, sir?"

Chiba checked the silhouette of the *Lapu Lapu*, barely visible in the moonlight straight ahead.

Yoshida said, "We're taking on water, sir. She's sinking."

Chiba said, "There's a highway that follows the shoreline. Head for shore. I'll radio the consul in Cebu City to have another vessel delivered to us in Danao. It's only twenty or thirty miles down the coast. Can you believe that treacherous old bastard? He had to be sixty if he was a day? When he saw that we'd had enough, he just jumped in the water and swam for it."

Yoshida, biting his lower lip, aimed *Nita's Baboy* toward the island as Chiba, holding his breath, plugged his ears with his fingers. It looked as though they had a chance to make it, but barely.

5

Tomi Kobayashi, Kip Smith, and Cading Rodriguez settled into Rudy's Carenderia, a local eatery where food was served from large aluminum pots. In the tropics there was no need at all for such fancy paraphernalia as walls and floors. A thatched roof for protection from the rain and sun was all that was needed. A dirt floor sufficed. A fancy *carenderia* might have simple tables and chairs where the customers could eat their food. Others served to go only, the food being dipped into plastic bags. Here was true Filipino home cooking. Meat being expensive in the Philippines, there was never a whole lot of it in anything. The food in a Filipino *carenderia* was freshest in the morning; as the day wore on it grew tepid. Eating hot foods was a luxury.

Tomi followed the lead of Smith and Rodriguez who leaned over the pots and removed the lids to see what was offered.

Smith liked *mongos* on rice, *mongos* being the beans that, if allowed to grow, turned into bean sprouts. He also tried some *sinaging*, fish soup seasoned with ginger and sour tamarind. Ding Rodriguez went for *mongo* beans plus stewed *canding*, goat, with chunks of potatoes and carrots—a spendy item in a *carenderia.*

Tomi was uncertain. On Smith's recommendation, she tried the fish soup and found that she liked it.

After they had finished their food, Smith and Rodriguez ordered another round of sweaty stubbies of San Miguel. Smith murmured, "They made it. They're setting up; see them there."

Rodriguez shook his head.

"By the side of the Sari Sari store."

"Under the palm tree," Tomi added.

"I see them. I knew they'd find us. They've got plenty of money to throw around, and in a town this size everybody knows we're here, guaranteed. Filipinos rarely see a Caucasian in these places. I'm just worried about Bong. I hope he's okay." Rodriguez suddenly brightened and leaped to his feet. "Bong!"

The old man strolled casually into the *carenderia*, his clothes still wet and a smile on his face. Bong gave Rodriguez a hug. "Uncle!"

Looking embarrassed, Bong said, "Nephew! I pulled the plug on the stern and jumped overboard about twenty miles north of here. Lucky we were close to shore."

"You're safe, that's all that matters, uncle. And *Nita's Baboy*?"

"The Japs beached her just as I snagged my ride. I had to do it, nephew. They were on to me and the old engine was about to blow. I could hardly believe that I could actually get it to run. It was making a racket you could probably hear all the way to Manila. *Oy!*"

Rodriguez grinned. "You go buy yourself some dry clothes and something to eat. I buy." Rodriguez dug a handful of peso notes from his pocket and gave them to his uncle. "You have a good time in Cebu City, uncle. Maybe buy yourself an overnighter with a young thing and sleep in an air-conditioned hotel. And my deal still stands. I'll buy you another engine. Is your new boat completed, by the way? Last time I saw it you were putting on the deck."

"Ready to go, nephew. Who would have thought I would ever take *Nita's Baboy* out to sea again. She was taking on water from the moment we left the dock. It was some kind of ride, I can tell you. You should have seen them two Japs suffer, wondering when the engine was going to go." Bong rolled his eyes and burst out laughing. "When I started singing, they really went wild." He laughed even louder, slapping his thighs in merriment.

Yoshida looked bitter. "I'd like to kill that treacherous old bastard right now, splash his brains into his food."

"Easy, easy, we've got work to do, Yoshida-san. He had me fooled, too, I have to admit. But we caught a ride. We're here with all our gear. All is well."

"What a liar! He wasn't even using that boat. He was building himself a new one. That piece of manure was just floating there rotting, waiting to sink."

Chiba grimaced. "Adjust the mike, Yoshida-san."

"And that singing of his! He was mocking us! A one-man karaoke. Can you believe he just jumped in and swam for it? A man his age!"

Kip Smith said, "Because of the secrecy involved, it's difficult to know the full story of the Sugamo Nineteen. The long of it is complicated. The short of it is that the favored war criminals released in the deal with Emperor Hirohito became a power behind the Liberal Democratic Party, an American creation. Among those released from Sugamo Prison on December 24, 1948, which I'll call the Class of '48, was an esteemed gentleman named Kishi Nobusuke, whose base of power was Manchukuo."

"That being?"

"The name of the puppet state the Japanese created after it invaded and occupied Manchuria. Kishi was the civilian in charge of the 'development,' read ripping-off, of Manchuria's resources by the Japanese Imperial Army from 1936 through 1939. During the war, he was Tojo's minister of trade and industry. You know from van der Elst's dossier on Kodama what that meant: the stripping of everything of value occupied by the Japanese Imperial

Army. Kishi used the resources of the M Fund to merge the Liberal Party with the Democratic Party to form the Liberal Democratic Party in 1955. By 1957, only nine years after being released from prison as a Class A war criminal, he became Prime Minister of Japan."

"Say again?"

"From war criminal to prime minister in nine years," Smith said. "Track the story, Tomi. In January 1960, Prime Minister Kishi flew to Washington and signed a revised mutual security pact for Ike, who gave him a warm welcome. Do you want to rate the performance of the press, Ding?"

Rodriguez reached into his daypack and pulled out an aged copy of *Time* magazine that had been rolled up in a tube. He flattened it on top of the table. It was the January 25, 1960, cover. On it a smiling Japanese was superimposed over bustling industrial activity.

Tomi's jaw dropped. "No!"

Smith said, "Kishi Nobusuke, war criminal Class of '48. The good folks at *Time* told their readers that Kishi's 134-pound body packed 'pride, power and passion—a perfect embodiment of his country's amazing resurgence.' *Newsweek* called him a 'Friendly, Savvy Salesman from Japan.' Those newsmagazine writers do love their alliteration, don't they? There was not a word in either magazine about Kishi's having signed a declaration of war against the United States in 1941 when he was a member of General Tojo's cabinet. Not a mention of his wartime activities as head of the Munitions Ministry, where he oversaw the use of slave labor of hundreds of thousands of Korean and Chinese prisoners who made weapons for the Japanese Imperial Army. The misery! The agony! The human suffering! And our reporters politely avoided the truth. Such a charming little war criminal. On top of that, hardly a sentence was published about opposition to the treaty back in Japan. Before you start shaking your head, remember that

Kurt Waldheim rose to become secretary-general of the UN before his Nazi background was revealed.

"Four months later, with growing resentment among students at the proposed U.S.-Japan defense pact, Prime Minister Kishi called on Kodama for help in providing security to protect President Eisenhower on a proposed visit. His old classmate from Sugamo organized eighteen thousand *yakuza kobun* and another ten thousand *yakuza*-protected street vendors to back up the Japanese police. Things got so out of hand that Ike's press secretary, James Hagert, and the U.S. Ambassador to Japan, Douglas MacArthur III, the general's nephew, had to be snatched by helicopter from a rioting mob. Ike's visit was called off, but the treaty was still signed. After Ike's visit was cancelled, Vice President Nixon met with the Japanese, who wanted complete control of the M Fund, claiming they needed an emergency source of funds in case war ever broke out with China. A Japanese who was privy to the arrangement once told one of my Company sources that Nixon agreed to relinquish American control over the fund if the government supported his bid for the White House and if they agreed to add substantially to the fund themselves. For his part, he promised to return Okinawa to Japan if he became President."

Yoshida looked up from his instruments. "That can't be, sir. That's impossible."

"What's that, Yoshida-san?"

"That a Japanese prime minister was once imprisoned for being a war criminal. I would have known about it. I've never heard of such a thing."

Chiba clenched his jaw. "I have to admit I haven't either."

"Why would Smith invent such a story? What motive could he possibly have? A lie like that can easily be checked."

"So one would think."

"I don't want to hear such lies," Yoshida said. "It's like they're driving spikes through my head."

Chiba closed his eyes, looking suddenly tired. "I don't like to hear it either. We just do our duty and record it for Suma-san and his colleagues."

"And did the Japanese live up to their end of the bargain?"

"Yes, they did. Although Nixon lost to Kennedy, the Japanese stuck to their end of the deal. Finance Minister Tanaka Kakuei undertook the task of raising money for the M Fund. Between 1960 and 1970, Tanaka sold 1,681 properties that the government had confiscated from aliens during the war—citizens of the United States and its allies who had failed to qualify for restitution after the war. Tanaka sold the properties to nominees at an artificially low price. The nominees resold them at market value and remitted the profit to the M Fund. Tanaka raised twenty-two billion dollars for the fund until 1970, when questions were raised in the Diet and he had to stop.

"And that, Tomi, was only part of the duping of the American public. Never accuse the Japanese of not being quick learners. They knew the secret of democratic rule. Money. Kishi's triumph preceded a wave of Sony transistors and Japanese-made television sets and automobiles dumped on our market with nary an objection from congressmen and senators who were receiving campaign contributions from the friendly, savvy salesman and his friends. The web of connections to the Class of '48, the M Fund, and the *yakuza* is astonishing.

"Lest you think the Class of '48 ever broke up, be reminded that in 1963 Kishi was an unembarrassed member of a committee that made the arrangements for a showy *yakuza* funeral. Can you imagine in your wildest dreams George W. Bush helping bury a Mafia don? Kishi's close advisor Kono Ichiro was Kodama's sworn *yakuza* brother. That's like Jimmy Carter having John Gotti on his staff. In that same year, another Kishi advisor, Ohno Bamboku, gave a rousing speech at the installation of the *oyabun* of one of Yamaguchi-gumi gangs, telling them that politicians and the *yakuza* were both devoted to the principles of *giri* and *ninjo*, and urging them to exert their devotion to chivalry to make Japan even better."

Tomi's eyes widened. "Whoa!"

Yoshida was furious. "Lies! Japanese prime ministers in league with the yakuza. *I've never heard any of this. Never."*

"Pay attention to your instruments."

Yoshida adjusted a knob. "Were you aware of this, sir?"

Chiba shrugged. "I've heard stories."

"Lies. Abominable, outrageous lies."

"Whether or not they're lies doesn't concern us. We have our duty."

"Same as Gerald Ford giving a gung ho speech to Sicilian mobsters. In 1971, Kishi guaranteed bail for a Yamaguchi-gumi *oyabun* accused of murder. Imagine Bill Clinton raising bail for Sammy 'The Bull' Gravano. By the way, Tanaka was prime minister when his sponsor Kodama got caught up in the Lockheed scandal, and his government went under in the ensuing scandal. In the late 1970s, a police raid of a Yamaguchi *oyabun* discovered a huge blown-up photo of Prime Minister Ohira getting loaded at a party of his *yakuza* pals. The connections between the *yakuza* and the LDP are legion and well known."

Rodriguez looked amused. "After Nixon relinquished American control, Kishi Nobusuke apparently dipped into the M Fund for about a trillion yen, then about three billion dollars. Tanaka was in control longer than any of the others. We think he lifted about ten trillion that he deposited in the Union Bank of Switzerland."

Smith said, "The Class of '48 was still making its influence felt as late as 1982, when a Kodama protégé, Nakasone Yasuhiro, became prime minister. Although several Kodama-sponsored politicians became prime minister, Tomi, you should always remember that while the M Fund has remained at the heart of the corruption, the Japanese government has never controlled it. Neither has the Liberal Democratic Party controlled it. It has been run by a handful of powerful individuals, some in government, some *yakuza oyabuns.*"

"And what about in more recent years? Who's controlled it most recently?"

"Tanaka Kakuei apparently controlled it through about 1986, when it came under Nakasone's control. Consider, Tomi, there are no Japanese government or institutional controls that can counter the secret power of such an astonishing wellspring wielded by an oligarchy of independent barons backed by *yakuza* muscle. Here you go, check this out." He handed Tomi a piece of paper.

Tomi glanced at it. "And this is?"

"A list of some of the prominent members of the Class of '48. Sasakawa Ryoichi, an M Fund heavyweight, is a story all to himself, as fascinating as Kodama, but it's far too complicated to get into here. Check out his 'philanthropy.' "

Yoshida's face was a mask of hatred. "They go too far, sir! Nishi-san was prime minister of Japan. It is absurd to say he put money in a Swiss bank account for his own benefit. Sasakawa-san was a great man. Everybody knows that. He was never jailed as a war criminal. Never! Why would anybody make up such stories? Why? This man Kip Smith is truly evil."

Chiba sighed.

"And they malign Nakasone-san and Tanaka-san. Why would anybody want to listen to this nonsense?"

"I have no idea. It's not our duty to ask such questions, Yoshida-san. We receive our orders. We follow them."

Smith said, "The reason gold is so valuable, Tomi, is that it doesn't interact with other elements. It doesn't rust. It doesn't tarnish. It doesn't disintegrate. It doesn't corrode in any way. Truth is the same way, if often less gaudy. It does not yield to ephemeral ideology, religious impulse, nationalism, cant, dogma, wishful thinking, or politics in its many forms. You journalists and scholars 'dig' for the truth. You follow hints and clues through a confusing thicket of self-serving half-truths. You pursue red herrings of lies. You grope your way through mazes of obfuscation in the ever-dimming light of time. How often does what is purported to be the truth turn out to be gilt or the deceiving glint of intellectual pyrite? Fukumitsu's ruse was fool's gold. The real gold was used to finance *kuroi kiri.*"

"No chance of this breaking in Japan?" Rodriguez asked.

Smith said, "The complicity of the emperor in the war is a taboo subject in Japan, as are the topics of the Golden Lily and the M Fund. Those who have inherited the legacy of the fund know generally what happened, but nothing specific. The truth is an intellectual hand-me-down, passed from generation to generation, getting more mangled with each telling. Japanese intellectuals suspect that MacArthur made some kind of deal giving the emperor a walk, but very little beyond that."

Smith turned and looked straight at Chiba and Yoshida. "Chiba-san and his *yakuza* companion who have been recording our briefings are among the handful of Japanese who have been privy to anything beyond rumor and fragments of the story. You're an historian of Japanese ancestry. Agree or disagree, Tomi?"

Tomi, too, looked at Chiba and Yoshida. "I think the ordinary Japanese citizen has received an expurgated, incomplete education about the country's recent past. A Japanese on the street owes *giri* to the royal family. What Emperor Hirohito did or did not do in World War II is beside the point. They don't want to hear this story. If they do hear it, they won't believe it. But the world would not stop if it knew the truth. The truth is liberating."

"So there it is. MacArthur worshippers don't want to hear it.

The Japanese public doesn't want to hear it. What do you think, Ding, rest our case and drink too much San Miguel?"

"I think so," Rodriguez said.

"These people cannot be allowed to spread their contemptible lies. Liars, they are. They lie as easily as they breathe. They lie and lie and lie! No more lies! Enough! They have to be stopped!" Yoshida was beside himself.

Chiba shook his head. "We now know their story, which was our primary objective. As long as they're following Kawana, we know where they are. When the Giri *is clear of Filipino waters and we're clear of possible witnesses, we send them under."*

6

It had been safe enough for Kawana Katchan to spend a day in Danao City waiting for Banzai One to get a proper craft. Nobody was going to mess with Kawana Katchan in Danao City; he was a profitable source of counterfeit weapons for the gunsmiths. The wait also enabled Kawana to experience a nighttime passage through the Surigao Strait—the route taken by Admiral Nishimura commanding the Southern Force on its way to join Admiral Kurita's Center Force in what would become the Battle of Leyte Gulf, the largest sea battle in history. In the early morning hours of October 26, 1944, the Southern Force encountered the American Admiral Jesse B. Oldendorf in the opening round—the Battle of Surigao Strait.

As the *Giri* proceeded southeast through the Canigoo Channel with Bohol and the setting sun on his starboard and the southern tip of Leyte on his port, Kawana struggled to answer several questions.

Suma had said he might be contacted by a support, Banzai One. Fair enough. But who specifically was Banzai One? Surely not another American. Roddy Baker, a desk officer not a field operative, had been pathetic. Judging from the code, Banzai One was Japanese.

Banzai One assumed somebody was following him, but if they

were, they must be just over the horizon because he couldn't see them. Kawana had pulled a neat hustle on Martinez and made a clean getaway, but Martinez had plenty of time to figure out that his archers were actually gilded lead.

The trailing vessel was either Martinez's or Smith and Rodriguez's. Martinez was never to be underestimated. Smith and Rodriguez were professionals. Kawana was unnerved by either possibility, and he didn't like it that Suma was butting in where he wasn't wanted. Suma was no more to be trusted than Martinez.

Kip Smith studied the *Taipei Darling* through night binoculars. The *Taipei Darling*, a sleek, modern powerboat, had appeared behind the *Lapu Lapu* shortly after they left Danao City late in the afternoon and had remained about a hundred yards off their stern ever since. "I have no idea what we should do next." He handed the binoculars to Rodriguez.

Rodriguez said, "No way in hell Chiba Wataru was going to make the same mistake twice."

"Looks like a fast boat," Tomi said. "Can we outrun them if we have to?"

Rodriguez said, "Hard to say."

Smith grinned ruefully. "Be honest, Ding. No way in hell."

"Plus she has larger fuel tanks, more range."

Chiba Wataru and Yoshida Akiri rode thoughtfully on the *Taipei Darling*. The Japanese consul had done well on short notice. The mellow diesel hummed comfortably. The young Taiwanese owner, An Luc, on Cebu visiting his wealthy uncle—a major investor in shopping mall—had been more than willing to accept too much money to accommodate two Japanese gentlemen. He was both competent and accommodating. Being from a rich and powerful family, he was virtually without fear—no matter what he did, his uncle would bail him out. In the Philippines, in fact, his family's fortune put him above the law. But he was also sensible. If he was curious about what was in the two heavy duffel bags, weapons most likely, he didn't ask questions.

As for Chiba and Yoshida, gone were the worries about a boat with a rotten hull and a motor that was coming apart. No more aging Captain Bong singing songs while he pretended to be innocent. If they had to make a run on the *Lapu Lapu*, they had plenty of power.

The *Taipei Darling* plunged easily into the waves. An had thermoses filled with hot tea. He had a refrigerator well stocked with Thai beer and catered Chinese food. He waited for instructions. When given them, he did as he was told. Being Chinese, An didn't care what they did; it was accepted wisdom in Japan that a Chinese would do anything if the price was right. While that belief was a stereotype held by most non-Chinese in East and Southeast Asia, it fairly described the ambitious An Luc, who liked it that Chiba addressed him as "Captain."

Kawana Katchan, a war buff since childhood, had the money and contacts to buy unadulterated accounts of World War II action from booksellers in Hong Kong, and because he regularly did business at Danao City on Cebu, he had taken a special interest in the Battle of Leyte Gulf. Gen. Douglas MacArthur had decided to begin his triumphant return to the Philippines by landing his force on the eastern shore of the Leyte, just east of Cebu and Bohol. Leyte Gulf faced the Philippine Sea at the westernmost edge of the Pacific Ocean. The Japanese, by then losing the war, decided on a dramatic ambush. They would attempt to surprise the Americans as they loaded their men and equipment on the beach and bombard them from the sea.

Five of Oldendorf's six battleships were obsolete vessels that had been resurrected from the bottom of Pearl Harbor three years earlier. Admiral Nishimura had two old battleships, *Fuso* and

Yamashiro. Vice Admiral Shima commanded the heavy cruisers *Nachii* and *Ashigara.*

Kawana was overcome by melancholy as he remembered the sequence of action in which Oldendorf employed classic tactics in what was to be the last sea battle in history employing big guns—the old dreadnoughts having been replaced by aircraft carriers in future years. Oldendorf sent torpedo boats to attack the Japanese in waves, and aimed his big guns in a crossfire at the Japanese proceeding through the narrow passage. In the end—in addition to three destroyers—both the *Fuso* and the *Yamashiro* went down.

By 5 A.M. on October 25, the routed Japanese were retreating to the south and the action was over. One of the heavy cruisers that survived the action was the *Nachii*, which retired to Manila for repairs; two months later the *Nachii*, loaded with Kampei-tai gold, was sunk on its way out of Manila Bay.

Admiral Nishimura had gone down with the *Yamashiro*, but on that same course in the dark of the night more than fifty years later, Kawana Katchan felt infused with Nishimura's spirit. Nishimura had bravely gone down with his ship. It was as though the ghost of Nishimura rode beside Kawana on the *Giri.*

7

At 2 P.M. the *Lapu Lapu* passed a small island, Homahon, on their port, and entered Asogoran Bay. The *Giri* bore to the north, heading for the town of Guiuan on the southern tip of Samar. Ding Rodriguez killed the engine. Behind them, the *Taipei Darling* came to rest.

Smith turned down the radio, which was reporting the approach of Tropical Storm Celing, which might well be Typhoon Celing by the time it reached the Visayan region of the Philippines. Smith studied the chart. "Kawana's likely topping off his fuel tanks, which means he's decided it's too risky to travel along the shoreline."

Rodriguez said, "Good if we had an opportunity to top off our tanks. The folks behind us probably have twice our range."

"If he makes good time to the northeast, he might be able to avoid Celing. He'll likely put in again at Casiguran in northern Luzon for more fuel."

"Playing it safe. I agree," Rodriguez said. "That means we have to put him down before he gets too far out to sea."

"Or risk losing everything in the Mindanao Deep."

Tomi wrinkled her brow. "The which?"

Smith said, "The southern end of the Philippine Trench, which is marked in deep blue here. We're looking at water as deep as twenty thousand feet. If we scuttle the *Giri* into the Mindanao Deep, nobody gets the archers unless they invest a fortune in a deep water submersible."

Rodriguez traced his finger along the chart. "But not to worry. He won't navigate at right angles. He'll proceed due north for a while. Plenty of shallow water for you to do your thing." He tapped the chart. "Say about here, off Panhinihian Point."

"Somewhere around there before Celing hits. Looks good to me," Smith said. He looked back at the *Taipei Darling*. "Do you suppose they're in radio contact with Kawana?"

"Very likely."

Smith thought for a moment. "If we sent Kawana under in shallow water they'd simply let him go and come back later for the archers. But what if we wait until he's over the Mindanao Deep then pop a hole in his hull? What would they do then?"

Having topped off his fuel tanks, Kawana Katchan was in a fabulous mood as the *Giri* passed Point Calicoan on the southernmost tip of Samar and headed northeast into the Philippine Sea. Once they were forty or fifty miles off the coast of Samar, they would bear slightly northeast until Celing passed, then they could turn northwest. While it was true that Typhoon Ceiling was on its way, the satellites all said it was turning west. The *Giri* could handle the rough water in front of the storm and the typhoon itself would serve to block any smaller vessel that might be pursuing him from the rear.

Kawana had bought a Filipino *lechon* and some *kinilaw* at Guiuan. The Filipinos knew how to roast a suckling pig; Kawana had to give them that. And *kinilaw*, the raw Spanish mackerel marinated in *kalamansi* juice, was also splendid. The peppers. The garlic. The onions. The coconut milk. All this made the *kinilaw* a little hot, but flavorful. Good stuff. Kawana was out of Sapporo and so had to make do with San Miguel. But while eating the pork and *kinilaw* and washing it down with San Miguel, he reconsidered the Filipino beer. Perhaps he had been too harsh in his judgement. It wasn't bad at all.

He wondered if the mere presence of the golden dragons on board, the source of blessing and power emanating from Emperor Hirohito, might not have something to do with making the San Miguel taste better.

The *Taipei Darling* was already rocking from the swells that preceded Celing. Chiba and Yoshida studied the charts. "Kawana's almost free. Time to put the *Lapu Lapu* under, do you think, Yoshida-san?"

"Yes, sir, I certainly do. Do that and our mission is complete."

Glancing up at the bank of black clouds on the horizon, Chiba started unfastening the snaps on one of the large duffel bags. Yoshida set to work on the second.

Glancing up from his work, Chiba said, "Please close now, Captain. Maximum speed if you please."

An nodded and put the *Taipei Darling* on full throttle. An could see what Chiba and Yoshida had in mind. Action! An thought it was far more fun than sitting around listening to his uncle talk about making money.

Smith and Rodriguez, too, were studying the charts.

Tomi, watching the *Taipei Darling* through the binoculars, said, "They're coming at us full speed."

Smith tapped his finger on the charts. "I checked it out, Ding, Kawana's over the Deep."

Rodriguez glanced at the chart, then back at the oncoming *Taipei Darling*. "You better be right."

Smith looked back. "Let's see if this works." He tapped a button on his remote detonator.

———

Kawana was knocked off the deck chair by an explosion that jarred the *Giri*. He leaped to his feet, swearing in Japanese, as water began welling through a hole in the stern of his vessel.

He leaped to the radio. "Banzai One! Banzai One! There has been an explosion on the *Giri*. I'm taking on water. Do you hear me, Banzai One?"

"We hear you, Kawana-san. We are just over the horizon. Give us your coordinates, please."

Kawana checked the monitor of his universal navigating instrument and gave Banzai One the position.

On the *Taipei Darling*, closing on the *Lapu Lapu* at full speed, Chiba and Yoshida also turned to the charts.

Chiba groaned aloud. "Smith and Rodriguez saw us coming and popped a charge by remote. Kawana's on the edge of the Mindanao Deep, maybe over it."

"Meaning, sir?"

"Meaning he could be over twenty thousand feet of water. If we let him go, the archers might be lost forever." Chiba looked up at the *Lapu Lapu*.

"What do we do, sir?"

Without answering, Chiba turned and aimed the Sabatini launching tube.

"Are we within range, sir?"

Chiba fired.

The slender missile streaked toward the *Lapu Lapu*.

Tomi Kobayashi spotted the oncoming rocket. "Heads up. Some kind of rocket headed our way."

The sleek white missile streaked just above the blue water, headed straight at them.

Smith said, "Good spot, Tomi. He's having to hold us in his sights, hard to do at this distance and on a pitching deck. Wait until the last second then take it hard port, Ding."

Rodriguez goosed the *Lapu Lapu,* getting all the speed he could. "Now we know where Kawana got the missiles for the Danao gunsmiths to copy."

"Likely used by the Japanese defense forces. On my call, Ding."

"Got it."

Closer.

"Get ready, Ding."

"Standing by."

Closer.

"Now!" Smith yelled.

Rodriguez piloted the *Lapu Lapu* hard to port.

The missile streaked harmlessly by.

Studying the *Taipei Darling* through her binoculars, Tomi murmured, "A second missile on its way."

Smith yelled, "Second launched. Same drill."

"On your call. Got it."

Tomi said, "It looks like two is all they have."

Concentrating on the oncoming missile, Smith said, "Wait, wait, wait."

Startled, Tomi yelled, "Kip!"

"Now, Ding!"

Chiba swore in Japanese and angrily threw the Sabatini launching tube into the sea. "So much for those."

Yoshida grimaced. "You did your best, sir. The *Lapu Lapu* was out of range and we're being tossed about by the swells."

Chiba said, "We go straight to the *Giri,* Captain An. You've got the coordinates. We'll need all the speed you can give us."

"That was close," Rodriguez said, catching his balance as the *Lapu Lapu* was pitched backward from a storm swell.

"Quick reactions, Ding. What do you think? See if we can't find a cove on Samar to hide in?"

"Our best bet," Rodriguez said. "We're low on fuel, and we don't want to risk being on open water when this storm hits."

"I agree. Go for it."

With the black bank of clouds closing, the wind suddenly kicked up, sending spray whistling across the deck of the *Lapu Lapu*. Rodriguez adjusted the course, heading for Samar; the pale blue silhouette of its shoreline was barely visible in the distance.

Tomi said, "We were lucky."

"That's possible. We were also a difficult target at that distance. You were watching through the binoculars; who did the firing, Chiba or Yoshida?"

"Chiba."

"Maybe they weren't misses at all."

Tomi said, "You think he deliberately fired wide? Why?"

Smith shrugged. "I suppose you'd have to ask Chiba. Right now all I want to do is find a hideout and shelter from this storm."

On the *Giri*, Kawana, waist deep in water, was frantic. "Banzai One, Banzai One, where are you? I'm sinking fast in heavy seas. Banzai One?"

"We're on our way Kawana-san."

"We're less than a minute from going under. I say again, we're taking on water very rapidly."

Kawana abandoned the radio, and with his crew of three set about launching the lifeboat as a huge swell pushed by Typhoon Celing rose like a mountain, headed directly at them.

On the *Taipei Darling*, Chiba scowled. "His radio is out. Kawana said he was sinking fast. In these seas, he won't last five minutes in a lifeboat."

"What happened to the *Giri*?" Yoshida said. "I don't understand. Kawana-san was over the horizon from Smith and Rodriguez. They couldn't possibly see him and I didn't see them fire anything."

Chiba said, "Smith likely used a remote to pop a charge he'd already mounted on the underside of the *Giri*'s hull. Got us confused. Gave the *Lapu Lapu* some space. Good move."

Yoshida said, "We've lost sight of the *Lapu Lapu*, sir. They're apparently headed for Samar."

"We know where the *Giri* went down. We can come back later and recover the archers with a submersible. Reverse course, please, Captain An. We will pursue the *Lapu Lapu* with all dispatch."

"Got it," An said, aiming the *Taipei Darling* in the direction of Samar.

Chiba said, "Sayonara, Kawana-san."

Above howl of wind, the *Taipei Darling*'s radio crackled. An said, "It's officially Typhoon Celing now, sir. We're looking at winds of up to a hundred and fifty miles an hour. Not good to stay on open water."

Chiba grimaced. "We'll have to find ourselves some shelter like the *Lapu Lapu*. Nothing else to do for now."

An stood to pick up some real money from his job for the Japanese consul; it was genuine fun, maybe not as much sport as cruising Cebu Doctors Hospital impressing the student nurses with his new Honda, but right up there. And the stories he'd have to tell later! He wondered who was aboard the *Lapu Lapu*. He also knew better than to ask questions.

8

Ding Rodriguez avoided Mataranao Bay, separated from the Philippine Sea by a sheltering peninsula, on the grounds that it was the likely destination of whoever was piloting the *Taipei Darling*. Instead he piloted the *Lapu Lapu* north in the howling wind and heavy seas, finding refuge an hour and a half later in the mouth of a small river that emptied into the sea near the village of Borongan. By then Celing was hard upon the coast, headed west across Samar toward Leyte and Cebu after that. Rodriguez's decision to go north meant that they would have to pass by Mataranao Bay on their way back to the Surigao Strait.

The chance remained that Chiba would lay in wait for them in Surigao Strait as Oldendorf had waited for Nishimura—only they would be sailing west, not east.

There was nothing to do but wait out the storm in the mountainous sea waves that rose from the Philippine Sea and went crashing into the *bankas* of the fishermen of Borongan. The fishermen were not home cowering in their huts; instead, they sat huddled on their craft ready to do what was necessary to keep their means of livelihood from being dashed into kindling.

The *Lapu Lapu* had a sheltering cabin, and in the cabin Rodriguez, Tomi, and Smith sat in the howl of wind and lashing rain.

Tomi said, "Tell me what you know about the widow Edie Compton."

Smith grinned. "*I* am Edie Compton. Did you really believe that van der Elst died of a heart attack in Japan and his journal lay in his niece's attic, unread all these years?"

Tomi clapped her hands over her ears. "You! You were the 'niece'! Of course! Bad eyes, you said. A cripple. Hands trembling from Parkinson's disease! Liar!"

"Got me. Yes, I am the crippled Edie. The beauty of communicating over the Internet is that nobody knows who you are for sure. I had lots of marks to choose from, but you were the closest, only ninety miles away up there in Pullman. Easy matter to check out your bona fides. Went so far as to shoot some pictures of you while you were working in your study."

"You did? You're calling me a 'mark?' "

"I never dreamed of scoring somebody exactly like you, what with your, uh, charms. Extraordinary!" Smith arched an eyebrow.

"Stop it."

"The real reason I chose you was because you're General Yamashita's granddaughter. You weren't just another academic on the make for something to help you score tenure. You were sore as hell. You wanted justice. You had fire in your belly that matched my own. Some abstract concept like the search for truth won't cut it on a quest like this. You have to want *justice* and want it *passionately*."

"Well, you picked the right woman. By the way, Ms. Compton, how did *you* happen to come by the journal?"

"Wim van der Elst was murdered hours after his interview with Kodama in 1948. A few years ago one of my sources in the Japanese underworld told me that a *yakuza oyabun* in Tokyo had a wartime journal kept by an AP correspondent who had followed Kodama's career from 1931. The handwriting was unreadable, but the *oyabun* held onto it on the grounds that it might one day be useful. Ding Rodriguez and I were curious about what was in it, so we did a second-story number on his compound one night, and I cracked the gentleman's safe."

"And you deliberately steered me to Baker, knowing he would send me to you."

"That too," Smith said. "After conducting e-mail correspondence with several other prospects, at least one of whom I suspect was working for the M Fund managers."

"The truth is hidden among Yamamoto-san's famous leaves."

"More accurately hidden among bank accounts."

Tomi, trying to take her mind off the pitching and heaving vessel that was making her sick, said, "There's gotta be a way to tell this story. Has to be."

Smith said, "The American public yearns for heroes and gods, Tomi. To challenge the mythical Douglas MacArthur is to risk the scorn of true believers."

She put her hand over her mouth, eyes wide. Then she looked momentarily relieved. She covered her mouth again.

Rodriguez looked sympathetic. "If you gotta hurl, go for it."

She swallowed, then looked relieved. "I'll be okay, thanks. Oh, God!" Eyes wide, she clapped her hand to her mouth and shot up the companionway to the deck.

At dawn, Typhoon Celing having passed, Tomi, Smith, and Rodriguez heard a helicopter overhead. Rodriguez scrambled topside and saw the chopper hovering above the fishing boats among which the *Lapu Lapu* was moored.

He went below, looking disconsolate, "The chopper was checking us out. Chiba knows where we are now."

"Now what do we do?" Tomi asked.

Smith got out their chart of Philippine waters, and he and Rodriguez studied it with Tomi peering over their shoulders.

Smith said, "The *Taipei Darling* is faster than the *Lapu Lapu*, so he can run us down pretty much whenever he wants. Our best bet is to stay either within sight of shore or of fishing boats, on the grounds that they won't want to attack us in front of witnesses."

"Agree," Rodriguez said.

"If we can stay out of harm's way long enough, maybe we can figure out a way to give them the slip."

"Best bet to make our move when it's dark, Ding."

"Makes sense. As I see it we have just two choices. We can either go the long way, north along the coast of Samar and west through the San Bernardino Strait. Or we can go the short way, south, then back through the Surigao Strait."

"You're the Filipino. Your druthers?"

Rodriguez said, "If we go north, I have to deal with Waray and Tagalog speakers. The Visayan speakers are to the south. Friendlier territory. Plenty of fishing boats to keep Chiba at bay. If we top off our tanks before we start and make good time, we should make the Surigao Strait at dark."

"You're the man. Sounds good to me. Tomi?"

"The Surigao Strait it is."

Smith briefly chewed on the fingernails of his left hand. "You have any scuba gear aboard, Ding?"

"Oxygen tanks and all that?" Rodriguez shook his head. "I've got several snorkels, though. I've got nieces and nephews clamoring to go snorkeling every time I take them on a picnic on Guimaras Island."

"Snorkels will do. We have to have at least three."

Rodriguez opened a compartment drawer. "Three you want. Three we've got."

Chiba Wataru scowled. He did not like the *Lapu Lapu*'s tactic of hugging the shoreline when there were villages to be seen, or seeking the company of fishing bankas when they were not. But Chiba was patient. The *Lapu Lapu* couldn't use that dodge forever. Eventually the Filipino vessel would round Cape Calicoan and there, in the open water of Asogoran Bay, she would be vulnerable.

Chiba concluded, and Yoshida agreed, that Smith and Rodriguez were most likely trying to time their arrival in the Surigao Strait at dusk so they could use the cover of darkness to make a run for it. Plenty of places to hide along the coast of Leyte on their starboard, or the islands of Dinagat or Mindanao on their port.

Chiba had night binoculars, but the danger remained. If Chiba couldn't find an opportunity to attack the *Lapu Lapu* without witnesses on Asogoran Bay, he would have to make his move at the entrance of the Surigao Strait.

All day long the *Taipei Darling* rode patiently about a hundred yards off the *Lapu Lapu*'s stern as an equally patient and determined Ding Rodriguez followed the nooks and crannies of the coast, occasionally darting out to join groups of fishing *bankas*. It was the practice of fishermen from a single village to spread out in groups, staying in eyesight of one another in case a comrade got into trouble.

At eleven degrees north latitude, the sun rose and set every day at plus or minus five minutes of 6 A.M. and 6 P.M. At 3 P.M., with the fishermen returning to shore, the *Lapu Lapu* reached Cape Calicoan. Behind them, the *Taipei Darling* began moving closer—with Chiba and Yoshida on deck brandishing assault rifles.

Rodriguez glanced back nervously. Smith chewed on his lower lip. "Not good. Maybe we should put in at Guiuan and try again in the morning."

Tomi pointed out to sea. "Look there, will that help?"

Chiba Wataru could hardly believe his bad luck. The lucky trio on the *Lapu Lapu* had spotted an American container vessel on its way to Cebu City. The pot-bellied Rodriguez had maneuvered his craft to within fifty yards of the starboard rail of *Georgie's Best* and stayed there. If the sailors aboard the Thompson Line vessel objected, they showed no sign of it.

Chiba muttered under his breath. To avoid identification by a casual sailor at the rail of the container ship, Chiba ordered An to fall father back, staying a half mile to the rear of the *Lapu Lapu*.

Since Typhoon Celing had moved into the central Visayas, the surface of Asogoran Bay was smooth and shiny as glass. Tomi, Smith, and Rodriguez rode the calm waters in thoughtful silence. Rodriguez kept the bow of the *Lapu Lapu* just starboard of the wake of the *Georgie's Best*. Behind them, the *Taipei Darling*, having fallen back a discreet distance, was a speck on the horizon.

As the sun sank slowly to the west, the shadows of *Georgie's Best* lengthened. The sun, reflecting on the water that was as a mirror, turned slowly from hot white to warming yellows and the cooling, dimming oranges and crimsons until it was a purplish red sliver that slipped beyond the horizon, gone for another twelve hours. At dusk the searing heat turned balmy in the gathering tropical night.

Looking back at the distant silhouette of the *Taipei Darling*, Rodriguez said, "When do you think, Kip?"

"When it gets dark enough, he'll make his move. The sailors will be off the rail of *Georgie's Best*, and if he attacks us quickly and gets out fast, it won't make any difference if they hear gunfire."

"When we see him making his move, we make ours," Rodriguez said.

"We watch him closely. When it's clear he's accelerating, we do it."

Studying the silhouette of their quarry dead ahead, Yoshida shook his head in disgust. "Do they really think they can cling to that container ship like a leech all the way to Cebu?"

Tracking the *Lapu Lapu* through his night glasses, Chiba said, "Possibly. Or they might make a run for it in the darkness, thinking they can find refuge on Leyte or Dinagat. Do you have everything ready and loaded, Yoshida-san? I want no mistakes. We simply run them down under cover of darkness and do what we have to do."

"Got it."

Chiba checked the clip of his assault rifle. "When we go, I want it to be top speed, Captain An, nothing less. We'll run them down and end these games."

"Just give the word."

"Okay then, let's see how much speed you can give us."

An straightened. "Now, sir?"

"Now, Captain An. Go."

"They're coming," Rodriguez said quietly. He gave Smith his binoculars and he turned sharply to port. Tomi and Smith quickly took their positions at the starboard rail. Rodriguez locked *Lapu Lapu*'s rudder into position and put the throttle on full speed as he leaped to join his companions.

The *Lapu Lapu* shot forward into the wash of the container vessel.

When the boat passed through the shadows behind the stern of *Georgie's Best*, Smith shouted, "Now!" and they went over the starboard rail, taking two uninflated life rafts with them.

The container ship moved. The trio waited, treading water.

"Did he go for it?" Tomi asked.

Smith waited, looking back at the *Taipei Darling*. "He's changing course."

"All right!" Rodriguez popped the tab on the inflating device of one of the rafts, a cylinder of compressed air. Smith pushed the uninflated raft into its inflated mate and gave Tomi a boost.

Within minutes the three were inside and paddling hard, heading west toward the southern tip of Leyte.

On the bow of the *Taipei Darling*, hurtling through the darkness at full throttle, Chiba Wataru studied the fleeing *Lapu Lapu* through his night glasses. "If they were closer to land they might try to jump out, but they would have to use a life raft to get to shore, and we'd still get them."

An called at him, "How do you want me to do this, sir?"

"Just circle to their starboard. We've got a rifle with a grenade launcher. No sense getting too close until we have to."

"Got it," An said. He was pumped.

Chiba looked concerned. "I don't see anybody on board."

"Nobody at the helm. They must be below."

Frowning, Chiba adjusted his glasses. "You'd think they'd have someone up on deck watching for us."

An piloted the *Taipei Darling* to the starboard as he had been ordered.

Yoshida fit a grenade launcher on the end of an M-16.

Chiba clenched his jaw. "Fire it into the stern, Yoshida-san. For the moment we just want her dead in the water. We need confirmed kills of our targets."

Yoshida pulled the trigger, and after a heartbeat the *Lapu Lapu*'s stern exploded. She glided to a halt in the water, kept afloat by her outriggers.

"Take us closer, Captain An. Quickly, quickly. Stay alert, Yoshida-san."

Chiba and Yoshida stood at the rail, their assault rifles at the ready.

Chiba hopped aboard, peered down the companionway, and

muttered under his breath. Aloud, he said, "She's empty." He scrambled back onto the *Taipei Darling*. "Quickly, quickly, Captain An. Take us back to the spot where Rodriguez turned port behind the container ship. All speed."

"All speed. Got it." Although it was clear that An wondered what had happened to the woman and two men aboard the *Lapu Lapu*, he said nothing.

It was a starry night with a full moon. Once Chiba figured out what they had done, he would be searching for them in ever widening circles.

Tomi, Smith, and Rodriguez rowed hard, taking turns with two on the oars, one watching the horizon with the night binoculars. They had the rest of the night to lose themselves in the darkness, but whether they could make it to Leyte before Chiba found them was debatable.

9

It was Yoshida who spotted the yellow life raft, floating in the glow of the morning sun with the hills of Leyte a pale blue silhouette barely visible on the horizon. "There," he said, pointing. He handed the binoculars to Chiba. "But it's empty."

Chiba adjusted the glasses, studying the raft.

"Where are they?" Yoshida asked.

Chiba looked puzzled. "They might have caught a ride with a fisherman, but it's hard to believe a Filipino leaving a perfectly good life raft behind. You see it, Captain?"

"Got it, Chiba-san." An swung the *Taipei Darling* to port.

Chiba and Yoshida, assault rifles in hand, stood on the bow as An piloted the *Taipei Darling* toward the life raft, riding gentle swells in the glow of the morning sun. An pulled alongside the empty raft and killed the engine.

"Gone," Yoshida said.

Chiba leaned over the rail, studying the bottom of the raft. "I want you to pull the life raft aboard, Yoshida-san. Do it decisively. Pull it out of the water in one swift motion."

Yoshida leaned over and snagged a rope at the bow of the life raft and yanked it aboard.

Chiba squatted, examining the bottom of the raft. Then he

shouted, "All full, Captain. Circle and come about. Stay alert, Yoshida-san."

Yoshida, grabbing for a rail to keep his balance, looked confused.

"If you look closely, you'll see three small holes in the bottom of the raft. One under each side and one under the stern. Unlikely that they got their hands on scuba gear that fast. The holes mean snorkels."

Yoshida still looked puzzled.

"Be patient. They can only hold their breath so long."

An uninflated raft popped to the surface, followed in short order by Rodriguez, Smith, then Tomi.

Chiba said, "Okay, Captain An, take her back slowly." As they got near the trio, he said, "Kill your engine, Captain An. Throw them back their raft, Yoshida-san."

Yoshida, at last understanding what their quarry had done, did as he was told.

To Tomi, Smith, and Rodriguez, treading water, Chiba said, "Good plan. Hide under our hull while we scratch our heads. You can get back in the life raft or I can shoot you in the water. Your choice."

Chiba waited patiently while Tomi, Smith, and Rodriguez crawled back onto the raft, looking wet, exhausted, and defeated. "No reason I shouldn't let you enjoy your last sunrise. No oddball Filipino or typhoon or container ship to save you now. You're . . . what is the American expression, Kip?"

"I can think of several. Toast. Dead meat. History."

"You're history. That's the one I like. Silenced forever. Out of curiosity, Kip, when did you and Colonel Rodriguez decide to try to double me? That *is* what you were up to, is it not?"

Smith, still breathing hard, mopped seawater from his brow and put his arm around Tomi. "At Aida's in Bacolod when the crippled young man showed us your image in a digital camera.

You wanted to find out what was in the van der Elst journal before you wasted us. We knew that. You were a critical audience of one, a Japanese trusted by the M Fund managers."

"So you decided to dump the whole story on me, the good, the bad, and the ugly, and see if you could turn me. You believe I'm somehow less Japanese because I was educated at the University of California? Or maybe that I would betray my countrymen because I have read Western histories of World War II? Or because I have memories of watching the Oakland Athletics at the Coliseum?" Chiba looked incredulous. "Do you really think that I have allowed a Big Mac to replace *sushi* as comfort food?"

"You'd have been the perfect mole."

Chiba shook his head in disgust. "Prime Minister Nakamura had his doubts, for which he was assassinated. While you were giving Dr. Kobayashi your so-called briefings, my *yakuza* companion and I had something of a running dialogue. The code of Bushido versus Western history. Is it best to keep the secrets and allow the people to keep the faith in their heroes? Or are we to watch in shame and humiliation as CNN craps on Japan: Look at the ignorant Japanese, serenely oblivious to the *kuroi kiri* surrounding their beginnings as a democracy. The old or the new Japan, which is to carry the day?"

"Well put," Smith said.

"At first I was skeptical of Yoshida-san's passionate defense of the emperor and his younger brother, but as time went on he made more and more sense. In the end, I concluded that Nakamura's doubts were misguided. An Arab proverb says it best: 'All truths are good, but not all truths are good to say.' In this case the truth is irrelevant. We've done well without it for a half century. By the way, Kip, I'm disappointed that you didn't mention the Ceremony of Mac's Pipe. Something you missed."

"I've heard of it. I just don't have any corroborating evidence."

Chiba smiled grimly. "Now you never will, guaranteed." He

turned and shot An in the chest with his Uzi, knocking him backward. "You picked the wrong man, Kip. I am no traitor to my people." He swung the muzzle of the Uzi toward the life raft.

Smith grabbed Tomi and pulled her into the water with him. Ding Rodriguez went the other way. Watching this, Yoshida Akiri casually raised his pistol and shot Chiba Wataru in the side of the head with an automatic pistol. He bowed to Chiba's corpse draped over the rail. Politely, he said, "If I convinced you to do your duty, Chiba-san, please accept my apology. It was I who was misguided. *You* convinced me that you should not kill them. This has been a most difficult decision for me. You honored what you thought was your duty. For that I respect you."

Looking out over the water, the respectful Yoshida was suddenly and without warning replaced by an alternate persona. The transformation was remarkable, both in quickness and intensity. His face grew tight as he addressed Chiba's corpse. His eyes blazed with fury. His voice rose in anger.

"I'm a *yakuza kobun,* Chiba-san! You instructed me to think for myself. I had no choice but to obey. You should never have done that. Why did you do that? Now look at what you did! You forced me to do this. Again I have no choice! Such lies! Such lies! Such incomprehensible, unspeakable, vile lies! All these years you and your kind mocked the Japanese people with your greed and whoring after power. Prime Minister Nakamura was right to have doubts. The shame!" He paused, and began shouting.

"The emperor led us to embarrassing defeat then hid from his shame without apologizing to the Japanese people. He bargained on behalf of his freedom and the Chrysanthemum throne, but made sure he got his cut of the Golden Lily. The treasure meant more to him than his duty to his people. He was our emperor. We believed in him. All the while he was a small man who thought only of himself."

Finally, at the top of his lungs, overcome by rage, his voice cracking, veins bulging on his neck, spittle flying, he screamed:

"Me! Me! Me! Me! How could the emperor do that? Where is the honor? What happened to honor?"

That said, Yoshida's fury dissipated as quickly as it had appeared.

Was that it, then? Was he now going to kill them himself?

Calmly, Yoshida said, "Please, return to your raft. I will cause you no harm."

He waited until Tomi, Smith, and Rodriguez had returned to the raft, then continued politely, his voice sincere. "Yamamoto Tsunetomo would vomit to hear this sorry tale. The conniving Japanese manipulated their countrymen and allowed the soiling of General Yamashita's reputation and the suffering of the Filipino people, twisting the meaning of the *Hagakure* beyond all recognition. You're right, Dr. Kobayashi, the world is entitled to know that General Yamashita Tomayuki was an honorable soldier. I am deeply sorry for the humiliation suffered by his family. Please accept the apologies of this humble *yakuza kobun.* Of course, Chiba-san could not have served as your spy. That would have been equally wrong."

He paused, then added, "Mr. Smith, you know the ways of Asia and speak some Japanese. Are you familiar with the requirements for *seppuku?*"

"I've read about it. I'm familiar with the ritual and the terms. I know what a *kozuka* is. And the requirement of a *daki-kubi.* But of course I have never witnessed it."

"Then you know a *kaishaku,* an assistant, is required. You acknowledge *giri* to your murdered wife. You feel *ninjo* for the Filipino people. I regard you as an American *samurai.* Will you honor me?"

Smith bowed deeply. "I would be pleased and genuinely honored, Yoshida-san. I will do my best."

"Then let us do our duty."

Saying no more, Smith climbed from the raft to the deck of the vessel.

Yoshida said, "If you would be so kind as to sink this vessel when we are finished, I think that would be best. I will provide you with a hand grenade for that purpose." To Tomi and Rodriguez, he said, "Miss Kobayashi, Mr. Rodriguez, I beg your forgiveness for being forced to witness this ceremony. It is not intended as spectacle. It is an act of conscience and personal duty, correctly performed in private, preferably in a Buddhist temple. If you'll excuse me for a moment."

Yoshida disappeared below and emerged two minutes later dressed in a dark blue kimono and carrying a knife with a blade about a foot long, plus a slightly curved sword with a long handle, a bottle of sake, a sake cup slightly larger than a shot glass, and a hand grenade. He gave all that to Smith.

Yoshida said, "I always travel with a kimono. Good for relaxing before I go to sleep at night. I have no pickle. I have no *sambo*, but we will make do. As we proceed, you might explain the ritual to your companions, Mr. Smith. Dr. Kobayashi likely is familiar with the Japanese terms and proper form, but not Mr. Rodriguez. If he is to be a witness, it is polite for us to tell him what he is seeing."

Smith said, "If he had a pickle I would serve it to him *mikire*, which means 'three slices' or 'cut flesh.' A *sambo* is a tray he would ordinarily use for his *kozuka*, the knife." To Yoshida, he said, "I can not guarantee a proper *daki-kubi*."

"I understand. Do your best. Explain to them, please."

Smith said, "I am to leave a flap of skin, a *daki-kubi*, so the head does not leave the body, but Yoshida-san's face is hidden."

Yoshida seemed pleased with Smith's explanation. "Let us proceed."

Smith placed the sake cup in front of Yoshida. He filled the cup with sake, pouring to the left with his left hand.

Yoshida drank the sake in two pairs of two sips.

Smith said, "Yoshida-san finished the cup in four sips. The Japanese word *shi*, four, also means death." Smith removed the sake cup and replaced it with the knife. "He will insert the *kozuka* into his abdomen and perform *jumonji*, a crosswise cut from left to right followed by an upward jerk."

Smith bowed again. "Yamamoto Joncho would be proud, Yoshida-san. You honor the code of Bushido. You are a true *samurai*, not a greedy, pretend warrior. Your *giri* is to the Japanese people, not personal profit or blind obedience. You die in the spirit of the noble forty-seven."

He placed the *kozuka* in front of Yoshida.

Yoshida let the front of his kimono fall open, revealing the tattooed dragons on his chest and stomach. He leaned forward and took the knife. Without hesitation, he calmly thrust the knife into his abdomen and executed the *jumonji*. His face was a mask. He showed no emotion whatever. Having disemboweled himself, Yoshida sat serenely, eyes peaceful, blood and entrails flowing onto the deck.

Smith stepped swiftly behind Yoshida and spread his legs wide. He gripped the handle of the sword with both hands. "A pleasure to have known you, however briefly, Yoshida-san. *Sayonara*." He swung the sword.

Yoshida's head flopped forward onto his chest, hanging by an inch-wide strip of skin.

Smith threw the hand grenade down the companionway into the cabin of the *Taipei Darling*, stepping back quickly as the grenade went off. With the vessel taking on water, he leapt back aboard the life raft. The *Taipei Darling* slid silently under the surface of the Camotes Sea.

Smith, overcome with emotion, wiped his watering eyes with the back of his forearm. "I did it. A perfect *daki-kubi*."

Tomi and Rodriguez remained silent. They, too, were affected by the grace and bravery that Yoshida had displayed in honoring the code of Bushido. His calm had been extraordinary.

Finally, Tomi said, "Did Chiba have it right? Was this all an elaborate attempt to recruit him to spy on the M Fund managers?"

Smith took a deep breath and exhaled slowly. "We started out trying to feed you what we knew of the story, just like we said. After Belize, we adjusted our tactics to fit the circumstances. Think of the story you'd have had if we had conned Chiba into feeding us information from the inside. Imagine!"

"Why didn't you tell me? You should have told me."

Smith did. "If you had known you might have behaved differently and tipped him off. For us to have any chance of turning Chiba, he had to believe it was entirely his decision. Didn't work, as it turned out."

"I suppose you're going to tell me to remember the mirrors."

Smith grinned. "Never forget the mirrors or the mist."

Tomi closed her eyes and shook her head slowly. "You two damn near got us all killed with your games. You want to tell us about the Ceremony of Mac's Pipe, Kip."

"Interesting that Chiba mentioned it. I had always thought the Ceremony of Mac's Pipe was apocryphal. One of those likely stories." Smith looped an arm around Tomi's shoulders. "Now I wonder. Maybe it's true after all."

10

Suma Obe eyed a kimono-clad waitress as he cut into his T-bone steak, flown in from Kansas City that afternoon. Suma found it amusing that Americans fussed so over Kobe beef, cut from steers fed beer to make them fat; the truth was there was no better steak in the world than a marbled T-bone cut from properly aged, corn-fed American Angus cooked rare over Texas mesquite charcoal. Eating a Kansas City T-bone tasted like triumph. The difference between Japanese and American beef was like Suntory whiskey, an imitation Scotch, and Johnnie Walker. Suntory was good, yes, but not close to the real thing; even while extolling Suntory's alleged virtues, every Japanese knew the truth.

Suma cut another piece of Kansas City T-bone and deftly speared the bloody chunk with a silver fork. "It's a pity we lost the archers, I have to admit."

Honda Atama had chosen a more traditional marinated whale steak, although he too ate with Western cutlery. Few members ate with chopsticks at Club Nippon. "Kawana could have been sent down by Typhoon Celing, although one would think the *Giri* would have handled it well enough. It was what, seventy feet long, something like that. A substantial vessel with a powerful engine and seasoned crew."

Suma, chewing thoughtfully, looked out over Tokyo Bay, which reflected the lights of the city. "If that happened and we can get the coordinates, we can recover the archers with a submersible. Perhaps we will someday. One never knows. For the moment, we will assume that Chiba and Yoshida completed their more important mission of getting rid of Mr. Smith and his troublesome companions."

Looking disgusted, Honda rolled his eyes. "They're easy enough to discredit. The woman is obviously running on emotion. An hysteric with a romantic view of her grandfather. The photographer is an embittered failure looking for a way to get even with the CIA. A conspiracy theorist. And what American sitting in an air-conditioned living room watching high-definition television will believe some pot-bellied 'colonel' from a hot, sweaty country? A Filipino!"

Suma flicked languidly at the air with the back of his hand as though dismissing an invisible irritant. "If one of them managed to survive, or their handiwork somehow pops up again, we continue precisely as before. Deny and ridicule. Deny and ridicule. A myth. A myth. A myth. The CIA knows how to keep its collective mouth shut."

Suma took a sip of red wine. He didn't know a whole lot about red wine, and so had selected a French Château Something-or-Other 1967 that cost six hundred U.S. dollars a bottle. The wine wasn't as sweet as he had expected, but if that's the way the French liked it, he supposed it must be good. "The Japanese understand how the world works. The trick to dealing with Americans is to secure their cooperation in such a way that they can justify to themselves that they did nothing wrong."

Kobayashi Katama had selected a live Maine lobster from the tank. He dipped a piece in melted New Zealand butter and savored it. "I agree entirely, Suma-san. I thought Glenn Barnes was incorruptible until I got the idea of setting him up with Matsuda Mikki."

Honda blinked. "Mr. Asian Correspondent and Matsuda Mikki? No!"

Kobayashi looked pleased. "Well, yes I did. She didn't come cheap. I had to produce 'A Dove in the Willows' to get her to do it." Kobayashi finished the last of his lobster. "Matsuda Miki is the sexiest movie star in Japan. A priceless fuck. Priceless. Can you imagine an IOU as good as that? And with Glenn Barnes?"

Honda grabbed his crotch and groaned. "Sweet, sweet Mikki! The flower of Nara. Ahhhhhhhh!"

Suma smiled. "Do you suppose Barnes was able to control himself long enough to get it in? I can just imagine little Mikki lying there all sweaty and juiced up, bracing herself for the big American hot dog, then oops! Squirt, squirt, squirt! All over her leg."

They all laughed.

Kobayashi said, "Of course, Barnes feels obliged to say something critical about us now and then to maintain credibility with his editors, but if the story truly gets serious, you can bet he'll remember Mikki."

They laughed again, then waited while the waiter cleared the table.

Suma said, "The CIA will continue to keep the secret. They don't want to lose face. Nobody pays any attention to scholars in the United States. They don't want to hear awful things said about Emperor Hirohito. They'd been taught he was a saintly little man who was dumped by militarists. The Americans will stop their channel surfing to hear a captain of industry or a football player, but Herbert Bix or Chalmers Johnson?" Suma made a farting sound with his tongue.

Kobayashi said, "A strange people, the Americans. They get all worked up over a president having a little fun with a fat girl, but do nothing when we dump our steel and automobiles on their market and buy their politicians."

"Why, that's no mystery!" Honda said. "Their television networks made money off the story of the fat girl and the presidential lollipop."

Dryly, Kobayashi said, "If it looks like this is all going public, we'll just dip into the fund and buy ourselves a congressional committee or two. The house speaker. Whatever."

Suma said, "Well, gentlemen, what do you think?"

"I think it's time," Honda said.

Kobayashi nodded. "I agree."

Suma raised his hand and caught the attention of the waiter, who bowed slightly. A moment later he brought a polished cherry-wood case to their table and carefully set it in the center.

Suma opened the lid, revealing a scrimshaw box cushioned securely in a felt-lined recession. An exquisitely rendered American bald eagle carved on top of the scrimshaw box clutched a tangle of delicate lilies with its mighty talons. He opened the box. It was lined with velvet. Nestled in the velvet, a corncob pipe.

Suma removed the pipe, admiring it. "The gift from Douglas MacArthur to Emperor Hirohito celebrating the division of the Golden Lily—what the American Indians call a peace pipe. The emperor sold. The General bought. We kept the Chrysanthemum throne. We prospered. The Americans got a Japanese Diet they could trust. They stopped the spread of communism in Asia. A good deal all around. The terms of the agreement and the pipe are in perfect condition after a half century. History has confirmed the righteousness and wisdom of their decision." Treating the pipe gingerly, he passed it to Honda. "Isn't this how the British colonists acquired Manhattan island from the native inhabitants?"

Honda accepted the pipe as though it were a precious jewel. The keepers of the M Fund had put a hardwood insert in the pipe's bowl to prolong its life. "The pipe should last virtually forever if it's only smoked each November 14." He gave it to Kobayashi.

Admiring it, Kobayashi said, "The insert will have to be replaced periodically to preserve the bowl. The stem will remain the same." He gave it back to Suma.

Suma opened the tin of tobacco and passed it under his nose, inhaling deeply. "Sweet." Suma remembered the line delivered by the American actor Robert Duvall in Francis Ford Coppola's movie *Apocalypse Now.* "I love the smell of napalm in the morning. It smells like victory." Suma felt the same way about smoking Douglas MacArthur's corncob pipe each December.

He took a pinch of tobacco with his thumb and forefinger and gently loaded the bowl. He lit a match and puffed the tobacco to life, releasing a grand cloud of sweet blue smoke that hung above the table, enveloping the trio in its odor. Thinning slowly, it drifted upward and outward. The aroma, carrying with it a hint of manly arrogance, was pungent with power and privilege.

He thought of the American expression 'smoking' gun, a phrase used to indicate undeniable evidence—fingerprints, DNA evidence, videotape, or an audio recording. Smoking gun? How about a smoking pipe? Could the DNA of Emperor Hirohito and Douglas MacArthur be lifted from the pipe stem after all these years? An amusing thought. Suma took another puff and released the smoke. "To Emperor Hirohito and General Douglas MacArthur and their agreement of November 14, 1947." He gave the pipe to Honda.

Honda took a puff. "To the losers go the spoils." He passed the pipe to Kobayashi.

Kobayashi sent a puff of sweet smoke rising toward the ceiling. "And the losers write the history."

Suma accepted MacArthur's pipe from Kobayashi. He gently scraped the interior of the bowl with a pen knife, emptying the contents into a heavy glass ashtray. He blew into the bowl and examined it. Thus satisfied, he carefully ran a pipe cleaner down the stem. He put the clean pipe back into the scrimshaw box and closed the lid. He returned everything to the cherrywood case.

The Ceremony of Mac's Pipe was finished until the next November 14.

Suma Obe tried the fancy French wine again and made a face. The aesthetic of the sour surely reflected something basic about Western culture. Just what that might be, Suma wasn't sure.

11

Tomi Kobayashi and Kip Smith settled into their seats on the Cathay Pacific Boeing 747, looking out onto the concourse of Ninoy Aquino International Airport in Manila. As they waited for the other passengers to stow their belongings and get settled in, Smith said quietly, "I'm curious about something. Tell me about MacArthur's meetings with Hirohito, Tomi. Which meetings were private, nonscripted and unrecorded."

"They met five times in all, two privately. The first private meeting was on September 25, 1945, a week after a joint resolution was introduced in the Senate declaring that the emperor should be tried as a war criminal. They met for forty minutes. There is no verbatim record of what they said."

"Hirohito clearly had more to lose."

"Yes, he did. Clearly. The first meeting convinced Hirohito that he stood to benefit by cooperating. MacArthur went away believing that Hirohito could be of use in furthering American objectives. We have no idea what transpired in their mysterious ninety-minute meeting of November 14, 1947, or why they wanted no witnesses."

On the screen in front of them a pretty Chinese girl began giving her spiel about safety belts and not smoking.

Watching the safety demonstration as though in rapt attention,

Smith said, "Mac had the hammer. The emperor had the gold. They both wanted something. You know, Tomi, I can feel it. We're right in this. When we get it all down, we'll know we're right."

"I hope the world knows."

"To hell with people who pooh-pooh a story because it has been scoffed at it in the past, or because they don't want to admit the U.S. might have been wrong. If the much ridiculed Imelda Marcos is telling the truth about the gold her husband recovered, then Douglas MacArthur might not have told us the whole truth about why he gave Emperor Hirohito a walk. Even the most honored old soldier might sometimes lie. Imelda Marcos versus Douglas MacArthur. Talk about black humor." Smith grinned ruefully. "Hard to give up on Imelda-baiting, I admit, but I'm betting Imelda told Ms. Herrera the truth. Our story is logical, based on complicated circumstances, admittedly. If the CIA will release all the details, it can be put to an honest and straightforward test. We've done our damndest. That's better than remaining silent for fear of embarrassment."

"Or because the truth might run contrary to the caricature of Imelda Marcos as the chronic liar." Tomi waited while a man stowed a carry-on bag in the compartment above their heads. When he had taken his seat, she said softly, "I promised Avi Feuer at the *Times* that he would get first dibs on the story of my investigation."

"Then Avi Feuer should get first dibs. What we're looking at here is guerrilla history. We brandish computers, not Kalashnikovs. We emerge from the jungle of rumor, lies, circumstance, connivance, canards, coincidence, disinformation, evasion, greed, self-interest, suppressed facts, willful ignorance, official denial, and perceived national interest and lay it on the public full, transparent automatic: means, motive, and opportunity."

Tomi looked amused. "A little wild image there."

Smith hesitated, then said, "Only if you believe that Emperor

Hirohito was a living god, does it make any sense that he was disinterested in the booty collected by the Japanese Imperial Army or that he was above such crass emotions as greed or love of treasure. But of course he was no living god. He was a mortal, just like all the kings, emperors, sultans, and potentates of whatever title who sent their armies forth on conquest. The gold did not belong to Hirohito's relatives, subordinates, or military officers. It was *his*. And MacArthur clearly had it wrong. Old soldiers are entirely mortal. They die. It's old lies that never die. They just fade away until they're eventually considered the truth. If the Company declines to comment or says it will neither confirm nor deny anything, we'll assert that as confirmation that our story is true. Drive 'em crazy."

Tomi said, "At the end of the war, the American public all thought Hirohito was guilty. MacArthur had to convince people otherwise. What if he had held Hirohito responsible, put him on trial, the works?"

Smith shrugged. "Good question. Supposing Mac had said to the emperor, 'Look pal, direct your people to unearth the booty publically, in front of God and everybody, or we're gonna hang your scrawny neck from the tallest tree.' No secret wheeling and dealing. No conniving. The war remains a black hole in Japanese schoolbooks. Maybe the Japanese people would have benefited from learning the whole truth all at once. Then again maybe not. By the way, I know we're going to Bali to put together our notes so we can fight the good fight, but do you suppose we can spring a little time to . . ." His voice trailed off.

"To what?"

"Bali is a beautiful place, Tomi. Exotic. Grand food. Splendid Hindu temples. Wonderful beaches."

She laughed. "So. Come on. Out with it."

He arched an eyebrow. "I was thinking of a little boy-girl fun. Heavy breathing and stuff."

"You know what, Whistling Man?" Tomi put her hand on his thigh. "I was wondering if you were ever going to make a move. I was beginning to think you were retarded."

The engines of the jumbo jet began to whine. The Cathay Pacific pilot began to taxi the plane away from the terminal.

Among the
Sugamo Nineteen

A partial list of those released by Gen. Douglas MacArthur and his G-2, Gen. Charles Willoughby, on December 24, 1948.

AMO, EIJI As chief of the intelligence section of the Ministry of Foreign Affairs, Amo issued the "Amo Statement" in 1934, calling on Western powers not to render assistance to China because Japan was responsible for maintaining the "East Asian order." He later became deputy minister of foreign affairs and the director of the Intelligence Bureau in Prime Minister Tojo's cabinet.

ANDO KICHIBURO Garrison commander at Port Arthur, Manchuria, and the minister of interior in Tojo's wartime cabinet.

AOKI, KAZUO Administrator of Manchurian affairs. He was minister of treasury in Prime Minister Abe Nobuyoki's cabinet and followed Abe to China as an advisor. Aoki was minister of Greater East-Asia under Prime Minister Tojo.

AYUKAWA, YOSHISUKE Sworn brother of Kuhara Fusanosuke, founder of the Japan Industrial Corporation. Ayukawa established the Manchurian Heavy Industry Development Company to dominate industry and mining in Manchuria.

KISHI, NOBUSUKE Kishi was in charge of industry and commerce in Manchuki between 1936 and 1940. He was minister of industry and commerce under Prime Minister Tojo. He served as prime minister of Japan between 1957 and 1960, in which position he advocated revision of the Japanese Constitution to enlarge the emperor's authority and curb the power of the Diet.

KODAMA, YOSHIO Radical nationalist involved in several coups and assassination attempts in the 1930s. Kodama established Kodama Kikan in occupied China to exploit Chinese resources. After the war he became a major leader of the *yakuza* and the most powerful *kuramaku* of the twentieth century.

KUHARA, FUSANOSUKE Leader of the militant Zaibatsu faction of Seiyukal (Political Friends Society).

NISHIO, TOSHIZO Chief of staff of the Kwangtung Army in Manchuria. He was commander-in-chief of the expeditionary army in China between 1939 and 1941 and minister of education under Prime Minister Tojo.

SASAKAWA, RYOICHI Sasakawa, a close friend of Kodama, was one of the leading Fascists and militarists of Japan. After the Kwangtung Army attacked Manchuria on September 18, 1931, Sasakawa organized a private army of 15,000 men, dressed in black shirts to emulate Mussolini, and equipped them with twenty warplanes. When the Pacific War broke out, his army massacred thousands of innocent Chinese and Malayans.

After the war, Sasakawa used his *yakuza* connections in drug trafficking, gambling, pornographic enterprises, and usury to amass an extraordinary fortune, in the process becoming one of the world's leading philanthropists. He gave handsome donations to the United Nations, to the library of former President Jimmy Carter, and numerous American universities.

In 1980, Sasakawa gave $48 million to establish the U.S.-Japan Foundation. The foundation's staff president was Richard W. Petree, a former political section chief at the U.S. Embassy in Tokyo and a likely CIA operative, a status he would neither confirm nor deny. The American "working group" of the foundation included tobacco heiress Angie Biddle Duke; James A. Linen, former president of Time, Inc.; former New York Mayor John Lindsay; former chairman of RCA Robert Sarnoff; and former Secretary of State Henry M. Kissinger.

SUMA YAKIJIRO Japanese general consul in Nanking at the time of the rape of that Chinese city. He served in the Japanese Embassy in Washington in 1938. After 1941, he was minister plenipotentiary to Spain.

TANI MASAYOKI Ambassador to Manchuko. Tani was later, concurrently, director of the Intelligence Bureau and ambassador to the Nanking puppet government. After the war, he served as ambassador to the United States.

List of Historical People, Places, and Things

This list is of historical persons, places, and alleged events that make up the complicated circumstances suggesting that Douglas MacArthur made a deal with Emperor Hirohito. In exchange for the war booty collected by the Japanese Imperial Army, MacArthur refrained from prosecuting Emperor Hirohito as a war criminal. Hirohito got to keep his throne plus a percentage of the treasure. MacArthur used the remainder of the gold to finance a pro-American political party in Japan and to reward American allies in the region. The characters, facts, and allegations supporting this circumstantial case are reported by Wim van der Elst in his journal entries, plus the briefings Rodriguez and Smith gave to Tomi Kobayashi.

Reports that the Kampei-tai buried gold under Pulak Pulakan is a separate issue. The geographical descriptions and place names in the competition for the alchemist archers of Xhingsui Gap on Negros island are accurate but not listed. Van der Elst's descriptions of the combat action on Negros and Hill 3155 are based on U.S. Army records.

LIST OF HISTORICAL PEOPLE, PLACES, AND THINGS

ALCHEMIST ARCHERS OF XHINGSUI GAP, *martyred archers in the form of golden dragons.*

ALL JAPAN COUNCIL OF PATRIOTIC ORGANIZATIONS, *offshoot of Kodama's Zen Ai Kagi.*

AMO, EIJI, *director of intelligence under Tojo, member of Sugamo Nineteen.*

ANDERSON, JACK, *published Curtis gold story in his nationally syndicated column in 1978.*

ANDO, KICHIBURO, *Tojo's minister of interior, member of the Sugamo Nineteen.*

ANG MGA MAHARLIKA (NOBLE STUDS), *Marcos's World War II group of thieves and hustlers.*

ANG PANGULO, *yacht the deposed Marcos used to ship gold to Hong Kong in 1968.*

AOKI, KAZUO, *administrator of Manchurian affairs, member of the Sugamo Nineteen.*

ASAKA, LT. GEN. PRINCE YASUHITO, *commander of Japanese troops that raped Nanking.*

ASIAN ANTI-COMMUNIST LEAGUE, *became World Anti-Communist League.*

AYUKAWA, YOSHISUKE, *head of Manchurian industry, member of the Sugamo Nineteen.*

BALMORES, BENJAMIN, *Japanese officer, a keeper of the Golden Lily maps.*

BARBA, MARCELINO, *Marcos's brother-in-law, confiscated Roxas's Golden Buddha.*

BATAAN BOYS, *MacArthur cronies, created the Yotsuya, Keenan, and M Funds.*

BENGUET, *site of Filipino gold mines.*

BENGUET CONSOLIDATED, *the corporation mining gold at Benguet.*

BLACK GOLD, *stolen gold, or gold illegally on the market.*

CAMP O'DONNELL, *American facilities used as a Japanese hospital in World War II.*

CANNU, GEN. RAMON, *in charge of flying Marcos's gold from Philippines.*

CASEY, WILLIAM, *director of the Central Intelligence Agency.*

CIA (CENTRAL INTELLIGENCE AGENCY), *formed in 1949, successor to OSS.*

CIC (COUNTERINTELLIGENCE CORPS), *army intelligence service.*

CHANG YU-SEN, *Chinese warlord who owned the alchemist archers in 1645.*

CHENNAULT, CLAIRE, *commander of Flying Tigers attacking Japanese from China.*

CHIANG KAI-SHEK, *Generalissimo, a major beneficiary of the M Fund.*

CHICHIBU, CROWN PRINCE YASUHITO, *in charge of operating Golden Lily.*

LIST OF HISTORICAL PEOPLE, PLACES, AND THINGS

CHRIST THE KING CHURCH, *Manila, a site where gold was buried.*

CLARK AIR FORCE BASE, *Luzon, origin of flights of gold shipped to Pine Gap, Australia.*

CLINE, RAY, *American intelligence operative in China, an intimate of the Chiang family.*

COLBY, WILLIAM, *ex-DCI, Nugan-Hand legal counsel, his card found on Nugan's body.*

CREW, HARRY, *U.S. ambassador to prewar Japanese government.*

CURTIS, ROBERT, *treasure hunter, employed by Marcos to excavate Golden Lily burial sites.*

DANTAI KAGI, *Kodama's* yakuza-*dominated patriotic organization, financed Liberal Party.*

DELTA INTERNATIONAL, *gold-recovery firm associated with Phoenix Exploration Services.*

DEMUKAI, *a* yakuza *welcome of released convict, usually carries reward for service.*

DON PACO ORTIGAS, *owner of estate where gold was buried.*

DUQUE, VENANCIO, *helped save Marcos from execution, helped Fukumitsu.*

ENGINEERING CONSTRUCTION CO. LTD., *Shirtly St., Nassau, the 1983 buyer of 716,045 ingots.*

EXECUTIVE X, *retired Air Force colonel, recruited to wash gold for* Shi Pa *in 1983.*

FLYING TIGERS, *an early threat to Japanese shipping from base in Kumming, China.*

FORT BONIFACIO, *one of the sites where gold was buried.*

FORT SANTIAGO, *Manila site of gold burial.*

FUKUMITSU, MINORU, *war crimes investigator.*

GOLDEN LILY, *the wartime booty collected by the Japanese Imperial Army.*

GOOD LONDON DELIVERY, *12.5 kilo gold bars.*

GREENSPUN, BRIAN, *published Curtis gold account in* Las Vegas Sun *in 1978.*

GRLS, *members of* Shi Pa *listed in 1983 gold contract proposed for Executive X.*

HAGAKURE, the bible of Japanese nationalism leading up to World War II.

HALL, ROBERT ASHLEY, *aide to Sen. Paul Laxalt, reviewed Curtis material in 1978.*

HAND, MICHAEL, *Nugan-Hand Bank principal vanished after Nugan was found dead in 1979.*

HASHIMOTO, COLONEL, *Japanese commander at Nanking.*

HELLIWELL, PAUL, *intelligence officer, formed the Asian Anti-Communist League.*

HERRERA, CHRISTINE, *reporter,* Philippine Daily Inquirer.

HIGASHIKUNI, TOSHIKIHO, *Gen. Prince, Hirohito's uncle, a major Golden Lily player.*

HIROHITO, EMPEROR, *an early sponsor and participant in Japanese military expansionism.*

HOKUTAN COAL MINES, *target of Kodama-led union busting on behalf of the United States.*

HONG KONG –SHANGHAI BANK, *Hong Kong, part of 1983 consortium of gold buyers.*

HUNT, CAPTAIN RAY, *American guerrilla commander who ordered Marcos's capture.*

INAGAWA, KAKUJII, *Japanese* oyabun *(godfather).*

INAGAWA-KAI, *the* yakuza *gang headed by Inagawa Kakujii.*

INTRAMUROS, *old walled city in Manila.*

IWABUCHI, SANJI, *Administration, the "Butcher of Manila, in Golden Lily chain of command.*

JAPAN POLICY RESEARCH INSTITUTE, *a think tank of Japanese and American scholars.*

JIGA, LEOPOLDO "PAUL," *Japanese officer and keeper of the maps.*

JOHN BIRCH SOCIETY, *source of loans given to treasure hunter Robert Curtis.*

JOHNSON, CHALMERS, *historian, sought to have CIA records declassified.*

JOHNSON MATTHEY, *London firm that went under after scandal involving Marcos gold.*

JONSSON, OLOF, *Swedish psychic called in by Marcos to help find the gold.*

KAMPEI-TAI, *Japanese military police, the SS of the Japanese Imperial Army.*

KASHII, KIJOMI, *Yamashita's personal driver, source of early Golden Lily report.*

KEENAN FUND, *early fund to finance Japanese institutions amenable to MacArthur.*

KIANGAN POCKET, *the place in central Luzon where Yamashita made his last stand.*

KISHI, PRIME MINISTER NOBUSUKE, *Kodama friend, member of the Sugamo Nineteen.*

KODAMA, YOSHIO, *bagman for the collection of Hirohito's Gold, postwar Kuramaku.*

KODAMA KIKAN, *Kodama company formed to relieve China of valuable minerals.*

KOKURU-KAI (BLACK DRAGON SOCIETY), *advocated Japanese takeover of Manchuria.*

KONO, ICHIRO, *Kodama's yakuza, brother, advisor to Prime Minister Kichii.*

KONOYE, FUMIMARO, *Prime minister, a reluctant militarist, attempt made on his life.*

KOTCHIAN, KARL, *Lockheed president, in charge during the bribery scandal of 1972.*

KUHARA, FUSANOSUKE, *leader of militant nationalists, member of the Sugamo Nineteen.*

KUMMING, CHINA, *base of raids made by the Flying Tigers.*

KURAMAKU, a behind-the-scenes person who pulls the strings, term from puppet theater.

KUROI KIRI, the Black Mist, Japanese term for corrupt politics.

KWANGTUNG ARMY, *renegade Japanese troops who first began collecting the Golden Lily.*

LAS VEGAS SUN, first published Robert Curtis's account in 1978.

LAXALT, PAUL, *U.S. senator, member of Senate Intelligence Committee.*

LEBER GROUP, *formed by Marcos to retrieve gold. Leber is "rebel" spelled backward.*

LIBERAL DEMOCRATIC PARTY (LDP), *merged with Democratic Party with CIA backing.*

LIBERAL PARTY (OF JAPAN), *early creation of American intelligence services.*

M FUND, *created by MacArthur to finance dependable Japanese institutions.*

MACHII, HISAYUKI, *Kodama crony, given rights to offshore recovery in the Philippines.*

MARCOS, FERDINAND, *Philippine president, washed Hirohito's Gold for* Shi Pa.

MARCOS, IMELDA, *Philippine first lady, claimed her husband washed Japanese gold.*

MARCOS, JOSEPHA, *Marcos's mother, tried to buy the Golden Buddha.*

MARCOS, MARIANO, *Marcos's father, allegedly executed as a spy by Filipino guerrillas.*

MARCOS, PIO, *Judge, Josepha Marcos's brother-in-law, ordered Roxas to give up Buddha.*

MARCOS'S BLACK EAGLE GOLD, *the name given Hirohito's Gold washed by Marcos in London.*

MACARTHUR, GENERAL DOUGLAS, *Supreme commander of Allied Powers.*

LIST OF HISTORICAL PEOPLE, PLACES, AND THINGS

MCCARTHY, JOSEPH R., *Senator, Wisconsin senator of Red Scare fame.*

MALACANANG PALACE, *the residence of the president of the Philippines.*

MARQUAT, GENERAL WILLIAM F., *MacArthur colleague, helped form the M Fund.*

MARVILES, *estate on the Bataan Peninsula where Marcos stored the gold.*

MASANUBU, LIEUTENANT GENERAL TSUJI, *led conspiracy to assassinate Konoye.*

MASE-WESTPAC, *Australian firm that bought Johnson Matthey after London gold scandal.*

MEIRAKI-GUMI, yakuza *gang.*

MERCANTILE INSURANCE CO., *insured 1983 shipment of 716,045 ingots to London gold pool.*

MINORITIES FINANCE, *the new name given Johnson Matthey by Mase-Westpac.*

MITSUBISHI BANK, *Las Vegas, proposed as a wash for Marcos gold.*

MOCCATA AND GOLDSMID, *a member of the London gold cartel in the early 1970s.*

MURPHY, LIEUTENANT COLONEL ARTHUR, *ordered execution of Japanese collaborator Ferdinand Marcos.*

NACHII, Japanese cruiser, sunk in Manila Bay while loaded with gold.

NAKAHAMA, AKIRA, *Kampei-tai commander-in-chief in Manila.*

NAKASONE, MAJOR, *Japanese officer in charge of digging tunnels under Manila.*

NAKASONE, PRIME MINISTER YASUHIRO, *sponsored by Kodama Yoshio.*

NANKING, *site of 1937 Japanese rape and looting.*

NIPPON STAR, *the new name of the Leber Group after Marcos was deposed in 1968.*

NISHIO, TOSHIZO, *leader of army in Manchuria, China, member of the Sugamo Nineteen.*

NORTH, COLONEL OLIVER M., *got Contra money from Sultan of Brunei, Marcos.*

NUGAN, FRANK, *cofounder of the Nugan-Hand Bank, found shot near Sydney in 1979.*

NUGAN-HAND BANK, *CIA sponsored bank used by Marcos to wash Hirohito's Gold.*

OSS (OFFICE OF STRATEGIC SERVICES), *World War II American intelligence organization.*

PARITY RIGHTS, *eliminated by Marcos who wanted to secretly buy Filipino corporations.*

PARK, *South Korean President Chung-hee.*

PERCIVAL, GENERAL, *surrendered to the Japanese in a Singapore bank.*

PHILIPPINE DAILY INQUIRER, published Imelda Marcos interview in 1998.

LIST OF HISTORICAL PEOPLE, PLACES, AND THINGS

PHILIPPINE NEWS, published by Filipino exiles in San Francisco.

PHOENIX EXPLORATION SERVICES LTD., *legal name of Nippon Star.*

PHOENIX OVERSEAS PROJECT, *John K. Singlaub's alleged gold exploration company.*

PINE GAP, *deep black American security base near Alice Springs, Australia.*

PLAZA MIRANDA, *where Marcos agents opened fire on his political enemies.*

QUIRINO, *Philippine President Elpido.*

QUIRINO, TONY, *brother of Elpido.*

REAGAN, NANCY, *U.S. First Lady.*

REAGAN, RONALD, *U.S. President.*

REWALD, RON, *of Bishop, Baldwin, Rewald, Dillingham & Wong, Honolulu.*

ROCKA, LUDWIG, *Marcos's brother-in-law.*

ROCKA, ELIZABETH MARCOS, *Ferdinand's sister.*

ROKKIEDO JIKEN, Japanese name for the Lockheed scandal.

ROTHCHILD'S, *a member of the London gold cartel in the early 1970s.*

ROXAS, ROGELIO, *the man who found the Golden Buddha.*

ST. PAUL'S COLLEGE, *Manila, site where gold was buried.*

SAITO, PRIME MINISTER, *object of Kodama assassination attempt.*

SAMUEL MONTAGU, *a member of the London gold cartel in the early 1970s.*

SAN AUGUSTIN CHURCH, *Manila, site where gold was buried.*

SAN SEBASTIAN CHURCH, *Manila, site where gold was buried.*

SANTA ROMANA, *Severino Garcia, OSS officer.*

SANTIAGO, KONSEHALA C. V., *Marcos employee, signed gold documents.*

SASAKAWA, RYOICHI, *Kodama crony, one of the Sugamo Nineteen.*

SHARPS PIXLEY, *a member of the London gold cartel in the early 1970s.*

SHI PA, Chinese for "eighteen," the name of those who got shares of Hirohito's Gold.

SINGLAUB, JOHN K., *OSS and CIA operative.*

STILLWELL, GENERAL JOSEPH, *AKA Vinegar Joe, commander of American force in China.*

STIMSON, HENRY L., *Secretary of State in prewar Japan.*

STUDEMAN, WILLIAM O. *Acting DCI, said CIA would "keep the faith" with aid recipients.*

SUGAMO PRISON, *where Japanese war criminals were held in Tokyo.*

SUKARNO, PRESIDENT OF INDONESIA, *member of the World Anti-Communist League.*

SULTAN OF BRUNEI, *Col. Oliver M. North sought Contra money from him in 1982.*

SUMA, YAKIJIRO, *Nanking general consul during the rape, one of the Sugamo Nineteen.*

SUMATRA LLOYD, *ingots cast in the Dutch East Indies.*

SWISS AMERICAN BANK, *Antigua, part of the 1983 consortium of gold buyers.*

TAKAO, KAZUO, *powerful Japanese godfather.*

TAKEDA, PRINCE, *traveled incognito with Prince Chichibu on Golden Lily mission.*

TAN, GENERAL SHENGZHI, *defeated at Nanking.*

TANAKA, KAKUEI, *raised money for the M Fund.*

TANI, MASAYOKI, *director of intelligence bureau, member of the Sugamo Nineteen.*

TERESA, *village near Manila, location of two burial sites of Hirohito's Gold.*

TERESA II, *site of 1975 excavation described by Robert Curtis.*

TRADING, HELMUT, *legal owner of Phoenix Exploration Services Ltd.*

TU, YUEH SHENG, *AKA Big-Eared Tu, Shanghai gangster who worked with Kodama.*

TWYMAN, VERNON R., *evangelical Christian, owner of Delta International.*

UNION BANK OF SWITZERLAND, *where Kishi allegedly stashed money.*

UNIT 731, *Japanese unit that conducted chemical and biological experiments on humans.*

VER, FABIAN, *Marcos strongman.*

VIPS, *members of* Shi Pa *listed on 1983 contract proposed to Executive X to wash gold.*

VOLCKMANN, COLONEL, RUSSELL W., *commander of the guerrilla force on Northern Luzon.*

WILLOUGHBY, GENERAL CHARLES, *MacArthur's intelligence advisor.*

WILSON, R. B., KERR & ASSOCIATES, *Sydney, asked to wash Marcos gold.*

WORLD ANTI-COMMUNIST LEAGUE, *led by American intelligence officer John K. Singlaub.*

WU TSE, *Emperor, had golden archers struck to honor martyred archers.*

YAMAGUCHI-GUMI, *major* yakuza *gang in Japan.*

YAMAMOTO, TSUNETOMO, *Japanese philosopher, inspired nationalists and militarists.*

LIST OF HISTORICAL PEOPLE, PLACES, AND THINGS

YAMASHITA, GENEAL TOMAYUKI, *wrongly blamed for the sacking of Manila.*

YOKOYAMA, SHIZUO, *General, relayed Yamashita's order to withdraw from Manila.*

YONG AN, *originally acquired the alchemist archers of Xhingsui Gap.*

YONG, ZHI-LU, *Yong An's son, the archers were in his vaults in 1937.*

YOTSUYA KAIDAN, a classical Kabuki play, source of the name Yotsuya Fund.

YOTSUYA FUND, *earliest of funds created by MacArthur and his cronies.*

ZEN NIPPON AIKOKUSH DANTAI KAGI, Zen Ai Kagi for short, Kodama's organization.

ZOBEL, ENRIQUE, *Filipino banker, friend of the Sultan of Brunei.*

Source Notes

The tunnels at Pulak Pulakan

The author lived near Bacolod in Negros Occidental for nine months in 1989. At *marienda* every afternoon, he drank San Miguel beer and Tanduay rum with a bespectacled Filipino intelligence officer. The officer told him numerous stories about Japanese tourists bearing metal detectors and wanting to visit Pulak Pulakan (as it was called in 1945), ostensibly to relive the scene of their stubborn last stand against American and Filipino troops and to honor their fallen comrades. He said the tourists were always escorted by "guides" provided by President Ferdinand Marcos and later by security people working for President Corazon Aquino.

An intermittent effort to recover treasure from Pulak Pulakan has apparently been ongoing since 1994. The Discovery Channel showed a documentary of the digging activity in 1995. In seeking investors on an Internet website, the recovery company did not name the island but described the piers and Japanese airfield at Silay on Negros.

The World War II combat action described by Wim van der Elst is based on U.S. Army records detailing the action on Negros and the struggle to take Pulak Pulakan. Staff Sergeant John C. Sjogren in fact won the Congressional Medal of Honor for his heroism.

Hirohito

Historian Herbert Bix wrote a definitive account of Emperor Hirohito's complicity in Japanese military expansionism in his Pulitzer Prize–winning *Hirohito and the Making of Modern Japan* (New York: HarperCollins, 2000).

The M Fund

For a description of the alleged origins of the M Fund, see "Working Paper #11," July 1995, by Chalmers Johnson, Norbert A. Schlei, and Michael Schaller of the Japan Policy Research Institution.

Kodama Yoshio

For Kodama's early activities in ultranationalist organizations see *Government by Assassination*, by Hugh Byas (New York: Alfred A. Knopf, 1942).

The main source of the details about Kodama Yoshio in Wim van der Elst's journal articles in Book One is the excellent *Yakuza: The Explosive Account of Japan's Criminal Underworld*, by David E. Kaplan and Alec Dubros (New York: Macmillan Publishing Company, 1986). Kaplan and Dubros were the lead writers of a team of researchers for the Center for Investigative Journalism, San Francisco.

SOURCE NOTES

Marcos collaboration

Special investigators for the U.S. Army checked Marcos's claims of heroism immediately after the war, but their reports were either lost or hidden for decades. While researching a book on another subject, the author Alfred McCoy found the Marcos files in the National Archives. He informed the *New York Times*. Articles based on those files were published by both the *New York Times* and the *Washington Post*.

Fukumitsu

Fukumitsu's investigation of "Yamashita's Gold" was detailed by the *Los Angeles Times* in an article published May 28, 1978.

CIA and the LDP

For the CIA's involvement in the Liberal Democratic Party, read "C.I.A. Spent Millions to Support Japanese Right in 50's and 60's," by Tim Weiner, Stephen Engelberg, and James Sterngold, *New York Times*, October 9, 1994.

Accounts by author Sterling Seagrave

Robert Curtis's alleged adventures with Marcos, as well as the stories of Executive X and reports of gold contracts and wheeling and dealing by Marcos's officers and associates are woven throughout Sterling Seagrave's *The Marcos Dynasty*, a biography of Ferdinand and Imelda Marcos, published by Harper & Row, New York, 1988.

In the source notes of his biography, Seagrave says he obtained a copy of the Luxembourg contracts passed on to the Central Intelligence Agency plus a copy of the insurance papers for the same transaction.

Although bits and pieces of the story of Hirohito's Gold may be gleaned from numerous publications, the involvement of Prince Chichibu is asserted in *The Yamato Dynasty,* by Sterling and Peggy Seagrave (New York: Broadway Books, 1999).

Nugan-Hand Bank

The details on the Nugan-Hand Bank emerged in sworn testimony in the trial of Imelda Marcos in Honolulu. For a look at the involvement of the Bank of England, see Stephen Fay's *Portrait of an Old Lady: Turmoil at the Bank of England* (Harmondsworth, Middlesex: Penguin Books, 1987).

Imelda Marcos's interviews with Christine Herrera

Imelda Marcos's revealing interviews with Ms. Herrera are to be found in December 1998 editions of the *Philippine Daily Inquirer.*